ENDER IN EXILE

By Orson Scott Card from Tom Doherty Associates

Empire
The Folk of the Fringe
Future on Fire (editor)
Future on Ice (editor)
Invasive Procedures (with Aaron Johnston)
Keeper of Dreams
Lovelock (with Kathryn Kidd)
*Maps in a Mirror: The Short Fiction of
    Orson Scott Card*
*Orson Scott Card's InterGalactic
    Medicine Show*
*Pastwatch: The Redemption of
    Christopher Columbus*
Saints
Songmaster
Treason
A War of Gifts
The Worthing Saga
Wyrms

THE TALES OF ALVIN MAKER

Seventh Son
Red Prophet
Prentice Alvin
Alvin Journeyman
Heartfire
The Crystal City

ENDER

Ender's Game
Ender's Shadow
Shadow of the Hegemon
Shadow Puppets
Shadow of the Giant
Speaker for the Dead
Xenocide
Children of the Mind
First Meetings
Ender in Exile

HOMECOMING

The Memory of Earth
The Call of Earth
The Ships of Earth
Earthfall
Earthborn

WOMEN OF GENESIS

Sarah
Rebekah
Rachel & Leah

From Other Publishers

Enchantment
Homebody
Lost Boys
Magic Street
Stonefather

Stone Tables
Treasure Box
*How to Write Science
    Fiction and Fantasy*
Characters and Viewpoint

ENDER IN EXILE

Orson Scott Card

TOR®

A TOM DOHERTY ASSOCIATES BOOK

NEW YORK

This is a work of fiction. All of the characters, organizations, and events portrayed in this novel are either products of the author's imagination or are used fictitiously.

ENDER IN EXILE

A Tor Book
Published by Tom Doherty Associates, LLC
175 Fifth Avenue
New York, NY 10010

www.tor-forge.com

Tor® is a registered trademark of Tom Doherty Associates, LLC.

Library of Congress Cataloging-in-Publication Data

Card, Orson Scott.
Ender in exile / Orson Scott Card.—1st ed.
      p.   cm.
"A Tom Doherty Associates book."
ISBN-13: 978-0-7653-0496-4
ISBN-10: 0-7653-0496-1
1. Wiggin, Ender (Fictitious character)—Fiction.   1. Title.
PS3553.A655 E498 2008
813'.54—dc22   2008034075

First Edition: November 2008

Printed in the United States of America

0   9   8   7   6   5   4   3   2   1

To

BAYDON HILTON

JORDAN HILTON

RICKY FENTON

Romeo, Mercutio, and Benvolio:
you continue to earn my trust and admiration
as fellow travelers on the twisted path of life.

ENDER IN EXILE

CHAPTER
1

To: jpwiggin@gso.nc.pub, twiggin@uncg.edu
From: hgraff%educadmin@ifcom.gov
Subj: When Andrew Returns Home

Dear John Paul and Theresa Wiggin,

You understand that during the recent attempt by the Warsaw Pact to take over the International Fleet, our sole concern at EducAdmin was the safety of the children. Now we are finally able to begin working out the logistics of sending the children home.

We assure you that Andrew will be provided with continuous surveillance and an active bodyguard throughout his transfer from the I.F. to American government control. We are still negotiating the degree to which the I.F. will continue to provide protection after the transfer.

Every effort is being made by EducAdmin to assure that Andrew will be able to return to the most normal childhood possible. However, I wish your advice about whether he should be retained here in isolation until the conclusion of the inquiries into EducAdmin actions during the late campaign. It is quite likely that testimony will be offered that depicts Andrew and his actions in damaging ways, in order to attack EducAdmin through him (and the other children). Here at IFCom we can keep him from hearing the worst of it; on Earth, no such protection will be possible and it is likelier that he will be called to "testify."

Hyrum Graff

Theresa Wiggin was sitting up in bed, holding her printout of Graff's letter. " 'Called to "testify." ' Which means putting him on exhibit as— what, a hero? More likely a monster, since we already have various senators decrying the exploitation of children."

"That'll teach him to save the human race," said her husband, John Paul.

"This is not a time for flippancy."

"Theresa, be reasonable," said John Paul. "I want Ender home as much as you do."

"No you don't," said Theresa fiercely. "You don't ache with the need for him every day." Even as she said it she knew she was being unfair to him, and she covered her eyes and shook her head.

To his credit, he understood and didn't argue with her about what he did and did not feel. "You can never have the years they've taken, Theresa. He's not the boy we knew."

"Then we'll get to know the boy he is. Here. In our home."

"Surrounded by guards."

"*That's* the part I refuse to accept. Who would want to hurt him?"

John Paul set down the book he was no longer pretending to read. "Theresa, you're the smartest person I know."

"He's a child!"

"He won a war against incredibly superior forces."

"He fired off *one* weapon. Which he did not design or deploy."

"He got that weapon into firing range."

"The formics are gone! He's a hero, he's not in danger."

"All right, Theresa, he's a hero. How is he going to go to middle school? What eighth-grade teacher is ready for him? What school dance is he going to be ready for?"

"It will take time. But here, with his family—"

"Yes, we're such a warm, welcoming group of people, a love nest into which he'll fit so easily."

"We *do* love each other!"

"Theresa, Colonel Graff is only trying to warn us that Ender isn't *just* our son."

"He's nobody *else's* son."

"You *know* who wants to kill our son."

"No, I don't."

"Every government that thinks of American military power as an obstacle to their plans."

"But Ender isn't going to *be* in the military, he's going to be—"

"This week he won't be in the American military. Maybe. He won a war at the age of twelve, Theresa. What makes you think he won't be drafted by our benevolent and democratic government the moment he gets back to Earth? Or put into protective custody? Maybe they'll let us go with him and maybe they won't."

Theresa let the tears flow down her cheeks. "So you're saying that when he left here we lost him forever."

"I'm saying that when your child goes off to war, you will never get him back. Not as he was, not the same boy. Changed, if he comes back at all. So let me ask you. Do you want him to go where he's in the greatest danger, or to stay where he's relatively safe?"

"You think Graff is trying to get us to tell him to keep Ender with him out there in space."

"I think Graff cares what happens to Ender, and he's letting us know— without actually saying it, because every letter he sends can be used against him in court—that Ender is in terrible danger. Not ten minutes after Ender's victory, the Russians made their brutal play for control of the I.F. Their soldiers killed thousands of fleet officers before the I.F. was able to force their surrender. What would they have done if they had won? Brought Ender home and put on a big parade for him?"

Theresa knew all of this. She had known it, viscerally at least, from the moment she read Graff's letter. No, she had known it even before, had known it with a sick dread as soon as she heard that the Formic War was over. He would not be coming home.

She felt John Paul's hand on her shoulder. She shrugged it off. His hand returned, stroking her arm as she lay there, facing away from him, crying because she knew she had already lost the argument, crying because she wasn't even on her own side in their quarrel.

"We knew when he was born that he didn't belong to us."

"He *does* belong to us."

"If he comes home, his life belongs to whatever government has the power to protect him and use him—or kill him. He's the single most important asset surviving from the war. The great weapon. That's all he'll be—that and such a celebrity he can't possibly have a normal childhood anyway. And would we be much help, Theresa? Do we understand what his life has been for the past seven years? What kind of parents can we be to the boy—the man—that he's become?"

"We would be *wonderful*," she said.

"And we know this because we're such perfect parents for the children we have at home with us."

Theresa rolled onto her back. "Oh, dear. Poor Peter. It must be killing him that Ender might come home."

"Take the wind right out of his sails."

"Oh, I'm not sure of that," said Theresa. "I bet Peter is already figuring out how to exploit Ender's return."

"Until he finds out that Ender is much too clever to be exploited."

"What preparation does Ender have for *politics*? He's been in the military all this time."

John Paul chuckled.

"All right, yes, of course the military is just as political as government."

"But you're right," said John Paul. "Ender's had protection there, people who intended to exploit him, yes, but he hasn't had to do any bureaucratic fighting for himself. He's probably a babe in the woods when it comes to maneuvering like that."

"So Peter really could use him?"

"That's not what worries me. What worries me is what Peter will do when he finds out that he *can't* use him."

Theresa sat back up and faced her husband. "You can't think *Peter* would raise a hand against Ender!"

"Peter doesn't raise his *own* hand to do anything difficult or dangerous. You know how he's been using Valentine."

"Only because she lets him use her."

"Exactly my point," said John Paul.

"Ender is *not* in danger from his own family."

"Theresa, we have to decide: What's best for Ender? What's best for Peter and Valentine? What's best for the future of the world?"

"Sitting here on our bed, in the middle of the night, the two of us are deciding the fate of the world?"

"When we conceived little Andrew, my dear, we decided the fate of the world."

"And had a good time doing it," she added.

"Is it good for Ender to come home? Will it make him happy?"

"Do you really think he's forgotten us?" she asked. "Do you think Ender doesn't care whether he comes home?"

"Coming home lasts a day or two. Then there's *living* here. The danger from foreign powers, the unnaturalness of his life at school, the constant infringements on his privacy, and let's not forget Peter's unquenchable ambition and envy. So I ask again, will Ender's life here be happier than it would be if . . ."

"If he stays out in space? What kind of life will *that* be for him?"

"The I.F. has made its commitment—total neutrality in regard to anything happening on Earth. If they have Ender, then the whole world—every government—will *know* they'd better not try to go up against the Fleet."

"So by not coming home, Ender continues to save the world on an ongoing basis," said Theresa. "What a useful life he'll have."

"The point is that nobody *else* can use him."

Theresa put on her sweetest voice. "So you think we should write back to Graff and tell him that we don't want Ender to come home?"

"We can't do anything of the kind," said John Paul. "We'll write back that we're eager to see our son and we don't think any bodyguard will be necessary."

It took her a moment to realize why he seemed to be reversing everything he'd said. "Any letters we send Graff," she said, "will be just as public as the letter he sent us. And just as empty. And we do nothing and let things take their course."

"No, my dear," said John Paul. "It happens that living in our own house, under our own roof, are two of the most influential formers of public opinion."

"But John Paul, officially we don't know that our children are sneaking around in the nets, manipulating events through Peter's network of correspondents and Valentine's brilliantly perverse talent for demagoguery."

"And they don't know that we have any brains," said John Paul. "They seem to think they were left at our house by fairies instead of having our genetic material throughout their little bodies. They treat us as convenient samples of ignorant public opinion. So . . . let's give them some public opinions that will steer them to do what's best for their brother."

"What's best," echoed Theresa. "We don't know what's best."

"No," said John Paul. "We only know what seems best. But one thing's certain—we know a lot more about it than any of our children do."

Valentine came home from school with anger festering inside her. Stupid teachers—it made her crazy sometimes to ask a question and have the teacher patiently explain things to her as if the question were a sign of Valentine's failure to understand the subject, instead of the teacher's. But Valentine sat there and took it, as the equation showed up in the holodisplay on everybody's desk and the teacher covered it point by point.

Then Valentine drew a little circle in the air around the element of the problem that the teacher had not addressed properly—the reason why the answer was not right. Valentine's circle did not show up on all the desks, of course; only the teacher's computer had that capability.

So the teacher then got to draw his own circle around that number and say, "What you're not noticing here, Valentine, is that even *with* this explanation, if you ignore *this* element you still can't get the right answer."

It was such an obvious ego-protective cover-up. But of course it was obvious only to Valentine. To the other students, who were barely grasping the material anyway (especially since it was being explained to them by an unobservant incompetent), it *was* Val who had overlooked the circled parenthetical, even though it was precisely because of that element that she had asked her question in the first place.

And the teacher gave her that simpering smile that clearly said, You aren't going to defeat me and humiliate me in front of this class.

But Valentine was not trying to humiliate him. She did not care about him. She simply cared that the material be taught well enough that if, God forbid, some member of the class became a civil engineer, his bridges wouldn't fall down and kill people.

That was the difference between her and the idiots of the world. They were all trying to look smart and keep their social standing. Whereas Valentine didn't care about social standing, she cared about getting it right. Getting the truth—when the truth was gettable.

She had said nothing to the teacher and nothing to any of the students and she knew she wouldn't get any sympathy at home, either. Peter would mock her for caring about school enough to let that clown of a teacher get under her skin. Father would look at the problem, point out the correct answer, and go back to his work without ever noticing that Val wasn't asking for *help,* she was asking for commiseration.

And Mother? She would be all for charging down to the school and *doing* something about it, raking the teacher over the coals. Mother wouldn't even *hear* Val explaining that she didn't want to shame the teacher, she just wanted somebody to say, "Isn't it ironic, that in this special advanced school for really bright kids, they have a teacher who doesn't know his own subject!" To which Val could reply, "It sure is!" and then she'd feel better. Like somebody was on her side. Somebody *got* it and she wasn't alone.

My needs are simple and few, thought Valentine. Food. Clothing. A comfortable place to sleep. And *no idiots.*

But of course a world with no idiots would be lonely. If she herself were even allowed there. It's not as if *she* never made mistakes.

Like the mistake of ever letting Peter rope her into being Demosthenes. He *still* thought he needed to tell her what to write every day after school—as if, after all these years, she had not completely internalized the character. She could write Demosthenes' essays in her sleep.

And if she needed help, all she had to do was listen to Father pontificate on world affairs—since he seemed to echo all of Demosthenes' warmongering jingoistic demagogic opinions despite claiming never to read the columns.

If he knew his sweet naive little daughter was writing those essays, he'd poop petunias.

She fumed into the house, headed straight for her computer, scanned the news, and started writing the essay she knew Peter would assign her—a diatribe on how the I.F. should not have ended the hostilities with the Warsaw Pact without first demanding that Russia surrender all her nukes, because shouldn't there be *some* cost to waging a nakedly aggressive war? All the usual spewings from her Demosthenes anti-avatar.

Or am I, as Demosthenes, Peter's *real* avatar? Have I been turned into a virtual person?

Click. An email. Anything would be better than what she was writing.

It was from Mother. She was forwarding an email from Colonel Graff. About Ender having a bodyguard when he came home.

"I thought you'd want to see this," Mother had written. "Isn't it just THRILLING that Andrew's homecoming is SO CLOSE?"

Stop shouting, Mother. Why do you use caps for emphasis like that? It's so—junior high school. It's what she told Peter more than once. Mother is such a *cheerleader.*

Mother's epistle went on in the same vein. It'll take NO time at ALL to get Ender's room back into shape for him and now there doesn't seem to be any reason to put off cleaning the room a SECOND longer unless what do you think, would Peter want to SHARE his room with his little brother so they could BOND and get CLOSE again? And what do you think Ender will want for his VERY FIRST meal home?

Food, Mother. Whatever it is will definitely be "SPECIAL enough to make him feel LOVED and MISSED."

Anyway. Mother was so naive to take Graff's letter at face value. Val went back and read it again. Surveillance. Bodyguard. Graff was sending her a warning, not trying to get her all excited about Ender's homecoming. Ender was going to be in danger. Couldn't Mother see that?

Graff asked if they should keep Ender in space till the inquiries were over. But that would take months. How could Mother have gotten the idea that Ender was coming home so soon it was time to clear out the junk that had gotten stacked in his room? Graff was asking her to request that he *not* be sent home just yet. And his reason was that Ender was in danger.

Instantly the whole range of dangers that Ender faced loomed before her. The Russians would assume that Ender was a weapon that America would use against them. The Chinese would think the same—that America, armed with this Ender-weapon, might become aggressive about intruding into China's sphere of influence again. Both nations would breathe easier if Ender were dead. Though of course they'd have to make it look like the assassination had been carried out by some kind of terrorist movement. Which meant that they wouldn't just snipe Ender out of existence, they'd probably blow up his school.

No, no, no, Val told herself. Just because that's the kind of thing Demosthenes would say doesn't mean it's what *you* have to think!

But the image of somebody blowing Ender up or shooting him or whatever method they used—all the methods kept flashing through her mind. Wouldn't it be ironic—yet typically human—for the person who saved the human race to be assassinated? It was like the murder of Abraham Lincoln or Mohandas Gandhi. Some people just didn't know who their saviors were. And the fact that Ender was still a kid wouldn't even slow them down.

He can't come home, she thought. Mother will never see it, I could never say it to her, but . . . even if they weren't going to assassinate him, what would his life be like here? Ender was never one to seek fame or status, and yet everything he did would end up on the vids with people commenting on how he did his hair (Vote! Like it or hate it?) and what classes he was taking in school (What will the hero be when he grows up? Vote on the career *you* think The Wiggin should prepare for!).

What a nightmare. It wouldn't be coming home. They could never bring Ender home anyway. The home he left didn't exist. The kid who was taken out of that home didn't exist either. When Ender was here—not even a whole year ago—when Val went to the lake and spent those hours with him, Ender seemed so old. Playful sometimes, yes, but he felt the weight of the world on his shoulders. Now the burden had been taken off—but the aftermath would cling to him, would tie him down, tear down his life.

The years of childhood were gone. Period. Ender didn't get to be a little boy growing up into an adolescent in his father's and mother's house. He was already an adolescent now—in years and hormones—and an adult in the responsibilities he'd borne.

If school feels empty to *me,* how will it feel to Ender?

Even as she finished writing her essay on Russia's nukes and the cost of defeat, she was mentally structuring another essay. The one explaining why Ender Wiggin should not be brought back to Earth because he'd be the target of every crank and spy and paparazzo and assassin and a normal life would be impossible.

She didn't write it, though. Because she knew there was a huge problem: Peter would hate it.

Because Peter already had his plans. His online persona, Locke, had already started laying the groundwork for Ender's homecoming. It was clear to Valentine that when Ender returned, Peter intended to come out of the closet as the real author of the Locke essays—and therefore the person who came up with the terms of the truce that was still holding between the Warsaw Pact and the I.F. Peter meant to piggyback on Ender's fame. Ender saved the human race from the formics, and his big brother Peter saved the world from civil war in the aftermath of Ender's victory. Double heroes!

Ender would hate the notoriety. Peter was so hungry for it that he intended to steal as much of Ender's as he could get.

Oh, he'd never admit that, thought Valentine. Peter will have all kinds of reasons why it's for Ender's own good. Probably the very reasons I've thought of.

And since that's the case, am I doing just what Peter does? Have I come up with all these reasons for Ender not to come home, solely because in my heart I don't want him here?

At that thought, such a wave of emotion swept over her that she found herself weeping at her homework table. She wanted him home. And even though she understood that he couldn't really come home—Colonel Graff was right—she still yearned for the little brother who was stolen from her. All these years with the brother I hate, and now, for the sake of the brother I love, I'll work to keep him from . . .

From me? No, I don't have to keep him from *me.* I hate school, I hate my life here, I hate hate hate being under Peter's thumb. Why should I stay? Why shouldn't I go out into space with Ender? At least for a while. I'm the one he's closest to. I'm the only one he's *seen* in the

past seven years. If he can't come home, one bit of home—me—can
come to him!

It was all a matter of persuading Peter that it wasn't in his best interest
to have Ender come back to Earth—without letting Peter *know* that she
was trying to manipulate him.

It just made her tired, because Peter wasn't easy to manipulate. He saw
through everything. So she had to be quite forthright and honest about
what she was doing—but do it with such subtle overtones of humility and
earnestness and dispassion and *whatever* that Peter could get past his own
condescension toward everything she said and decide that he had thought
that way all along and . . .

And is my real motive that I want to get off planet myself? Is this
about Ender or about me getting free?

Both. It can be both. And I'll tell Ender the truth about that—I won't
be giving up *anything* to be with him. I'd rather be with him in space and
never see Earth again than stay here, with or without him. Without him:
an aching void. With him: the pain of watching him lead a miserable,
frustrated life.

Val began to write a letter to Colonel Graff. Mother had been careless
enough to include Graff's address. That was almost a security breach.
Mother was so naive sometimes. If she were an I.F. officer, she would
have been cashiered long ago.

At dinner that night, Mother couldn't stop talking about Ender's homecoming. Peter listened with only half his attention, because of course
Mother couldn't see past her personal sentimentality about her "lost little
boy coming back to the nest" whereas Peter understood that Ender's
return would be horribly complicated. So much to prepare for—and not
just the stupid bedroom. Ender could have Peter's own bed, for all he
cared—what mattered was that for a brief window of time, Ender would
be the center of the world's attention, and *that* was when Locke would
emerge from the cloak of anonymity and put an end to the speculation
about the identity of the "great benefactor of humanity who, because
of his modesty in remaining anonymous, cannot receive the Nobel prize

that he so richly deserves for having led us to the end of the last war of mankind."

That from a rather gushy fan of Locke's—who also happened to be the head of the opposition party in Great Britain. Naive to imagine even for a moment that the brief attempt by the New Warsaw Pact to take over the I.F. was the "last war." There's only one way to have a "last war," and that's to have the whole of Earth under a single, effective, powerful, but popular leader.

And the way to introduce that leader would be to find him on camera, standing beside the great Ender Wiggin with his arm flung across the hero's shoulders because—and who should be surprised by this?—the "Boy of War" and the "Man of Peace" are brothers!

And now Father was blathering about something. Only he had addressed something to Peter directly and so Peter had to play the dutiful son and listen as if he cared.

"I really think you need to commit to the career you want to pursue *before* your brother gets home, Peter."

"And why is that?" asked Peter.

"Oh, don't pretend to be so naive. Don't you realize that Ender Wiggin's brother can get into *any college he wants*?"

Father pronounced the words as if they were the most brilliant ever spoken aloud by someone who had not yet been deified by the Roman senate or sainted by the Pope or whatever. It would never occur to Father that Peter's perfect grades and his perfect score on all the college-entry tests would already get him into any school he wanted. He didn't have to piggyback on his brother's fame. But no, to Father everything good in Peter's life would always be seen as flowing from Ender. Ender Ender Ender Ender what a stupid name.

If Father's thinking this way, no doubt everybody else will, too. At least everybody below a certain minimum intelligence.

All Peter had been seeing was the publicity bonus that Ender's homecoming would offer. But Father had reminded him of something else— that everything he did would be discounted in people's minds precisely because he was Ender the Great's older brother. People would see them standing side by side, yes—but they'd wonder why Ender's brother had not been taken into Battle School. It would make Peter look weak and inferior and vulnerable.

There he'd stand, noticeably taller, the brother who stayed home and didn't do anything. "Oh, but I wrote all the Locke essays and shut down the conflict with Russia before it could turn into a world war!" Well, if you're so smart, why weren't *you* helping your little brother save the human race from *complete destruction*?

Public relations opportunity, yes. But also a nightmare.

How could he use the opportunity Ender's great victory offered, yet not have it *look* like he was nothing but a hanger-on, sucking at his brother's fame like a remora? How ghastly if his announcement sounded like some sad kind of me-too-ism. Oh, you think my brother's cool? Well, I'll have you know that I saved the world *too*. In my own sad, needy little way.

"Are you all right, Peter?" asked Valentine.

"Oh, is something wrong?" asked Mother. "Let me look at you, dear."

"I'm not taking my shirt off or letting you use a rectal thermometer on me, Mother, because Val is hallucinating and I look just fine."

"I'll have you know that if and when I start hallucinating," said Val, "I can think of something better than seeing your face looking pukish."

"What a great commercial idea," said Peter, almost by reflex now. "Choose Your Own Hallucination! Oh, wait, they have that one—they call it 'illegal drugs.'"

"Don't sneer at us needy ones," said Val. "Those who are addicted to ego don't need drugs."

"Children," said Mother. "Is *this* what Ender will find when he comes home?"

"Yes," said Val and Peter simultaneously.

Father spoke up. "I'd like to think he might find you a bit more mature."

But by now Peter and Val were laughing uproariously. They couldn't stop, so Father sent them from the table.

Peter glanced through Val's essay on Russian nukes. "This is so boring."

"I don't think so," said Valentine. "They have the nukes and that keeps other countries from slapping them down when they need it—which is often."

"What's this thing you've got against Russia?"

"It's Demosthenes who has something against Russia," said Val with fake nonchalance.

"Good," said Peter. "So Demosthenes will not be worried about Russian nuclear weapons, he'll be worried about Russia getting its hands on the most valuable weapon of them all."

"The Molecular Disruption Device?" asked Val. "The I.F. will never bring it within firing range of Earth."

"Not the M.D. Device, you poor sap. I'm referring to our brother. Our civilization-destroying junior sib."

"Don't you dare talk about him with scorn!"

Peter's expression turned into a mocking simper. But behind his visage there was anger and hurt. She still had the power to get to him, just by making it clear how much more she loved Ender.

"Demosthenes is going to write an essay pointing out that America must get Andrew Wiggin back to Earth immediately. No more delays. The world is too dangerous a place for America not to have the immediate services of the greatest military leader the world has ever known."

Immediately a fresh wave of hatred for Peter swept over Valentine. Partly because she realized *his* approach would work far better than the essay she had already written. She hadn't internalized Demosthenes as well as she thought. Demosthenes would absolutely call for Ender's immediate return and enlistment in the American military.

And that would be as destabilizing, in its own way, as a call for forward deployment of nukes. Demosthenes' essays were watched very carefully by the rivals and enemies of the United States. If he called for Ender to come home at once, they would all start maneuvering to keep Ender in space; and some, at least, would openly accuse America of having aggressive intentions.

It would then be Locke's place, in a few days or weeks, to come up with a compromise, a statesmanlike solution: Leave the kid in space.

Valentine knew exactly why Peter had changed his mind. It was that stupid remark of Father's at dinner—his reminder that Peter would be in Ender's shadow, no matter what he did.

Well, even political sheep sometimes said something that had a good result. Now Val wouldn't even have to persuade Peter of the need to keep Ender away from Earth. It would be all his idea instead of hers.

Theresa once again sat on the bed, crying. Strewn about her were printouts of the Demosthenes and Locke essays that she knew would keep Ender from returning home.

"I can't help it," she said to her husband. "I know it's the right thing—just as Graff *wanted* us to understand it. But I thought I'd see him again. I really did."

John Paul sat beside her on the bed and put his arms around her. "It's the hardest thing we ever did."

"Not giving him up in the first place?"

"That was hard," said John Paul, "but we didn't have a choice. They were going to take him anyway. This time, though. You know that if we went on the nets and put up vids of us pleading for our son to come home—we'd have a pretty good chance."

"And our little boy is going to wonder why we *don't* do it."

"No he's not."

"Oh, you think he's so smart he'll figure out what we're doing? Why we're doing *nothing*?"

"Why wouldn't he?"

"Because he doesn't know us," said Theresa. "He doesn't know what we think or feel. As far as he can tell, we've forgotten all about him."

"One thing I feel good about, in this whole mess," said John Paul. "We're still good at manipulating our genius children."

"Oh, that," said Theresa dismissively. "It's easy to manipulate your children when they're absolutely sure you're stupid."

"What makes me saddest," said John Paul, "is that Locke is getting credit for caring about Ender more than anybody. So when his identity does come out, it'll look as though he loyally stepped in to protect his brother."

"He's our boy, that Peter," said Theresa. "Oh, what a piece of work he is."

"I have a philosophical question. I wonder if what we call 'goodness' is actually a maladaptive trait. As long as most people have it, and the rules of society promote it as a virtue, then the *natural* rulers have a clear field of action. It's because of Ender's goodness that it's Peter we'll have at home on Earth."

"Oh, Peter's good," said Theresa bitterly.

"Yes, I forgot," said John Paul. "It's for the good of the human race that he'll become ruler of the world. An altruistic sacrifice."

"When I read his simpering essays I want to claw his eyes out."

"He's our son, too," said John Paul. "As much a product of our genes as Ender or Val. And we did goad him into this."

Theresa knew he was right. But it didn't help. "He didn't have to enjoy himself so much, did he?"

CHAPTER

2

To: hgraff%educadmin@ifcom.gov
From: demosthenes@LastBestHopeOfEarth.pol
Subj: You know the truth

You know who decides what to write. No doubt you can even guess why. I'm not going to try to defend my essay, or how it's being used by others.

You once used the sister of Andrew Wiggin to persuade him to go back into space and win that little war you were fighting. She did her job, didn't she? Such a good girl, fulfills all her assignments.

Well I have an assignment for her. You once sent her brother to her, for comfort and company. He'll need her again, more than ever, only he can't come to her. No house by the lake this time. But there's no reason she can't go out into space to be with him. Enlist her in the I.F., pay her as a consultant, whatever it takes. But she and her brother need each other. More than either of them needs Life On Earth.

Don't second-guess her on this. Remember that she's smarter than you are, and she loves her younger brother more than you do, and besides, you're a decent man. You know this is right and good. You always try to bring about what's right and good, don't you?

Do us both a favor. Take this letter and shred it and stick it where the sun don't shine.

Your devoted and humble servant—everybody's devoted and humble servant—the humble and devoted servant of truth and noble jingoism—Demosthenes.

How does a thirteen-year-old admiral spend his days?

Not commanding a ship—that was made plain to Ender from the day he received his commission. "You have a rank commensurate with your achievements," said Admiral Chamrajnagar, "but you will have duties commensurate with your training."

What was his training? To play at virtual war on the simulator. Now there was no one left to fight, so he was trained for . . . nothing.

Oh, one other thing: to lead children into combat, to squeeze the last ounce of effort and concentration and talent and intelligence from them. But the children had no purpose here, and one by one, they were going home.

They each came to Ender to say good-bye. "You'll be home soon," said Hot Soup. "They've got to prepare a hero's welcome." He was heading to Tactical School, to complete the bits of work remaining before he could earn his high school diploma. "So I can get into college right away."

"Fifteen-year-olds always do great in college," said Ender.

"I have to concentrate on my studies," said Han Tzu. "Finish college, find out what I'm supposed to do with my life, and then find someone to marry and start a family."

"Get on with the cycle of life?" said Ender.

"A man without a wife and babies is a menace to civilization," said Han Tzu. "One bachelor is an irritation. Ten thousand bachelors are a war."

"I love it when you recite Chinese wisdom."

"I'm Chinese, so I get to make it up." Han Tzu grinned at him. "Ender, come see me. China's a beautiful country. More variety inside China than in the rest of the world."

"I will if I can," said Ender. He didn't have the heart to point out that China was full of human beings, and that the mix of good and bad, strong and weak, courageous and fearful was bound to be about the same as in any other country or culture or civilization . . . or village, or house, or heart.

"Oh, you'll be able to!" said Han Tzu. "You led the human race to victory, and everyone knows it. You can do whatever you want!"

Except go home, said Ender silently. Out loud, he answered, "You don't know my parents."

He had meant it to be in the same jocular tone that Han Tzu was using, but nothing came out right these days. Maybe there was a moroseness in him that colored all his speech without his knowing it. Or maybe it was Han Tzu who couldn't hear a joke coming from Ender's mouth; maybe he and the other kids all had too many memories of how it was near the end, when they worried that Ender might be losing his mind.

But Ender knew that he wasn't losing it. He was finding it. The deep mind, the utter soul, the heartlessly compassionate man—able to love others so deeply he can understand them, yet remain so detached that he can use that knowledge to destroy them.

"Parents," said Han Tzu joylessly. "Mine's in prison, you know. Or maybe he's out now. He set me up to cheat on my test, to make sure I got in here."

"You didn't need to cheat," said Ender. "You're the real thing."

"But my father needed to bestow it on me. It was no good if I earned it myself. It's how he made himself feel necessary. I understand that now. My plan is to be a better father than him. I am the Good Man-Parent!"

Ender laughed and then embraced him and they said good-bye. But the conversation stuck with him. He realized that Han Tzu would take his training and turn himself into the perfect father. And much of what he had learned in Battle School and here in Command School would probably serve him well. Patience, absolute self-control, learning the capabilities of those under you so you can make up for their deficits through training.

What was I trained for?

I am Tribal Man, thought Ender. The chief. They can trust me utterly to do exactly what's right for the tribe. But that trust means that I am the one who decides who lives and dies. Judge, executioner, general, god. That's what they trained me for. They did it well; I performed as trained.

Now I scan the help wanted ads on the nets and can't find a single job on offer for which those are the qualifications. No tribes applying for chieftains, no villages in search of a king, no religions in search of a warrior-prophet.

Officially, Ender was never supposed to have been informed of the court martial proceedings against ex-colonel Hyrum Graff. Officially, Ender was too young and too personally involved and the juvenile psychologists declared, after several tedious psychological evaluations, that Ender was too fragile to be exposed to the consequences of his own actions.

Oh, right, *now* you're worried.

But that's what the trial was going to be about, wasn't it? Whether Graff and other officials—but mostly Graff—acted properly in the use they made of the children who were put in their care. It was all being taken very seriously, and from the way adult officers fell silent or looked away when Ender came into a room, Ender was reasonably sure that there had been some terrible consequence of something he had done.

He came to Mazer just before the trial began and laid out his hypotheses about what was really going on. "I think Colonel Graff is being put on trial because they're holding him responsible for things I did. But I doubt that it's because I blew up the formics' home world and destroyed an entire sentient species—they approve of that."

Mazer had nodded wisely but said nothing—his normal mode of response, left over from his days as Ender's trainer.

"So it's something else I did," said Ender. "I can think of only two things I've done that they'd put a man on trial for letting me do them. One was a fight I was in at Battle School. A bigger kid cornered me in a bathroom. He'd been bragging that he was going to beat me till I wasn't so smart anymore, and he brought his gang with him. I shamed him into fighting me alone, and then I put him down in a single move."

"Really," said Mazer.

"Bonzo Madrid. Bonito de Madrid. I think he's dead."

"Think?"

"They took me out of Battle School the next day. They never spoke of him. I assumed that meant I had really hurt him. I think he's dead. That's the kind of thing they'd hold a court martial for, isn't it? They have to account to Bonzo's parents for why their son is dead."

"Interesting line of thought," said Mazer. Mazer said that whether his guesses were right or wrong, so Ender didn't try to interpret it. "Is that all?" asked Mazer.

"There are governments and politicians that would like to discredit me. There's a move to keep me from coming back to Earth. I read the nets, I know what they're saying, that I'll just be a political football, a target for assassins, or an asset that my country will use to conquer the world or some such nonsense. So I think there are those who intend to use Graff's court martial as a way to publish things about me that would ordinarily be kept under seal. Things that will make me look like some kind of monster."

"You do know that it sounds suspiciously like paranoia, to think that *Graff's* trial is about *you.*"

"Which makes it all the more appropriate that I'm in this loony bin," said Ender.

"You understand that I can't tell you anything," said Mazer.

"You don't have to," said Ender. "I'm also thinking that there was another boy. Years ago. When I was just little. He was hardly that much bigger than me. But he had a gang with him. I talked him out of using them—made it personal, one-on-one. Just like Bonzo. I wasn't a good fighter then. I didn't know how. All I could do was go crazy on him. *Hurt* him so bad he'd never dare to come after me again. Hurt him so bad that his gang would leave me alone, too. I had to *be* crazy in order to scare them with how crazy I was. So I think that incident is going to be part of the trial, too."

"Your self-absorption is really quite sweet—you really are convinced you're the center of the universe."

"Center of the court martial," said Ender. "It's about me, or people wouldn't be so anxious to keep me from knowing about it. The absence of information *is* information."

"You kids are so smart," said Mazer, with just enough sarcasm to make Ender smile.

"Stilson's dead, too, isn't he," said Ender. It wasn't really a question.

"Ender, not everyone you fight with dies." But there was just a titch of hesitation *after* he said it. And so Ender knew. Everyone he had fought with—really *fought*—was dead. Bonzo. Stilson. And all the formics, every hive queen, every bugger, every larva, every egg, however they reproduced, it was over.

"You know," said Ender quietly, "I think about them all the time. How they'll never have any more children. That's what being alive is, isn't it? The ability to replicate. Even people without children, their bodies are still making new cells all the time. Replicating. Only that's over for Bonzo and Stilson. They never lived long enough to reproduce. Their line is cut off. *I* was nature, red in tooth and claw, for them. I determined their unfitness."

Ender knew even as he said it that this was unfair. Mazer was under orders not to discuss these matters with him and even if he guessed right, not to *confirm* them. But ending the conversation would confirm it, and even denying the truth had confirmed it. Now Ender was practically forcing him to speak, to reassure him, to answer his perceived need. "You don't have to respond," said Ender. "I'm not really as depressed as I sound. I don't blame myself, you know."

Mazer's eyes flickered.

"No, I'm not insane," said Ender. "I regret their deaths. I know that I'm *responsible* for killing Stilson and Bonzo and all the formics in the universe. But I'm not to blame. I didn't seek out Stilson or Bonzo. They came to *me,* with a threat of real damage. A credible threat. Tell them that in the court martial. Or run the recording you're doubtless making of this conversation. My intention was not to kill them, but my intention was definitely to stop them from damaging me. And the only way to do that was to act brutally. I'm sorry that they died from their injuries. I'd undo that if I could. But I didn't have the skill to hurt them enough to prevent future attacks, and yet not kill them. Or whatever it was that I did to them. If they're mentally damaged or crippled, I'll do what I can for them, unless their families would rather I stay away. I don't want to cause any more harm.

"But here's the thing, Mazer Rackham: I knew what I was doing. It's ridiculous for Hyrum Graff to be on trial for this. He had no idea of the way I thought, when it came to Stilson. He couldn't have known what I'd do. Only I knew. And I meant to hurt him—I meant to hurt him bad. Not

Graff's fault. The fault was Stilson's. If he had left me alone—and I gave him every chance to walk away. I begged him to leave me alone. If he'd done that, he'd be alive. He chose. Just because he thought I was weaker than him, just because he thought I couldn't protect myself, doesn't mean it stopped being his fault. He chose to attack me precisely because he thought there would be no consequences. Only there *were* consequences."

Mazer cleared his throat a little. And then spoke. "This has gone far enough."

"With Bonzo, however, Graff was taking a terrible risk. What if Bonzo and his friends hurt me? What if I died? Or was brain-damaged? Or was simply made fearful and timid? He would lose the weapon he was forging. Bean would have won the war even if I was out of the picture, but Graff couldn't know that. It was a terrible gamble. Because Graff also knew that if I got out of that confrontation with Bonzo alive—victorious—then I would believe in myself. My ability to win under any circumstances. The game didn't give me that—it was just a game. Bonzo showed me that in real life I could win. As long as I understood my enemy. *You* understand what that means, Mazer."

"Even if anything you're saying were true . . ."

"Take this vid and introduce it into evidence. Or if, by some remote chance, nobody's recording our conversation, then testify on his behalf. Let them know—the court martial—let them know that Graff acted properly. I was angry at him for doing it that way, and I suppose I still am. But if I were in his place, I would have done the same. It was part of winning the war. People die in war. You send your soldiers into combat and you know some of them won't come back. But Graff didn't send Bonzo. Bonzo was a volunteer for the duty he assigned himself—attacking me and allowing us all to learn that no, I would not allow myself to lose, ever. Bonzo volunteered. Just like the buggers volunteered by coming here and trying to wipe out human life. If they'd left us alone, we wouldn't have hurt them. The court martial has to understand. I am what Battle School was designed to create, what the whole world *wanted* it to create. Graff cannot be blamed for shaping and sharpening the weapon. He did not wield it. No one did. Bonzo found a knife and cut himself on it. That's how they have to look at it."

"Are you done?" Mazer had asked.

"Why, are you running out of recording room?"

Mazer got up and left.

When he came back, he said nothing about their discussion. But Ender was now free to come and go anywhere. They no longer tried to hide things from him. He was able to read the transcript of Graff's arraignment.

He had been right on every point.

Ender also understood that Graff would not be convicted of anything serious—he would not go to prison. The court martial existed only to damage Ender and make it impossible for America to use him as a military leader. Ender was a hero, yes, but he was now officially a really scary kid. The court martial would cement that image in the public mind. People might have rallied around the savior of the human race. But a monstrous kid who killed other children? Even if it was self-defense, it was just too terrible. Ender's political future on Earth was nonexistent.

Ender tracked how the commentator Demosthenes responded as things began to come out in the trial. For months—ever since it became clear that Ender was *not* being sent home immediately—the famous American chauvinist had been agitating on the nets to "bring the hero home." Even now, as Ender's private killings were being used against Graff at the trial, Demosthenes still declared, more than once, that Ender was a "weapon that belongs to the American people."

This practically guaranteed that no one from any other nation would consent to that weapon getting into American hands.

Ender thought at first that Demosthenes must be a complete idiot, playing his hand completely wrong. Then he realized that Demosthenes might be doing it on purpose, energizing the opposition, because the last thing Demosthenes wanted was a rival for American political leadership.

Was the man that subtle? Ender pored over his essays—what else did he have to do?—and saw a pattern of self-defeat. Demosthenes was eloquent, but he always pushed a little too hard. Enough to energize the opposition, inside and outside America. Discrediting his own side of every argument.

Deliberately?

Probably not. Ender knew the history of leaders—especially of the original Demosthenes. Eloquence didn't imply intelligence or deep analysis. True believers in a cause often behaved in self-defeating ways because they expected other people to see the rightness of their cause if they just stated it clearly enough. As a result, they tipped their hand in every game and couldn't understand why everyone ganged up against them.

Ender had watched the arguments unfold on the nets, watched the teams form, saw how the "moderates" led by Locke kept benefiting from Demosthenes' provocations.

And now, as Demosthenes continued to agitate in support of Ender, he was actually the one doing Ender the most damage. To everyone who feared Demosthenes' movement—which was the whole world outside America—Ender would not be a hero, he'd be a monster. Bring *him* home, to lead America on a nuevo-imperialista rampage? Let him become an American Alexander, Genghis Khan, Adolf Hitler, conquering the world or forcing the world to unite in brutal war against him?

Fortunately, Ender did not want to be a conqueror. So he wouldn't be hurt by missing out on the chance to try it.

Still, he'd love to have a chance to explain things to Demosthenes.

Not that the man would ever consent to be alone in a room with the killer hero.

Mazer never discussed the actual court martial with Ender, but they could talk about Graff.

"Hyrum Graff is the consummate bureaucrat," Mazer told him. "He's always thinking ten steps ahead of everyone else. It doesn't really matter what office he holds. He can use anybody—below him or above him or complete strangers who've never met him—to accomplish whatever he thinks is needful for the human race."

"I'm glad he chooses to use this power of his for good."

"I don't know that he does," said Mazer. "He uses it for what he believes is good. But I don't know that he's particularly good at knowing what 'good' is."

"In philosophy class I think we finally decided that 'good' is an infinitely recursive term—it can't be defined except in terms of itself. Good is good because it's better than bad, though why it's better to be good than bad depends on how you define good, and on and on."

"The things the modern fleet teaches to its admirals."

"You're an admiral too, and look where it got *you.*"

"Tutor to a bratty boy who saves the human race but doesn't do his chores."

"Sometimes I wish I were bratty," said Ender. "I dream about it—about defying authority. But even when I absolutely decide to, what I can't get rid of is responsibility. People counting on me—that's what controls me."

"So you have no ambition except duty?" asked Mazer.

"And I have no duties now," said Ender. "So I envy Colonel . . . Mister Graff. All those plans. All that purpose. I wonder what he plans for *me.*"

"Are you sure he does?" asked Mazer. "Plan anything for you, I mean?"

"Maybe not," said Ender. "He worked awfully hard to shape this tool. But now that it will never be needed again, maybe he can set me down and let me rust and never think of me."

"Maybe," said Mazer. "That's the thing we have to keep in mind. Graff is not . . . *nice.*"

"Unless he needs to be."

"Unless he needs to *seem* to be," said Mazer. "He's not above lying his face off to frame things in such a way that you'll *want* to do what he wants you to do."

"Which is how he got you here, to be my trainer during the war?"

"Oh, yes," said Mazer, with a sigh.

"Going home now?" asked Ender. "I know you have family."

"Great-grandchildren," said Mazer. "And great-great-grandchildren. My wife is dead and my only surviving child is gaga with senility, my grandchildren tell me. They say it lightly, because they've accepted that their father or uncle has lived a full life and he's getting really old. But how can I accept it? I don't know any of these people."

"Hero's welcome won't be enough to make up for losing fifty years, is that it?" asked Ender.

"Hero's welcome," muttered Mazer. "You know what the hero's welcome is? They're still deciding whether to charge me along with Graff. I think they probably will."

"So if they charge you along with Graff," said Ender, "then you'll be acquitted along with him."

"Acquitted?" said Mazer ruefully. "We won't be jailed or anything. But we'll be reprimanded. A note of censure placed in our files. And Graff will probably be cashiered. The people who brought this court martial can't be made to look foolish for doing it. They have to turn out to have been correct."

Ender sighed. "So for their pride, you both get slapped. And Graff maybe loses his career."

Mazer laughed. "Not so bad, really. My record was full of notes of reprimand *before* I beat the buggers in the Second Formic War. My career has been forged out of reprimands and censures. And Graff? The military was never his *career.* It was just a way to get access to the influence and power he needed in order to accomplish his plans. Now he doesn't need the military anymore, so he's willing to be drummed out of it."

Ender nodded, chuckled. "I bet you're right. Graff is probably planning to exploit it somehow. The people who benefit from his being kicked out, he'll take advantage of how guilty they feel in order to get what he really wants. A consolation prize that turns out to be his real objective."

"Well, they can't very well give him medals for the exact same thing that he was court-martialed for," said Mazer.

"They'll give him his colonization project," said Ender.

"Oh, I don't know if guilt goes *that* far," said Mazer. "It would cost billions of dollars to equip and refit the fleet into colony ships, and there's no guarantee that anyone from Earth will volunteer to go away forever. Let alone crews for the ships."

"They have to do something with this huge fleet and all its personnel. The ships have to go somewhere. And there are those surviving I.F. soldiers on all the conquered worlds. I think Graff's going to get his colonies—we won't send ships to bring them home, we'll send new colonists to join them."

"I see you've mastered all of Graff's arguments."

"So have you," said Ender. "And I bet you'll go with them."

"Me? I'm too old to be a colonist."

"You'd pilot a ship," said Ender. "A colony ship. You'd go away again. Because you've already done it once. Why not go again? Lightspeed travel, taking the ship to one of the old formic planets."

"Maybe."

"After you've lost everybody, what's left to lose?" asked Ender. "And you believe in what Graff is doing. It's his real plan all along, isn't it? To spread the human race out of the solar system so we aren't held as hostages to the fate of a single planet. To spread ourselves out among star systems as far as we can go, so that we're unkillable as a species. It's Graff's great cause. And you also think that's worth doing."

"I've never spoken a word on the subject."

"Whenever it's discussed, you don't make that little lemon-sucking face when Graff's arguments are presented."

"Oh, now you think you can read my face. I'm Maori, I don't show anything."

"You're half-Maori, and I've studied you for months."

"You can't read my mind. Even if you've deluded yourself into thinking you can read my face."

"The colonization project is the only thing left out here in space that's worth doing."

"I haven't been asked to pilot anything," said Mazer. "I'm old for a pilot, you know."

"Not a pilot, a commander of a ship."

"I'm lucky they let me aim by myself when I pee," said Mazer. "They don't trust me. That's why I'm going on trial."

"When the trial's over," said Ender, "they'll have no more use for you than they have for me. They've got to send you somewhere far away so that the I.F. will be safe for the bureaucrats again."

Mazer looked away and waited, but there was an air about him that told Ender that Mazer was about to say something important.

"Ender, what about you?" Mazer finally asked. "Would you go?"

"To a colony?" Ender laughed. "I'm thirteen years old. On a colony, what would I be good for? Farming? You know what my skills are. Useless in a colony."

Mazer barked a laugh. "Oh, you'll send *me,* but you won't go yourself."

"I'm not sending anybody," said Ender. "Least of all myself."

"You've got to do *something* with your life," said Mazer.

And there it was: The tacit recognition that Ender wasn't going home. That he was never going to lead a normal life on Earth.

One by one the other kids got their orders, each saying good-bye before they left. It was increasingly awkward with each one, because Ender was more and more a stranger to them. He didn't hang out with them. If he happened to join in a conversation, he didn't stay long and never really engaged.

It wasn't a deliberate choice, he just wasn't interested in doing the things they did or talking about what they discussed. They were full of their studies, their return to Earth. What they'd do. How they'd find a way to get together again after they'd been home for a while. How much money they'd get as severance pay from the military. What they might choose as a career. How their families might have changed.

None of that applied to Ender. He couldn't pretend that it did, or that he had a future. Least of all could he talk about what really preyed on his mind. They wouldn't understand.

He didn't understand it himself. He had been able to let go of everything else, all the things he'd concentrated on so hard for so long. Military tactics? Strategy? Not even interesting to him now. Ways that he might have avoided antagonizing Bonzo or Stilson in the first place? He had strong feelings about that, but no rational ideas, so he didn't waste time trying to think it through. He let go of it, just the way he let go of his deep knowledge of everyone in his jeesh, his little army of brilliant kids whom he led through the training that turned out to be the war.

Once, knowing and understanding those kids had been part of his work, had been essential to victory. During that time he had even come to think of them as his friends. But he was never one of them; their relationship was too unequal. He had loved them so he could know them, and he had known them so he could use them. Now he had no use for them— not his choice, there simply wasn't a purpose to be served by keeping the group together. They didn't, as a group, exist. They were just a bunch of kids who had been on a long, difficult camping trip together, that's how

Ender saw them now. They had pulled together to make it back to civilization, but now they'd all go home to their families. They weren't connected now. Except in memory.

So Ender had let go of them all. Even the ones who were still here. He saw how it hurt them—the ones who had wanted to be closer than mere pals—when he didn't let things change, didn't let them into his thoughts. He couldn't explain to them that he wasn't keeping them out, that there was simply no way they'd understand what it was that occupied him whenever he wasn't forced to think about something else:

The hive queens.

It made no sense, what the formics had done. They weren't stupid. Yet they had made the strategic mistake of grouping all their queens—not "their" queens, they *were* the queens, the queens *were* the formics—they had all gathered on their home planet, where Ender's use of the M.D. Device could—and did—destroy them utterly, all at once.

Mazer had explained that the hive queens must have gathered on their home planet years before they could have known that the human fleet *had* the M.D. Device. They knew—from the way Mazer had defeated their main expedition to Earth's star system—that their greatest weakness was that if you found the hive queen and killed her, you had killed the whole army. So they withdrew from all their forward positions, put the hive queens together on their home world, and then protected that world with everything they had.

Yes, yes, Ender understood *that.*

But Ender had used the M.D. Device early on in the invasion of the formic worlds, to destroy a formation of ships. The hive queens had instantly understood the capabilities of the weapon and never allowed their ships to get close enough together for the M.D. Device to be able to set up a self-sustaining reaction.

So: Once they knew that the weapon existed, and that humans were willing to use it, why did they *stay* on that single planet? They must have known that the human fleet was coming. As Ender won battle after battle, they must have known that the possibility of their defeat existed. It would have been easy for them to get onto starships and disperse from their home planet. Before that last battle began, they could all have been out of range of the M.D. Device.

Then we would have had to hunt them down, ship by ship, queen by queen. Their planets would still be inhabited by the formics, and so they could have fought us in bloody confrontations on every world, meanwhile building new ships, launching new fleets against us.

But they had stayed. And died.

Was it fear? Maybe. But Ender didn't think so. The hive queens had bred themselves for war. All the speculations of the scientists who had studied the anatomy and molecular structure of the formic corpses left over from the Second Formic War led to that conclusion: The formics were created, first and foremost, to fight and kill. That implied that they had evolved in a world where such fighting was necessary.

The best guess—at least the one that made the most sense to Ender—was that they weren't fighting some predatory species on their home world. Like humans, they would surely have wiped out any really threatening predator early on. No, they had evolved to fight each other. Queens fighting queens, spawning vast armies of formics and developing tools and weapons for them, each of them vying to be the dominant—or sole surviving—queen.

Yet somehow they had gotten over it. They had stopped fighting each other.

Was it before they had developed spaceflight and colonized other worlds? Or was it one particular queen who developed near-lightspeed ships and created colonies and then used the power that she had developed to crush the others?

It wouldn't have mattered. Her own daughters would surely have rebelled against her—it would go on and on, each new generation trying to destroy the one before. That was how hives on Earth worked, anyway—the rival queen must be driven off or killed. Only the non-reproducing workers could be allowed to stay, because they weren't rivals, they were servants.

It was like the immune system of an organism. Each hive queen had to make sure that any food their workers grew was used *only* to nurture her workers, her children, her mates, and herself. So any formic—queen or worker—that tried to infiltrate her territory and use her resources had to be driven off or killed.

Yet they had stopped fighting with each other and now cooperated.

If they could do that with each other, the implacable enemies that had driven each other's evolution long enough to become the brilliant sentient beings they were, then why couldn't they have done it with us? With the humans? Why couldn't they have tried to communicate with us? Made some sort of settlement with us, just as they had done with each other? Divided the galaxy between us? Live and let live?

In any of these battles, Ender knew that if he had seen a sign of an effort to communicate, he would have known instantly that it wasn't a game—there would have been no reason for the teachers to simulate any attempt to parley. They didn't regard that as Ender's business—they wouldn't train him for it. If some effort at communication had really happened, surely the adults would have stopped Ender at once, pretended that the "exercise" was over, and tried to deal with it on their own.

But the hive queens did not attempt to communicate. Nor did they use the obvious strategy of dispersal to save themselves. They had sat there, waiting for Ender to come. And then Ender had won, the only way he could: with devastating force.

It was how Ender always fought. To make sure that there was no further fighting. To use this victory to ensure that there was no more danger.

Even if I had known the war was real, I would have tried to do exactly what I did.

So in his mind he now asked the hive queens, over and over, though he knew they were dead and could not answer: Why?

Why did you decide to let me kill you?

His rational mind introduced all the other possibilities—including the chance that perhaps they were really quite stupid. Or perhaps they had so little experience at running a society of equals that they were unable to reach a rational decision together. Or, or, or, or, over and over he ran through possible explanations.

Ender's study now, when he wasn't pursuing the schoolwork that someone—Graff, still? Or Graff's rivals?—kept assigning him, was to read over the reports from the soldiers that he had once unknowingly commanded. On every formic colony world, humans now walked. And from every exploratory team the reports were the same: All the formics dead and rotting, with vast farms and factories now available for the taking. The soldiers-turned-explorers were always alert to the possibility of ambush, but as the months passed and there were no attacks, their reports became full of the things they were learning from the xenobiologists that had been sent with them: Not only can we breathe the air on every formic world, we can eat most of their food.

And so every formic planet became a human colony, the soldiers settling down to live among the relics of their enemies. There were not enough women among them, but they began to work out social patterns that would maximize reproduction and keep from having too many males without a hope of mating. Within a generation or two, if babies came in the usual proportions, half male and half female, the normal human pattern of monogamy could be restored.

But Ender took only peripheral interest in what the humans were doing on the new worlds. What he studied were the formic artifacts. The patterns of formic settlement. The warrens that had once been the hive queens' breeding grounds, full of larvae that were so hard-toothed they could gnaw through rock, creating more and more tunnels. They had to farm on the surface, but they went underground to breed, to raise their young, and the young themselves were every bit as lethal and powerful as the adults. Chewing through rock—the explorers found the larval bodies, rotting quickly but still there to be photographed, dissected, studied.

"So this is how you spend your days," said Petra. "Looking at pictures of formic tunnels. Is this a return-to-the-womb thing?"

Ender smiled and set aside the pictures he had been studying. "I thought you'd already gone home to Armenia."

"Not till I see how this stupid court martial turns out," she said. "Not until the Armenian government is ready to receive me in high style. Which means they have to decide whether they want me."

"Of course they want you."

"They don't know what they want. They're politicians. Is it good for them to have me back? Is keeping me up here *worse* for them than having me come home? It's so very, very hard when you have no convictions except your lust to remain in power. Aren't we glad we're not in politics?"

Ender sighed. "É. I will never hold office again. Commander of Dragon Army was too much for me, and that was just a kids' game."

"That's what I tried to assure them. I don't want anybody's job. I'm not going to endorse anybody for office. I want to live with my family and see if they remember who I am. And vice versa."

"They'll love you," said Ender.

"And you know this because . . . ?"

"Because *I* love you."

She looked at him in consternation. "How can I possibly answer a comment like *that*?"

"Oh. What was I supposed to say?"

"I don't know. Am I supposed to write scripts for you now?"

"OK," said Ender. "Should it have been banter? 'They'll love you because somebody has to, and it sure isn't anybody up here.' Or maybe the ethnic slur: 'They'll love you because hey, they're Armenian and you're a female.'"

"What does *that* mean?"

"I got that from an Azeri I talked to during that whole flap about Sinterklaas Day back in Battle School. Apparently the idea is that Armenians know that the only people who think Armenian women are . . . I don't have to explain ethnic insults, Petra. They're infinitely transferable."

"When are they letting *you* go home?" asked Petra.

Instead of sidestepping the question or giving it a lazy answer, Ender answered truthfully for once. "I'm thinking maybe it won't happen."

"What do you mean? You think this stupid court martial is going to end up convicting *you*?"

"I'm the one on trial, aren't I?"

"Definitely *not*."

"Only because I'm a child and therefore not responsible. But it's all about what an evil little monster I am."

"It is not."

"I've seen the highlights on the nets, Petra. What the world is seeing is that the savior of the world has a little problem—he kills children."

"You defended yourself from bullies. Everybody understands that."

"Except the people who post comments about how I'm a worse war criminal than Hitler or Pol Pot. A mass murderer. What makes you think I *want* to go home and deal with all that?"

Petra wasn't playing now. She sat down next to him and took his hands. "Ender, you have a family."

"Had."

"Oh, don't say that! You *have* a family. Families still love their children even if they've been away for eight years."

"I've only been away for seven. Almost. Yes, I know they love me. Some of them at least. They love who I was. A cute little six-year-old. I must have been so huggable. Between killing other children, that is."

"So is that what this obsession with formic porn is?"

"Porn?"

"The way *you* study it. Classic addiction. Got to have more and more of it. Explicit photos of rotting larva bodies. Autopsy shots. Slides of their molecular structure. Ender, they're gone, and *you* didn't kill them. Or if you did, then *we* did. But we didn't. We played a game! We were training for war, that's all it was."

"And if it had really been just a game?" asked Ender. "And then they assigned us to the fleet after we graduated, and we actually piloted those ships or commanded those squadrons? Wouldn't we have done it for real?"

"Yes," said Petra. "But we didn't. It didn't happen."

"It happened. They're gone."

"Well, studying the structure of their bodies and the biochemistry of their cells is not going to bring them back."

"I'm not trying to bring them back," said Ender. "What a nightmare *that* would be."

"No, you're trying to persuade yourself that you deserve the merdicious things they're saying about you in the court martial, because if that's true, then you don't deserve to go back to Earth."

Ender shook his head. "I want to go home, Petra, even if I can't stay. And I'm not conflicted about the war. I'm glad we fought and I'm glad we won and I'm glad it's over."

"But you keep your distance from everybody. We understood, or sympathized, or pretended we did. But you've kept us all at arm's length. You make this show of dropping everything whenever one of us comes around to chat, but it's an act of hostility."

What an outrageous thing to say. "It's common courtesy!"

"You never even say, 'Just a sec,' you just drop everything. It's so . . . *obvious.* The message is: 'I'm really busy but I still think you're my responsibility so I'll drop whatever I'm doing because you need my time.' "

"Wow," said Ender. "You sure understand a lot of things about me. You're so smart, Petra. A girl like you—they could really make something out of you in Battle School."

"Now *that's* a real answer."

"Not as real as what I said before."

"That you love me? You're not my therapist, Ender. Or my priest. Don't coddle me, don't tell me what you think I need to hear."

"You're right," said Ender. "I *shouldn't* drop everything when one of my friends drops by." He picked his papers back up again.

"Put those down."

"Oh, *now* it's OK because you asked me so rudely."

"Ender," Petra said, "we all came back from the war. You didn't. You're still in it. Still fighting . . . something. We talk about you all the time. Wondering why you won't turn to us. Hoping there's *somebody* you talk to."

"I talk to anybody and everybody. I'm quite the chatterbox."

"There's a stone wall around you and those words you just said are some of the bricks."

"Bricks in a stone wall?"

"So you *are* listening!" she said triumphantly. "Ender, I'm not trying to violate your privacy. Keep it all in. Whatever it is."

"I'm not keeping anything in," said Ender. "I don't have any secrets. My whole life is on the nets, it belongs to the human race now, and I'm really not that worried about it. It's like I don't even live in my body. Just in my mind. Just trying to solve this question that won't leave me alone."

"What question?"

"The question I keep asking the hive queens, and they never answer."

"What question?"

"I keep asking them, 'Why did you die?' "

Petra searched his face for . . . what, a sign that he was joking? "Ender, they died because we—"

"Why were they still on that planet? Why weren't they in ships, speeding away? They chose to stay, knowing we had that weapon, knowing what it did and how it worked, they *stayed* for the battle, they waited for us to come."

"They fought us as hard as they could. They didn't want to die, Ender. They didn't commit suicide by human soldier."

"They knew we had beaten them time after time. They had to think it was at least a possibility that it would happen again. And they stayed."

"So they stayed."

"It's not like they had to prove their loyalty or courage to the footsoldiers. The workers and soldiers were like their own body parts. That would be like saying, 'I have to do this because I want my hands to know how brave I am.'"

"I can see you've given this a lot of thought. Obsessive, borderline crazy thought. But whatever keeps you happy. You *are* happy, you know. People all over Eros talk about it—how cheerful that Wiggin boy always is. You've got to cut back on the whistling, though. It's driving people crazy."

"Petra, I've done my life's work. I don't think they're going to let me go back to Earth, not even to visit. I hate that, I'm angry about it, but I also understand it. And in a way it's *fine* with me. I've had all the responsibility I want. I'm done. I'm retired. No more duty to anybody. So now I get to think about what actually bothers me. The problem I have to solve."

He slid the pictures forward on the library table. "Who *are* these people?" he asked.

Petra looked at the pictures of the dead larvae and formic workers and said, "They aren't people, Ender. They're *formics*. And they're gone."

"For years I've bent every thought to understanding them, Petra. To knowing them better than I know any human being in my life. To *loving* them. So I could use that knowledge to defeat them and destroy them. Now they're destroyed, but that doesn't mean that I can switch off my *attention* to them."

Petra's face lit up. "I get it. I finally get it!"

"Get what?"

"Why you're so weird, Ender Wiggin, sir. It's not weird at all."

"If you think I'm not weird, Petra, it proves you *don't* understand me."

"The rest of us, we fought a war and we won it and we're going home. But you, Ender, you were *married* to the formics. When the war ended you were *widowed*."

Ender sighed and rolled his chair back from the table.

"I'm not joking," said Petra. "It's like when my great-grandpa died. Great-grandma had always taken care of him, it was pathetic the way he bossed her around, and she just did whatever he wanted, and my mother would say to me, 'Don't you ever marry a man who treats you like that,' but when he died, you'd think Great-grandma would have been liberated. Free at last! But she wasn't. She was *lost.* She kept looking for him. She kept talking about things she was working on for him. Can't do this, can't do that, Babo wouldn't like it, until my grandpa—her son—said, 'He's gone.'"

"I know the formics are gone, Petra."

"And so did Great-grandma. That's what she said. 'I know. I just can't figure out why I'm not gone too.'"

Ender slapped his forehead. "Thank you, doctor, you finally revealed my innermost motivations and now I'm able to get on with my life."

Petra ignored his sarcasm. "They died without giving you answers. That's why you hardly notice what's going on around you. Why you can't act like a regular friend to anybody. Why you don't even seem to care that there are people down there on Earth who are trying to keep you from ever coming home. You win the victory and they want to exile you for life and you *don't care* because all you can think about is your lost formics. They're your dead wife and you can't let go."

"It wasn't much of a marriage," said Ender.

"You're still in love."

"Petra, cross-species romance just isn't for me."

"You said it yourself. You had to love them to defeat them. You don't have to agree with me now. It will come to you later. You'll wake up in a cold sweat and you'll shout, 'Eureka! Petra was right!' Then you can start fighting for the right to return to the planet you saved. You can start *caring* about something again."

"I care about *you,* Petra," said Ender. What he didn't say was: I already care about understanding the hive queens, but you don't count that because you don't get it.

She shook her head. "No getting through the wall," she said. "But I thought it was worth one last try. I'm right, though. You'll see. You can't let these hive queens deform the rest of your life. You have to let them be dead and move on."

Ender smiled. "I hope you find happiness at home, Petra. And love. And I hope you have the babies that you want and a good life full of meaning and accomplishment. You are so ambitious—and I think you'll have it all, true love and domesticity and great achievements."

Petra stood up. "What makes you think I want babies?" she said.

"I know you," said Ender.

"You *think* you know me."

"The way you think you know me?"

"I'm not a lovesick girl," said Petra, "and if I were, it wouldn't be over *you.*"

"Ah, so it bothers you when somebody presumes to know your deepest inner motivation."

"It bothers me that you're such an oomo."

"Well, you've cheered me up marvelous well, Miss Arkanian. We oomos are grateful when the fine folk from the big house come to visit us."

Petra's voice was angry and defiant when she fired her parting shot. "Well, I actually *love* you and *care* about you, Ender Wiggin." Then she turned and walked away.

"And I love and care about *you,* only you wouldn't believe me when I said it!"

At the door she turned back to face him. "Ender Wiggin, *I* wasn't being sarcastic or patronizing when I said that."

"Neither was I!"

But she was gone.

"Maybe I've been trying to study the wrong alien species," he said softly.

He looked at the display above his desk. It was still in motion, though muted, showing bits from Mazer's testimony. He looked so cold, so aloof, as if he had contempt for the whole business. When they asked about Ender's violence and whether that made it hard to train him, Mazer turned to face the judges and said, "I'm sorry, I misunderstood, isn't this a court *martial*? Aren't we all soldiers here, trained to commit acts of violence?"

The judge gaveled him down and reprimanded him, but the point was made. Violence was what the military existed for—controlled violence, directed against appropriate targets. Without actually having to say a word about Ender, Mazer had made it clear that violence wasn't a drawback, it was the point.

It made Ender feel better. He could switch off the newslink and get back to work.

He stood up to reach across the table and retrieve the photos that Petra had moved. The face of a dead formic farmer from one of the faroff planets stared up at him, the torso open and the organs arranged neatly around the corpse.

I can't believe you *gave up,* Ender said silently to the picture. I can't believe that a whole species lost its will to live. Why did you let me kill you?

"I will not rest until I know you," he whispered.

But they were gone. Which meant that he could never, never rest.

CHAPTER

3

To: mazerrackham%nonexistent@unguessable.com/imaginary.heroes
From: hgraff%educadmin@ifcom.gov
{self-shred protocol}
Subj: How about a little voyage?

Dear Mazer,

I know as well as anyone that you almost refused to come home from your last voyage, and I'm certainly not going to let them send you anywhere now. But you took too big a risk testifying for me (or for Ender; or for truth and justice; I don't presume to guess your motives) and the heat is on. The best way, I think, for you to become less visible and therefore less likely to be further interfered with is to let it be known that you will be the commander of a certain colony ship. The one that's going to carry Ender away to safety.

Once you're fully ignored because you're supposedly going on a forty-year voyage, it will be easy enough to reassign you at the last minute to another ship that isn't leaving till later. No publicity that time. You'll just happen not to go.

As for Ender, we'll let him in on the lie from the start. He doesn't need or deserve any more surprises. But he also doesn't need you or me to protect him. I think he's proven that many times over.

—Hyrum

PS: It's just too cute for you to use your real name as your secret identity on Unguessable.com. Who knew you had a sense of irony?

Mother and Father were both out of the house. That was a bad thing, because it meant Peter could get in full carpet-chewing mode if he felt like it, and things were definitely heading that way.

"I can't believe I got suckered into this," said Peter.

"Suckered into what?"

"Having Locke and Demosthenes push for Ender not to come home."

"You haven't been paying attention," said Valentine. "Demosthenes is pushing for Ender to come back and restore America to its former greatness. And Locke is the conciliatory moderate, trying to find a middle way, as he always does, the miserable appeaser."

"Oh shut up," said Peter. "It's too late for you to start playing dumb. But I had no way of knowing they were going to turn that stupid court martial into a smear campaign against the Wiggin name!"

"Oh, I see," said Valentine. "It's not Ender, it's the fact that you can't take advantage of being Locke without revealing who you are, and who you are is Ender's brother. Now that won't be such a nice boost for you."

"I can't accomplish anything unless I get into a position of influence, and now it's going to be a lot harder because Ender *killed* people."

"In self-defense."

"When he was a *baby.*"

"I distinctly remember," said Valentine, "that you once promised to kill him."

"I didn't mean it."

Valentine had her doubts. She was the only one who didn't trust Peter's sudden bout of niceness several Christmases ago, when apparently he was anointed by Saint Nick—or Uriah Heap—with the unguent of altruism. "My point is that Ender didn't kill *everybody* who threatened him."

And there it was—a flash of the old rage. She watched, amused, as Peter fought it down, got it under control.

"It's too late to change our position on Ender's return." He said it like an accusation, as if this had all been her idea.

Well, in a way, it had. But not the actual implementation—that was all Peter's script.

"But before we let it be discovered who Locke really is, we have to re-habilitate Ender's reputation. That's not going to be easy. I just can't fig-ure out which of us should do it. On the one hand, Demosthenes would be right in character—but nobody would trust his motives. On the other hand, if Locke does it openly, then everybody will think I had an ulterior motive when it comes out who I really am."

Valentine didn't even smirk, though she knew—had known for years— that Colonel Graff and probably half the I.F. command knew who Locke and Demosthenes really were. They had kept the secret so that it wouldn't compromise Ender. But at some point, somebody was going to let it slip— and it wasn't going to be on Peter's own timing.

"No, I think what we have to do," said Peter, "is bring Ender home after all. But not to the United States, or at least not under the control of the U.S. government. I think Locke needs to speak with compassion about the young hero who can't help how he was exploited." Peter put on his Locke voice—a conciliatory whine that if he ever used it in public, Locke would be out of business in a trice. "Let him come home, as a cit-izen of the world he saved. Let the Hegemon's Council protect him. If no one threatens him, the boy poses no danger." Peter looked at her tri-umphantly and went back to his own voice. "See? We bring him home, and then when my identity comes out, I'm a loyal brother, yes, but I also acted for the good of the whole world, and not for the advantage of the United States."

"You're forgetting a couple of things," said Valentine.

Peter glared at her. He hated it when she accused him of making a mistake, but he had to listen to her because she was often right. Even though he usually pretended that he had already thought of her objection.

"First, you're assuming that Ender wants to come home."

"Of course he wants to come home."

"You don't know that. We don't know him. Second, you're assuming that if he does come home, he'll be such a cuddly kid that everybody will decide he isn't *really* a child-killing monster."

"We've both watched the vids of the court martial," said Peter. "Those men love Ender Wiggin. You could see it in everything they said and did. All that mattered to them was protecting him. Which is exactly how everybody used to act when Ender lived here."

"He never actually lived *here*," said Valentine. "We moved after he left, remember?"

Another glare. "Ender makes people want to die for him."

"Or kill him," she said with a smile.

"Ender makes *adults* love him."

"So we're back to the first problem."

"He wants to come home," said Peter. "He's human. Humans want to go home."

"But where is Ender's home?" asked Valentine. "He's spent more than half his life in Battle School. What does he even remember about living with us? An older brother who was constantly bullying him, threatening to kill him—"

"I'll apologize," said Peter. "I really *am* sorry I acted like that."

"But you can't apologize if he doesn't come home. Besides, Peter, he's a smart kid. Smarter than us—there's a reason we weren't taken into Battle School and he was. So he'll figure out exactly how you're using him. Hegemon's Council—that is such itshay. He won't stay under your thumb."

"He's been trained for war. Not for politics," said Peter.

His hint of a smile was so smug Valentine wanted to smash a baseball bat into his face a little. "It doesn't matter," said Valentine. "You can't bring him home no matter what Locke writes."

"And why is that?"

"Because you didn't create the forces that dread him and fear his return, you just exploited them. They aren't going to change their minds, not even for Locke. And also, Demosthenes won't let you."

Peter looked at her with amused contempt. "Oh, going freelance, eh?"

"I think I can scare people into keeping Ender in space better than you can make them pity him enough to bring him home."

"I thought you loved him best. I thought you wanted him home."

"I wanted him home for the past seven years, Peter," said Valentine, "and you were glad he was gone. But now—to bring him home so that he can be under the protection of the Hegemon's Council—which means under *your* control, since you've got the thing packed with your toadies—"

"Locke's toadies," Peter corrected her.

"I'm not helping you bring Ender home so he can be a tool to advance your career."

"So you'd make your beloved little brother stay in permanent exile in space, just to spite your nasty older brother?" asked Peter. "Wow, I'm glad *I'm* not the one you love."

"You nailed it, Peter," said Valentine. "I've spent all these years under your thumb. I know exactly how it feels. Ender would hate it. I know, because I hate it."

"You've loved the whole thing. Being Demosthenes—you know what power feels like."

"I know what it feels like to have power flow through me and into your hands," said Valentine.

"Is that what this is about? You're suddenly power hungry?"

"Peter, you're such an idiot about the people you supposedly know best. I'm not telling you I want your power. I'm telling you that I'm getting out from under your thumb."

"Fine, I'll just write the Demosthenes essays myself."

"No you won't, because people would know something was wrong. You can't do Demosthenes."

"Anything you can do . . ."

"I've changed all the passwords. I've hidden all of Demosthenes' memberships and money and you can't get to any of it."

Peter gazed at her with pity. "I'll find it all if I want to."

"It wouldn't do you any good. Demosthenes is retiring from politics, Peter. He's going to plead ill health and offer a ringing endorsement . . . of Locke!"

Peter looked horrorstruck. "You can't! It would destroy Locke to have Demosthenes' endorsement!"

"You see? I do have some weapons you fear."

"Why would you do this? All these years, and suddenly *now* you've decided to pack up your dolls and dishes and leave the tea party?"

"I never played with dolls, Peter. Apparently you did."

"Stop this," said Peter sternly. "Really. It's not funny. Let's get Ender home. I won't try to control him the way you're saying."

"You mean the way you control me."

"Come on, Val," said Peter. "Just a couple more years and I can unmask myself as Locke—and as Ender's brother. Sure, salvaging his reputation will help me, but it'll help Ender, too."

"I think you should do it. Salvage away, Peter. But I don't think Ender should come home. Instead, I'll go to *him*. Mom and Dad will, too, I bet."

"They're not going to pay for you to have a jaunt into space—not all the way to Eros. That would take months anyway. Right now it's practically on the other side of the sun."

"Not a jaunt," said Valentine. "I'm leaving Earth. I'm joining Ender in exile."

For a moment Peter believed her. It was gratifying to see genuine alarm on his face. Then he relaxed. "Mom and Dad won't let you," he said.

"Fifteen-year-old females don't have to have their parents' consent to volunteer to be colonists. We're the ideal age for reproduction, and are assumed to be dumb enough to volunteer."

"What do the colonies have to do with anything? Ender's not going to be a colonist."

"What else will they do with him? It's the only task remaining for the I.F., and he's their responsibility. That's why I'm making arrangements to get assigned to the same colony as him."

"Where did you get these imasen ideas?" If she didn't understand Battle School slang, too bad. "Colonies, voluntary exile, it's just crazy. The future is here on Earth, not out at the far reaches of the galaxy."

"The formics' worlds were all in the same arm of the galaxy as us, and not all that far away, as galaxies go," said Valentine primly, to goad him. "And Peter, just because *your* future is all tied up with trying to become the ruler of the world doesn't mean that I want to spend my whole future as your sidekick. You've had my youth, you've used me up, but I will spend my declining years without you, my love."

"It's sickening when you talk as if we were married."

"I'm talking as if we were in an old movie," said Valentine.

"I don't watch movies," said Peter, "so I wouldn't know."

"There's so much you 'wouldn't know,'" said Valentine. For a moment she was tempted to tell him all about Ender's visit to Earth, when Graff tried to use Valentine to persuade a burnt-out Ender to get back to work. And to tell Peter that Graff knew all about their secret identities on the nets. That would take the smirk off his face.

But what would that accomplish? It was better for everyone to leave Peter in blissful ignorance.

While they were talking, Peter had been doing some desultory pointing and typing on his desk. Now he was seeing something in his holo that made him as angry as she had ever seen him. "What?" she asked, assuming it was some dreadful world news.

"You shut down my back doors!"

It took her a moment to understand what he meant. Then she realized—he had apparently thought she wouldn't notice that he had secret access points to all of Demosthenes' vital sites and identities. What an idiot. When he made a big deal about how he had created all these wonderful identities and accounts for her, of *course* she assumed that he had created back doors to all of them so he could always come in and change what she did. Why would he imagine she'd leave things that way? She found them all within a few weeks; anything he could do with Demosthenes on the nets, she could undo. So when she changed all the passwords and access codes, of course she closed the back doors, too. What did he think?

"Peter," she said, "they wouldn't be locked if I let you have a key, now, would they?"

Peter rose to his feet, his face turning red, his fists clenched. "You ungrateful little bitch."

"What are you going to do, Peter? Hit me? I'm ready. I think I can take you down."

Peter sat back down. "Go," he said. "Go into space. Shut down Demosthenes. I don't need you. I don't need anybody."

"That's why you're such a loser," said Valentine. "You'll never rule the world until you figure out that you can't do it without *everybody's* cooperation. You can't fool them, you can't force them. They have to *want* to follow you. Like Alexander's soldiers wanted to follow him and fight for him. And the moment they stopped wanting to, his power evaporated. You need *everybody* but you're too narcissistic to know it."

"I need the willing cooperation of key people here on Earth," said Peter, "but you won't be one of them, will you? So go, tell Mom and Dad what you're doing. Break their hearts. What do *you* care? You're going off to see your precious Ender."

"You still hate him," said Valentine.

"I never hated him," said Peter. "But at this moment, I certainly do hate you. Not a lot, but enough to make me want to piss on your bed."

It was a standing joke between them. She couldn't help it. It made her laugh. "Oh, Peter, you're such a *boy*."

—

Mother and Father took her decision surprisingly well. But they refused to come with her. "Val," Father said, "I think you're right—Ender won't be coming home. It broke our hearts to realize it. And it's wonderful of you to want to join him, even if neither of you ends up going with a colony. Even if it's just a few months in space. Even a few years. It's a good thing for him to be with you again."

"It would be better to have the two of you out there, too."

Father shook his head. Mother pressed a finger to each eye—her gesture that said, I'm not going to cry.

"We can't go," said Father. "Our work is here."

"They could spare you for a year or two."

"That's easy for you to say," said Father. "You're young. What's a couple of years to you? But we're older. Not old, but older than you. Time means something different to us. We love Ender, but we can't spend months or years just going out to visit him. We don't have that much time left."

"That's exactly the point," said Valentine. "You don't have much time— and still less time to get a chance to see Ender again."

"Val," said Mother, her voice quavering. "Nothing we do now will give us back the years we've lost."

She was right, and Valentine knew it. But she didn't see the relevance. "So you're going to treat him as if he's dead?"

"Val," said Father. "We know he's not dead. But we also know he doesn't want us. We've written to him—since the war ended. Graff—the one who's on trial—he wrote back. Ender doesn't want to write letters to us. He reads them, but he told Graff that he had nothing to say."

"Graff's a liar," said Valentine. "He probably hasn't shown Ender anything."

"That's possible," said Father. "But Ender doesn't need us. He's thirteen. He's becoming a man. He's done brilliantly since he left us, but he also went through terrible things, and we weren't there. I'm not sure he'll ever forgive us for letting him go."

"You had no choice," said Valentine. "They would have taken him to Battle School whether you liked it or not."

"I'm sure he knows that in his head," said Mother. "But in his heart?"

"So I'm going without you," she said. It had never crossed her mind that they wouldn't even want to go.

"You're going to leave us behind," said Father. "It's what children do. They live at home until they leave. Then they're gone. Even if they visit, even if they move back, it's never the same. You think it will be, but it won't. It happened with Ender, and it'll happen with you."

"The good thing," said Mother, who was crying a little now, "is that you won't be with Peter anymore."

Valentine couldn't believe her mother was saying such a thing.

"You've spent too much time with him," said Mother. "He's a bad influence on you. He makes you unhappy. He sucks you into his life so you can't have one of your own."

"That'll be our job now," said Father.

"Good luck," was all Valentine could say. Was it possible that her parents really did understand Peter? But if they did, why had they let him have his way for all these years?

"You see, Val," said Father, "if we went to Ender now, we'd want to be his parents, but we don't have any authority over him. Nor anything to offer him. He doesn't need parents anymore."

"A sister, now," said Mother. "A sister, he can use." She took Valentine's hand. She was asking for something.

So Valentine gave her the only thing she could think of that she might want. A promise. "I'll stick with him," said Valentine, "as long as he needs me."

"We would expect nothing less of you, dear," said Mother. She squeezed Valentine's hand and let go. Apparently that was what she had wanted.

"It's a kind and loving thing," said Father. "It's always been your nature. And Ender was always your darling baby brother."

Valentine winced at the old phrase from childhood. Darling baby brother. Ick. "I'll make sure to call him that."

"Do," said Mother. "Ender likes to be reminded of good things."

Did Mother really imagine that anything she knew about Ender at age six would still apply to him now, at age thirteen?

As if she had read Valentine's mind, Mother answered her. "People don't change, Val. Not their fundamental character. Whatever you're going to be as an adult is already visible to someone who really knows you from your birth onward."

Valentine laughed. "So . . . why did you let Peter live?"

They laughed, but uncomfortably. "Val," said Father, "we don't expect you to understand this, but some of the things that make Peter . . . difficult . . . are the very things that might also make him great someday."

"What about me?" asked Valentine. "As long as you're telling fortunes."

"Oh, Val," said Father. "All you have to do is live your life, and everyone around you will be happier."

"No greatness, then."

"Val," said Mother, "goodness trumps greatness any day."

"Not in the history books," said Valentine.

"Then the wrong people are writing history, aren't they?" said Father.

CHAPTER

4

To: qmorgan%rearadmiral@ifcom.gov/fleetcom
From: chamrajnagar%polemarch@ifcom.gov/centcom
{self-shred protocol}
Subj: In or out?

My dear Quince, I'm quite aware of the difference between combat command and flying a colony ship for a few dozen lightyears. If you feel your usefulness in space is over, then by all means, retire with full benefits. But if you stay in, and remain in near space, I can't promise you promotion within the I.F.

We suddenly find ourselves afflicted with peace, you see. Always a disaster for those whose careers have not reached their natural apex.

The colony ship I have offered you is not, contrary to your too-often-stated opinion (try discretion now and then, Quince, and see if it might not work better), a way to send you to oblivion. Retirement is oblivion, my friend. A forty- or fifty-year voyage means that you will outlive all of us who remain behind. All your friends will be dead. But you'll be alive to make new friends. And you'll be in command of a ship. A nice, big, fast one.

This is what the whole fleet faces. We have heroes out there who fought this war that The Boy is credited with winning. Have we forgotten them? ALL our most significant missions will involve decades of flight. Yet we must send our best officers to command them. So at any given moment, most of our best officers will be strangers to everyone at CentCom because they've been in flight for half a lifetime.

Eventually, ALL the central staff will be star voyagers. They will look down their noses at anyone who has NOT taken decades-long flights between stars. They will have cut themselves loose from Earth's timeline. They will know each other by their logs, transmitted by ansible.

What I'm offering you is the only possible source of career-making voyages: colony ships.

And not only a colony ship, but one whose governor is a thirteen-year-old boy. Are you seriously going to tell me that you don't understand that you are not his "nanny," you are being entrusted with the highly responsible position of making sure that The Boy stays as far from Earth as possible, while also making sure that he is a complete success in his new assignment so that later generations cannot judge that he was not treated well.

Naturally, I did not send you this letter, and you did not read it. Nothing in this is to be construed as a secret order. It is merely my personal observation about the opportunity that you have been offered by a polemarch who believes in your potential to be one of the great admirals of the I.F.

Are you in? Or out? I need to draw up the papers one way or the other within the week.

Your friend, Cham

Ender knew that making him the nominal governor of the colony was a joke. When he got there, the colony would already be a going concern, with its own elected leaders. He would be a thirteen-year-old—well, by then a fifteen-year-old—whose only claim to authority was that forty years before he commanded the *grandparents* of the colonists, or at least their parents, in a war that was ancient history by then.

They would have bonded together into a closed community, and it would be outrageous for the I.F. to send them any governor at all, let alone a teenager.

But they'd soon find out that if nobody wanted him to govern, Ender would go along quite happily. All he cared about was getting to a formic planet to see what they had left behind.

The bodies that had so recently been dissected would have long since rotted away; but there's no way the colonists could have settled or even explored more than a tiny fraction of the formic civilization's buildings and artifacts. Governing the colony would be an annoyance—all Ender wanted was to see if there was some way to understand the enemy he had loved and vanquished.

Still, he had to go through the motions of preparing to be governor. For instance, training sessions with legal experts who had drafted the constitution that was being imposed on all the colonies. And even though Ender didn't actually care, he could see that an honest effort had been made to reflect what had been reported by all the soldiers-turned-colonists so far. He should have expected that. Anything Graff did, or caused to be done, was done well.

And then there were the even-less-relevant lessons on the workings of starships. What did Ender care? He was never going to be regular fleet. He had no interest in captaining any vessel of any size.

On the third day of his walk-through of the ship that would carry him and his colonists, Ender was so tired of phony nautical terminology transferred to starships that he found himself making sarcastic remarks. Fortunately, he didn't actually say them, he only thought them. Do we swab the decks, matey? Will the bosun pipe us aboard? How many degrees will she tack into the wind, sir?

"You know," said the captain who had Ender duty today, "the real barrier to interstellar flight wasn't just getting up to lightspeed. It was overcoming the collision problem."

"You mean with all of space to work in . . ." Then, from the captain's smirk, Ender realized he had fallen into a little trap. "Ah. You mean collisions with space debris."

"All those old vids showing spaceships dodging through asteroid clusters—they weren't actually far off. Because when you hit a molecule of hydrogen when you're near lightspeed, it releases a huge amount of energy. Like hitting a huge rock at a much slower speed. Tears you up. Any shielding scheme our ancestors came up with involved so much additional mass, or cost so much energy and therefore fuel, that it simply wasn't practical. You had so much mass that you couldn't carry enough fuel to get anywhere."

"So how did we finally solve it?" asked Ender.

"Well of course we didn't," said the captain.

Again, Ender could see that this was an old prank to play on novices, and so he gave the man the pleasure of showing off his superior knowledge. "Then how are we getting from star to star?" asked Ender. Instead of saying, Ah, so it's formic technology.

"The formics did it for us," said the captain with delight. "When they got here, yes, they devastated parts of China and damn near whupped us in the first two wars. But they also taught us. The very fact that they got here told us that it could be done. And then they thoughtfully left behind dozens of working starships for us to study."

The captain had by now led Ender to the very front of the ship, through several doors that required the highest security clearance to enter. "Not everybody gets to see this, but I was told that you were to see *everything*."

It was crystalline in substance and ovoid in shape, except that it came to a sharp point at the back. "Please don't tell me it's an egg," said Ender.

The captain chuckled. "Don't tell anybody, but the engines of this ship, and all that fuel—they're just for maneuvering near planets and moons and such. And getting the ship going. Once we get up to one percent of lightspeed, we switch on this baby, and from then on, it's just a matter of controlling the intensity and direction."

"Of what?"

"Of the drive field," said the captain. "It was such an elegant solution, but we hadn't even discovered the *area* of science that would have gotten us to this."

"And what area is that?"

"Strong force field dynamics," said the captain. "When people speak of it, they almost always say that the strong force field breaks apart molecules, but that's not the real story. What it really does is change the direction of the strong force. Molecules simply can't hold together when the nuclei of all the constituent atoms start to prefer a particular direction of movement at lightspeed."

Ender knew he was pouring on technical terms, but he was tired of the game. "What you're saying is that the field generated by this device takes all the molecules and objects it runs into in the direction of movement and uses the nuclear strong force to make them move in a uniform direction at lightspeed."

The captain grinned. "Touché. But you're an admiral, sir, and so I was giving you the show I give all the admirals." He winked. "Most of them don't have a clue what I'm saying, and they're too stuffed to admit it and ask me to translate."

"What happens to the energy from the breaking of the molecules into their constituent atoms?" asked Ender.

"That, sir, is what powers the ship. No, I'll be more specific. That's what actually *moves* the ship. It's so beautiful. We move forward under rockets, and then we switch off the engines—can't be generating molecules of our own!—and turn on the egg—yeah, we call it the egg. The field goes up—it's shaped exactly like the crystal ball here—and the leading edges start colliding with molecules and tearing them up. The atoms are channeled along the field and they all emerge at the trailing point. Giving us an incredible amount of thrust. I've talked to physicists who still don't get it. They say there isn't enough energy stored in the molecular bonds to produce the thrust—they've come up with all kinds of theories about where the extra energy is coming from."

"And we got this from the formics."

"There was one terrible accident the first time we turned on one of these. Of course they weren't using them in-system. But we had one of our cruisers simply disappear because it was docked right up against a formic ship when the egg got turned on. Poof. Every molecule in the cruiser—including the unluckiest crew in history—got incorporated into the field, then got spit out the back, and made the formic ship itself jump like a bullet halfway across the solar system."

"Didn't that kill the people on the formic ship, too? To jump that fast?"

"No. Because the formic anti-grav—technically, anti-inertial—was on. Powered by the egg reaction, too, of course. It's like all the molecules in space were put there to be cheap fuel for our ships and everything on them. Anyway, the anti-gravs compensated for the jump and the only problem was communicating with IFCom to tell them what happened. Without the cruiser, no communications except short-range radio."

The captain went on to tell about the clever way the men on the formic ship attracted the attention of rescuers, but Ender's concentration was on something else—something so disturbing that it made him lightheaded and a little nauseated from the shock of it.

The egg, the strong force field generator, obviously was the source of the molecular disruption device. What the captain had just described was the reaction that was in the M.D. Device, the "Little Doctor," which Ender had used to destroy the formic home planet and kill all the hive queens.

Ender thought it was a technology that humans had come up with on their own. But it was clearly based on formic technology. You just take away the controls that shape the field, and you've got a field that chews up everything in its path and spits it out as raw atoms. A field that sustains itself on the energy it generates by playing with the strong nuclear force. A planet-eater.

The formics had to recognize it when Ender used it the first time. It wasn't mysterious to them—they'd recognize it immediately as a raw, uncontrolled weaponization of the principle that powered every formic starship.

Between the time of that battle and the final one, the formics surely had the time to do the same thing—to weaponize the strong force field generator and use it against the humans before they came in range.

They absolutely knew what the weapon was. They could have made their own whenever they wanted. But they didn't do it. They just sat there waiting for Ender.

They gave us the stardrive we used to get to them, and the weapon we used to kill them. They gave us everything.

We humans are supposed to be so clever. So inventive. Yet this was completely beyond our reach. *We* make desks with clever holodisplays that we can play really fun games on. Plus send each other letters over vast distances. But compared to them, we didn't even know how to *kill* properly. While they knew how—but chose not to use the technology that way.

"Well, this part of the tour usually bores people," said the captain.

"No, I wasn't bored. Truly. I was just thinking."

"About what?"

"Stuff that's too classified to talk about using any method but telepathy," said Ender. Which was true—the existence of the M.D. Device was only on a need-to-know basis, and the secret had been well kept. Even the men who deployed and used the weapons didn't understand what they were and what they could do. The soldiers who had seen the Little Doctor consume a planet were dead, lost in the same vast chain reaction. The soldiers who had seen it used in one of the early battles just thought of it as an incredibly big bomb. Only the top brass understood it—and Ender, because Mazer Rackham had insisted that he had to be told what the weapons he carried actually were and how they worked. As Mazer told him later, "I told Graff, You don't give a man a bag of tools and not tell him what they are and what they do and how they might go wrong."

Graff again. Graff who decided Mazer was right and allowed them to tell Ender what it was and how it worked.

My slaughter of the formics—it's all here in the egg.

"You've gone off again," said the captain.

"Thinking about what a miracle starflight is. Whatever else we might think of the buggers, they did give us our road to the stars."

"I know," said the captain. "I've thought of that before. If they had just bypassed our system instead of coming in and trying to wipe Earth clean, we'd never have known they existed. And at our level of technology, we probably wouldn't have gotten out into the stars until so much later that we'd have found every nearby planet completely occupied by formics."

"Captain, this was a most excellent and productive tour."

"I know. How else would you have learned how to find the head on every deck?"

Ender laughed at the joke. Partly because it was true. He'd need to find a bathroom several times a day through the whole voyage.

"I assume you're staying awake for the flight," said the captain.

"Wouldn't want to miss any of the scenery."

"Oh, there's no scenery, because at lightspeed you—oh, a joke. Sorry, sir."

"Got to work on my sense of humor, when my jokes make other people apologize to me."

"Begging your pardon, sir, but you don't talk like a kid."

"Do I talk like an admiral?" asked Ender.

"Since you *are* an admiral, however you talk is like an admiral, sir," said the captain.

"Very cleverly sidestepped, sir. Tell me, are you coming on the voyage with me?"

"I have a family on Earth, sir, and my wife doesn't want to join a colony on another world. No pioneer spirit, I'm afraid."

"You have a life. A good reason for staying home."

"But you're going," said the captain.

"Have to see the formic homeland," said Ender. "Or the next best thing, considering that their home planet doesn't exist anymore."

"Which I'm damned happy about, sir," said the captain. "If you hadn't whupped them for good and all, sir, we'd be looking over our shoulder through the next ten thousand years of human history."

There was a stab of insight there. Ender caught it and then it immediately slipped away. Something about the way the hive queens thought. Their purpose in letting Ender kill them.

Well, if it's true, then I'll think of it again.

Ender hoped that optimistic thought was right.

———

When all of Ender's tours and training sessions were finished, he finally got an interview with the Minister of Colonization.

"Please don't call me Colonel," said Graff.

"I can't call you MinCol."

"Officially, a Hegemony minister is addressed as 'Your Excellency.' "

"With a straight face?"

"Sometimes," said Graff. "But we're colleagues, Ender. I call you by your first name. You can call me by mine."

"Never in my life," said Ender. "You're Colonel Graff to me, and that will never change."

"Doesn't matter," said Graff. "I'll be dead before you get to your destination."

"Hardly seems fair. Come with us."

"I have to be here to get my own work done."

"My work *is* done."

"I don't know about that," said Graff. "The work *we* had for you is done. But you don't even know yet what your own work is going to be."

"I know it won't be governing a colony, sir."

"And yet you accepted the job."

Ender shook his head. "I accepted the title. When I get to the colony, *then* we'll see just how much of a governor I'll be. The Constitution you came up with is good, but the real constitution is always the same: The leader only has as much power as his followers give him."

"And yet you're going to make the voyage awake instead of in stasis."

"It's only a couple of years," said Ender. "And it'll make me fifteen when we arrive. I'm hoping I'll get taller."

"I hope you're bringing a lot of books to read."

"They stocked a few thousand titles for me in the ship's library," said Ender. "But what matters to me is that you use the ansible to give us all the information about the formics that comes out while we're in flight."

"Of course," said Graff. "That will be sent to all the ships."

Ender smiled slightly.

"All right, yes, of course I'll send them directly to you as well. What, are you suspecting that the ship's captain will try to control your access to information?"

"If you were in his place, wouldn't you do the same?"

"Ender, I would never let myself get in the position of trying to control you against your will."

"You just spent the last six years doing that."

"And got court-martialed for it, you'll notice."

"And your punishment was to get the job you've wanted all along. Let me see. Minister of Colonization doesn't go to Earth to be under the thumb of the Hegemon. He stays in space, nicely ensconced with the International Fleet. So even if they change hegemons, it won't involve you. And if they fire you—"

"They won't," said Graff.

"You're so sure of that."

"It's not a prediction, it's an intention."

"You, sir, are a piece of work," said Ender.

"Oh, speaking of pieces of work," said Graff, "did you hear that Demosthenes has retired?"

"The guy on the nets?" asked Ender.

"I don't mean the Greek author of the Philippics."

"I don't actually care," said Ender. "It's just the nets."

"The nets, and this rabble-rouser's screeds in particular, are where the battle was played out and you lost," said Graff.

"Who says I lost?" asked Ender.

"Touché," said Graff. "My point is that the person behind the online identity is actually younger than most people imagined. So the retirement isn't about age, it's about leaving home. Leaving Earth."

"Demosthenes is becoming a colonist?"

"Isn't that an odd choice," said Graff, sounding as if it weren't odd to him at all.

"Please don't tell me he's coming on my ship."

"Technically, it's Admiral Quincy Morgan's ship. You don't take over till you set foot on the ground in your colony. That's the law."

"Dodging the question as usual."

"Yes, you'll have Demosthenes on your ship. But of course no one will be using that name."

"You've been avoiding the use of the masculine pronoun—of any pronoun," said Ender. "So Demosthenes is a woman."

"And she's eager to see you."

Ender sagged in his chair. "Oh, sir, please."

"Not your normal hero-worshiper, Ender. And since she's also going to be awake through your whole voyage, I think you'll want to be prepared by seeing her in advance."

"When is she coming?"

"She's here."

"On Eros?"

"In my cozy little antechamber," said Graff.

"You're going to make me meet her *now*? Colonel Graff, I don't *like* anything she wrote. Or the result."

"Give her credit. She was warning the world about the Warsaw Pact's attempt to take over the fleet long before anybody else took the threat seriously."

"She was also crowing about how America could conquer the world once it had me."

"You can ask her about that."

"I have no such intention."

"Let me tell you one pure and simple truth. In everything she wrote about you, Ender, her only concern was to protect you from the terrible things people would have done to exploit you or destroy you if you ever set foot on Earth."

"I could have dealt with it."

"We'll never know, will we?"

"If I know you, sir, what you just told me is that you were behind this. Keeping me off Earth."

"Not really," said Graff. "I went along with it, yes."

Ender wanted to cry. From sheer moral exhaustion. "Because you know better than me what's in my best interest."

"In this case, Ender, I think you could have dealt with any challenge that came to you. Except one. Your brother, Peter, is determined to rule the world. You would have been either his tool or his enemy. Which would you have chosen?"

"Peter?" asked Ender. "Do you think he really has a chance of it?"

"He's done incredibly well so far—for a teenager."

"Isn't he twenty by now? No, I guess he'd still be seventeen. Or eighteen."

"I don't keep track of your family's birthdays," said Graff.

"If he's doing such a great job," said Ender, "why haven't I heard of him?"

"Oh, you have."

That meant Peter was using a pseudonym. Ender quickly thought through all the online personalities that might be considered close to some kind of world domination and when he got it, he sighed. "Peter is Locke."

"So, clever boy, who is Demosthenes?"

Ender rose to his feet and to his own chagrin he was crying, just like that. He didn't even *know* he was crying till his cheeks were wet and he couldn't see for the blur. "Valentine," he whispered.

"I'm going to leave my office now and let the two of you talk," said Graff.

When he left, the door stayed open. And then she came in.

CHAPTER

5

To: imo%testadmin@colmin.gov
From: hgraff%mincol@heg.gov
Subj: What are we screening for?

Dear Imo,

I've been giving our conversation a great deal of thought, and I think you may be right. I had the foolish idea that we should test for desirable and useful traits so that we could assemble ideally balanced teams to the colonies. But we're not getting such a flood of volunteers that we can afford to be really choosy. And as history shows us, when colonization is voluntary, people will self-select better than any testing system.

It's like those foolish attempts to control immigration to America based on the traits that were deemed desirable, when in fact the only trait that defines Americans historically is "descended from somebody willing to give up everything to live there." And we won't go into the way Australian colonists were selected!

Willingness is the single most important test, as you said. But that means all the other tests are . . . what?

Not useless, as you suggested. On the contrary, I think the test results are a valuable resource. Even if the colonists are all insane, shouldn't the governor have a good dossier on each individual's particular species of madness?

I know, you're not letting through anyone who needs to maintain functional sanity with drugs. Or known addicts and alcoholics and sociopaths, or people with genetic diseases, etc. We always agreed on that, to avoid overburdening the colonies. They'll develop their own genetic and brain-based quirks in a few generations anyway, but for now, let them have a little breathing room.

But the family you queried about, the ones with a plan for marrying off a daughter to the governor—surely you will agree with me that in the long history of motives for joining a faraway colony, marriage was one of the noblest and most socially productive.

—Hyrum

"Do you know what I did today, Alessandra?"

"No, Mother." Fourteen-year-old Alessandra set her book bag on the floor by the front door and walked past her mother to the sink, where she poured herself a glass of water.

"Guess!"

"Got the electricity turned back on?"

"The elves would not speak to me," said Mother. It had once been funny, this game that electricity came from elves. But it wasn't funny now, in the sweltering Adriatic summer, with no refrigeration for the food, no air-conditioning, and no vids to distract her from the heat.

"Then I don't know what you did, Mother."

"I changed our lives," said Mother. "I created a future for us."

Alessandra froze in place and uttered a silent prayer. She had long since given up hope that any of her prayers would be answered, but she figured each unanswered prayer would add to the list of grievances she would take up with God, should the occasion arise.

"What future is that, Mother?"

Mother could hardly contain herself. "We are going to be colonists."

Alessandra sighed with relief. She had heard all about the Dispersal

Project in school. Now that the formics had been destroyed, the idea was for humans to colonize all their former worlds, so that humanity's fate would not be tied to that of a single planet. But the requirements for colonists were strict. There was no chance that an unstable, irresponsible— no, pardon me, I meant "feckless and fey"—person like Mother would be accepted.

"Well, Mother, that's wonderful."

"You don't *sound* excited."

"It takes a long time for an application to be approved. Why would they take us? What do we know how to do?"

"You're such a pessimist, Alessandra. You'll have no future if you must frown at every new thing." Mother danced around her, holding a fluttering piece of paper in front of her. "I put in our application *months* ago, darling Alessandra. Today I got word that we have been accepted!"

"You kept a secret for all this time?"

"I can keep secrets," said Mother. "I have all kinds of secrets. But this is no secret, this piece of paper says that we will journey to a new world, and on that new world you will not be part of a persecuted surplus, you will be needed, all your talents and charms will be noticed and admired."

All her talents and charms. At the coleggio, no one seemed to notice them. She was merely another gawky girl, all arms and legs, who sat in the back and did her work and made no waves. Only Mother thought of Alessandra as some extraordinary, magical creature.

"Mother, may I read that paper?" asked Alessandra.

"Why, do you doubt me?" Mother danced away with the letter.

Alessandra was too hot and tired to play. She did not chase after her. "Of course I doubt you."

"You are no fun today, Alessandra."

"Even if it's true, it's a horrible idea. You should have asked me. Do you know what colonists' lives will be like? Sweating in the fields as farmers."

"Don't be silly," said Mother. "They have machines for that."

"And they're not sure we can eat any of the native vegetation. When the formics first attacked Earth, they simply destroyed all the vegetation in the part of China where they landed. They had no intention of eating anything that grew here naturally. We don't know if our plants can grow on their planets. All the colonists might die."

"The survivors of the fleet that defeated the formics will already have those problems resolved by the time we get there."

"Mother," said Alessandra patiently. "I don't want to go."

"That's because you have been convinced by the dead souls at the school that you are an ordinary child. But you are not. You are magical. You must get away from this world of dust and misery and go to a land that is green and filled with ancient powers. We will live in the caves of the dead ogres and go out to harvest the fields that once were theirs! And in the cool evening, with sweet green breezes fluttering your skirts, you will dance with young men who gasp at your beauty and grace!"

"And where will we find young men like *that*?"

"You'll see," said Mother. Then she sang it: "You shall see! You shall see! A fine young man with prospects will give his heart to you."

Finally the paper fluttered close enough for Alessandra to snatch it out of Mother's hands. She read it, with Mother bending down to hover just behind the paper, smiling her fairy smile. It was real. Dorabella Toscano (29) and daughter Alessandra Toscano (14), accepted into Colony I.

"Obviously there's no sort of psychological screening after all," said Alessandra.

"You try to hurt me but I will not be hurt. Mother knows what is best for you. You shall not make the mistakes that I have made."

"No, but I'll pay for them," said Alessandra.

"Think, my darling, beautiful, brilliant, graceful, kind, generous, and poutful girl, think of this: What do you have to look forward to here in Monopoli, Italia, living in a flat in the unfashionable end of Via Luigi Indelli?"

"There is no *fashionable* end of Luigi Indelli."

"You make my point for me."

"Mother, I don't dream of marrying a prince and riding off into the sunset."

"That's a good thing, my darling, because there are no princes—only men and animals who pretend to be men. I married one of the latter but he at least provided you with the genes for those amazing cheekbones, that dazzling smile. Your father had very good teeth."

"If only he had been a more attentive bicyclist."

"It was not his fault, dear."

"The streetcars run on tracks, Mother. You don't get hit if you stay out from between the tracks."

"Your father was not a genius but fortunately I am, and therefore you have the blood of the fairies in you."

"Who knew that fairies sweat so much?" Alessandra pulled one of Mother's dripping locks of hair away from her face. "Oh, Mother, we won't do well in a colony. Please don't do this."

"The voyage takes forty years—I went next door and looked it up on the net."

"Did you *ask* them this time?"

"Of course I did, they lock their windows now. They were thrilled to hear we were going to be colonists."

"I have no doubt they were."

"But because of magic, to us it will be only two years."

"Because of the relativistic effects of near-lightspeed travel."

"Such a genius, my daughter is. And even those two years we can sleep through, so we won't even age."

"Much."

"It will be as if our bodies slept a week, and we wake up forty years away."

"And everyone we know on Earth will be forty years older than we are."

"And mostly dead," sang Mother. "Including *my* hideous hag of a mother, who disowned me when I married the man I loved, and who therefore will never get her hands on my darling daughter." The melody to this refrain was always cheery-sounding. Alessandra had never met her grandmother. Now, though, it occurred to her that maybe a grandmother could get her out of joining a colony.

"I'm not going, Mother."

"You are a minor child and you will go where I go, tra-la."

"You are a madwoman and I will sue for emancipation rather than go, tra-lee."

"You will think about it first because I am going whether you go or not and if you think your life with me is hard you should see what it's like without me."

"Yes, I should," said Alessandra. "Let me meet my grandmother."

Mother's glare was immediate, but Alessandra plowed ahead. "Let me live with her. You go with the colony."

"But there's no reason for me to go with the colony, my darling. I'm doing this for you. So without you, I will not go."

"Then we're not going. Tell them."

"We *are* going, and we are thrilled about it."

Might as well get off the merry-go-round; Mother didn't mind endlessly repeating circular arguments, but Alessandra got bored with it. What lies did you have to tell, to get accepted?"

"I told no lies," said Mother, pretending to be shocked at the accusation. "I only proved my identity. They do all the research, so if they have false information it's their own fault. Do you know why they want us?"

"Do *you*?" asked Alessandra. "Did they actually tell you?"

"It doesn't take a genius to figure it out, or even a fairy," said Mother. They want us because we are both of childbearing age."

Alessandra groaned in disgust, but Mother was preening in front of an imaginary full-length mirror.

"I am still young," said Mother, "and you are just flowering into womanhood. They have men from the fleet there, young men who have never married. They will be waiting eagerly for us to arrive. So I will mate with very eager old man of sixty and bear him babies and then he will die. I used to that. But you—you will be a prize for a young man to marry. You will be a treasure."

"My *uterus* will, you mean," said Alessandra. "You're right, that's exactly what they're thinking. I bet they took practically any healthy female who applied."

"We fairies are always healthy."

It was true enough—Alessandra had no memory of ever being sick, except for food poisoning that time when Mother insisted they would eat supper from a street vendor's cart at the end of a very hot day.

"So they're sending a herd of women, like cows."

"You're only a cow if you choose to be," said Mother. "The only question I have to decide now is whether we want to sleep through the voyage wake up just before landing, or stay awake for the two years, receiving training and acquiring skills so we're ready to be productive in the wave of colonists."

Alessandra was impressed. "You actually read the documentation?"

"This is the most important decision of our lives, my darling Alessa. I am being extraordinarily careful."

"If only you had read the bills from the power company."

"They were not interesting. They only spoke of our poverty. Now I see that God was preparing us for a world without air-conditioning and vids and nets. A world of nature. We were born for nature, we elvish folk. You will come to the dance and with your fairy grace you will charm the son of the king, and the king's son will dance with you until he is so in love his heart will break for you. Then it will be for *you* to decide if he's the one for you."

"I doubt there'll be a king."

"But there'll be a governor. And other high officials. And young men with prospects. I will help you choose."

"You will certainly *not* help me choose."

"It's as easy to fall in love with a rich man as a poor one."

"As if you'd know."

"I know better than you, having done it badly once. The rush of hot blood into the heart is the darkest magic, and it must be tamed. You must not let it happen until you have chosen a man worthy of your love. I will help you choose."

No point in arguing. Alessandra had long since learned that fighting with Mother accomplished nothing, whereas ignoring her worked very well.

Except for this. A colony. It was definitely time to look up Grandmother. She lived in Polignano a Mare, the next city of any size up the Adriatic coast, that's all that she knew of her. And Mother's mother would not be named Toscano. Alessandra would have to do some serious research.

A week later, Mother was still going back and forth about whether they should sleep through the voyage or not, while Alessandra was discovering that there's a lot of information that they won't let children get at. Snooping in the house, she found her own birth certificate, but that wasn't helpful, it only listed her own parents. She needed Mother's certificate, and that was not findable in the apartment.

The government people barely acknowledged she existed and when they heard her errand sent her away. It was only when she finally thought of the Catholic Church that she made any headway. They hadn't actually attended Mass since Alessandra was little, but at the parish, the priest on duty helped her search back to find her own baptism. They had a record of baby Alessandra Toscano's godparents as well as her parents, and Alessandra figured that either the godparents *were* her grandparents, or they would know who her grandparents were.

At school she searched the net and found that Leopoldo and Isabella Santangelo lived in Polignano a Mare, which was a good sign, since that was the town where Grandmother lived.

Instead of going home, she used her student pass and hopped the train to Polignano and then spent forty-five minutes walking around the town searching for the address. To her disgust, it ended up being on a stub of a street just off Via Antonio Ardito, a trashy-looking apartment building backing on the train tracks. There was no buzzer. Alessandra trudged up to the fourth floor and knocked.

"You want to knock something, knock your own head!" shouted a woman from inside.

"Are you Isabella Santangelo?"

"I'm the Holy Virgin and I'm busy answering prayers. Go away!"

Alessandra's first thought was: So Mother lied about being a child of the fairies. She's really Jesus' younger sister.

But she decided that flippancy wasn't a good approach today. She was already going to be in trouble for leaving Monopoli without permission, and she needed to find out from the Holy Virgin here whether or not she was her grandmother.

"I'm so sorry to trouble you, but I'm the daughter of Dorabella Toscano and I—"

The woman must have been standing right at the door, waiting, because it flew open before Alessandra could finish her sentence.

"Dorabella *Toscano* is a dead woman! How can a dead woman have daughters!"

"My mother isn't dead," said Alessandra, stunned. "You were signed as my godmother on the parish register."

"That was the worst mistake of my life. She marries this pig boy, this bike messenger, when she's barely fifteen, and why? Because her belly's getting fat with you, that's why! She thinks a wedding makes it all clean and pure! And then her idiot husband gets himself killed. I told her, this proves there is a God! Now go to hell!"

The door slammed in Alessandra's face.

She had come so far. Her grandmother couldn't really mean to send her away like this. They hadn't even had time to do more than *glance* at each other.

"But I'm your granddaughter," said Alessandra.

"How can I have a granddaughter when I have no daughter? You tell your mother that before she sends her little quasi-bastard begging at my door, she'd better come to me herself with some serious apologizing."

"She's going away to a colony," said Alessandra.

The door was yanked open again. "She's even more insane than ever," said Grandmother. "Come in. Sit down. Tell me what stupid thing she's done."

The apartment was absolutely neat. Everything in it was unbelievably cheap, the lowest possible quality, but there was a lot of it—ceramics, tiny framed art pieces—and everything had been dusted and polished. The sofa and chairs were so piled with quilts and throws and twee little embroidered pillows that there was nowhere to sit. Grandmother Isabella moved nothing, and finally Alessandra sat on top of one of the pillow piles.

Feeling suddenly quite disloyal and childish herself, telling on Mother like a schoolyard tattletale, Alessandra now tried to softpedal the outrage. "She has her reasons, I know it, and I think she truly believes she's doing it for me—"

"What what what is she doing for you that you don't want her to do! I don't have all day!"

The woman who embroidered all of these pillows has all day *every* day. But Alessandra kept her sassy remark to herself. "She has signed us up for a colony ship, and they accepted us."

"A colony ship? There aren't any colonies. All those places are countries of their own now. Not that Italy ever *did* have any real colonies, not since the Roman Empire. Lost their balls after that, the men did. Italian men have been worthless ever since. Your grandfather, God keep him buried, was worthless enough, never stood up for himself, let everybody push him around, but at least he worked hard and provided for me until my ungrateful daughter spat in my face and married that bike boy. Not like that worthless father of yours, never made a dime."

"Well, not since he died, anyway," said Alessandra, feeling more than a little outraged.

"I'm talking about when he was alive! He only worked the fewest hours he could get by with. I think he was on drugs. You were probably a cocaine baby."

"I don't think so."

"How would *you* know anything?" said Grandmother. "You couldn't even talk then!"

Alessandra sat and waited.

"Well? Tell me."

"I did but you wouldn't believe me."

"What was it you said?"

"A colony ship. A *starship* to one of the formic planets, to farm and explore."

"Won't the formics complain?"

"There aren't any more formics, Grandmother. They were all killed."

"A nasty piece of business but it needed doing. If that Ender Wiggin boy is available, I've got a list of other people that need some good serious destruction. What do you want, anyway?"

"I don't want to go into space. With Mother. But I'm still a minor. If you would sign as my guardian, I could get emancipated and stay home. It's in the law."

"As your guardian?"

"Yes. To supervise me and provide for me. I'd live here."

"Get out."

"What?"

"Stand up and get out. You think this is a hotel? Where exactly do you think you'd sleep? On the floor, where I'd trip on you in the night and break my hip? There's no room for you here. I should have known you'd be making demands. Out!"

There was no room for argument. In moments Alessandra found herself charging down the stairs, furious and humiliated. This woman was even crazier than Mother.

I have nowhere to go, thought Alessandra. Surely the law doesn't allow my mother to *force* me to go into space, does it? I'm not a baby, I'm not a *child,* I'm fourteen, I can read and write and make rational choices.

When the train got back to Monopoli, Alessandra did not go directly home. She had to think up a good lie about where she'd been, so she might as well come up with one that covered a longer time. Maybe the Dispersal Project office was still open.

But it wasn't. She couldn't even get a brochure. And what was the point? Anything interesting would be on the net. She could have stayed after school and found out all she wanted to know. Instead she went to visit her grandmother.

That's proving what good decisions I make.

Mother was sitting at the table, a cup of chocolate in front of her. She looked up and watched Alessandra shut the door and set down her book bag, but she said nothing.

"Mother, I'm sorry, I—"

"Before you lie," said Mother softly, "the witch called me and screamed at me for sending you. I hung up on her, which is what I usually end up doing, and then I unplugged the phone from the wall."

"I'm sorry," said Alessandra.

"You didn't think I had a *reason* for keeping her out of your life?"

For some reason, that pulled the trigger on something inside Alessandra and instead of trying to retreat, she erupted. "It doesn't matter whether you had a reason," she said. "You could have ten million reasons, but you didn't tell any of them to me! You expected me to obey you blindly. But you don't obey *your* mother blindly."

"*Your* mother isn't a monster," said Mother.

"There are many kinds of monsters," said Alessandra. "You're the kind that flits around like a butterfly but never lands near me long enough to even know who I am."

"Everything I do is for you!"

"Nothing is for me. Everything is for the child you imagine you had, the one that doesn't exist, the perfect, happy child that was bound to result from your being the exact opposite of your mother in every way. Well, I'm not that child. And in your mother's house, the electricity is on!"

"Then go live there!"

"She won't let me!"

"You would hate it. Never able to touch anything. Always having to do things *her* way."

"Like going off on a colony ship?"

"I signed up for the colony ship *for you*."

"Which is like buying me a supersized bra. Why don't you look at who I am before you decide what I need?"

"I'll tell you what you are. You're a girl who's too young and inexperienced to know what a woman needs. I'm ten kilometers ahead of you on that road, I know what's coming, I'm trying to get you what you'll need to make that road easy and smooth, and you know what? In spite of you, I've done it. You've fought me every step of the way, but I've done a great job with you. You don't even *know* how good a job I've done because you don't know what you could have been."

"What could I have been, Mother? You?"

"You were never going to be me," said Mother.

"What are you saying? That I would have been *her*?"

"We'll never know what you would have been, will we? Because you already are what I made you."

"Wrong. I *look* like whatever I have to *look* like in order to stay alive in your home. Down inside, what I really am is a complete stranger to you. A stranger that you intend to drag off into space without even asking me if I wanted to go. They used to have a word for people you treated like that. They called them *slaves*."

Alessandra wanted more than ever before in her life to run to her bedroom and slam the door. But she didn't have a bedroom. She slept on the sofa in the same room with the kitchen and the kitchen table.

"I understand," said Mother. "I'll go into my bedroom and you can slam the door on me."

The fact that Mother really did know what she was thinking was the most infuriating thing of all. But Alessandra did not scream and did not scratch at her mother and did not fall on the floor and throw a tantrum and did not even dive onto the sofa and bury her face in the pillow. Instead she sat down at the table directly across from her mother and said, "What's for dinner?"

"So. Just like that, the discussion is over?"

"Discuss while we cook. I'm hungry."

"There's nothing *to* eat, because I haven't turned in our final acceptance because I haven't decided yet whether we should sleep or stay awake through the voyage, and so we haven't got the signing bonus, and so there's no money to buy food."

"So what are we going to do about dinner?"

Mother just looked away from her.

"I know," said Alessandra excitedly. "Let's go over to Grandma's!"

Mother turned back and glared at her.

"Mother," said Alessandra, "how can we run out of money when we're living on the dole? Other people on the dole manage to buy enough food and pay their electric bills."

"What do *you* think?" said Mother. "Look around you. What have I spent all the government's money on? Where's all the extravagance? Look in my closet, count the outfits I own."

Alessandra thought for a moment. "I never thought about that. Do you owe money to the mafia? Did Father, before he died?"

"No," said Mother contemptuously. "You now have all the information you need to understand completely, and yet you still haven't figured it out, smart and grown up as you are."

Alessandra couldn't imagine what Mother was talking about. Alessandra didn't have *any* new information. She also didn't have anything to eat.

She got up and started opening cupboards. She found a box of dry radiatori and a jar of black pepper. She took a pan to the sink and put in some water and set it on the stove and turned on the gas.

"There's no sauce for the pasta," said Mother.

"There's pepper. There's oil."

"You can't eat radiatori with just pepper and oil. It's like putting fistfuls of wet flour in your mouth."

"That's not my problem," said Alessandra. "At this point, it's pasta or shoe leather, so you'd better start guarding your closet."

Mother tried to turn things light again. "Of course, just like a daughter, you'd eat *my* shoes."

"Just be glad if I stop before I get to your leg."

Mother pretended she was still joking when she airily said, "Children eat their parents alive, that's what they do."

"Then why is that hideous creature still living in that flat in Polignano a Mare?"

"I broke my teeth on her skin!" It was Mother's last attempt at humor.

"You tell me what terrible things daughters do, but you're a daughter, too. Did you do them?"

"I married the first man who showed me any hint of what kindness and pleasure could be. I married stupidly."

"I have half the genes of the man you married," said Alessandra. "Is that why I'm too stupid to decide what planet I want to live on?"

"It's obvious that you want to live on any planet where I am not."

"You're the one who came up with the colony idea, not me! But now I think you've named your *own* reason. Yes! You want to colonize another planet because *your* mother isn't there!"

Mother slumped in her seat. "Yes, that is part of it. I won't pretend that I wasn't thinking of that as one of the best things about going."

"So you admit you *weren't* doing it all for me."

"I do not admit such a lie. It's all for you."

"Getting away from your mother, that is for you," said Alessandra.

"It is for you."

"How can it be for me? Until today I didn't even know what my grandmother looked like. I had never seen her face. I didn't even know her name."

"And do you know how much that cost me?" asked Mother.

"What do you mean?"

Mother looked away. "The water is boiling."

"No, that's my temper you're hearing. Tell me what you meant. What did it cost *you* to keep *me* from knowing my own grandmother?"

Mother got up and went into her bedroom and closed the door.

"You forgot to slam it, Mother! Who's the parent here, anyway? Who's the one who shows a sense of responsibility? Who's fixing *dinner*?"

The water took three more minutes before it got to a boil. Alessandra threw in two fistfuls of radiatori and then got her books and started studying at the table. She ended up overcooking the pasta and it was so cheaply made that it clumped up and the oil didn't bind with it. It just pooled on the plate, and the pepper barely helped make it possible to swallow the mess. She kept her eyes on her book and her paper as she ate, and swallowed mechanically until finally the bite in her mouth made her gag and she got up and spat it into the sink and then drank down a glass of water and almost threw the whole mess back up again. As it was, she retched twice at the sink before she was able to get her gorge under control. "Mmmmm, delicious," she murmured. Then she turned back to the table.

Mother was sitting there, picking out a single piece of pasta with her fingers. She put it in her mouth. "What a good mother I am," she said softly.

"I'm doing homework now, Mother. We've already used up our quarreling time."

"Be honest, darling. We almost never quarrel."

"That's true. You flit around ignoring whatever I say, being full of happiness. But believe me, *my* end of the argument is running through my head all the time."

"I'm going to tell you something because you're right, you're old enough to understand things."

Alessandra sat down. "All right, tell me." She looked her mother in the eye.

Mother looked away.

"So you're *not* going to tell me. I'll do my homework."

"I'm going to tell you," said Mother. "I'm just not going to look at you while I do."

"And I won't look at you either." She went back to her homework.

"About ten days into the month, my mother calls me. I answer the phone because if I don't she gets on the train and comes over, and then I have a hard time getting her out of the house before you get home from school. So I answer the phone and she tells me I don't love her, I'm an ungrateful daughter, because here she is all alone in her house, and she's out of money, she can't have anything lovely in her life. Move in with me, she says, bring your beautiful daughter, we can live in my apartment and share our money and then there'll be enough. No, Mama, I say to her. I will not move in with you. And she weeps and screams and says I am a hateful daughter who is tearing all joy and beauty out of her life because I leave her alone and I leave her penniless and so I promise her, I'll send you a little something. She says, don't send it, that wastes postage, I'll come get it and I say, No, I won't be here, it costs more to ride the train than to mail it, so I'm mailing it. And somehow I get her off the phone before you get home. Then I sit for a while not cutting my wrists, and then I put some amount of money into an envelope and I take it to the post office and I mail it, and then she takes the money and buys some hideous piece of garbage and puts it on her wall or on a little shelf until her house is so full of things I've paid for out of money that should go to my daughter's upbringing, and I pay for all of that, I run out of money every month even though I get the same money on the dole that *she* gets, because it's worth it. Being hungry is worth it. Having you be angry with me is worth it, because you do not have to know that woman, you do not have to have her in your *life*. So yes, Alessandra, I do it *all* for you. And if I can get us off this planet, I won't have to send her any more money, and she won't phone me anymore, because by the time we reach that other world she will be dead. I only wish you had trusted me enough that we could have arrived there without your ever having to see her evil face or hear her evil voice."

Mother got up from the table and returned to her room.

Alessandra finished her homework and put it into her backpack and then went and sat on the sofa and stared at the nonfunctioning television. She remembered coming home every day from school, for all these years, and there was Mother, every time, flitting through the house, full of silly talk about fairies and magic and all the beautiful things she did during the day and all the while, the thing she did during the day was fight the monster to keep it from getting into the house, getting its clutches on little Alessandra.

It explained the hunger. It explained the electricity. It explained everything.

It didn't mean Mother wasn't crazy. But now the craziness made a kind of sense. And the colony meant that finally Mother would be free. It wasn't Alessandra who was ready for emancipation.

She got up and went to the door and tapped on it. "I say we sleep during the voyage."

A long wait. Then, from the other side of the door, "That's what I think, too." After a moment, Mother added, "There'll be a young man for you in that colony. A fine young man with prospects."

"I believe there will," said Alessandra. "And I know he'll adore my happy, crazy mother. And my wonderful mother will love him too."

And then silence.

It was unbearably hot inside the flat. Even with the windows open, the air wasn't stirring so there was no relief for it. Alessandra lay on the sofa in her underwear, wishing the upholstery weren't so soft and clinging. She lay on the floor, thinking that maybe the air was a tiny bit cooler there because hot air rises. Only the hot air in the flat below must be rising and heating the floor so it didn't help, and the floor was too hard.

Or maybe it wasn't, because the next morning she woke up on the floor and there was a breath of a breeze coming in off the Adriatic and Mother was frying something in the kitchen.

"Where did you get eggs?" asked Alessandra after she came back from the toilet.

"I begged," said Mother.

"One of the neighbors?"

"A couple of the neighbors' chickens," said Mother.

"No one saw you?"

"No one stopped me, whether they saw me or not."

Alessandra laughed and hugged her. She went to school and this time was not too proud to eat the charity lunch, because she thought: My mother paid for this food for me.

That night there was food on the table, and not just food, but fish and sauce and fresh vegetables. So Mother must have turned in the final papers and received the signing bonus. They were going.

Mother was scrupulous. She took Alessandra with her when she went to both of the neighbors' houses where chickens were kept, and thanked them for not calling the police on her, and paid them for the eggs she had taken. They tried to refuse, but she insisted that she could not leave town with such a debt unpaid, that their kindness was still counted for them in heaven, and there was kissing and crying and Mother walked, not in her pretend fairy way, but light of step, a woman who has had a burden taken from her shoulders.

Two weeks later, Alessandra was on the net at school and she learned something that made her gasp out loud, right there in the library, so that several people rushed toward her and she had to flick to another view and then they were all sure she had been looking at pornography but she didn't care, she couldn't wait to get home and tell Mother the news.

"Do you know who the governor of our colony is going to be?"

Mother did not know. "Does it matter? He'll be an old fat man. Or a bold adventurer."

"What if it's not a man at all? What if it's a boy, a mere boy of thirteen or fourteen, a boy so brilliantly smart and good that he saved the human race?"

"What are you saying?"

"They've announced the crew of our colony ship. The pilot of the ship will be Mazer Rackham, and the governor of the colony will be Ender Wiggin."

Now it was Mother's turn to gasp. "A boy? They make a *boy* the governor?"

"He commanded the fleet in the war, he can certainly govern a colony," said Alessandra.

"A boy. A little boy."

"Not so little. My age."

Mother turned to her. "What, you're so big?"

"I'm big enough, you know. As you said—of childbearing age!"

Mother's face turned reflective. "And the same age as Ender Wiggin."

Alessandra felt her face turning red. "Mother! Don't think what I know you're thinking!"

"And why not think it? He'll have to marry somebody on that distant lonely world. Why not you?" Then Mother's face also turned red and she fluttered her hands against her cheeks. "Oh, oh, Alessandra, I was so afraid to tell you, and now I'm glad, and you'll be glad!"

"Tell me what?"

"You know how we decided to sleep through the voyage? Well, I got to the office to turn in the paper, but I saw that I had accidentally checked the other box, to stay awake and study and be in the first wave of colonists. And I thought, What if they don't let me change the paper? And I decided, I'll make them change it! But when I sat there with the woman I became afraid and I didn't even mention it, I just turned it in like a coward. But now I see I wasn't a coward, it was God guiding my hand, it truly was. Because now you'll be awake through the whole voyage. How many fourteen-year-olds will there be on the ship, awake? You and Ender, that's what I think. The two of you."

"He's not going to fall in love with a stupid girl like me."

"You get very good grades and besides, a smart boy isn't looking for a girl who is even smarter, he's looking for a girl who will love him. He's a soldier who will never come home from the war. You will become his friend. A good friend. It will be years before it's time for him and you to marry. But when that time comes he'll *know* you."

"Maybe you'll marry Mazer Rackham."

"If he's lucky," said Mother. "But I'll be content with whatever old man asks me, as long as I can see you happy."

"I will not marry Ender Wiggin, Mother. Don't hope for what isn't possible."

"Don't you *dare* tell me what to hope for. But I will be content for you merely to become his friend."

"I'll be content merely to see him and not wet my pants. He's the most famous human being in the world, the greatest hero in all of history."

"Not wetting your pants, that's a good first step. Wet pants don't make a good impression."

The school year ended. They received instructions and tickets. They would take the train to Napoli and then fly to Kenya, where the colonists from Europe and Africa were gathering to take the shuttle into space. Their last few days were spent in doing all the things they loved to do in Monopoli—going to the wharf, to the little parks where she had played as a child, to the library, saying good-bye to everything that had been pleasant about their lives in the city. To Father's grave, to lay their last flowers there. "I wish you could have come with us," whispered Mother, but Alessandra wondered—if he had not died, would they have needed to go into space to find happiness?

They got home late on their last night in Monopoli, and when they reached the flat, there was Grandmother on the front stoop of the building. She rose to her feet the moment she saw them and began screaming, even before they were near enough to hear what she was saying.

"Let's not go back," said Alessandra. "There's nothing there that we need."

"We need clothing for the journey to Kenya," said Mother. "And besides, I'm not afraid of her."

So they trudged on up the street, as neighbors looked out to see what was going on. Grandmother's voice became clearer and clearer. "Ungrateful daughter! You plan to steal away my beloved granddaughter and take her into space! I'll never see her again, and you didn't even tell me so I could say good-bye! What kind of monster does that! You never cared for me! You leave me alone in my old age—what kind of duty is that? You in this neighborhood, what do you think of a daughter like that? What a monster has been living among you, a monster of ingratitude!" And on and on.

But Alessandra felt no shame. Tomorrow these would not be her neighbors. She did not have to care. Besides, any of them with sense would realize: No wonder Dorabella Toscano is taking her daughter away from this vile witch. Space is barely far enough to get away from *this* hag.

Grandmother got directly in front of Mother and screamed into her face. Mother did not speak, merely sidestepped around her and went to the door of the building. But she did not open the door. She turned around and held out her hand to stop Grandmother from speaking.

Grandmother did not stop.

But Mother simply continued to hold up her hand. Finally Grandmother wound up her rant by saying, "So now she wants to speak to me! She didn't want to speak to me for all these weeks that she's been planning to go into space, only when I come here with my broken heart and my bruised face will she bother to speak to me, only now! So speak already! What are you waiting for! Speak! I'm listening! Who's stopping you?"

Finally Alessandra stepped between them and screamed into Grandmother's face, "Nobody can speak till you shut up!"

Grandmother slapped Alessandra's face. It was a hard slap, and it knocked Alessandra a step to the side.

Then Mother held out an envelope to Grandmother. "Here is all the money that's left from our signing bonus. Everything I have in all the world except the clothes we take to Kenya. I give it to you. And now I'm done with you. You've taken the last thing you will ever get from me. Except this."

She slapped Grandmother hard across the face.

Grandmother staggered, and was about to start screaming when Mother, lighthearted fairy-born Dorabella Toscano, put her face into Grandmother's and screamed, "Nobody ever, ever, ever hits my little girl!" Then she jammed the envelope with the check in it into Grandmother's blouse, took her by the shoulders, turned her around, and gave her a shove down the street.

Alessandra threw her arms around her mother and sobbed. "Mama, I never understood till now, I never knew."

Mother held her tight and looked over her shoulder at the neighbors who were watching, awestruck. "Yes," she said, "I am a terrible daughter. But I am a very, very good *mother*!"

Several of the neighbors applauded and laughed, though others clucked their tongues and turned away. Alessandra did not care.

"Let me look at you," said Mother.

Alessandra stepped back. Mother inspected her face. "A bruise, I think, but not too bad. It will heal quickly. I think there won't be a trace of it left by the time you meet that fine young man with prospects."

CHAPTER

6

To: GovNom%Colony1@colmin.gov
From: GovAct%Colony1@colmin.gov
Subj: Naming the colony

I agree that calling this place Colony I is going to get tiresome. I agree that naming it now instead of REnaming it when you and your colony ship get here in fifty years will be much better.

But your suggestion of "Prospero" would not play well here right now. We're burying former fighter pilots at the rate of one every other day while our xeno-biologist struggles to find drugs or treatments that will control or eliminate the airborne worms that we inhale and that burrow through our veins until they're so perforated we bleed out internally.

Sel (the XB) assures me that the drug he just gave us will slow them down and buy us time. So there's a chance there'll actually be a colony here when you arrive. If you have questions about the dustworm itself, you'll have to ask him at SMenach%Colony1@colmin.gov\xbdiv.

My address is my job title but my name is Vitaly Kolmogorov and my permanent title is Admiral. Do you have a name? Whom am I writing to?

To: GovAct%Colony1@colmin.gov
From: GovNom%Colony1@colmin.gov
Subj: Re: Naming the colony

Dear Admiral Kolmogorov,

I have read with great relief the recent report that the dustworm has been completely controlled by the drug cocktail your xb Sel Menach developed. The worm is being named for him, but the actual name will be held up while committees argue endlessly about whether Latin should be used for naming xenospecies. Some are arguing for a different language for each colony world; others for standardization across all the colonies; others for linguistic differentiation between species native to each planet and the species from the formic home world that were transplanted to all the colony worlds. Thus the Earthbound keep themselves busy while you do the real work of trying to establish a bridgehead in an alien ecosphere.

I am part of the problem, with my fussing about the colony's name. Please forgive my wasting your time on this; yet it must be done, and you have already prevented me from a faux pas that would have hurt the relations between your colonists and the Ministry and its minions (including me). You were right that Prospero doesn't work, but for some reason I am quite drawn to using a name from The Tempest by William Shakespeare. Perhaps Tempest itself, or Miranda, or Ariel. I suspect Caliban would not be a good choice. Gonzalo? Sycorax?

As to my name, there is debate about whether to inform your colonists of who I am. I am strictly forbidden to tell even you, the "acting" governor. Meanwhile, my name is being bandied about on the nets, with no great secret made of the fact that I am appointed governor of Colony I. The information will simply not be transmitted to you by ansible. So easy to deceive you or leave you ignorant—something that I will keep in mind when I receive information from ColMin as governor 40 years from now. Unless I can get them to change this foolish practice before I depart.

I believe that the powers-that-be think that having a child of thirteen appointed as governor of your colony might hurt morale among your colonists, though it will be forty years before I arrive. At the same time, others think that having the victorious commander as governor will help morale. While they decide, I trust both your powers of deduction and your discretion.

To: GovNom%Colony1@colmin.gov
From: GovAct%Colony1@colmin.gov
Subj: Re: Naming the colony

Dear Governor-Nominate Wiggin,

I am impressed with the alacrity with which ColMin acted on your petition for ansible bandwidth to be made available for unrestricted access to the nets by colonists, at the discretion of the governors.

My first thought was to inform everyone in the colony about the identity of their governor-in-transit. The name of Ender Wiggin is revered here. After our own victory, we studied your battles and debated about just which superlative was most appropriate when applied to your degree of military brilliance. But I have also seen the reports of the court martial of Col. Graff and Admiral Rackham. Your reputation was savaged and I don't want to provide an incentive for the colonists, when they finally have the leisure for connecting to the home of humanity, to brood about whether you are a savior or a sociopath. Not that any of the soldiers and pilots among us has the slightest doubt that you are the former; but there will be children born here during the fifty years of your voyage who did not fight under your command.

I confess to having had to reread The Tempest upon receiving your list of names. Sycorax indeed! And yet, obscure as the name is in the play, it is astonishingly appropriate for our situation. The mother of Caliban, the witch who made the unmapped island rich with magic—Sycorax would then be the appropriate name for the hive queen who once ruled this world but now is gone, leaving behind so many artifacts . . . and traps.

Our xb—a remarkable young man, who refuses to hear of our gratitude for his having saved our lives—says that the formic bodies were riddled with damage from the dustworms. Apparently the individual formics were regarded as so expendable that there was no attempt to control or prevent the disease. The waste of life! Fortunately, Sel has found that the dustworm life cycle has a phase that requires feeding on a certain species of plant. He is working on a means of wiping out that entire plant species. Ecocide, he calls it—a monstrous biological crime. He broods with guilt. Yet the alternative is to keep injecting ourselves forever, or to genetically alter all the children born to us in this world so our blood is poisonous to the dustworms.

In short, Sel IS Prospero. The hive queen was Sycorax. The formics, Caliban. So far, no Ariels, though every female of reproductive age is venerated here. We're about to have a lottery for mating purposes. I have taken myself out of the running, lest I be accused of making sure I got one of them. No one likes this unromantic, unfree plan—but we voted on the method of allocating scarce reproductive resources and Sel persuaded a majority that this was the way to go. We have no time for wooing here, or for hurt feelings, or rejection.

I talk to you because I can't talk to anyone here, not even Sel. He has burdens enough without my spilling any of mine onto his back.

By the way, the captain of your ship keeps writing to me as if he thought he could give me orders about the governance of Colony I, without reference to you. I thought you should be aware of this so you can take appropriate steps to avoid having to deal with a would-be regent when you arrive. He strikes me as being the kind of officer I call a "man of peace"—a bureaucrat who thrives in the military only when there is no war, because his true enemy is any officer who has a position or assignment he wants. You are the thing he hates worst: a man of war. Look behind you; that's where the man of peace always tries to stay, dirk in hand.

—Vitaly Denisovitch

To: GovAct%Colony1@colmin.gov
From: GovNom%Colony1@colmin.gov
Subj: Re: I have the name

Dear Vitaly Denisovitch,

I have it: Shakespeare. As the name for both the planet and the first settlement. Then later settlements can be named for characters in The Tempest and other plays.

Meanwhile, we can refer to a certain admiral as Thane of Cawdor, to remind ourselves of the inevitable result of overweening ambition.

Are you content with Shakespeare as the name? It seems appropriate to me that a new world be named for that great writer of human souls. But if you think it is too English, too tied to a particular culture, I will start over on another track entirely.

I am grateful for your confidence. I hope it will continue during the voyage, even though time dilation will make it take weeks to send and receive each message. Of course that means I will not be in stasis—arriving at age fifteen will be better than at age thirteen.

And, so you know, the voyage will not take fifty years, but closer to forty—refinements have been made in the eggs that power the ships and in the inertial protection of the ships, so we can accelerate and decelerate faster in-system and spend more time at relativistic speeds. We may have gotten all our technology from the formics, but that doesn't mean we can't improve on it.

—Ender

To: GovNom%Colony1@colmin.gov
From: GovAct%Colony1@colmin.gov
Subj: Re: Naming the colony

Dear Ender,

Shakespeare belongs to everyone, but now especially to our colony. I sounded out a few colonists and those who cared at all thought it was a good name.

We will do our best to stay alive until you come with more to augment our numbers. But I remember from my own voyage leading up to the war: Your two years will feel longer than our forty. We will be doing something. You will feel frustrated and bored. Those who opted for stasis were happier. Yet your argument for arriving at age fifteen instead of thirteen is a wise one. I understand better than you do the sacrifice you will be making.

I will send you reports every few months—every few days to you—so that you have some idea of who the colonists are and how the village works, socially, agriculturally, and technologically, as well as our achievements and the problems we will have overcome. I will do my best to help you get to know the leading people. But I will not tell them that I am doing this, because they would feel spied upon. When you arrive, try not to let them know how much I have told you. It will make you appear to be insightful. This is a good reputation to have.

I would do the same for Admiral Morgan, since there is a chance that he will actually be in control—the soldiers on your ship will answer to him, not you, and the nearest law enforcement is forty years distant if he should choose to illegally deploy them on our planet's surface. Our colonists will be unarmed and untrained in military action so he would face no resistance.

However, Admiral Morgan persists in sending me orders without once inquiring about conditions here, beyond what he may or may not have read in my official reports. He is also becoming quite testy about my failure to respond in a satisfactory way (though I have responded fully to all his legitimate inquiries and requests). I suspect that if he is in control when he arrives, removing me from office will be his first priority. Fortunately, demographics suggest that I will be dead before he gets here so that issue will be moot.

Thirteen you may be, but at least you understand that you cannot lead strangers, you can only coerce or bribe them.

—Vitaly

Sel Menach's back and neck ached from his hours staring at alien molds through a microscope. *If I keep this up, I'll be bent over like an old hag before I'm thirty-five.*

But it would be the same out in the fields, hoeing, trying to keep the vines from growing up the maize and blocking out the sun. His back would bend there, too, and his skin turn brown. You could hardly tell one race from another in this savage sunlight. It was like a vision of the future: Personnel chosen from all the races of earth to be surgeons and geologists and xenobiologists and climatologists—and also combat pilots, so they could kill the enemy who once owned this world—and now that the war was over, they'd interbreed so thoroughly that in three generations, maybe two, there would be no concept of race or national origin here.

And yet each colony world would get its own look, its own accent of I.F. Common, which was merely English with a few spelling changes. As colonists began to go from world to world, new divisions would arise. Meanwhile, Earth itself would keep all the old races and nationalities and many of the languages, so that the distinction between colonist and Earthborn would become more and more clear and important.

Not my problem, thought Sel. *I can see the future, anyone can; but there'll be no future here on the planet now called Shakespeare unless I can find a way to kill this mold that infests the grain crops from Earth. How could there be a mold that is already specific to grasses, when the grasses of Earth, including the grains, have no genetic analogue on this world?*

Afraima came in with more samples from the test garden in the green-house. It was so ironic—all the high-tech agricultural equipment that had been carried along with the fighters in the belly of the transport starship, and yet when it failed there would be no parts, no replacements for fifty years. Maybe forty, if the new stardrive actually brought the colony ship sooner. By the time it gets here, we might be living in the woods, digging for roots and utterly without any working technology.

Or I might succeed in adjusting and adapting our crops so that they thrive in this place, and we have huge food surpluses, enough to buy us leisure time for the development of a technological infrastructure.

We arrive at an extremely high level of technology—but with nothing under it to hold it up. If we crash, we crash all the way down.

"Look at this," said Afraima.

Dutifully, Sel stood up from his microscope and walked over to hers. "Yes, what am I looking at here?"

"What do you see?" she asked.

"Don't play games with me."

"I'm asking for independent verification. I can't tell you anything."

So this was something that mattered. He looked closely. "This is a section of maize leaf. From the sterile section, so it's completely clean."

"But it's not," she said. "It's from D-4."

Sel was so relieved he almost wept; yet at the same moment, he was angry. Anger won, in the moment. "No it's not," he said sharply. "You've mixed up the samples."

"That's what I thought," she said. "So I went back and got a new selection from D-4. And then again. You're looking at my triple check."

"And D-4 is easy to make out of local materials. Afraima, we did it!"

"I haven't even checked to see if it works on the amaranth."

"That would be too lucky."

"Or blessed. Did you ever think God might *want* us to succeed here?"

"He could have killed this mold before we got here," said Sel.

"That's right, sound impatient with his gift and piss God off."

It was banter, but there was truth behind it. Afraima was a serious Jew—she had renamed herself in Hebrew to a word meaning "fertile" when they held the vote on mating, in hopes that it would somehow induce God to let her have a Jewish husband. Instead, the governor simply assigned her to work for the only orthodox Jew among the colonists. Governor Kolmogorov had respect for religion. So did Sel.

He just wasn't sure that God knew this place. What if the Bible was exactly right about the creation of that particular sun, moon, and earth—only that was the whole of God's creation, and worlds like this one were the creation of alien gods with six limbs, or trilateral symmetry or something, like some of the life forms here—the ones that seemed to Sel to be the native species.

Soon they were back in the lab, with the amaranth samples that had been treated the same way. "So that's it—good enough for starters, anyway."

"But it takes so long to make it," said Afraima.

"Not our problem. The chems can figure out how to make it faster and in larger quantities, now that we know which one works. It doesn't seem to have damaged either plant, does it?"

"You are a genius, Dr. Menach."

"No Ph.D."

"I define the word 'doctor' as 'person who knows enough to make species-saving discoveries.' "

"I'll put it on my resume."

"No," she said.

"No?"

Her hand touched his arm. "I'm just coming into my fertile period, doctor. I want your seed in this field."

He tried to make a joke of it. "Next thing you'll be quoting from the Song of Solomon."

"I'm not proposing romance, Dr. Menach. We have to work together, after all. And I'm married to Evenezer. He won't have to know the baby isn't his."

This sounded like she had really thought things through. Now he was genuinely embarrassed. And chagrined. "We have to work together, Afraima."

"I want the best possible genes for my baby."

"All right," he said. "You stay here and head up the adaptation studies. I'll go work in the fields."

"What do you mean? There are plenty of people who can do that."

"It's either fire you or fire me. We're not working together anymore after this."

"But no one had to know!"

"Thou shalt not commit adultery," said Sel. "You're supposed to be the believer."

"But the daughters of Midian—"

"Slept with their own father because it was more important to have babies than to practice exogamy." Sel sighed. "It's also important to respect the rules of monogamy absolutely, so we don't see the colony torn up with conflict over women."

"All right, forget I said anything," said Afraima.

"I can't forget it," said Sel.

"Then why don't you—"

"I lost the lottery, Afraima. It's now illegal for me to have offspring. Especially by poaching another man's mate. But I also can't take the libido suppressants because I need to be sharp and energetic in order to conduct my study of the life forms on this world. I can't have you in here, now that you've offered yourself to me."

"It was just an *idea*," she said. "You need me to work with you."

"I need someone," said Sel. "Doesn't have to be you."

"But people will wonder why you fired me. Evenezer will guess that there was something between us."

"That's your problem."

"What if I tell them that you got me pregnant?"

"You're definitely fired. Right now. Irrevocably."

"I was kidding!"

"Get your brain back inside your head. There'll be a paternity test. DNA. Meanwhile, your husband will be made a figure of ridicule, and every other man will look at his wife, wondering if she's offering herself to someone else to put a cuckoo in the nest. So you're out. For the sake of everyone."

"If you make it that obvious, then it'll do the same damage to people's trust in marriage as if we'd actually done it!"

Sel sat down on the greenhouse floor and buried his face in his hands.

"I'm sorry," said Afraima. "I only half meant it."

"You mean that if I had said yes, you'd have told me you were just kidding and left *me* humiliated for having agreed to adultery?"

"No," she said. "I'd do it. Sel, you're the smartest, everyone knows it.

And you shouldn't be cut off without having children. It's not right. We need your genes in the pool."

"That's the genetic argument," said Sel. "Then there's the social argument. Monogamy has been proven, over and over, to be the optimum social arrangement. It's not about genes, it's about children—they have to grow up into the society we want them to maintain. We *voted* on this."

"And I vote to carry one baby of yours. Just one."

"Please leave," said Sel.

"I'm the logical one, since I'm Jewish and so are you."

"Please go. Close the door behind you. I have work to do."

"You can't turn me away," she said. "It would hurt the colony."

"So would killing you," said Sel, "but you're making that more and more tempting the longer you stay here to torture me."

"It's only torture because you want me."

"My body is human and male," said Sel, "and so of course I want to engage in mating behavior regardless of consequences. My logical functions are being suppressed already so it's a good thing I made the decision irrevocably. Don't make me turn my decision into a painful reality by cutting the little suckers off."

"So that's it? You castrate yourself, one way or the other. Well, I'm a human female, and I hunger for the mate that will give me the best offspring."

"Then look for somebody big and strong and healthy if you want to commit adultery, and don't let me catch you because I'll turn you in."

"Brain. I want your brain."

"Well, the kid would probably have your brain and my face. Now go and get the reports on the D-4 treatment and take it over to chem."

"I'm not fired?"

"No," said Sel. "I'm resigning. I'm going out into the fields and leaving you here."

"I'm just the backup XB. I can't do the work."

"You should have thought of that before you made it impossible for us to work together."

"Who ever heard of a man who didn't want a little roll in the hay on the side?"

"This colony is my life now, Afraima. Yours too. You don't shit in your own soup. Can I put it any plainer than that?"

She began to cry.

"What have I done that God would punish me like this?" said Sel. "What comes next? Interpreting dreams for Pharaoh's baker and butler?"

"I'm sorry," she said. "You have to stay on as the XB, you really are a genius at it. I wouldn't even know where to start. Now I've ruined everything."

"Yes, you have indeed," said Sel. "But you're right about all my solutions, too. They'd be almost as damaging as your original idea. So here's what we'll do."

She waited, the tears still coming out of her eyes.

"Nothing," he said. "You will never mention this again. Never. You won't touch me. You'll dress with perfect modesty around me. Your communication with me will be work only. Scientific language, as formal as possible. People will think you and I detest each other. Because I can't afford to drug down my libido and still try to do this work. Get it?"

"Yes."

"Forty years till the colony ship arrives with a new XB and I can quit this lousy job."

"I didn't mean to make you miserable. I thought you'd be happy."

"My hormones were thrilled. They thought it was the best idea they'd ever heard."

"Well, then I feel better," she said.

"You feel *better* because I'm going to be going through hell for the next forty years?"

"Don't be stupid," she said. "As soon as I'm having babies, I'll get fat and unattractive and way too busy to come here to help. Child production is everything, right? And soon the next generation will provide you with an apprentice to train. The most it will bother you is a few months. Maybe a year."

"Easy for you to say."

"Dr. Menach, I'm truly sorry. We're scientists, I start to think of human reproduction just like the animals. I didn't mean to be disloyal to Evenezer, I didn't mean to make you miserable. I just felt a wave of desire. I just knew that if I was going to have a baby, it should be yours, it should be the baby most worth having. But I'm still a rational person. A scientist. I will do exactly as you said—all business. As if we disliked each other and neither could ever desire the other. Let me stay until I need to quit this work to have babies."

"All right. Get up, take the formula to chem, and leave me alone to work on the next problem."

"And what is that? After the dustworm and the corn and amaranth mold, what are we working on?"

"The next problem I'm working on," said Sel, "is burying myself in whatever tedious task I can find that does not involve you in any way. Will you *please* go away now?"

She went.

Sel wrote his report and sent it to the governor's machine so it could be queued up for ansible transmission. If it turned out that the mold was something that cropped up on other worlds, his solution might work there, too. Besides, that's what science was—the sharing of information, the pooling of knowledge.

That's my gene pool, Afraima, he thought. The meme pool, the collective knowledge of science. What I discover here, what I learn, the problems I solve—those will be my children. They will be part of every generation that lives on this planet.

When the report was done, Afraima was still not back. Good, thought Sel. Let her spend all day with chem.

Sel walked through the village and out into the communal fields. Fernão McPhee was foreman on duty. "Give me a job," Sel said to him.

"I thought you were working on the mold problem."

"I think it's solved. It's up to chem now to figure out how to deliver it to the plants."

"I've already got all the crews working on all the jobs. Your time is too valuable to waste on manual labor."

"Everybody does manual labor. The governor does manual laborer."

"The crews are full. You don't know the jobs, you know *your* job, which is much more important. Go do your job, don't bother me!"

He said it jokingly, but he meant it. And what could Sel answer? I need you to give me a hot, sweaty job so I can work off the steam from my beautiful assistant having offered me her body to put babies into!

"You're no help to me at all," said Sel to Fernão.

"Then we're even."

So Sel went on a long walk. Out beyond the fields, into the woods, gathering samples. When you don't have an emergency to deal with, you do science. You collect, classify, analyze, observe. Always work to do.

No fantasizing about her, about what might have happened. Sexual fantasies are scripts for future behavior. What good will it do to say no today, and yes six months from now, after rehearsing the adultery over and over in my mind?

It would be so much easier if I weren't determined to do what's best for everybody. Whoever said virtue was its own reward was full of crap.

CHAPTER

7

To: jpwiggin@gso.nc.pub, twiggin@uncg.edu
From: vwiggin%Colony1@colmin.gov/citizen
Subj: Ender is fine

By "fine" I mean of course that his body and mind seem to be functioning normally. He was happy to see me. We talked easily. He seems at peace about everything. No hostility toward anyone. He spoke of both of you with real affection. We shared lots of childhood memories.

But as soon as that conversation ended, I saw him almost visibly crawl inside a shell. He is obsessed with the formics. I think he's burdened with guilt over having destroyed them. He knows that this is not appropriate—that he did not know what he was doing, they were trying to destroy us so it was self-defense anyway—but the ways of conscience are mysterious. We evolved consciences so that we would internalize community values and police ourselves. But what happens when you have a hyperactive conscience and make up rules that nobody else knows about, just so you can punish yourself for breaking them?

Nominally, he is governor, but I have been warned by two different people that Admiral Quincy Morgan has no intention of letting Ender govern anything. If

Peter were in such a position, he would already be conspiring to have Morgan removed before the voyage began. But Ender just chuckles and says, "Imagine that." When I pressed him, he said, "He can't have a contest if I won't play." And when I pressed him harder, he got irritable and said, "I was born for one war. I won it and I'm done."

So now I'm torn. Do I try to maneuver for him? Or do what he asks and ignore the whole situation? He thinks I should spend my time on the voyage either in stasis, so we'd be the same age when we arrived, both fifteen—or, if I'm awake, then I should write a history of Battle School. Graff has promised to give me all the documents about Battle School—though I can get those from the public records, since they all came out in the court martial.

Here's my philosophical question: What is love? Does my love for Ender mean that I do what I think is good for him, even if he asks me not to? Or does love mean I do what he asks, even though I think he would find being a figurehead governor a hellish experience?

It's like piano lessons, dear parents. So many adults complain about the hideous experience of being forced to practice and practice. And yet there are others who say to their parents, "Why didn't you MAKE me practice so today I'd be able to play well?"

Love, Valentine

To: vwiggin%Colony1@colmin.gov/citizen
From: Twiggin@uncg.edu
Subj: re: Ender is fine

Dear Valentine,

Your father says that you will be irritated if I say how shocking it is to discover that one of my children does not know everything, and admits it, and even asks her parents for advice. For the past five years, you and Peter have been as closed off as twins with a private language. Now, only a few weeks out from under Peter's influence, you have discovered parents again. I find this gratifying. I hereby declare you to be my favorite child.

We continue to be devastated—a slow, corrosive kind of devastation—that Ender chooses not to write to us. You say nothing of anger toward us. We do not understand. Doesn't he realize we were forbidden to write to him? Why doesn't he read our letters now? Or does he read them and then choose not to poke the reply box and say even as little as "Got your letters"?

As to your questions, the answers are easy. You are not his mother or father. We are the ones with the right to meddle and do what's good for him whether he likes it or not. You are his sister. Think of yourself as companion, friend, confidante. Your responsibility is to receive what he gives, and to give him what he asks only if you think it's good. You do not have either the right or the responsibility to give him what he specifically asks you not to give. That would be no gift; that is neither friend nor sister.

Parents are a special case. He has built a wall exactly in the place where Battle School first built it. It keeps us out. He thinks he does not need us. He is mistaken. I suspect we are exactly what he is hungry for. It is a mother who can provide the ineffable comfort to a wounded soul. It is a father who can say, "Ego te absolvo" and "well done, thou good and faithful servant" and be believed by the inmost soul.

If you were better educated and hadn't lived in an atheistic establishment, you would understand those references. When you look them up, please remember that I did not have to.

> Love,
> Your sarcastic, overly analytical,
> deeply wounded yet quite satisfied,
> Mother

To: jpwiggin@gso.nc.pub, twiggin@uncg.edu
From: vwiggin%Colony1@colmin.gov/citizen
Subj: Ender is fine

I know all about Father's confessionals and your King James Version and I did not have to look anything up either. Do you think your and Father's religions were a secret from your children? Even Ender knew, and he left home when he was six.

I am taking your advice because it is wise and because I have no better ideas. And I'm going to follow Ender's and Graff's advice, too, and write a history of Battle School. My goal is a simple one: to get it published as quickly as possible so it can be part of the task of erasing the vile slanders of the court martial, rehabilitating the reputations of the children who won this war and the adults who trained and aimed them. Not that I don't still hate them for taking Ender from us. But I find it quite possible to hate someone and still see their side of the argument between us. This is perhaps the only worthwhile gift Peter ever gave me.

Peter has not written to me, nor I to him. If he asks, tell him that I think about him often, I notice that I don't see him anymore, and if that counts as "missing him," then he is missed.

Meanwhile, I had a chance to meet Petra Arkanian in transit and I have spoken—well, literally WRITTEN—to "Bean," Dink Meeker, Han Tzu, and have letters out to several others. The better I understand from them what Ender went through (since Ender's not telling), the better I will know what I should be doing but am not because, as you point out, I am not his mother and he has asked me not to do it. Meanwhile, I am pretending that it's only about writing the book.

I am an astonishingly fast writer. Are you sure we have no genes of Winston Churchill in us? Some dalliance of his, for instance, with a Pole-in-exile during World War II? I feel him to be a kindred spirit of mine, except for the political ambitions, the constant blood alcohol level, and walking around the house naked. He did those things, by the way, not me.

> Love,
> Your equally sarcastic, just-analytical-enough,
> not-yet-wounded-nor-satisfied daughter,
> Valentine

Graff had disappeared from Eros soon after the court martial, but now he was back. It seems that as Minister of Colonization, he could not miss the opportunity for publicity that the departure of the first colony ship would offer.

"Publicity is good for the Dispersal Project," said Graff when Mazer laughed at him.

"And you don't love the camera?"

"Look at me," said Graff. "I've lost twenty-five kilos. I'm a mere shadow of myself."

"All through the war, you gain weight, bit by bit. You balloon during the court martial. And now you lose weight. Was it Earth gravity?"

"I didn't go to Earth," said Graff. "I was busy turning Battle School into the assembly point for the colonists. No one understood why I insisted that all the beds be adult-sized. Now they talk about my foresight."

"Why are you lying to *me*? You weren't in charge when Battle School was built."

Graff shook his head. "Mazer, I wasn't in charge of anything when I talked you into coming home, was I?"

"You were in charge of the get-Rackham-home-to-help-train-Ender-Wiggin project."

"But no one knew there was such a project."

"Except you."

"So I was also in charge of the make-sure-Battle-School-is-fitted-out-for-the-Human-Genome-Dispersal-Project project."

"And that's why you're losing weight," said Mazer. "Because you finally got the funding and authority to carry out the real project that you've had in mind all along."

"Winning the war was the most important thing. I had my mind on my job of training children! Who knew we'd win it in circumstances that gave us all these uninhabited already-terraformed completely habitable planets? I expected Ender to win, or Bean if Ender failed, but I thought we'd then be battling the buggers world to world, and racing to found new colonies in the opposite direction, so we wouldn't be vulnerable to their counterattack."

"So you're here to have your picture taken with the colonists."

"I'm here to have my smiling picture taken with you and Ender and the colonists."

"Ah," said Mazer. "The court martial crowd."

"The cruelest thing about that court martial was the way they savaged Ender's reputation. Fortunately, most people remember the victory, not the evidence from the court martial. Now we place another image in their minds."

"So you actually care about Ender."

Graff looked hurt. "I have always loved that boy. It would take a moral idiot not to. I know deep goodness when I see it. I hate having his name tied to the murder of children."

"He did kill them."

"He didn't know that he did."

"Those weren't like winning the war while thinking it was a game, Hyrum," said Mazer. "He knew he was in a real fight for his life, and he knew that he had to win decisively. He had to know that the death of his opponent was always a possibility."

"So you're saying he's as guilty as our enemies said he was?"

"I'm saying that he killed them and he knew what he was doing. Not the exact outcome, but that he was taking actions that could cause real and permanent damage to those boys."

"They were going to kill him!"

"Bonzo was," said Mazer. "Stilson was a petty bully."

"But Ender was so untrained he had no idea of the damage he was doing, or that his shoes had steel toes. Weren't we clever to keep him safe by insisting he wear shoes like that."

"Hyrum, I think Ender's actions were perfectly justified. He didn't choose to fight those boys, so the only choice he had was how thoroughly to win."

"Or lose."

"Ender never has the choice to lose, Hyrum. It's not in him, even when *he* thinks it is."

"All I know is that he promised to try to work a picture with me and you into his schedule."

Mazer nodded. "And you think that meant that he'd do it."

"He doesn't *have* a schedule. I thought he was being ironic. Except for hanging with Valentine, what does he have to do?"

Mazer laughed. "What he's been doing for more than a year—studying the formics so obsessively that we all worried about his mental health.

Only I have to say that with the colonists' arrival, he's been preparing to be governor in more than just name."

"Admiral Morgan will be disappointed."

"Admiral Morgan expects to get his way," said Mazer, "because he doesn't realize Ender is serious about governing the colony. What Ender was doing was memorizing the dossiers of all the colonists—their test results, family relationships with other colonists *and* with family members who were left home, their towns and countries of origin and what those places look like and what's been going on there in the past year, during the time they were signing up."

"And Admiral Morgan doesn't get the point?"

"Admiral Morgan is a *leader*," said Mazer. "He gives orders and they're passed down the chain. Knowing the grunts is the job of the petty officers."

Graff laughed. "And people wonder why we used children to command the final campaign."

"Every officer learns how to function within the system that promoted him," said Mazer. "The system is still sick—it always has been and always will be. But Ender learned how *real* leadering is done."

"Or was born knowing it."

"So he's greeting every colonist by name and making a point of conversing with them all for at least a half hour."

"Can't he do that on the ship after they take off?"

"He's meeting the ones who are going into stasis. The ones who are staying awake he'll meet after launch. So when he says he'll try to fit you into his schedule, he was not being ironic. Most of the colonists are sleepers and he barely has time for a real conversation with all of them."

Graff sighed. "Isn't he even *sleeping*?"

"I think he figures he'll have time to sleep after launch—when Admiral Morgan is commanding his vessel and Ender will have no official duties that he doesn't assign to himself. At least that's how Valentine and I decode his behavior."

"He doesn't talk to her?"

"Of course he does. He just doesn't admit to having any plans or any reasons for the things he does."

"Why would he keep secrets from her?"

"I'm not sure they're secrets," said Mazer. "I think he might not *know* that he has plans of any kind. I think he's greeting the colonists because that's what they need and expect. It's a duty because it means a lot to them, so he does it."

"Nonsense," said Graff. "Ender always has plans within plans."

"I believe you're thinking of you."

"Ender is better at this than I am."

"I doubt it," said Mazer. "Peacetime bureaucratic maneuvering? Nobody does it better than you."

"I wish I were going with them."

"Then go," said Mazer, laughing. "But you wish nothing of the kind."

"Why not?" said Graff. "I can run ColMin by ansible. I can see first-hand what our colonists have accomplished during the years they've been waiting for relief. And the advantages of relativistic travel will keep me alive to see the end of my great project."

"Advantages?"

"To you, a horrible sacrifice. But you'll notice that I did not marry, Mazer. I had no secret reproductive dysfunction. My libido and my desire for a family are as strong as any man's. But I decided years ago to marry Mother Eve posthumously and adopt all her children as my own. They were all living in the same crowded house, where one bad fire would kill the whole bunch of them. My job was to move them out into widely dispersed houses so they'd go on living forever. Collectively, that is. So no matter where I go, no matter whom I'm with, I am surrounded by my adopted children."

"You really are playing God."

"I most certainly am not *playing.*"

"You old actor—you think there were auditions and you got the part."

"Maybe I'm an understudy. When he forgets a bit of business, I fill in."

"So what are you going to do about getting a picture with Ender?"

"Simple enough. I'm the man who decides when the ship will go. There will be a technical malfunction at the last minute. Ender, having done his duty, will be encouraged to take a nap. When he wakes up, we'll take some pictures, and then the technical problems will be miraculously resolved and the ship will sail."

"Without you on board," said Mazer.

"I have to be here to keep fighting for the project," said Graff. "If I weren't here to stymie my enemies at every step, the project would be killed within months. There are so many powerful people in this world who refuse to see any vision they didn't think of."

———

Valentine enjoyed watching the way Graff and Rackham treated Ender. Graff was one of the most powerful men in the world; Rackham was still regarded as a legendary hero. Yet both of them quietly deferred to Ender. They never ordered him to do anything. It was always, "Will it be all right for you to stand here for the picture?" "Would 0800 be a good time for you?" "Whatever you're wearing will be fine, Admiral Wiggin."

Of course Valentine knew that calling him "Admiral Wiggin" was for the benefit of the admirals and generals and political brass who were watching, most of them seething because they weren't in the picture. But as she watched, she saw many instances of Ender expressing an opinion—or just seeming to be hesitant about something. Graff usually deferred to Ender. And when he didn't, Rackham smilingly made Ender's point for him, and insisted on it.

They were taking care of him.

It was genuine love and respect. They might have created him like a tool in a forge, they might have hammered him and ground him into the shape they wanted, and then plunged him into the heart of the enemy. But now they truly loved this weapon they had made, they cared about him.

They thought he was damaged. Dented from all he had been through. They thought his passivity was a reaction to trauma, to finding out what he had really done—the deaths of the children, of the formics, of the thousands of human soldiers who had perished during that last campaign when Ender thought he was playing a game.

They just don't know him the way I do, thought Valentine.

Oh, she knew the danger of such a thought. She was constantly on the alert, lest she entrap herself in a web of her own conceit. She had not assumed she knew Ender. She had approached him like a stranger, watching everything to see what he did, what he said, and what he seemed to *mean* by all he did and said. ·

Gradually, though, she learned to recognize the child behind the young man. She had seen him obeying his parents—immediately, without question, though he surely could have argued or pleaded his way out of onerous tasks. Ender accepted responsibility and accepted also the idea that he would not always get to decide which responsibilities were his, or when they needed to be carried out. So he obeyed his parents with few hesitations.

But it was more than that. Ender really *was* damaged, they were right. Because his obedience was more than that of the happy child springing up at his parents' request. It had strong overtones of the kind of obedience Ender had given to Peter—compliance in order to avoid conflict.

Somewhere between the two attitudes: eagerness versus resignation mixed with dread.

Ender was eager for the voyage, for the work he would do. But he understood that being governor was the price he was paying for his ticket. So he was acting the part, performing all his duties, including the pictures, including the formal good-byes, the speeches from the very commanders who had allowed his name to be so badly tarnished during the court martial of Graff and Rackham.

Ender stood there smiling—a real smile, as if he liked the man—while Admiral Chamrajnagar bestowed on him the highest medal the International Fleet could offer. Valentine watched the whole thing sourly. Why wasn't that medal given during the court martial, when it would have been an open repudiation of the terrible things being said about Ender? Why had the court martial been opened to the public, when Chamrajnagar had the complete power to suppress it all? Why was there even a court martial? No law required it. Chamrajnagar had never, for a moment, been Ender's friend—though Ender gave him the victory that he could not otherwise have achieved.

Unlike Graff and Rackham, Chamrajnagar showed no sign of real respect for Ender. Oh, he called him Admiral, too, with only a couple of instances of "my boy"—both immediately corrected by Rackham, to Chamrajnagar's visible annoyance. Of course, Chamrajnagar could do nothing about Rackham, either—except make sure he was in all the pictures, too, since having two heroes associated with the great Polemarch would be an even more memorable picture.

What was plain to Valentine was that Chamrajnagar was very happy, and the happiness clearly came from the prospect of having Ender get on that starship and go away. Things could not go quickly enough for Chamrajnagar.

Yet they all waited for the pictures to be printed out in physical form so that Ender, Rackham, and Chamrajnagar could all sign copies of that most excellent souvenir.

Rackham and Ender were each given signed copies with a great flourish, as if Chamrajnagar imagined he was honoring them.

Then, at last, Chamrajnagar was gone—"to the observation station, to watch the great vessel sail forth on its mission of creation instead of destruction." In other words, to have his picture taken with the ship in the background. Valentine doubted any of the press would be allowed to take pictures of the event that did *not* include Chamrajnagar's smiling face.

So it was actually a great concession that the picture of Graff, Rackham, and Ender had been allowed to exist at all. Perhaps Chamrajnagar did not even know it had been taken. It was the official fleet photographer, but perhaps he was disloyal enough to take a picture he knew that his boss would hate.

Valentine knew Graff well enough to know that appearances of the Polemarch's pictures would be rare compared to the picture of Graff, Rackham, and Ender, which would be pasted on every possible surface on Earth: electronic, virtual, and physical. It would serve Graff's purpose to have everyone on Earth reminded that the I.F. existed for only two purposes now—to support the colonization program, and to punish from space any power on Earth that dared to use, or threaten to use, nuclear weapons.

Chamrajnagar had not yet reconciled himself to the idea that most of the continued funding for the I.F. and its bases and stations came through Graff's hands as Minister of Colonization—MinCol. At the same time, Graff was perfectly aware that it was fear of what a disgruntled I.F. might do—like seizing worldwide power from the politicians, which the Warsaw Pact had tried to do—that kept the funding coming to *his* project.

What Chamrajnagar would never understand was why he was somehow the adjunct in all of this, why his lobbying came to nothing—except for allowing Ender's diminishment in the court martial.

Which led Valentine once again to her suspicion that Graff, too, could have prevented the court martial if he had wanted to, that perhaps it was a price he paid in order to gain some other advantage. Even if all it did for Graff was "prove" that not everything was going his way, that would be a great source of complacency for Graff's rivals and opponents, and Valentine well knew that complacency was the best possible attitude for one's rivals and opponents to have.

Graff loved and respected Ender, but he was not above allowing something very unfortunate to happen to him if it served the larger purpose. Hadn't Graff proved it over and over?

Well, my dear MinCol, by the time we get to Shakespeare Colony, you will almost certainly be either dead or very, very old. I wonder if you'll still be running everything then?

Poor Peter. Aspiring to rule the world, while Graff had already done it. The difference was that Peter needed to be *known* to rule the world; all the outward forms of government needed to be seen to lead to Peter's throne. Whereas Graff only needed to use his control of whatever he wanted to control in order to accomplish his single, lofty purpose.

But aren't they the same person, apart from that? Manipulators, letting anyone else pay whatever cost was required to accomplish the end in view. It was a good end, in Graff's case. Valentine agreed with it, believed in it, happily cooperated with it. But wasn't Peter's goal also a good one? The end of war, because the world was united under a single good government. If he brought it off, wouldn't it be as much a blessing to the human race as anything Graff accomplished?

She had to give both Peter and Graff credit for this: They weren't monsters. They didn't require that all costs be paid by others, none by themselves. They would also make whatever personal sacrifices were required. They really did serve a cause bigger than themselves.

But couldn't that also have been said of Hitler? Unlike Stalin and Mao, who wallowed in luxury while others did all the work and made all the sacrifices, Hitler lived sparingly and truly believed himself to be living for a cause greater than himself. That's precisely what made him such a monster. So Valentine was not quite sure that Peter's and Graff's self-sacrifices were quite enough to absolve them of monsterhood.

Well, they would both be someone else's problem now. Let Rackham watch out for Graff and kill him if he gets out of hand, which he probably won't. And let Father and Mother do their pathetic best to keep Peter from becoming the devil. Do they even realize that Peter's whole goodson attitude was an act? That Peter had obviously made the conscious decision several years back to pretend to be just like the boy Ender had been? All an act, dear parents—do you see it? Sometimes I think you do, but other times you are so oblivious.

You will be lost in the past by the time I get where I'm going, all of you. My present will be Ender and whatever he's doing. He is my whole flock, and I must shepherd him without ever letting him see the crook I use to guide him and protect him.

What am I thinking? Who's the megalomaniac here? I think *I* will know better than Ender what is good for him, where he should go, what he should do, and what he should be protected from?

Yet that is exactly what I think, because it's true.

———

Ender was so sleepy he could hardly stand, yet he stood, through all the pictures, making the smile as warm and real as he could. These are the pictures Mother and Father will see. The pictures for Peter's children, if he has any, to remember that once they had an Uncle Ender who did something very famous before he was in his teens and then went away. This is how he looked when he left. See? He's very happy. See, Mom and Dad? You didn't hurt me when you let them take me. Nothing has hurt me. I'm fine. Look at my smile. Don't see how tired I am, or how glad I am to go, when they let me go.

Then at last the pictures were done. Ender shook hands with Mazer Rackham and wanted to say, I wish you were coming. But he could not say he wished that, because he knew that Mazer did not want to go, and so it would be a selfish wish. So he said only this: "Thank you for all you taught me, and for standing by me." He did not add "standing by me at the trial" because the words might be picked up by some stray microphone.

Then he shook hands with Hyrum Graff and said, "I hope this new job works out for you." It was a joke, and Graff got it, or at least enough to smile a little. Maybe the thinness of Graff's smile was because he had heard Ender thank Mazer and wondered why Ender had no thanks for him. But Graff had not been his teacher, only his master, and it was not the same. Nor had Graff stood by him, as far as Ender could tell. Hadn't Graff's whole program of teaching been to get Ender to believe to the depth of his soul that there would never be anyone standing by him?

"Thanks for the nap," he said to Graff.

Graff chuckled out loud. "May you always have as many as you need."

Then Ender paused, looking at nothing, at the empty room, and thought, Good-bye, Mom. Good-bye, Dad. Good-bye, Peter. Good-bye, all the men and women and children of Earth. I've done all I could for you, and had all I could receive from you, and now someone else is responsible for you all.

Ender walked up the ramp to the shuttle, Valentine directly behind him.

The shuttle took them off Eros for the last time. Good-bye, Eros, and all the soldiers on it, the ones who fought for me and the other children, the ones who manipulated us and lied to us for the good of humanity, the ones who conspired to defame me and keep me from returning to Earth, all of you, good and bad, kind and selfish, good-bye to you, I am no longer one of you, neither your pawn nor your savior. I resign my commission.

Ender said nothing to Valentine beyond the trivial comments of travel. It was only about a half hour of jockeying until the shuttle was docked against the surface of the transport ship. It had been meant to carry soldiers and their weapons into war. Now it was carrying a vast amount of equipment and supplies for the agricultural and manufacturing needs of Shakespeare Colony, and more people to join them, to improve their gene pool, to help buy them enough productivity that there'd be leisure for science and creativity and luxury, a life closer to what the societies of Earth offered.

But all of that had been loaded, and all the people. Ender was last. Ender and Valentine.

At the bottom of the ladderway that would take them up into the ship, Ender stopped and faced Valentine. "You can still go back now," he said. "You can see that I'll be fine. The people of the colony that I've met so far are very nice and I won't be lonely."

"Are you afraid to go up the ladder first?" asked Valentine. "Is that why you've stopped to make a speech?"

So Ender went up the ladder and Valentine followed, making her the last of the colonists to cut the thread connecting them to Earth.

Below them, the hatch of the shuttle closed, and then the hatch of the ship. They stood in the airlock until a door opened and there was Admiral Quincy Morgan, smiling, his hand already extended. How long did he strike that pose before the door opened, Ender wondered. Was he there, perhaps, for hours, posed like a mannequin?

"Welcome, Governor Wiggin," said Morgan.

"Admiral Morgan," said Ender, "I'm not governor of anything until I set foot on the planet. On this voyage, on your ship, I'm a student of the xenobiology and adapted agriculture of Shakespeare Colony. I hope, though, that when you're not too busy, I'll have a chance to talk to you and learn from you about the military life."

"You're the one who's seen combat," said Morgan.

"I played a game," said Ender. "I saw nothing of war. But there are colonists on Shakespeare who made this voyage many years ago, and never had a hope of returning home to Earth. I want to get some idea of what their training was, their life."

"You'll have to read books for that," said Morgan, still smiling. "This is my first interstellar voyage, too. In fact, as far as I know, no one has ever made two of them. Even Mazer Rackham only made a single voyage, which ended at its starting place."

"Why, I believe you're right, Admiral Morgan," said Ender. "It makes us all pioneers together, here in your ship." There—had he said "your ship" often enough to reassure Morgan that he knew the order of authority here?

Morgan's smile was unchanged. "I'll be happy to talk to you any time. It's an honor to have you on my ship, sir."

"Please don't 'sir' me, sir," said Ender. "We both know that I'm an admiral in name only, and I don't want the colonists to hear anyone call me by a title other than Mr. Wiggin, and preferably not that. Let me be Ender. Or Andrew, if you want to be formal. Would that be all right, or would it interfere with shipboard discipline?"

"I believe," said Admiral Morgan, "that it won't interfere with discipline, and so it shall be entirely as you prefer. Now Ensign Akbar will show you and your sister to your stateroom. Since so few passengers are making the voyage awake, most families have quarters of similar size. I say this because of your memo requesting that you not have an exorbitantly oversized space on the ship."

"Is your family aboard, sir?" asked Ender.

"I wooed my superiors and they gave birth to my career," said Morgan. "The International Fleet has been my only bride. Like you, I travel as a bachelor."

Ender grinned at him. "I think your bachelorhood and mine are both going to be much in question before long."

"Our mission is reproduction of the species beyond the bounds of Earth," said Morgan. "But the voyage will go more smoothly if we guard our bachelorhood zealously while in transit."

"Mine has the safety of ignorant youth," said Ender, "and yours the distance of authority. Thank you for the great honor of greeting us here. I've underslept a little the past few days, and I hope I'll be forgiven for indulging myself in about eighteen hours of rest. I fear I'll miss the beginning of acceleration."

"Everyone will, Mr. Wiggin," said Morgan. "The inertia suppression on this ship is superb. In fact, we are already accelerating at the rate of two gravities, and yet the only apparent gravity is imparted by the centrifugal force of the spin of the ship."

"Which is odd," said Valentine, "since centrifugal force is also inertial, and you'd think it would also be suppressed."

"The suppression is highly directionalized, and affects only the forward movement of the ship," said Morgan. "I apologize for ignoring you so nearly completely, Ms. Wiggin. I'm afraid your brother's fame and rank have distracted me and I forgot courtesy."

"None is owed to me," said Valentine with a light laugh. "I'm just along for the ride."

With that they separated and Ensign Akbar led them to their stateroom. It was not a huge space, but it was well equipped, and it took the ensign several minutes to show them where their clothing, supplies, and desks had been stowed, and how to use the ship's internal communications system. He insisted on setting down both their beds and then raising them up again and locking them out of the way, so Ender and Valentine had seen a complete demonstration. Then he showed them how to lower and raise the privacy screen that turned the stateroom into two sleeping areas.

"Thank you," said Ender. "Now I think I'll take the bed down again so I can sleep."

Ensign Akbar was full of apologies and took both the beds down again, ignoring their protests that the point of his demonstration was so they could do it themselves. When he was finally done, he paused at the door. "Sir," he said, "I know I shouldn't ask. But. May I shake your hand, sir?"

Ender thrust out his hand and smiled warmly. "Thank you for helping us, Ensign Akbar."

"It's an honor to have you aboard this ship, sir." Then Akbar saluted. Ender returned the salute and the ensign left and the door closed behind him.

Ender went to his bed and sat down on it. Valentine sat on hers, directly across from him. Ender looked at her and started to laugh. She joined in his laughter.

They laughed until Ender was forced to lie down and rub the tears out of his eyes.

"May I ask," said Valentine, "if we're both laughing at the same thing?"

"Why? What were you laughing at?"

"Everything," said Valentine. "The whole picture-taking thing before we left, and Morgan greeting us so warmly, as if he weren't preparing to stab you in the back, and Ensign Akbar's hero worship despite your insistence that you were just 'Mr. Wiggin'—which is, of course, an affectation too. I was laughing at the whole of it."

"I see that all of that is funny, if you look at it that way. I was too busy to be amused with it. I was just trying to stay awake and say all the right things."

"So what were *you* laughing at?"

"It was pure delight. Delight and relief. I'm not in charge of anything now. For the duration of the voyage, it's Morgan's ship, and I'm a free man for the first time in my life."

"Man?" asked Valentine. "You're still shorter than me."

"But Val," said Ender, "I have to shave every week now, or the whiskers show."

They laughed again, just a little. Then Valentine spoke the command to bring down the barrier between their beds. Ender stripped down to his underwear, crawled under a single sheet—nothing more was needed in this climate-controlled environment—and in moments he was asleep.

CHAPTER
8

To: GovDes%ShakespeareCol@ColMin.gov/voy
From: MinCol@ColMin.gov
Fwd: Report on Planet Making

Dear Ender,

I was conflicted about whether to send you this. On the one hand, it is fascinating, even heartening; on the other hand, I know you have suffered greatly because of the destruction of the formic home world and reminders might be painful. I risk the pain—your pain, so it was not much risk to me, was it?—because if there is anyone who should be receiving these reports, it is you.

—Hyrum

Forwarded Message:
To: MinCol@ColMin.gov
From: LPo%formcent@IFCom.gov/bda
Subj: Report on Planet Making

Dear Hyrum,

I'm not sure you're in the need-to-know loop, since it will be a long time before

the subject planet will be ready for colonization, but since there is also no further enemy presence there, I thought you'd want to know something of the
aftermath—our official "damage assessment" reports. (You'll note that in my
new assignment, I do NOT get to follow normal military abbreviations and
call my area "DamAss" or "AssDam." We have to use mere initials, BDA. As
the kids say, kuso.)

SecureLinka7977@rTTu7&!a**********bdA.gov

I've set it so your full name is a nonce password for the next week.

In case you don't have time to read the whole report at the above site, here's
the gist: The former formic home world, destroyed last year by molecular disruption, is re-forming. Our follow-up ship, instead of trying to salvage a losing
battle, is finding that its mission is astronomical: to watch the formation of a
planet out of, quite literally, elemental dust.

Since the md field broke everything into its constituent atoms, it is coalesc-
ing with remarkable quickness. Our observer ship has recently been in a
position to see the dust cloud with the star directly behind it, and during the
passage sufficient spectrometry and mass measurements were taken to assure us that the vast majority of the atoms have re-formed into the common,
expected molecules, and that the gravity of the cloud was sufficient to hold
most of the material in place. There has been some loss from escape ve-
locity and further loss to solar gravity, solar wind, etc., but our best estimate
is that the new planet will be at no less than 80 percent of the original
mass, and perhaps more. At that size, there will still be atmosphere, potentially breathable. There will also be molten core and mantle, ocean,
and the probability of tectonic movement of thicker areas of crust—i.e.,
continents.

In short, while no artifacts of the former civilization can possibly be found, the
planet itself will be back in a nice wad, in stellar orbit, within the next thousand
years, and perhaps cool enough to explore in ten thousand years. Colonizable
in a hundred thousand, if we seed it with oxygenating bacteria and other life as
soon as the oceans are fully formed.

We humans can be destructive, but the universe's thirst for creation goes on unslaked.

—Li

Public spaces were few on the "Good Ship Lollipop" (as Valentine called it), also known as "IFcoltrans1" (which was painted on its side and broadcast continuously from its beacon), or "Mrs. Morgan" (as the ship's officers and crew called it behind their captain's back).

There was the mess hall, where no one could linger long, since one dining shift or another started every hour. The library was for serious research by ship's personnel; passengers had full access to the contents of the library on their own desks in their staterooms and so were not particularly welcome in the library itself.

The officers' and crew's lounges were open to passengers by invitation only, and such invitations were rare. The theater was good for viewing holos and vids, or for gathering all the passengers for a meeting or announcement, but private conversations tended to be shushed, with some hostility.

For conviviality, this left the observation deck, whose walls offered a view only when the stardrive was off and the ship was maneuvering close to a planet; and the few open spaces in the cargo hold—which would increase in number and size as they used up supplies during the voyage.

It was to the observation deck, then, that Ender betook himself every day after breakfast. Valentine was surprised at his apparent sociability. On Eros, he had been private, reluctant to converse, obsessed with his studies. Now he greeted everyone who entered the observation deck and chatted amiably with anyone who wanted his time.

"Why do you let them interrupt you?" asked Valentine one night, after they returned to their stateroom.

"They don't interrupt me," said Ender. "My purpose is to converse with them; I do my other work when no one wants me."

"So you're being their governor."

"I am not," said Ender. "I'm not governor of anything at the moment. This is Admiral Morgan's ship, and I have no authority here."

It was Ender's standard answer when anyone wanted him to solve a problem—to judge a dispute, to question a rule, to ask for a change or a privilege. "I'm afraid that my authority doesn't begin until I set foot on the surface of the planet Shakespeare," he'd say. "But I'm sure that you'll get satisfaction from whatever officer Admiral Morgan has delegated to deal with us passengers."

"But you're an admiral, too," several people mentioned. A few even knew that Ender had a higher rank, among admirals, than Morgan. "You outrank him."

"He's captain of the ship," said Ender, always smiling. "There *is* no higher authority than that."

Valentine wasn't going to settle for such answers, not when they were alone. "Mierda, mi hermano," said Valentine. "If you don't have any official duties and you're not being governor, then why are you spending so much time being—*affable*?"

"Presumably," said Ender, "we will arrive at our destination someday. When that happens, I need to know every person who will stay with the colony. I need to know them well. I need to know how they fit together in their families, among the friendships they form on the ship. I need to know who speaks Common well and who has trouble communicating outside their native language. I must know who is belligerent, who is needy of attention, who is creative and resourceful, what education they have, how they think about unfamiliar ideas. For the passengers who are in cold storage, I had only a half hour meeting with each group. For those who are making the voyage awake, like us, I have much more time. Time enough, maybe, to find out why they chose not to sleep through the trip. Afraid of stasis? Hoping for some advantage when we get there? As you can see, Valentine, I'm working constantly out there. It makes me tired."

"I've been thinking of teaching English," said Valentine. "Offering a class."

"Not English," said Ender. "Common. It's spelled better—no *ugh*s and *igh*s—and there's some special vocabulary and there's no subjunctive, no 'whom,' and the word 'of' is spelled as the single letter 'v.' To name just a few of the differences."

"So I'll teach them Common," said Valentine. "What do you think?"

"I think it'll be harder than you think, but it would really help the people who took the class—if the ones who need it take it."

"So I'll see what language-teaching software there is in the library."

"First, though, I hope you'll check with Admiral Morgan."

"Why?"

"It's his ship. Offering a course can be done only with his permission."

"Why would he care?"

"I don't know that he does care. I just know that on his ship, we have to find out if he cares before we start something as formal and regular as a class."

As it turned out, the passenger liaison officer, a colonel named Jarrko Kitunen, was already planning to organize Common classes and he accepted Valentine as an instructor the moment she volunteered. He also flirted with her shamelessly in his Finnish accent, and she found that she rather enjoyed his company. With Ender always busy talking with somebody or reading whatever he'd just received by ansible or downloaded from the library, it was good to have a pleasant way to pass the time. She could only stand to work on her history of Battle School for a few hours at a time, so it was a relief to have human company.

She had come on this voyage for Ender, but until he was willing to take her fully into his confidence, she had no obligation to mope around wishing for more of Ender's soul than he was willing to share. And if it turned out that Ender never wished to take her into his life, to restore their old bond, then she would need to make a life for herself, wouldn't she?

Not that Jarrko would be that life. For one thing, he was at least ten years older than she was. For another, he was crew, which meant that when the ship was loaded up with whatever artifacts and trade goods and supplies Shakespeare was able to supply them with, it would be turning around and heading back to Earth, or at least to Eros. She would not be on it. So any relationship with Jarrko was going to end. He might be fine with that, but Valentine was not.

As Father always said, "Monogamy is what works best for any society in the long run. That's why half of us are born male and half female—so we come out even."

So Valentine wasn't always with Ender; she was busy, she had things to do, she had a life of her own. Which was more than Peter had ever given her, so she rather enjoyed it.

It happened, though, that Valentine *was* with Ender in the observation deck, working on the book, when an Italian woman and her teenage daughter walked up to Ender and stood there, saying nothing, waiting to be noticed. Valentine knew them because they were both in her Common class.

Ender noticed them at once and smiled at them. "Dorabella and Alessandra Toscano," he said. "What a pleasure to meet you at last."

"We were not ready," said Dorabella in her halting Italian accent. "On till your sister could taught us English good enough." Then she giggled. "I mean 'Common.' "

"I wish I spoke Italian," said Ender. "It's a beautiful language."

"The language of love," said Dorabella. "Not is French, nasty language of kissy lips and spitting."

"French is beautiful, too," said Ender, laughing at the way she had imitated the French accent and attitude.

"To French and deaf peoples," said Dorabella.

"Mother," said Alessandra. She had very little Italian accent, but rather spoke like an educated Brit. "There are French speakers among the colonists, and he can't offend any of them."

"Why will they be any offended? They make the kissy mouth to talk, we pretend we not to notice it?"

Valentine laughed aloud. Dorabella really was quite funny, full of attitude. Sassy, that was the word. Even though she was old enough to be Ender's mother—considering her daughter was Ender's age—she could be seen as flirting with Ender. Maybe she was one of those women who flirted with everybody because they knew of no other way to relate to them.

"Now we are ready," said Dorabella. "Your sister teaching us good, so we ready for our half hour with you."

Ender blinked. "Oh, did you think—I took a half hour with all the colonists who were going to travel in stasis because that's all the time I had before they became unavailable. But the colonists on the ship—we have a year or two, plenty of time. No need to schedule a half hour. I'm here all the time."

"But you are very important man, saving of the whole world."

Ender shook his head. "That was my old job. Now I'm a kid with a job that's too big for me. So sit down, let's talk. You're learning English very well—Valentine has mentioned you, actually, and how hard you work—and your daughter has no accent at all, she's fluent."

"Very intelligent girl my Alessandra," said Dorabella. "And pretty, too, yes? You think so? Nice figure for fourteen."

"Mother!" Alessandra shrank down into a chair. "Am I a used car? Am I a street vendor's sandwich?"

"Street vendors," sighed Dorabella. "I miss them yet."

"Already," Valentine corrected her.

"I am already miss them," said Dorabella, proudly correcting herself. "So small Shakespeare planet will be. No city! What you said, Alessandra? Tell him."

Alessandra looked flustered, but her mother pressed her. "I just said that there are more characters in Shakespeare's plays than there will be colonists on the planet named after him."

Ender laughed. "What a thought! You're right, we probably couldn't put on all of his plays without having to use several colonists for more than one part. Not that I have any particular plan to put on a Shakespearean play. Though maybe we should. What do you think? Would anyone want to be ready to put on a play for the colonists who are already there?"

"We don't know whether they like the new name," said Valentine. She also thought: Does Ender have any idea how much work it is to put on a play?

"They know the name," Ender assured her.

"But do they like it?" asked Valentine.

"It doesn't matter," said Alessandra. "Not enough women *ruoli, parti*— how do you say it?" She turned to Valentine helplessly.

" 'Role,' " said Valentine. "Or 'part.' "

"Oh." Alessandra giggled. It was not an annoying giggle, it was a rather charming one. It didn't make her sound stupid. "The same words! Of course."

"She's right," said Valentine. "The colonists are about half and half, and Shakespeare's plays are what, five percent female parts?"

"Oh well," said Ender. "It was a thought."

"I wish we could put on a play," said Alessandra. "But maybe we can read them together?"

"In theater," said Dorabella. "The place for *holografi*. We all read. Me, I listen, my English is not good enough."

"It's a good idea," said Ender. "Why don't you organize it, Signora Toscano?"

"Please call me of Dorabella."

"There's no 'of' in that sentence," said Alessandra. "There isn't in Italian, either."

"English has so much 'of,' everywhere 'of,' except where I put it!" As Dorabella laughed, she touched Ender's arm. Probably Dorabella didn't see how he suppressed his instinct to flinch—Ender didn't like being touched by strangers, he never had. But Valentine saw it. He was still Ender.

"I've never seen a play," said Ender. "I've read them, I've seen holos and vids of them, but I've never actually been in a room where people actually said the lines aloud. I could never put it together, but I'd love to be there and listen as it happens."

"Then you must!" said Dorabella. "You are governor, you make it happen!"

"I can't," said Ender. "Truly. You do it, please."

"No, I cannot," said Dorabella. "My English is too bad. *Il teatro* is for young persons. I will watch and listen. You and Alessandra do it. You are students, you are children. Romeo and Juliet!"

Could she possibly be any more obvious? thought Valentine.

"Mother thinks that if you and I are together a lot," said Alessandra, "we'll fall in love and get married."

Valentine almost laughed aloud. So the daughter wasn't a co-conspirator, she was a draftee.

Dorabella feigned shock. "I have no plan like such!"

"Oh, Mother, you've been planning it from the start. Even back in the town we came from—"

"Monopoli," said Ender.

"She was calling you a 'young man with prospects.' A likely candidate for my husband. My personal opinion is that I'm very young, and so are you."

Ender was busy mollifying the mother. "Dorabella, please, I'm not offended and of course I know you weren't planning anything. Alessandra is teasing me. Teasing us both."

"I'm not, but you can say whatever it takes to make Mother happy," said Alessandra. "Our lives together are one long play. She makes me . . . not the star of my own autobiography. But Mother always sees the happy ending, right from the start."

Valentine wasn't sure what to make of the relationship between these two. The words were biting, almost hostile. Yet as she said them, Alessandra gave her mother a hug and seemed to mean it. As if the words were part of a long ritual between them, but they no longer were meant to sting.

Whatever was going on, between Ender and Alessandra, Dorabella seemed mollified. "I like the happy ending."

"We should put on a Greek play," said Alessandra. "*Medea.* The one where the mother kills her own children."

Valentine was shocked at this—what a cruel thing to say in front of her mother. But no, from Dorabella's reaction Alessandra wasn't referring to her. For Dorabella laughed and nodded and said, "Yes, yes, Medea, spiteful mama!"

"Only we'll rename her," said Alessandra. "Isabella!"

"Isabella!" cried Dorabella at almost the same moment. The two of them laughed so hard they almost cried, and Ender joined with them.

Then, to Valentine's surprise, while the other two were still hiccuping through the end of their laughter, Ender turned to her and explained. "Isabella is Dorabella's mother. They had a painful parting."

Alessandra stopped laughing and looked at Ender searchingly—but if Dorabella was surprised that Ender knew so much of their past, she didn't show it. "We come on this colony to be free of my perfect mother. Santa Isabella, we will not pray to you!"

Then Dorabella leapt to her feet and began to do some kind of dance, a waltz perhaps, holding an imaginary full skirt in one hand, and with the other hand tracing arcane patterns in the air as she danced. "Always I have a magic land where I can be happy, and I take my daughter there with me, always happy." Then she stopped and faced Ender. "Shakespeare Colony is our magic land now. You are king of the . . . *folletti*?" She looked to her daughter.

"Elfs," said Alessandra.

"Elves," said Valentine.

"Gli elfi!" cried Dorabella in delight. "Again same word! Elfo, elve!"

"Elf," said Valentine and Alessandra together.

"King of the elves," said Ender. "I wonder what email address I'll get for that one. ElfKing@Faerie.gov." He turned to Valentine. "Or is that the title Peter aspires to?"

Valentine smiled. "He's still torn between Hegemon and God," she said.

Dorabella didn't understand the reference to Peter. She returned to her dancing, and this time she sang a wordless but haunting tune with it. And Alessandra shook her head but still joined in the song, harmonizing with it. So she had heard it before and knew it and had sung with her mother. Their voices blended sweetly.

Valentine watched Dorabella's dance, fascinated. At first it had seemed like a childish, rather mad thing to do. Now, though, she could see that Dorabella knew she was being silly, but still meant it from the heart. It gave the movement, and her facial expression, a sort of irony that made it easy to forgive the silliness and affectation of it, while the sincerity turned it into something quite winning.

The woman isn't old, thought Valentine. She's still young and quite good looking. Beautiful, even, especially now, especially in this strange fairyish dance.

The song ended. Dorabella kept dancing in the silence.

"Mother, you can stop flying now," said Alessandra gently.

"But I can't," said Dorabella, and now she was openly teasing. "In this starship we fly for fifty years!"

"Forty years," said Ender.

"Two years," said Alessandra.

Apparently Ender liked the idea of doing a play, because he brought them all back to the topic. "Not *Romeo and Juliet*," he said. "We need a comedy, not a tragedy."

"*The Merry Wives of Windsor*," said Valentine. "Lots of women's parts."

"The Taming of the Shrew!" cried Alessandra, and Dorabella almost collapsed with laughter. Another reference, apparently, to Isabella. And when they stopped laughing, they insisted that *Shrew* was the perfect play. "I will read the part of the madwoman," said Dorabella. Valentine noticed that Alessandra seemed to be biting back some kind of comment.

So it was that the plan was conceived for a play reading in the theater three days later—days by ship's time, though the whole concept of time seemed rather absurd to Valentine, on this voyage where forty years would pass in less than two. What would her birthday be *now*? Would she count her age by ship's time or the elapsed calendar when she arrived? And what did Earth's calendar mean on Shakespeare?

Naturally, Dorabella and Alessandra came to Ender often during the days of preparation, asking him endless questions. Even though he made it clear that all the decisions were up to them, that he was not in charge of the event, he was never impatient with them. He seemed to enjoy their company—though Valentine suspected that it was not for the reason Dorabella had hoped. Ender wasn't falling in love with Alessandra—if he was infatuated with anyone, it was likely to be the mother. No, what Ender was falling in love with was the family-ness of them. They were close in a way that Ender and Valentine had once been close. And they were including Ender in that closeness.

Why couldn't I have done that for him? Valentine was quite jealous, but only because of her own failure, not because she wished to deprive him of the pleasure he was getting from the Toscanos.

It was inevitable, of course, that they enlisted Ender himself to read the part of Lucentio, the handsome young suitor of Bianca—played, of course, by Alessandra. Dorabella herself read Kate the Shrew, while Valentine was relegated to the part of the Widow. Valentine didn't even pretend not to want to read the part—this was the most interesting thing going on in the ship, and why not be at the heart of it? She was Ender's sister; let people hear her voice, especially in the ribald, exaggerated part of the Widow.

It was entertaining for Valentine to see how the men and boys who were cast in the many other parts focused on Dorabella. The woman had an incredible laugh, rich and throaty and contagious. To earn a laugh from her in this comedy was a fine thing, and the men all vied to please her. It made Valentine wonder if getting Ender and Alessandra together was really Dorabella's agenda? Perhaps it's what she *thought* she was doing, but in fact Dorabella held the center of the stage herself, and seemed to love having all eyes on her. She flirted with them all, fell in love with them all, and yet always seemed to be in a world of her own, too.

Has Kate the Shrew ever been played like this before?

Does every woman have what this Dorabella has? Valentine searched in her heart to find that kind of ebullience. I know how to have fun, Valentine insisted to herself. I know how to be playful.

But she knew there was always irony in her wit, a kind of snottiness in her banter. Alessandra's timidity covered everything she did—she was bold in what she said, but it was as if her own words surprised and embarrassed her after the fact. Dorabella, however, was neither ironic nor frightened. Here was a woman who had faced all her dragons and slain them; now she was ready for the accolades of the admiring throng. She cried out Kate's dialogue from the heart, her rage, her passion, her petulance, her frustration, and finally her love. The final monologue, in which she submits to her husband's will, was so beautiful it made Valentine cry a little, and she thought: I wonder what it would be like to love and trust a man so much that I'd be willing to abase myself as Kate did. Is there something in women that makes us long to be humbled? Or is it something in human beings, that when we are overmastered, we rejoice in our subjection? That would explain a lot of history.

Since everyone who was interested in the play was already in it, and attending the rehearsals, it wasn't as if the actual performance was going to surprise anyone. Valentine almost asked the whole group, at the last rehearsal, "Why bother to put it on? We just did it, and it was wonderful."

But there was still a kind of excitement throughout the ship about the coming performance, and Valentine realized that rehearsal was not performance, no matter how well it went. And there would be others there after all, who had not been at the last rehearsal: Dorabella was going around inviting members of the crew, many of whom promised to come. And passengers who weren't in the play seemed excited about coming, and some were openly rueful about having declined to take part. "Next time," they said.

When they got to the theater at the appointed time, they found Jarrko standing at the door, a stiff, formal expression on his face. No, the theater would not be opened; by order of the admiral, the play reading had been canceled.

"Ah, Governor Wiggin," said Jarrko.

A bad sign, if the title was back, thought Valentine.

"Admiral Morgan would like to see you at once, if you please, sir."

Ender nodded and smiled. "Of course," he said.

So Ender had *expected* this? Or was he really that perfectly poised, so it *seemed* that nothing surprised him?

Valentine started to go with him, but Jarrko touched her shoulder. "Please, Val," he whispered. "Alone."

Ender grinned at her and took off with real bounce in his step, as if he was truly excited to be going to see the admiral.

"What's this about?" Valentine asked Jarrko quietly.

"I can't say," he said. "Truly. Just have my orders. No play, theater closed for the night, would the governor please come see the admiral immediately."

So Valentine stayed with Jarrko, helping soothe the players and other colonists, whose reactions ranged from disappointment to outrage to revolutionary fervor. Some of them even started reciting lines there in the corridor, until Valentine asked them not to. "Poor Colonel Kitunen will be in trouble if you keep this up, and he's too nice to stop you himself."

The result was that everyone was quite angry with Admiral Morgan for his arbitrary cancellation of a completely harmless event. And Valentine herself couldn't help but wonder: What was the man thinking? Hadn't he ever heard of morale? Maybe he'd heard of it, but was against it.

Something was going on here, and Valentine began to wonder if somehow Ender was behind it. Could it be that in his own way, Ender was just as sneaky and snaky as Peter?

No. Not possible. Especially because Valentine could always see through Peter. Ender wasn't devious at all. He always said what he meant and meant what he said.

What is the boy doing?

CHAPTER

9

To: demosthenes@LastBestHopeOfEarth.pol
From: PeterWiggin@hegemony.gov/hegemon
Re: While you were out

I had one of my staff run a set of calculations about how long it has been for you since you began your relativistic voyage into the future. At best he could give me only a range of possible subjective durations—a few weeks, anyway. For me, a couple of years. So I am fairly safe in saying that I miss you a great deal more than you miss me. At present you probably still think that you will never miss me at all. The world is full of people who are convinced of the same thing. They vaguely remember that I was elected to the office of Hegemon. They just can't remember what that office does. They think my name is Locke when they think of me at all.

Yet I am at war. My force is tiny, commanded by—of all people—Ender's old friend Bean. The other children from Ender's jeesh—Battle School slang for "army," but it's caught on here and that's what they're called—were all kidnapped by the Russians, inspired by a conniving little bastard named Achilles, who was kicked out of Battle School. It appears that Achilles chose his main enemy better than Bonito de Madrid did—it was Bean who confronted him in a dark air vent, or so the story goes, and instead of killing him, turned him over to the authorities. Have you ever heard that tale? Did Ender know about it when it happened? Achilles is Hitler with stealth, Stalin with brains, Mao with energy, Pol Pot with subtlety—name your monster, and Achilles has all the inconvenient virtues to make him very hard to stop and even harder to kill. Bean swears he will do it, but he had the chance before and blew it, so I'm skeptical.

I wish you were here.

More than that, I actually wish Ender were here. I'm waging war with the help of an army of a few hundred men—very loyal, brilliantly trained, but only two hundred of them! Bean is not the most reliable of commanders. He always wins, but he doesn't always do what he's told or go where I want him to. He picks and chooses among his assignments. To his credit, he doesn't argue with me in front of his (supposedly "my") men.

The trouble is that these Battle School kids are all so cynical. They don't believe in anything. Certainly they don't believe in ME. Just because Achilles keeps trying to assassinate Bean and has all the Battle School kids terrified, they think they don't owe Ender Wiggin's big brother their lifelong personal service. (That was a joke. They owe me nothing.)

Wars here and there around the world, shifting alliances—it's what I predicted would happen after the Battle School kids came home. They're such excellent weapons—potentially devastating, but no fallout, no mushroom clouds. Somehow, though, I always saw myself riding the crest of the wave. Now I find myself sucked down to the bottom of the wave so I can barely tell which way is up and I'm constantly running out of air. I get to the top, gasp, and then a new wave crashes me back down.

A few privileges inhere to this office, for the time being, anyway. Minister of Colonization Graff tells me I have unlimited access to the ansible—I can talk to you whenever I want. Congratulate me for not abusing it. I know you're writing a history of Battle School, and I thought you could use some information about the careers of the more prominent Battle School grads, for an epilogue, perhaps. Ender's jeesh fought the formics and won; but all the others are now involved, one way or another, as captives or servants or leaders or figureheads or victims, in the military planning and action of every nation lucky enough to have a single graduate and strong enough to hold on to him.

So steel yourself for reams of information. Graff tells me that it will take weeks to send it all from his office (in the old Battle School station now), but that at your end it will seem to arrive all at once. I hope it doesn't annoy your ship's captain too much—I understand it's a nobody, not Mazer Rackham after all— but what I'm sending goes with hegemony priority, which means he won't be able to read any of this and any messages HE'S expecting will have to wait. Give him my apologies. Or not, as you see fit.

I have never been so alone in my life. I wish for you every day. Fortunately, Father and Mother have turned out to be surprisingly useful. No, I should have said "helpful." But I'll leave the "useful" there so you can say, "He hasn't changed." They also miss you, and among the information you're getting are letters from both Father and Mother. Also letters from them to Ender. I hope the boy gets over the snit he's in and writes back to them. Missing you has given me some idea of how they feel about Ender (and now you): If he wrote to them it would mean the world. And what would it cost him?

No, I'm not going to write to him myself. I have no stock in that company. Mom and Dad are miserable, having only me as visible proof that they re- produced. Brighten their lives, both of you. What ELSE do you have to do? I picture you gliding along at lightspeed, with servants bringing you juleps and the fawning colonists begging Ender to tell them once again about how the formic home world went boom.

Writing this sometimes feels as if I'm talking to you like old times. But at this moment it's a painful reminder that it's nothing like talking to you at all.

As the official monster of the family, I hope you will compare me to a real monster like Achilles and give me some points for not being as awful as it is possible to be. I also have to tell you that I've learned that when no one else can be trusted—and I mean no one—there is family. And somehow I managed to be complicit in driving away two of the four people I could trust. Clumsy of me, n'est-ce pas?

I love you, Valentine. I wish I had treated you better from childhood on up. Ender too. Now, happy reading. The world is such a mess, you're glad you aren't here. But I promise you this: I will do all I can to put things back in order and bring peace. Without, I hope, waging too much war along the way.

With all my heart, your bratty brother,
Peter

Admiral Morgan kept Ender waiting outside his office for two full hours. It was exactly what Ender expected, however, so he closed his eyes and used the time to take a long, refreshing nap. He awoke to hear someone shouting from the other side of a door: "Well, wake him up and send him in, I'm ready!"

Ender sat up immediately, instantly aware of his surroundings. Even though he had never knowingly been in combat, he had acquired the military habit of remaining alert even when asleep. By the time the ensign whose duty was to waken him arrived, Ender was already standing up and smiling. "I understand it's time for my meeting with Admiral Morgan."

"Yes sir, if you please sir." The poor kid (well, six or seven years older than Ender, but still young to have an admiral yelling at him all day) was all over himself with eagerness to please Ender. So Ender made it a point to be visibly pleased. "He's in a temper," the ensign whispered.

"Let's see if I can cheer him up a little," said Ender.

"Not bloody likely," whispered the ensign. Then he had the door open. "Admiral Andrew Wiggin, sir." Ender stepped in as he was announced; the ensign beat a hasty retreat and shut the door behind him.

"What the hell do you think you're doing?" demanded Admiral Morgan, his face livid. Since Ender had been napping for two hours, that meant either that Morgan had maintained his lividity throughout the interim, or he was able to switch it on at will, for effect. Ender was betting on the latter.

"I'm meeting with the captain of the ship, at his request."

"*Sir*," said Admiral Morgan.

"Oh, you don't need to call me *sir*," said Ender. "Andrew will do. I don't like to insist on the privileges of rank." Ender sat down in a comfortable chair beside Morgan's desk, instead of the stiff chair directly in front of it.

"On my ship you have no rank," said Morgan.

"I have no authority," said Ender. "But my rank travels with me."

"You are fomenting rebellion on my ship, coopting vital resources, subverting a mission whose primary purpose is to deliver *you* to the colony that you purport to be ready to govern."

"Rebellion? We're reading *Taming of the Shrew,* not *Richard II.*"

"I'm still talking, boy! You may think you're heroism personified because you and your little chums played a videogame that turned out to be real, but I won't put up with this kind of subversion on my own ship! Whatever you did that made you famous and got you that ridiculous rank is *over.* You're in the real world now, and you're just a snot-nosed boy with delusions of grandeur."

Ender sat in silence, regarding him calmly.

"*Now* you can answer."

"I have no idea what you're talking about," said Ender.

Whereupon Morgan let fly with such a string of obscenities and vulgarities that it sounded like he had collected the favorite sayings of the entire fleet. If he had been red-faced before, he was purple now. And through it all, Ender struggled to figure out what it was about a play reading that had the man so insanely angry.

When Morgan paused for breath, leaning—no, slumping—on the desk, Ender rose to his feet. "I think you had better prepare the charges for my court martial, Admiral Morgan."

"Court martial! I'm not going to court-martial you, boy! I don't have to! I can have you put in stasis for the duration of the voyage on the authority of my signature alone!"

"Not a person of admiralty rank, I'm afraid," said Ender. "And it seems that formal charges in a court martial are the only way I'm going to get a coherent statement from you about what I have supposedly done to offend your dignity and cause such alarm."

"Oh, you want a formal statement? How about this: Hijacking all ansible communications for three hours so that we are effectively cut off
from the rest of the known universe, how about that? Three hours means
more than two days back in real time—for all I know there's been a revolution, or my orders have changed, or any number of things might be
happening and I can't even send a message to inquire!"

"That's a problem, certainly," said Ender. "But why would you think I
have anything to do with it?"

"Because it's got your name all over it," said Morgan. "The message is
addressed to you. And it's still coming in, coopting our entire ansible
bandwidth."

"Doesn't it occur to you," said Ender gently, "that the message is *to*
me, not *from* me?"

"*From* Wiggin, *to* Wiggin, eyes only, so deeply encrypted that none of
the shipboard computers can crack it."

"You tried to crack a secure communication addressed to a ranking officer, without first asking the permission of that officer?"

"It's a subversive communication, boy, that's why I tried to crack it!"

"You know it's subversive because you can't crack it, and you tried to
crack it because you know it's subversive," said Ender. He kept his voice
soft and cheerful. Not because he knew that it would drive Morgan crazy
that Ender remained unflappable—that was just a bonus. He simply assumed that the entire exchange was being recorded to be used as evidence later, and Ender was not going to say a word or reveal an emotion
that would not redound to his credit in some later court proceeding. So
Morgan could be as abusive as he pleased—Ender was not going to make
a single statement that could be excerpted and used to make him look
subversive or angry.

"I don't have to justify my actions to you," said Morgan. "I brought
you here and canceled your supposed play reading so that you could open
the transmission in front of me."

"Eyes only, secure communication—I'm not sure it's proper for you
to insist on watching."

"Either you open it right now, in front of me, or you go into stasis
and you never get off this ship until it returns to Eros for your court
martial."

Someone's court martial, thought Ender, but probably not mine.

"Let me have a look at it," said Ender. "Though I can't promise to open it, since I have no idea what it is or who it's from."

"It's from *you,*" said Morgan acidly. "You arranged this before you left."

"I did not do so, Admiral Morgan," said Ender. "I assume you have a secure access point here in your office?"

"Come around here and open it now," said Morgan.

"I suggest you rotate the terminal, Admiral Morgan," said Ender.

"I said come sit here!"

"Respectfully, Admiral Morgan, there will be no vid of me sitting at your desk."

Morgan stared at him, his face growing redder again. Then he reached down and rotated the holodisplay on his desk so it faced Ender.

Ender leaned forward and poked a couple of menu choices in the holodisplay as Admiral Morgan came around behind him to watch. "Move slowly so I can see what you're doing."

"I'm doing nothing," said Ender.

"Then you're going into stasis, boy. You were never fit to be governor of anything. Just a child who's been praised way too much and completely spoiled. Nobody on that colony is going to pay any attention to you! The only way you could ever survive as governor would be if I backed you up—and after this, you can be sure I'll do no such thing. You're finished in this game of let's pretend."

"As you wish, Admiral," said Ender. "But I'm doing nothing with this message because there's nothing I *can* do. It isn't addressed to me and I have no way of opening a secure comm that isn't mine."

"Do you think I'm a fool? Your name is all over it!"

"On the outside," said Ender, "it specifies Admiral Wiggin, which is me, because it was sent from IFCom through a secure military channel and the intended recipient has no standing in the fleet. But as soon as you open it—and this is a level of opening that your techs did immediately, I'm sure—you'll see that the Wiggin to whom the secure portion of the message is addressed is not A. Wiggin or E. Wiggin, which would be me, but V. Wiggin, which is my sister, Valentine."

"Your *sister*?"

"Didn't your techs tell you that? And while the actual authority for the message is the Minister of Colonization himself, again, the real sender is P. Wiggin, and his title is given as Hegemon. I find that interesting. The only P. Wiggin I'm personally acquainted with is my older brother, Peter, and this would seem to imply that my brother is now Hegemon. Did you know that? I certainly didn't. He wasn't when I left."

A long silence came from Admiral Morgan behind him. Ender finally turned and looked at him—again, doing his best to keep any hint of triumph from showing in his face. "I think my brother, the Hegemon, is writing a private communication to my sister, with whom he had a long collaborative relationship. Perhaps he seeks her counsel. But it has nothing to do with me. You know that I haven't seen my brother or communicated with him in any way since I first entered Battle School at the age of six. And I only entered into communication with my sister for a few weeks before our ship was launched. I'm sorry that it tied up your communications, but as I said, I don't know anything about it, and it has nothing to do with me."

Morgan walked back and sat down behind his desk. "I am astonished," said Morgan.

Ender waited.

"I am embarrassed," said Morgan. "It seemed to me that my ship's communications were under attack, and that the agent of this attack was Admiral Wiggin. In that light, your repeated meetings with a subset of the colonists, to which you have been inviting members of my crew, looked suspiciously like mutiny. So I treated it as mutiny. Now I find that my fundamental premise was incorrect."

"Mutiny is a serious business," said Ender. "Of course you were alarmed."

"It happens that your brother *is* Hegemon. Word came to me a week ago. Two weeks ago. A year ago Earth time, anyway."

"It's perfectly all right that you didn't tell me," said Ender. "I'm sure you thought I would have found out by other means."

"It did not cross my mind that this communication might be from him, and *not* to you."

"It's easy to overlook Valentine. She keeps to the background. It's just the way she is."

Morgan looked at Ender gratefully. "So you understand."

I understand you're a paranoid, power-hungry idiot, said Ender silently. "Of course I do," said Ender.

"Do you mind if I send for your sister?"

Suddenly it was "do you mind"—but Ender had no interest in making Morgan squirm. "Please do. I'm as curious about this message as you are."

Morgan sent an ensign to bring her, and then sat down and tried to make small talk while they waited. He told two ostensibly amusing stories from his own training days—he was never Battle School material, he came up "the hard way, through the ranks." It was clear that he resented Battle School and the implied inferiority of anyone who wasn't invited to attend.

Is that all this is? Ender wondered. The traditional rivalry between graduates of a service academy and those who didn't have such a head start?

Valentine came in to find Ender laughing at Morgan's story. "Val," said Ender, still chuckling. "We need you to help us with something." In a few moments he explained about the message that had preempted hours of ansible time, shutting everything else out. "It caused a lot of consternation, and naturally, Admiral Morgan has been concerned. It'll put our minds at ease if you can open the message right here and give us some idea of what it's about."

"I'll need to watch you open it," said Morgan.

"No you won't," said Valentine.

They looked at each other for a long moment.

"What Valentine meant to say," said Ender, "is that she doesn't want you to see her actual security procedures—on a message from the Hegemon, you can understand her caution. But I'm sure that she'll let us know the contents of the message in some readily verifiable way." Ender looked at Valentine and gave her a mockingly cute smile and shrug. "For me, Val?"

He knew she would recognize this as a mockery of their relationship, put on entirely for Morgan's benefit; of course she played along. "For you, Mr. Potato Head. Where's the access?"

In moments, Valentine was sitting at the end of the desk, poking her way through the holodisplay. "Oh, this is only semi-secure," she said. "Just a fingerprint. Anybody could have gotten into it just by cutting off my finger. I'll have to tell Peter to use full security—retina, DNA, heartbeat—so that they have to keep me alive in order to get in. He just doesn't value me highly enough."

She sat there reading for a little while, then sighed. "I can't believe what an idiot Peter is. *And* Graff, for that matter. There's nothing in here that couldn't have been sent unsecured, and there's no reason why it couldn't have been sent piecemeal instead of in a single uninterruptible top-priority flow. It's just a bunch of articles and summaries and so on about events on Earth for the past couple of years. It seems that there are wars and rumors of wars." She glanced at Ender.

He got the King James Version reference—he had memorized long passages of it as part of his strategy for dealing with a minor crisis in Battle School several years back. "Well, transmitting it certainly took time, and times, and half a time," he said.

"I'll need to—I'd like to see some evidence that this is what you say," said Morgan. "You have to understand that anything that seemed to threaten the security of my ship and my mission must be verified."

"Well, that's the awkward thing," said Valentine. "I'm perfectly happy to let you see the entire infodump—in fact, I suggest that it be put into the library so everyone can have access to it. It's bound to be fascinating to people to have an idea of the things that have been happening on Earth. I can't wait to read it myself."

"But?" asked Ender.

"It's the cover letter itself." She looked genuinely embarrassed. "My brother makes slighting references to you. I hope you understand that neither Ender nor I discussed you with Peter in any way—anything he says is his own assumption. I can assure you that Ender and I hold you in the highest respect."

With that, she rotated the holodisplay and Ender and Valentine sat silently to watch Morgan read.

At the end, he sighed, then leaned forward, resting his elbows on the table, his forehead on his fingertips. "Well, I am embarrassed indeed."

"Not at all," said Ender. "A perfectly understandable mistake. I'd rather fly with a captain who takes every potential threat to his ship seriously than one who thinks that losing communications for three hours is no big deal."

Morgan took the olive branch. "I'm glad you see it that way, Admiral Wiggin."

"Ender," Ender corrected him.

Valentine stood up, smiling. "So if you don't mind, I'll leave the whole thing unencrypted here on your desk, as long as you assure me that every speck of it will be downloaded into the library—except my brother's personal letter." She turned to Ender. "He says he loves me and misses me and he wants me to tell you to write to our parents. They aren't getting any younger, and they're very hurt not to have heard from you."

"Yes," said Ender. "I should have done that as soon as the ship left. But I didn't want to take up ansible time on personal matters." He smiled ruefully at Morgan. "And then we end up doing *this,* all because Peter and Graff have an inflated sense of their own importance."

"I'll tell my egocentric brother to send future messages a different way," said Valentine. "I assume you won't mind my sending such a message by ansible."

They were heading for the door, Morgan shepherding them, full of smiles and "I'm glad you're so understanding," when Ender stopped.

"Oh, Admiral Morgan," said Ender.

"Please call me Quincy."

"Oh, I could never do that," said Ender. "Our respective ranks allow it, but if anybody heard me address you that way, there'd be no way to erase the visual image of a teenager speaking to the captain of the ship in a way that could only seem disrespectful. I'm sure we agree on that. Nothing can undermine the authority of the captain."

"Very wisely said," Morgan replied. "You're taking better care of my position than I am myself. But you wanted to say something?"

"Yes. The play reading. It really is just that—we're reading *Taming of the Shrew.* I'm playing Lucentio. Val has a small part, too. Everyone was looking forward to it. And now it's been canceled without a word of explanation."

Morgan looked puzzled. "If it's just a play reading, then go ahead and do it."

"Of course we will," said Ender, "now that we have your permission. But you see, some of the participants invited crew members to attend. And the cancellation might leave some bad feelings. Hard on morale, don't you think? I wanted to suggest a sort of gesture from you, to show that it really *was* a misunderstanding. To patch up any bad feelings."

"What sort of gesture?" asked Morgan.

"Just—when we reschedule it, why don't you come and watch? Let them see you laughing at the comedy."

"He could play a part," said Valentine. "I'm sure the man playing Christopher Sly—"

"My sister is joking," said Ender. "This is a comedy, and *every* part in it is beneath the dignity of the captain of the ship. I'm only suggesting that you attend. Perhaps just for the first half. You can always plead urgent business at the break halfway through. Everyone will understand. Meanwhile, though, they'll all see that you really do care about them and what they do during this voyage. It will go a long way toward making them feel good about your leadership, during the voyage and after we arrive."

"After we arrive?" asked Valentine.

Ender looked at her in wide-eyed innocence. "As Admiral Morgan pointed out to me during our conversation, none of the colonists will be likely to follow the leadership of a teenage boy. They'll need to be assured that Admiral Morgan's authority is behind whatever I do, officially, as governor. So I think that makes it all the more important that they see the admiral and get to know him, so they'll trust him to provide strong leadership."

Ender was afraid Valentine was going to lose control right there and either laugh or scream at him. But she did neither. "I see," she said.

"That's actually a good idea," said Admiral Morgan. "Shall we go start it up?"

"Oh, no," said Valentine. "Everybody's too upset. Nobody will be at their best. Why not let us go smooth things over, explain that it was all a mistake and completely *my* fault. And then we can announce that you're going to attend, that you're glad the reading can go on after all, and we get a chance to perform for you. Everyone will be excited and happy. And if you can let off-duty crew come too, so much the better."

"I don't want anything that lessens ship's discipline," said Morgan.

Valentine's answer was immediate. "If you're right there with them, laughing at the play and enjoying it, then I can't see that it will cause any weakening of the crew. It might even help morale. We actually do a pretty good job with the play."

"It would mean a lot to all of us," said Ender.

"Of course," said Morgan. "You do that, and I'll be there tomorrow at 1900. That was the starting time today, wasn't it?"

Ender and Valentine made their good-byes. The officers they passed looked amazed and relieved to see them smiling and chatting comfortably as they left.

Not till they were back in the stateroom did they let down the façade, and then only long enough for Valentine to say, "He's planning for you to be a figurehead while he rules behind the throne?"

"There's no throne," said Ender. "It solves a lot of problems for me, don't you think? It was going to be tough for a fifteen-year-old kid to lead a bunch of colonists who've already been living and farming on Shakespeare for forty years by the time I get there. But a man like Admiral Morgan is used to giving orders and being obeyed. They'll fall right in line under his authority."

Valentine stared at him like he was insane. Then Ender gave that little twitch of his lower lip that had always been the giveaway that he was being ironic. He hoped she would leap to the correct conclusion—that Admiral Morgan certainly had the means of listening in on all their conversations and was bound to be using it right now, so nothing they said could be regarded as private.

"All right," said Valentine. "If you're happy with it, I'm happy with it." Whereupon she did that momentary bug-eyed thing *she* did to let him know she was lying.

"I'm done with responsibility, Val," said Ender. "I had quite enough in Battle School and on Eros. I intend to spend the voyage making friends and reading everything I can get my hands on."

"And at the end, you can write an essay called 'How I Spent My Summer Vacation.' "

"It's always summer when your heart is full of joy," said Ender.

"You are so full of crap," said Valentine.

CHAPTER
10

To: PeterWiggin@hegemony.gov/hegemon
From: vwiggin%Colony1@colmin.gov/citizen
Subj: you arrogant bastard

Do you have any idea how much trouble you caused, sending that package with such high priority that it shut down all other ansible communications with our ship? Certain persons thought it was some kind of attack on the ansible link and Ender was almost put into stasis for the duration—and that would have meant there AND back again.

Once we sorted it all out, though, the package itself was very informative. Apparently you were cursed by some pseudo-Confucian to live in interesting times. Please send follow-ups. But make them low enough priority, please, that regular ship's communications can continue. And don't let Graff address it to Ender. It comes to me as a colonist, not to the governor-designate.

Seems to me that you're doing all right. Though that all might have changed between your sending and my reply. Ain't space travel grand?

Has Ender written to the parents yet? I can't ask him (well, I HAVE asked him, but I can't get answers) and I can't ask THEM or they'll know I've been trying to get him to write, which would hurt them all the more if he hasn't written and discount the emotional value of his letters if he has.

Stay smart. They can't take that away from you.

Your former puppet,
Demosthenes

Alessandra was happy when word came that the play reading was back on again. Mother had been devastated, though she showed it only to Alessandra in the privacy of their stateroom. She made a great show of not weeping, which was good, but she stalked around the tiny space, opening and closing things and slamming things and stomping her feet at every opportunity, and now and then emitting some fierce but gnomic statement like:

"Why are we always in the backwash of somebody else's boat?"

Then, in the midst of a game of backgammon: "In the wars of men, women always lose!"

And through the bathroom door: "There is no pleasure so simple that somebody won't take it away just to hurt you!"

In vain did Alessandra try to mollify her. "Mother, this wasn't aimed at you, it was clearly aimed at Ender."

Such responses always triggered a long emotional diatribe in which no amount of logic could cause Mother to change her mind—though moments later, she might have completely adopted Alessandra's point of view after all, acting as if that's how she had felt all along.

Yet if Alessandra didn't answer her mother's epigrammatic observations, the storming about got worse and worse—Mother *needed* a response the way other people needed air. To ignore her was to smother her. So Alessandra answered, took part in the meaningless but intense conversation, and then ignored her mother's inability to admit that she had changed her mind even though she had.

It never seemed to occur to her mother that Alessandra herself was disappointed, that playing Bianca to Ender's Lucentio had made her feel . . . what? Not love—she was definitely not in love. Ender was nice enough, but he was exactly as nice to Alessandra as to everyone else, so it was plain she was nothing special to him, and she was not interested in bestowing her affection on someone who had not first bestowed his on her. No, what Alessandra felt was glory. It was reflected, of course, from her mother's quite stunning performance of Kate and from Ender's fame as savior of the human race—and his notoriety as a child-killing monster, which Alessandra did not *believe* but which certainly added to the fascination.

All disappointment was forgotten the moment the message came through to everyone's desk: The reading was back on for the following night, and the admiral himself would attend.

Alessandra immediately thought: *The* admiral? There are two admirals on this voyage, and one of them was part of the program from the start. Was this a calculated slight, that the message sounded as if only one officer held that lofty rank? The very fact that Ender had been summoned so peremptorily to see Admiral Morgan was another sign—did Ender really warrant so little respect? It made her a little angry on his behalf.

Then she told herself: I have no bond with Ender Wiggin that should make me protective of his privileges. I've been infected with Mother's disease, of acting as if her plans and dreams were already real. Ender is not in love with me, any more than I am with him. There will be girls on Shakespeare when we get there; by the time he's old enough to marry, what will I be to him?

What have I done, coming on this voyage to a place where there won't be enough people my age to fill a city bus?

Not for the first time, Alessandra envied her mother's ability to make herself cheerful by sheer force of will.

They dressed in their finest for the reading—not that there had been room for much in the way of clothes during the voyage. But they had spent some of their signing bonus buying clothing, before the rest got turned over to Grandmother. Most of the clothing had to meet the description on the list from the Ministry of Colonization—warm clothes for a chilly but not-too-cold winter, light-but-tough clothing for summer work, and at least one long-lasting frock for special occasions. Tonight's reading was such an occasion—and here was where Mother had made sure that a bit of money was spent on gewgaws and accessories. They were over the top, really, and obviously costume jewelry. Then there were Mother's bedazzling scarves, which looked almost ironically extravagant on her, but would look pathetic and needy on Alessandra. Mother was dressed to kill; Alessandra could only strive not to disappear completely in Mother's penumbra.

They arrived just at the moment when the event was supposed to begin. Alessandra immediately rushed to her stool at the front, but Mother made a slow progress, greeting everyone, touching everyone, bestowing her smiles on everyone. Except one.

Admiral Morgan was seated in the second row, with a few officers around him, insulating him from any contact with the public—it was so obvious he considered himself a breed apart and wanted no contact with mere colonists. That was the privilege of rank, and Alessandra did not begrudge it. She rather wished she had the power to create a cordon around herself to keep unwanted persons from intruding into her privacy.

To Alessandra's horror, once Mother got down front, she continued her grand progress by passing along the front row of seats, greeting people there—and in the second row as well. She was going to try to force Admiral Morgan to speak to her!

But no, Mother's plan was even worse. She made a point of introducing herself to—and flirting with—the officers on either side of the admiral. But she did not so much as pause in front of Morgan himself; it was as if he didn't exist. A snub! Of the most powerful man in their little world!

Alessandra could hardly bear to look at Morgan's face, yet could not bring herself to look away, either. At first, he had watched Mother's approach with resignation—he was going to have to speak to this woman. But when Mother passed right over him, his barely contained sneer gave way to consternation and then to seething anger. Mother had indeed made an enemy. What was she thinking? How could this help anything?

But it was time to begin. The leading actors were seated on stools; the rest were on the front row, prepared to stand and face the audience when their parts came. Mother finally made her way to the stool in the center of the stage. Before sitting, she looked out over the audience beneficently and said, "Thank you so much for coming to our little performance. The play is set in Italy, where my daughter and I were born. But it is written in English, which comes to us only as a second language. My daughter is fluent, but I am not. So if I mispronounce, remember that Katharina was Italian, and in English she too would have my same accent."

It was all said with Mother's trademark glow, her light-and-happy air. What had become so annoying to Alessandra that there were times she wanted to scream in rage when she heard it now seemed absolutely charming, and her little speech was answered by the rest of the colonists and crew with chuckles and some applause. And the actor playing Petruchio—who had an obvious crush on Mother, despite his having brought along a wife and four children—even said, "Brava! Brava!"

The play thus began with all eyes on Mother, even though she didn't enter until the second act. Through sidelong glances, Alessandra could see that Mother was in a perfect trance of self-absorption during the scenes in which the men did all the exposition and made their bargain with Petruchio. As the other actors repeatedly mentioned beautiful Bianca and monstrous Katharina, Alessandra could see how Mother's pose was working—as her reputation grew, the audience would keep glancing at her and would find perfect stillness.

But that would not be right for Bianca, thought Alessandra. She remembered something Ender had said during their last rehearsal. "Bianca is perfectly aware of the effect she has on men." So where Katharina should be as still as Mother made her, Bianca's job was to be bright, happy, desirable. So Alessandra smiled and glanced away as the men spoke of beautiful Bianca, as if she were blushing and shy. It did not matter that Alessandra was *not* beautiful—as Mother always taught her, the plainest of women became movie stars because of how they presented themselves, unashamed of their worst features. What Alessandra could never do in real life—greet the world with an open smile—she could do as Bianca.

Then it dawned on her for the first time. Mother is *not* able to change her mood by simply deciding to be happy. No, she's an actress. She has always been an actress. She merely *acts* happy for the audience. I have been her audience all my life. And even when I didn't applaud her show, she put it on for me all the same; and now I see why. Because Mother knew that when she was in her fairy-dancing mode, it was impossible to look at or think about anything else but her.

Now, though, the fairy queen was gone, and in her place just the queen:

Mother, regal and still, letting the peons and courtiers talk, for she knew that when she wanted to, she could blow them all off the stage with a breath.

And so it was. It came time for act II, scene i, when Katharina is supposedly dragging Bianca about, her hands tied. Alessandra made herself melting and sweet, pleading with her mother to let her go, swearing that she loved no one, while Mother railed at her, so on fire with inner rage that it really frightened Alessandra, for a moment at least. Even in rehearsal Mother had not been so vehement. Alessandra doubted that Mother had been holding back before—Mother was not skilled at holding back. No, the special fire came because of the audience.

But not the whole audience, it became apparent as the scenes progressed. All of Katharina's lines about the unfairness of her father and the stupidity of men were invariably shot directly at Admiral Morgan! It wasn't just Alessandra's imagination. Everybody could see it, and the audience at first tittered, then laughed outright as barb after barb was directed, not just at the characters in the play, but also at the man sitting in the middle of the second row.

Only Morgan himself seemed oblivious; apparently, with Mother's eyes directly upon him, he merely thought that the performance, not the meaning of the words, was aimed at him.

The play went well. Oh, the Lucentio scenes were as boring as ever—not Ender's fault, really, Lucentio was simply not one of the funny roles. It was a fate that Bianca shared, so Alessandra and Ender were designed only to be a "sweet couple" while the focus of attention—of laughter *and* of romance—was entirely on Katharina and Petruchio. Which meant, despite the best efforts of a pretty good Petruchio, that all eyes were on Mother. He would be shouting, but it was her face, her reactions that got the laughs. Her hunger, her sleepiness, her despair, and finally her playful acquiescence when Katharina finally understands and begins to play along with Petruchio's mad game, all were fully communicated by Mother's face, her posture, her tone when she spoke.

Mother is brilliant, Alessandra realized. Absolutely brilliant. And she knows it. No wonder she suggested a play reading!

And then another thought: If Mother could do this, why wasn't she an actress? Why didn't she become a star of stage or screen and let us live in wealth?

The answer, she realized, was simple: It was Alessandra's birth when Mother was only fifteen.

Mother conceived me when she was exactly the age I am now, Alessandra realized. She fell in love and gave herself to a man—a boy—and produced a child. It was unbelievable to Alessandra, since she herself had never felt any kind of passion for any of the boys at school.

Father must have been remarkable.

Or Mother must have been desperate to get away from Grandmother. Which was far more likely to be the truth. Instead of waiting a few more years and becoming a great actress, Mother married and set up housekeeping and had this baby—not in that order—and because she had me, she was never able to use this talent to make her way in the world.

We could have been rich!

And now what? Off to a colony, a place of farmers and weavers and builders and scientists, with no time for art. There'll be no leisure in the colony, the way there is on the ship during the voyage. When will Mother ever have a chance to show what she can do?

The play neared the end. Valentine played the widow with surprising wit and verve—she absolutely understood the part, and not for the first time Alessandra wished she could be a genius and a beauty like Valentine. Yet something else overshadowed that wish—for the first time in Alessandra's life, she actually envied her mother, and wished she could be more like *her*. Unthinkable, yet true.

Mother stepped away from her stool and delivered her soliloquy straight to the front—straight to Admiral Morgan—speaking of the duty a woman owes to a man. Just as all her barbs had been aimed at Morgan, now this speech—this sweet, submissive, graceful, heartfelt, love-filled homily—was spoken straight into Morgan's eyes.

And Morgan was riveted. His mouth was slightly open, his eyes never wavered from full attention on Mother. And when she knelt and said "my hand is ready, may it do him ease," there were tears in Morgan's eyes. Tears!

Petruchio roared his line: "Why there's a wench! Come on and kiss me, Kate!"

Mother rose gracefully to her feet, not attempting to pantomime a kiss, but rather showing the face that a woman shows to her lover when she is about to kiss him—and her eyes, yet again, were directly on Morgan's.

Now Alessandra understood Mother's game. She was making Morgan fall in love with her!

And it worked. When the last lines were spoken and the audience stood and cheered for them all as the readers bowed and curtseyed, Morgan literally stepped onto the first row of seats so that as the applause continued, he walked onto the stage and shook Mother's hand. Shook it? No, seized it and simply would not let it go, while talking to her about how wonderful she was.

Mother's aloofness, her snub of him at the beginning, was all part of the plan. She was the shrew, punishing him for his presumption in canceling their reading; but by the end, she was tamed; she belonged to him completely.

All that evening, as Morgan invited everyone to the officers' mess—where previously he had absolutely forbidden the colonists to go—he hovered around Mother. It was so obvious he was smitten that several of the officers mentioned it, obliquely, to Alessandra. "Your mother seems to have melted the great stone heart," said one. And she overheard two officers speaking to each other, when one of them said, "Am I mistaken, or are his pants already coming off?"

If they thought *that* would happen, they didn't know Mother. Alessandra had lived through years of Mother's advice about men. Don't let them this, don't let them that—tease, hint, promise, but they get nothing at all until they have made their vows. Mother had done it the other way in her youth, and paid for it the past fifteen years. Now she would surely follow her own sadder-but-wiser advice and seduce this man with words and smiles only. She wanted him besotted, not satisfied.

Oh, Mother, what a game you're playing.

Do you really . . . is it possible . . . are you really *attracted* to him? He's a good-looking man, in military trim. And around you he is not cold at all, not aloof; or if he is, he includes you in his lofty place.

One telling moment: As he was talking to someone else—one of the few officers who had brought a wife along—Morgan's hand came to rest on Mother's shoulder, a light embrace. But Mother instantly reached up, removed the hand, but then turned at the same moment to speak to Morgan with a warm smile, making a little joke of some kind, because everyone laughed. The message was mixed, yet clear: Touch me not, thou mortal, but yes, I will bestow this smile on you.

You are mine, but I am not yet yours.

This is what Mother meant for me to do with Ender Wiggin, my supposed "young man with prospects." But I could no more come to own a man that way than I could fly. I will always be the supplicant, never the seducer; always grateful, never gracious.

Ender came up to her. "Your mother was brilliant tonight," he said.

Of course that's what he said. That's what everyone was saying.

"But I know something they don't know," he said.

"What's that?" asked Alessandra.

"I know that the only reason my performance was good at all was because of you. All of us who played the suitors of Bianca, all that comedy, everything rested on the audience believing that we would yearn for you. And you were so lovely, no one doubted it for a moment."

He smiled at her and then walked away to rejoin his sister.

Leaving Alessandra gasping.

CHAPTER
11

To: vwiggin%ShakespeareCol@ColMin.gov/voy ==PosIDreq
From: GovDes%ShakespeareCol@ColMin.gov/voy
Subj: How clean is your desk?

My desk is completely tamper-proof—though the ship's computer tries to install snoops many times a day. Also, I'm assuming every room, corridor, toilet, and cupboard on this ship is wired at least for sound. On a voyage like this, with no outsider force to buttress the captain's authority, the danger of mutiny is ever present, and it is not paranoia for Morgan to monitor all conversations of people he thinks pose a danger to the ship's internal security.

It is unfortunate but predictable that he would regard me as such a danger. I have authority that does not depend in any way on him or his good wishes. His threat to have me put in stasis and returned to Eros—eighty years from now—is one that he can, in fact, carry out, and even though he might be censured it would not be regarded as a criminal act. There is a strong presumption that the captain of a ship is always to be believed when he makes a charge of mutiny or conspiracy. It is dangerous for me even to encrypt this message. However, there is no other safe way for us to talk. (You'll notice that unlike Peter, I required proof that you be alive, not just your finger inserted into holospace.)

I am doing things that are certainly driving Quincy crazy. I get almost daily (monthly) messages from Acting Governor Kolmogorov, keeping me abreast of events in Shakespeare Colony as they transpire. Morgan has no idea what we say to each other; he simply has to pass along the encrypted notes when they come through the ansible.

I also get all the scientific papers and reports filed by the chem and bio teams. XB Sel Menach is the Linnaeus and Darwin of this planet. He is facing the ONLY non-formic-homeworld biota yet discovered (besides Earth's, of course), and he has done a brilliant job of making the genetic adaptations that create human-edible varieties of native plants and animals, and varieties of Earth species that can thrive on this world. Without him, we would probably be coming to a ragged and destitute colony; instead, they generate surpluses of food and will be able to resupply this ship for immediate departure (inshallah).

All of this scientific information is available to Admiral Morgan, if he's interested. He seems not to be. I am the only person who is accessing the Shakespeare Colony XB papers on this ship, since our XBs are in stasis and won't wake up until we drop from relativistic speeds.

You can see why I chose not to go into stasis—I had visions of Admiral Morgan not bothering to rouse me until he was firmly in control of the colony, say six months after arrival. It wouldn't have been within his rights, but it would certainly have been in his power. And who is to contradict him, with his forty marines whose sole duty is to make sure his will is uncontested, and a crew whose survival and freedom are tied to his pleasure?

Now, though, anything I do is a potential provocation—that's what he made very clear with his actions and threats. I don't think that was his purpose—I think he really believed he was facing some kind of attack. But he was too hasty to leap to the conclusion that I was responsible for it, and he was paranoid enough to try to resolve it as if it were an attack on his authority, rather than on the ship itself. We are on notice, and not a word can pass between us that mocks him, denigrates him, or questions his decisions.

Nor can we trust anyone else. While Governor Kolmogorov is completely in my confidence (and vice versa), no one else on the planet can be trusted to agree that having a fifteen-year-old boy as their governor is a good idea. Therefore I can take no preemptive actions using my future authority as governor. So my only alternative is to appear as if I really look up to Quincy in a fatherly way, and intend to be guided by him in every way. When you see me sucking up shamelessly, it is the moral equivalent of war. I am passing an army under his nose, masquerading as a bunch of simple farmers. That you and I are the entire army is not a problem for me—as long as you're willing to pretend to be all innocence. You and Peter were doing that for years, weren't you?

This letter is not going to be followed by many others—only in a real emergency. I don't want him wondering what we're saying to each other. He has the right to seize our desks and force us to disclose all contents. Therefore, you will eradicate this message, as will I. Of course, I AM taking the precaution of copying it, fully secure, to Graff. In case there is someday a court martial determining whether Morgan was right to put me in stasis and take me back to Eros, I want this to be available as evidence of my state of mind after our little incident over Peter's message.

There is always the chance, however, that Morgan's plan is even more dire—that he plans to send the ship back rather than taking it, while he remains on Shakespeare as governor-for-life. By the time anyone from Eros can be sent to put down his rebellion, he will have finished out his lifespan or be so old as to be not worth prosecuting.

However, I do not believe that is in his character. He is a creature of bureaucracy—he wants supremacy, not autonomy. Also, my judgment of him so far is that he can only do perfidious acts that he can morally justify in his own mind. Thus he must work himself into a frenzy over my supposed sabotage of ansible communications in order to justify what would have amounted to a coup d'etat against me as governor.

This only refers to what he consciously plans, not what he unconsciously desires. That is, he will think that he is responding to events as they unfold, but in fact he will be interpreting events to justify actions that he wants to take—even though he does not know he wants to take them. Thus when we arrive on Shakespeare, there is always the chance that he will find there's an "emergency" that requires him to stay longer than the ship can stay, "forcing" him to send it back and remain behind.

The need to understand Quincy is why I am remaining so close to the Toscanos. The mother is clearly betting on Quincy rather than me as the future power, though in her mind she is no doubt merely hedging her bets, to make sure that no matter who governs, either she or her daughter will be married to the powerful figure.

But the mother has no intention of letting her daughter out from under her thumb, as she would be if we married and I actually become governor in fact as well as name. So, deliberately or not, the mother will be my enemy in this; however, at present she is my best guide to Quincy's state of mind, since she is with him as often as possible. I must get to know this man. Our future depends on knowing what he is going to do before he does it.

Meanwhile, you have no idea what a relief it is to me that there is someone who shares this with me. In all my years in Battle School, the closest I came to having a confidant was Bean. Yet I could only burden him up to a certain point; this letter is my first exercise in genuine candor since I talked to you on the lake in North Carolina so long ago.

Oh, wait. It was only three years. Less? Time is so confusing. Thank you for being with me, Valentine. I only hope that I can keep it from being a meaningless exercise that takes us back to Eros in stasis, with eighty years of human history gone and absolutely nothing accomplished except my being defeated by a bureaucrat.

Ender

What Virlomi hadn't counted on was the way it would affect her, returning to Battle School after all that she had been through, all that she had done.

She turned herself over to her enemies when she could see there was nothing left to the war but slaughter. She knew with a sinking desperation in her heart that it was all her fault. She had been warned, by friends and would-be friends: This is too much. It was enough to drive the Chinese out of India and liberate your homeland. Don't seek to punish them.

She had been the same kind of fool that Napoleon and Hitler and Xerxes and Hannibal had been: She thought that because she had never been defeated, she could not be. She had bested enemies with far greater strength than hers; she thought she always would.

Worst of all, she told herself, I believed my own legend. I had deliberately cultivated the notion of myself as goddess, but at first I remembered that I was pretending.

In the end, it was the Free People of Earth—the FPE, Peter Wiggin's Hegemony under a new name—that defeated her. It was Suriyawong, a Thai from Battle School who had once loved her, who arranged her surrender. At first she refused—but she could see that the only difference between surrendering now and waiting until all her men had died was her pride. And her pride was not worth the life of a single soldier.

"Satyagraha," Suriyawong said to her. "Bear what must be born."

Satyagraha was her final cry to her people. I command you to live and bear this.

So she saved the life of her armies and surrendered her own body to Suriyawong. And, through him, to Peter Wiggin.

Wiggin, who had shown mercy to her in his victory. That was more than his little brother, the legendary Ender, had shown to the formics. Had they, too, seen in him the hand of death, repudiating them? Had they any gods, to pray to or resign themselves to or curse as they saw their destruction? Perhaps they had it easier, to be obliterated from the universe.

Virlomi remained alive. They could not kill her—she was still worshiped throughout India; if they executed her or imprisoned her, India would be a continuous revolution, impossible to govern. If she simply disappeared, she would become a legend of the goddess who left and would someday return.

So she made the vids they asked her to make. She begged her people to vote to freely join the Free People of Earth, to accept the rule of the

Hegemon, to demobilize and dismantle their army, and in return, to have the freedom to govern themselves.

Han Tzu did the same for China, and Alai, once her husband until she betrayed him, did so for the Muslim world. More or less, it worked.

All of them accepted exile. But Virlomi knew that only she deserved it.

Their exile consisted of being made governors of colonies. Ah, if only I had been appointed when Ender Wiggin was, and had never returned to Earth to shed so much blood! Yet it was only because she had so spectacularly won India's freedom from an overwhelming Chinese army, had united an ununitable country, that she was deemed capable of governing. Only because of the monstrous things I did, she thought, am I being entrusted with the foundation of a new world.

In her captivity on Earth—months spent in Thai and then Brazilian custody, watched over but never mistreated—she had begun to chafe and wish she could leave the planet and begin her new life.

What she hadn't counted on was that the new staging area was the space station that once was Battle School.

It was like waking up from a vivid dream and finding herself in the place of her childhood. The corridors were unchanged; the color-coded lights along the walls still did their service, guiding colonists to their dormitories. The barracks had been changed, of course—the colonists were not going to put up with the crowding and regimentation that the Battle School students had endured. Nor was there any nonsense about a game in zero gee. If the battleroom was being used for anything, they didn't tell her.

But the mess halls were there, both the officers' and soldiers'—though she ate now in the one that she had never entered as a student, the teachers' dining room. Her own colonists were not allowed there; it was her place of refuge from them. In their place, she was surrounded by Graff's people of the Ministry of Colonization. They were discreet, leaving her alone, which she was grateful for; they were aloof, keeping away from her, which she resented. Opposite responses, opposite assumptions about their motives; she knew they were being kind but it still hurt as if she were a leper, kept apart. If she wanted friendship, she could probably have it; they were probably waiting for her to let them know whether she would welcome their conversation. She longed for human company. But she never crossed the short space between her table and anyone else's. She ate alone. Because she did not believe she merited any human society.

What galled her was the worshipful way the colonists treated her. When she had been a student in Battle School, she was merely ordinary. Being a girl made her different, and she had to struggle to hold her own—but she was no Ender Wiggin, no legend. She wasn't much of a leader. That would come later, when she was back in India, with people she understood, blood of her blood.

The problem was that these colonists were overwhelmingly Indian. They had volunteered for the colonization program precisely because Virlomi would be the governor of the colony—several of them told her that they had competed in a lottery for the chance to come. When she went among them, to talk to them, get to know them, she found it nearly futile. They were in such awe of her they became tongue-tied, or when they managed to speak, their words were so formal, their language so lofty, that there was no chance of real communication.

They all acted as if they thought they were talking to a goddess.

I did my work too well during the war, she told herself. To Indians, defeat was not a sign of the disfavor of the gods. What mattered was how she bore it. And she could not help it—she kept her dignity, and to them she seemed godlike because of it.

Maybe this will make it easier to govern them. Or maybe it will make the day of their disillusionment a terrible thing to behold.

A group of colonists from Hyderabad came to her with a petition. "The planet has been named Ganges, for the holy river," they said, "and that is right. But can we not also remember the many of us from the south? We speak Telugu, not Hindi or Urdu. Can we not have a part of this new colony that belongs to us?"

Virlomi answered them in fluent Telugu—she had learned it because she could not have fully united India if she spoke only Hindi and English—and told them that she would do what the colonists allowed her to do.

It was the first test of her leadership. She went among the people and asked them, dormitory by dormitory, whether they would accept naming the village they would build in the new world "Andhra," after the province whose capital was Hyderabad.

Everyone agreed with her proposal instantly. The world would be named Ganges, but the first village would be Andhra.

"Our language must be Common," she said. "This breaks my heart, to submerge the beautiful languages of India, but we must all be able to speak to each other with one voice, one language. Your children must learn Common in their homes, as the first language. You may also teach them Hindi or Telugu or any other language, but Common first."

"The language of the Raj," said one old man. Immediately the other colonists shouted at him to be respectful to Virlomi.

But Virlomi only laughed. "Yes," she said. "The language of the Raj. Conquered once by the British, and again by the Hegemony. But it is the language we all have in common. We of India because the British ruled us for so long, and then we did so much business with America; the non-Indians because it is a requirement to speak Common or you cannot come on this voyage."

The old man laughed with her. "So you remember," he said. "We have a longer history with this so-called 'Common' than anyone but the English and the Americans themselves."

"We have always been able to learn the languages of our conquerors and then make them our own. Our literature becomes their literature, and theirs becomes ours. We speak it our own way, and think our own thoughts behind their words. We are who we are. Nothing changes."

This was how she spoke to the Indian colonists. But there were others, about a fifth of the colonists, who were not from India. Some had chosen her because she was famous, and her struggle for freedom had captured their imagination. She was the creator of the Great Wall of India, after all, and so they thought of her as a celebrity and sought after her for that reason.

But there were others who were assigned to Ganges Colony by the luck of the draw. It was Graff's decision, to allow no more than four-fifths of the colonists to come from India. His memo had been concise: "There may come a day when colonies can be founded by one group alone. But the law of these first colonies is that all humans are equal citizens. We are taking a risk letting you have so many Indians. Only the political realities in India made me bend from the normal policy of no more than *one*-fifth from any one nation. As it is, we have now demands from Kenyans and Darfurians and Kurds and Quechua speakers and Mayans and other groups that feel the need for a homeland that is exclusively their own. Since we're giving one to Virlomi's Indians, why not to them? Do they need to fight a bloody war in order to . . . etc., etc. That is why I have to be able to point to the twenty percent who are not Indian, and why I need to know that you will in fact make them equal citizens."

Yes, yes, Colonel Graff, you will have it all your way. Even after we arrive on Ganges and you are lightyears away and can no longer influence what we do, I will keep my word to you and encourage intermarriage and equal treatment and will insist on English—pardon me, Common—as the language of all.

But despite my best efforts, the twenty percent will be swallowed up. In six generations, five generations, three perhaps, visitors will come to Ganges and find blond and redheaded Indians, freckled white skins and ebony black skins, African faces and Chinese faces and yet they will all say, "I am Indian," and treat you with scorn if you insist that they are not.

Indian culture is too strong for anyone to control. I ruled India by bowing to Indian ways, by fulfilling Indian dreams. Now I will lead Ganges Colony—the village of Andhra—by teaching the Indians to pretend to be tolerant of the others, even as they befriend them and bring them inside our ways. They will soon realize that on this strange new world, we Indians will be the natives, and the others the interlopers, until they "go native" and become part of us. It can't be helped. This is human nature combined with Indian stubbornness and patience.

Still, Virlomi made it a point of reaching out to the non-Indians here in Battle School—here on the Way Station.

They accepted her well enough. Now her fluency in Battle School Common and its slang stood her in good stead. After the war, Battle School slang had caught on with children all over the world, and she was fluent in it. It intrigued the children and young people, and amused the adults. It made her more approachable to them, not so much of a celebrity.

In the barracks—no, the dormitory—that used to be for newly arrived students—launchies, as they were called—there was one woman with a babe in arms who remained steadfastly aloof. Virlomi was content with that—she didn't have to be everyone's favorite person—but soon it became clear, as she visited that barracks more and more, that Nichelle Firth was not just shy or aloof, she was actively hostile.

Virlomi became fascinated by her and tried to find out more about her. But the biography in her file was so sparse that it made Virlomi suspect it was bogus; there were several like that, belonging to people who were joining the colony specifically to leave all their past, even their identity, behind them.

There was no talking to the woman directly, however. Her face became a pleasant blank and she answered succinctly or not at all; when she chose not to answer, she smiled with a set jaw, so that despite the toothy grin Virlomi was aware of the anger behind it. She did not push the matter further.

But she did watch for Nichelle's reactions to things Virlomi and others said when Nichelle was within earshot, but not part of the group. What seemed to set her off, what made her huffy in her body language, was any mention of the Hegemony or Peter Wiggin or the wars on Earth or the Free People of Earth or the Ministry of Colonization. Also the names of Ender Wiggin, Graff, Suriyawong, and, above all, Julian Delphiki—"Bean"—seemed to make her hold tightly to her baby and start to whisper some sort of incantation to the child.

Virlomi introduced some of these names herself, as a test. Nichelle Firth was certainly not someone who had taken part in the war in any way—her picture got no response from Peter's staff when she sent an inquiry. Yet she seemed to take the events of recent history quite personally.

Only toward the end of the preparation period did it occur to her to try one other name. She worked it into a conversation with a pair of Belgians, but made sure they were near enough to Nichelle that she could hear them. "Achilles Flandres," she said, referring to him as the most famous Belgian in recent history. Of course they were offended and denied that he was really Belgian, but while she was smoothing things over with them, she was also watching Nichelle.

Her reaction was strong, yes, and at first glance seemed to be the same as always—hold the baby close, nuzzle it, speak to it.

But then Virlomi realized: She was not stiff. She was not huffy. Instead she was tender with the child. She was gentle and seemed happy. She was smiling.

And she was whispering the name "Achilles Flandres" over and over.

This was so disturbing that Virlomi wanted to go over to her and scream at her: How dare you venerate the name of that monster!

But she was too keenly aware of her own monstrous deeds. There were differences between her and Achilles, yes, but there were similarities, too, and it was not wise of her to condemn him too vehemently. So the woman felt some affinity for him. What of that?

Virlomi left the barracks then and searched again. No record of Achilles ever being in a place where he might have met this definitely American woman. Virlomi could not imagine her speaking French, not even badly. She didn't seem educated enough—like most Americans, she would have only the one language, spoken raggedly but loudly. The baby could not possibly be Achilles'.

But she had to check. The woman's behavior pointed so clearly toward that possibility.

She did not allow Firth mother-and-child to go into stasis and be stowed on the ship until she got back the results of a comparison between the baby's genetic print and the records of Achilles Flandres's genes.

No match. He could not possibly be the father.

All right then, thought Virlomi. The woman is strange. She'll be a problem. But not one that can't be handled with time. Far away from Earth, whatever it was that made her such a devotee of the monster will fade. She will accept the pressure of the friendship of others.

Or she won't, and then her offense will be self-punishing, as she earns ostracism from those whose friendship she refused. Either way, Virlomi would deal with it. How much trouble can one woman be, out of thousands of colonists? It's not as if Nichelle Firth was any kind of leader. No one would follow her. She would amount to nothing.

Virlomi gave orders clearing the Firths for stasis. But because of the delay, they were still there when Graff came in person to speak to those who were going to be awake during the voyage. It was only about a hundred colonists—most of them preferred the sleeping option—and Graff's job was to make clear to them that it was the ship's captain who ruled absolutely, and to impress on them the captain's almost unlimited powers of punishment. "You will do whatever you are asked to do by a crew member, and you will do it instantly."

"Or what?" asked someone.

Graff did not take umbrage—the voice sounded more frightened than challenging. "The captain's power extends to life and death. Depending on the seriousness of the infraction. And he is the sole judge of how serious your offense is. There are no appeals. Am I clear?"

Everyone understood. A few of them even took the last-minute option to travel in stasis—not because they intended to mutiny, but because they didn't like the idea of being cooped up for years with someone who had that kind of power over them.

When the meeting ended, there was a tremendous amount of noise and bustle, as some headed for the table where last-minute stasis could be arranged, and others headed for their dormitories, and a few gathered around Graff—the celebrity hounds, of course, since he was almost as famous, in his own way, as Virlomi, and he hadn't been available till now.

Virlomi was making her way to the stasis sign-up table when she heard a loud noise—many gasps and exclamations at once—from the people around Graff. She looked over but couldn't see what was going on. Graff was just standing there, smiling at somebody, and seemed perfectly normal. Only the glances—glares, really—of a few of the bystanders drew her eye to the woman huffing her way out of the room, clearly coming from Graff's little crowd.

It was Nichelle Firth, of course, holding her dear little infant Randall.

Well, whatever she had done, apparently it didn't bother Graff, though it bothered other people.

Still, it was a worry that Nichelle had sought out an opportunity to confront Graff. Her hostility led to action; bad news.

Why hasn't she been openly hostile to me? I'm just as famous as . . .

Famous, but why? Because the Hegemony defeated me and took me into captivity. And the enemies arrayed against me? Suriyawong. Peter Wiggin. The whole civilized world along with them. Pretty much the same list that opposed and hated Achilles Flandres.

No wonder she volunteered for my colony, and not one of the others. She thinks that I'm a kindred soul, having been beaten by the same foes. She doesn't understand—or at least she didn't when she signed up for my colony—that I agree with those who defeated me, that I was wrong and needed to be stopped. I am not Achilles. I am not like Achilles.

If the goddess wanted to punish Virlomi for having impersonated her to gain power and unite India, there would be no surer way than this: to have everyone think she was like Achilles—and like her for it.

Fortunately, Nichelle Firth was only one person, and nobody liked her because she liked nobody. Whatever her opinions were, they would not affect Virlomi.

I keep reassuring myself of that, thought Virlomi. Does that mean that in the deepest recesses of my mind, this woman's strange opinions are already affecting me?

Of course it does.

Satyagraha. This, too, I will bear.

CHAPTER 12

To: GovDes%ShakespeareCol@ColMin.gov/voy
From: MinCol@ColMin.gov
Subj: Strange encounter

Dear Ender,

Yes, I'm still alive. I've been going into stasis for ten months out of each year so that I can see this project through. This is only possible because I have a staff that I literally trust with my life. Actuarial tables suggest that I will still be alive when you reach Shakespeare.

I'm writing to you now, however, because you were close to Bean. I have attached documentation concerning his genetic illness. We know now that Bean's real name was Julian Delphiki; he was kidnapped as a frozen embryo and was the sole survivor of an illegal genetic experiment. The alteration in his genes made him extraordinarily intelligent. Alas, it also affected his growth pattern. Very small in childhood—the Bean you knew. No growth spurt at puberty. Just a steady onward progress until death from giantism. Bean, not wishing to be hospitalized and pathetic at the end of his life, has embarked on a lightspeed voyage of exploration. He will live as long as he lives, but to all intents and purposes, he is gone from Earth and from the human race.

I don't know if anyone has told you, but Bean and Petra married. Despite Bean's fear that any children he might have would inherit his condition, they fertilized nine eggs—because they were hoaxed, alas, by a doctor who claimed he could repair the genetic malady in the children. Petra gave birth to one, but the other eight embryos were kidnapped—echoing what happened to Bean himself as an embryo—and implanted in surrogates who did not know the source of their babies. After a search both deep and wide, we found seven of the lost babies. The last was never found. Till now.

I say this because of a strange encounter earlier today. I'm at Ellis Island—our nickname for what used to be Battle School. All the colonists pass through here to be sorted out and sent on to wherever their ship is being sorted out—Eros is too far away in its orbit right now to be convenient, so we're refitting and launching the ships from closer in.

I was giving an orientation lecture, full of my usual wit and wisdom, to a group that was going to Ganges Colony. Afterward, a woman came up to me—American, by her accent—carrying a baby. She said nothing. She just spat on my shoe and walked on.

Naturally, this piqued my interest—I'm a sucker for a flirtatious woman. I looked her up. Which is to say, I had one of my friends on Earth do a thorough background check on her. It turns out that her colony name is a phony—not that unusual, and we don't care, you can be whoever you want to be, as long as you're not a child molester or serial killer. In her previous life, she was married to a grocery store assistant manager who was completely sterile. So the boy she has with her is not her ex-husband's—again, not that unusual. What's unusual is that it also isn't hers.

I am about to confess something that I'm somewhat ashamed of. I promised Bean and Petra that no record of their children's genetic prints would remain anywhere. But I kept a copy of the record we used in the search for the children, on the chance that someday I might run into the last missing child.

Somehow, this woman, Randi Johnson (nee Alba), now known as Nichelle Firth, was implanted with Bean's and Petra's missing child. This child is afflicted with Bean's genetic giantism. He will be brilliant, but he will die in his twenties (or earlier) of growth that simply does not stop.

And he is being raised by a woman who, for some reason, thinks it is important to spit on me. I am not personally offended by this, but I am interested, because this action makes me suspect that, unlike the other surrogates, she may have some knowledge of whose child she bore. Or, more likely, she might have been told false stories. In any event, I cannot quiz her on this because by the time I secured this information, she was gone.

She is going to Ganges Colony, which, like yours, is headed by a young Battle School graduate. Virlomi was not as young as you when she left—she had had enough years on Earth post–Battle School to become the savior of India under Chinese occupation, and then the instigator of an ill-fated (and ill-planned) invasion of China. She became quite the self-destructive fanatic by the end of her rise to power, believing her own propaganda. She is back to sanity now, and instead of trying to decide whether to honor her for the liberation of her own people or condemn her for the invasion of the nation of their oppressors, she has been made the head of a colony that, for the first time, takes into account the culture of origin on Earth. Most of the colonists are Indians of the Hindu persuasion—but not all.

Bean's son will be brilliant—like his father, plus his mother. And Randi may be feeding him with stories that will bend his character in awkward ways.

Why am I telling you all this? Because Ganges Colony is our first effort at colonizing a world that was NOT originally a formic possession. They are traveling at a slightly smaller fraction of lightspeed, so they will not arrive until the XBs have a chance to do their work and have the planet ready for colonization.

If you are happy governing Shakespeare and wish to spend the rest of your life there, then this information will not be of any particular interest to you. But if, after a few years, you decide that government is not your metier, I would ask you to travel by courier to Ganges. Of course, the colony will not even be established by the time you have spent five (or even ten) years on Shakespeare. And the voyage to Ganges will be of such a distance that you can leave Shakespeare and reach Ganges within fourteen (or nineteen) years of its founding. At that point, the boy (named Randall Firth) will be adult size—no, larger—and may be so shockingly brilliant that Virlomi has no chance of keeping him from being a danger to the peace and safety of the colony. Or he may already be the dictator. Or the freely elected governor that saved them from Virlomi's madness. Or he might already be dead. Or a complete nonentity. Who knows?

Again: The choice is yours. I have no claim upon you; Bean and Petra have no claim upon you. But if it should be interesting to you, more interesting than remaining on Shakespeare, this would be a place where you could go and perhaps help a young governor, Virlomi, who is brilliant but also prone to the occasional very poor decision.

Alas, it's all a pig in a poke. By the time you would have to leave Shakespeare with time enough to be effective on Ganges, the Ganges colonists won't even have debarked from their ship! We might be sending you to a colony with no problems at all and therefore nothing for you to do.

Thus you see how I plan for things that can't be planned for. But sometimes I'm oh so glad that I did. But if you decide you want no part of my plans from now on, I will understand better than anyone!

Your friend,
Hyrum Graff

PS: On the chance that your captain has not informed you, five years after you left, the I.F. agreed with my urgent request and launched a series of couriers, one departing every five years, to each of the colonies. These ships are not the huge behemoths that carry colonists, but they have room for some serious cargo and we are hoping they become the instrument of trade among the colonies. Our endeavor will be to have a ship call on each colony world every five years—but then they will travel colony to colony and return to Earth only after making a full circuit. The crews will have the option of completing the whole voyage, or training their replacements on any colony world and remaining behind while someone else completes their mission. Thus no one will be trapped on any one world for their whole life, and no one will be trapped in the same spaceship for the rest of their life. As you can guess, we did not lack for volunteers.

Vitaly Kolmogorov lay in bed, waiting to die and getting rather impatient about it.

"Don't hurry things," said Sel Menach. "It sets a bad example."

"I'm not hurrying anything. I'm just *feeling* impatient. I have a right to feel what I feel, I think!"

"And a right to think what you think, I feel," said Sel.

"Oh, *now* he develops a sense of humor."

"You're the one who decided this was your deathbed, not me," said Sel. "Black humor seems appropriate, though."

"Sel, I asked you to visit me for a reason."

"To depress me."

"When I'm dead, the colony will need a governor."

"There's a governor coming from Earth, isn't there?"

"Technically, from Eros."

"Ah, Vitaly, we all come from Eros."

"Very funny, and very classical. I wonder how much longer there'll be anybody capable of being amused by puns based on Earth-system asteroids and Greek gods."

"Anyway, Vitaly, please don't tell me you're appointing me governor."

"Nothing of the kind," said Vitaly. "I'm giving you an errand."

"And no one but an aging xenobiologist will do."

"Exactly," said Vitaly. "There is a message—encrypted, and no, I won't give you the key—a message waiting in the ansible queue. I ask only this: When I'm well and thoroughly dead, but before they've chosen a new governor, please send the message."

"To whom?"

"The message already knows where it's going."

"Very clever message. Why doesn't it figure out when you're dead, and go by itself?"

"Promise?"

"Yes, of course."

"And promise me something else."

"I'm getting old. Don't count on my remembering too many promises all at once."

"When they elect you governor, do it."

"They will not."

"If they don't, then fine," said Vitaly. "But when they do elect you, as everyone but you fully expects they will, do it."

"No."

"And here's why you must," said Vitaly. "You are best qualified for the job because you don't want it."

"Nobody in their right mind wants it."

"Too many men crave it, not because they want to do it, but because they fancy the honor of it. The prestige. The rank." Vitaly laughed, and the laugh turned into an ugly coughing jag till he was able to get a drink of water and calm the spasms in his chest. "I won't miss *that* sort of thing when I'm dead."

"Rank?"

"I was speaking of my cough. That constant tickling deep in my chest. Wheezing. Flatulence. Blurred vision no matter how good my glasses are and no matter how much light I have. All the nasty decay of old age."

"What about your bad breath?"

"*That* is designed to make *you* glad I'm dead. Sel, I'm serious about this. If someone else is elected governor, it will be someone who wants the job and won't be happy to give it up when the new governor comes."

"That's what they get for deciding, clear off in Eros, that along with supplies, equipment, and expertise, they'll also send us a dictator."

"I was a dictator at first," said Vitaly.

"When we were starting and survival looked impossible, yes, you kept things calm till we could find a way to handle the things this planet came up with to kill us off. But those days are over."

"No they're not," said Vitaly. "Let me lay it out plainly. The ship that is coming to us contains two admirals. One is our future governor. And one is the captain of the ship. Guess which one believes he should be our governor."

"The captain of the ship, of course, or you wouldn't have said it that way."

"A bureaucrat. A climber. I didn't know him before we set out on our own voyage, but I know the type."

"So the ship is bringing us everything we need, plus a power struggle."

"I don't want war here. I don't want bloodshed. I don't want the newcomers to have to conquer an upstart acting governor here on Shakespeare. I want our colony to be ready to welcome the new colonists and all they bring with them—and to unify behind the governor that was appointed for us back on Eros. They knew what they were doing when they appointed him."

"You know who it is," said Sel. "You know, and you haven't told a soul."

"Of course I know," said Vitaly. "I've been corresponding with him for the past thirty-five years. Ever since the colony ship launched."

"And didn't breathe a word. Who is it? Anyone I'd have heard of?"

"How do I know what you've heard and haven't heard?" said Vitaly. "I'm a dying man, don't bother me."

"So you still aren't telling."

"When he comes out of lightspeed, he'll make contact with you. Then you can deal with telling the colonists about him—whatever he tells you, you can tell them."

"But you don't trust me to keep the secret."

"Sel, you don't keep secrets. You say whatever's on your mind. Deception isn't in you. That's why you'll be such a splendid governor, and why I'm not telling you a single thing that you can't tell everybody as soon as you know it."

"I can't lie? Well, then, I won't bother promising you to accept the governorship, because I won't do it. I won't have to. They'll choose somebody else. Nobody likes me but you, Vitaly. I'm a grumpy old man who bosses people around and makes clumsy assistants cry. Whatever I did for this colony is long in the past."

"Oh shut up," said Vitaly. "You'll do what you do and I'll do what I do. Which in my case is die."

"I'm going to do that too, you know. Probably before you."

"Then you'll have to get a move on."

"This new governor—has he any idea of what it will take for these new people to live here? The injections? The regular diet of modified pig, so they can get the proteins that starve the worms? I hope they haven't sent us any vegetarians. It really stinks that these new people will out-number us from the moment they get off the ship."

"We need them," said Vitaly.

"I know. The gene pool needs them, the farms and factories need them."

"Factories?"

"We're tinkering with one of the old formic solar power generators. We think we can get it to run a loom."

"The industrial revolution! Only thirty-six years after we got this planet! And you say you haven't done anything for the people lately."

"I'm not *doing* it," said Sel. "I just talked Lee Tee into giving it a look."

"Oh, well, if that's all."

"Say it."

"Say what? I said what I was going to say."

"Say that persuading somebody to *try* something is exactly the way you've governed for the past three-and-a-half decades."

"I don't have to say what you already know."

"Don't die," said Sel.

"I'm so touched," said Vitaly. "But don't you see? I want to. I'm done. Used up. I went off to war and we fought it and won it and then Ender Wiggin won the battle of the home world and all the buggers down here died. Suddenly I'm not a soldier anymore. And I *was* a soldier, Sel. Not a bureaucrat. Definitely not a governor. But I was admiral, I was in com-mand, it was my duty, and I did it."

"I'm not as dutiful as you."

"I'm not talking about you now, dammit, you'll do whatever you want. I'm talking about me. I'm telling you what to say at my damn funeral!"

"Oh."

"I didn't want to be governor. I fully expected to die in the war, but the truth is, I no more thought about the future than you did. We were coming to this place, we were trained to be ready to survive on this formic colony world, but I thought that would all be *your* job, you and the other techs, while I commanded the fighting, the struggle against the hordes of formics coming over the hill, burrowing up underneath us—you have no idea the nightmares I had about the occupation, the clearing, the holding. I was afraid there wouldn't be enough bullets in the world. I thought we'd die."

"Then Ender Wiggin disappointed you."

"Yes. Selfish little brat. I'm a soldier, and he took my war out from under me."

"And you loved him for it."

"I did my duty, Sel. I did my duty."

"So have I," said Sel. "But I won't do yours."

"You will when I'm gone."

"You won't be alive to see."

"I have hopes of an afterlife," said Vitaly. "I'm not a scientist, I'm allowed to say so."

"Most scientists believe in God," said Sel. "Certainly most of us here."

"But you don't believe I'll be alive to see what you're doing."

"I'd like to think that God has better things for you to do. Besides, the heaven around here is a formic heaven. I hope God will let whatever part of you lives on go back to the heaven where all the humans are."

"Or the hell," said Vitaly.

"I forgot what pessimists you Russians are."

"It's not pessimism. I just want to be where all my friends are. Where my father is, the old bastard."

"You didn't like him? But you want to be with him?"

"I want to beat up the old drunkard! Then we'll go fishing."

"So it won't be heaven for the fish."

"It'll be hell for everybody. But with good moments."

"Just like our lives right now," said Sel.

Vitaly laughed. "Soldiers shouldn't do theology."

"Xenobiologists shouldn't do government."

"Thank you for making my deathbed so full of uncertainty."

"Anything to keep you entertained. And now, if you don't mind, I have to feed the pigs."

Sel left and Vitaly lay there, wondering if he should get out of bed and just send the message himself.

No, his decision was right. He didn't want to have any sort of conversation with Ender. Let him get the letter when it's too late to answer it, that was the plan and it was a good one. He's a smart kid, a good boy. He'll do what he needs to do. I don't want him asking my advice because he doesn't need it and he might follow it.

CHAPTER
13

To: GovDes%ShakespeareCol@ColMin.gov/voy
From: GovAct%ShakespeareCol@colmin.gov
Re: You will get this when I'm dead

Dear Ender,

I put it bluntly in the subject line. No beating around the bush. I'm writing this as I feel the seeds of death in me. I will arrange for it to be sent after they have done with me.

I expect my successor to be Sel Menach. He doesn't want the job, but he is widely liked and universally trusted, which is vital. He will not try to cling to his office when you arrive. But if it is not him, you'll be on your own and I wish you luck.

You know how hard it will be for my little community. For thirty-six years, we've been living and giving in marriage. The new generation has already restored the gender balance; there are grandchildren nearly of marrying age. Then your ship will come and suddenly we will be five times the population, and only one in five will be of our original group. It will be hard. It will change everything. But I believe that I know you now, and if I'm right, then my people have nothing to fear. You will help the new colonists adapt to our ways, wherever our ways make sense for this place. You will help my people adapt to the new colonists, wherever they must because the ways of Earth make sense.

In a way, Ender, we are the same age, or at least in the same stage of life. We long since left our families behind. As far as the world is concerned, we stepped into an open grave and disappeared. This has *been* the afterlife for me, the career after my career ended, the life after my life ended. And it has been a good one. It has been heaven. Busy, frightening, triumphant, and finally peaceful. May it be the same for you, my friend. However long it is, may you be glad of each day of it.

I have never forgotten that I owe our victory, and therefore this second life, to you and the other children who led us in the war. I thank you again from this grave of mine.

> With love and respect,
> Vitaly Denisovitch Kolmogorov

"I don't like what you're doing to Alessandra," said Valentine.

Ender looked up from what he was reading. "And what would that be?"

"You know perfectly well that you've made her fall in love with you."

"Have I?"

"Don't pretend to be oblivious to it! She looks at you like a hungry puppy."

"I've never owned a dog. They didn't allow team mascots in Battle School, and there weren't any strays."

"And you deliberately made her do it."

"If I can make a woman fall in love with me at will, I should have bottled it and sold it and gotten rich on Earth."

"You didn't make a *woman* fall in love with you, you made an emotionally dependent, shy, sheltered *girl* fall in love with you, and that's pathetically easy. All it took was being extraordinarily nice to her."

"You're right. If I hadn't been so selfish, I would have slapped her."

"Ender, it's me you're talking to. Do you think I haven't been watching? You seek out opportunities to praise her. To ask her advice on the most meaningless things. To thank her all the time for nothing at all. And you smile at her. Has anyone ever mentioned that when you smile, it would melt steel?"

"Inconvenient, in a spaceship. I'll smile less."

"You switch it on like . . . like the stardrive! That smile—with your whole face, as if you were taking your soul out and putting it into her hands."

"Val," said Ender. "This is kind of an important letter. What is your point?"

"What are you planning to do with her, now that you own her?"

"I don't own anybody," said Ender. "I haven't laid a hand on her—literally. Not shaking hands, not a pat on the shoulder, nothing. No physical contact. I also haven't flirted with her. No sexual innuendoes. No inside jokes. And I haven't gone off alone with her, either. Month after month, as her mother conspires to leave us alone, I've simply not done it. Even if it took walking out of a room quite rudely. What part of that is making her fall in love with me, exactly?"

"Ender, I don't like it when you lie to me."

"Valentine, if you want an honest answer, write me an honest letter."

She sighed and sat down on her bed. "I can't wait for this voyage to end."

"A bit more than two months to go. Almost over. And you did finish your book."

"Yes, and it's very good," said Valentine. "Especially when you consider I barely met any of them and *you* were almost no help to me."

"I answered every question you asked."

"Except to evaluate the people, to evaluate the school, to—"

"My opinions aren't history. It wasn't supposed to be '*Ender Wiggin's School Days* as told to his sister, Valentine.'"

"I didn't come on this voyage to quarrel with you."

Ender looked at her with such overdone astonishment that she threw a pillow at him.

"For what it's worth," she said, "I've never been as mean to you as I was to Peter all the time."

"Then all's right with the world."

"But I'm angry at you, Ender. You shouldn't toy with a girl's feelings. Unless you really plan to marry her—"

"I do not," said Ender.

"Then you shouldn't lead her on."

"I have not," said Ender.

"And I say you have."

"No, Valentine," said Ender. "What I have done is exactly what is needed for her to have the thing she wants most."

"Which is you."

"Which is definitely *not* me." Ender sat beside her on her bed, leaned close to her. "You will help me most by scrutinizing someone else."

"I scrutinize everybody," said Val. "I judge everybody. But you're my brother. I get to boss you around."

"And you're my sister. I have to tickle you until you pee or cry. Or both." Which he proceeded to attempt, though he didn't really go quite that far. Or at least, she only peed a little. And then punched him hard in the arm and made him say, "Ow," in a really snotty, sarcastic way, so she knew he was pretending it didn't hurt, but it really did. Which he deserved. He really was being rotten to Alessandra, and he didn't even care, and worse yet, he thought he could deny it. Just pitiful.

All that afternoon, Ender thought about what Valentine said. He knew what he was planning, and it really was for Alessandra's good, but he *had* miscalculated if the girl was actually falling in love with him. It was supposed to be friendship, trust, gratitude maybe. Brother-and-sister. Only Alessandra wasn't Valentine. She couldn't keep up. She didn't leap to conclusions as quickly as Val—or at least not to the same conclusions. She couldn't really hold up her end.

Where am I going to find anyone I *can* marry? Ender wondered. Nowhere and never, if I compare them all to Valentine.

All right, yes, I knew I was causing Alessandra to have feelings. I like it when she looks at me like that. Petra never looked at me that way. Nobody did. It feels good. The hormones wake up and get excited. It's fun. I'm fifteen. I haven't said anything to mislead her about my intentions, and I haven't done anything, not ever, to signal any kind of physical attraction. So shoot me for liking that she likes me and doing the things that make her feel that way. What's the rule here? Either totally ignore her and grind her face in her nothingness, or marry her on the spot? Are those the only choices?

But gnawing at the back of his mind was this question: Am I Peter? Am I using other people for whatever plan I have? Does it make a difference that my intention is to have a result that will give her a chance at happiness? I'm not asking her, I'm not giving her a choice, I'm manipulating her. Shaping her world so she makes certain choices and takes certain actions that make other people do what I want *them* to do and . . .

And what? What's the other choice? To passively let things happen and then say, "Tut-tut, what a botch *that* was"? Don't we all manipulate people? Even if we openly ask them to make a choice, don't we try to frame it so they'll choose as we think they should?

If I tell her what I'm up to, she'll probably go along with me. Do it voluntarily.

But is she a good enough actor to keep her mother from knowing something's going on? Forcing it out of her? Alessandra was still so much her mother's creature that Ender didn't believe she could keep a secret from her mother, not for long. And if she does give away the game, then it will cost Alessandra nothing—she'll be right where she already is—while I will lose everything. Don't I have a right to count myself in the balance here, my own happiness, my own future? And on the off chance that I'd be a better governor than Admiral Morgan, don't I owe it to the colonists to make sure things work out to put me in as governor, rather than him?

It's still war, even if there are no weapons but smiles and words. I have to take the forces I have, the advantages of the terrain, and try to face a more powerful enemy under circumstances that neutralize his advantages. Alessandra is a person, yes—so is every soldier, every pawn in the great game. I was used to win a war. Now I'll use someone else. All for the "good of the whole."

But underneath all his moral reasoning, there was something else. He could feel it. An itch, a hunger, a yearning. It was his inner chimp, as he and Valentine called it. The animal that smelled womanhood on Alessandra. Did I choose this plan, these tools, because they were best? Or because they would put me near a girl who *is* pretty, who desires my affection?

So maybe Valentine was completely right.

But if she was . . . what then? I can't undo all the attention I've paid to Alessandra. Do I suddenly turn cold to her, for no reason at all? Is that any less manipulative?

Sometimes can't I switch off my brain and be the hairless chimp with an eye for an available female?

No.

"How long are you going to play this little game with Ender Wiggin?" asked Dorabella.

"Game?" asked Alessandra.

"He's obviously interested in you," said Dorabella. "He always homes in on you, I've seen how he smiles at you. He likes you."

"Like a sister," sighed Alessandra.

"He's shy," said Dorabella.

Alessandra sighed.

"Don't sigh at me," said Dorabella.

"Oh, when I'm around you, I'm not allowed to exhale?"

"Don't make me pinch your nose and stuff cookies in your mouth."

"Mother, I can't control what he does."

"But you can control what you do."

"Ender isn't Admiral Morgan."

"No, he isn't. He's a boy. With no experience at all. A boy who can be led and helped and shown."

"Shown what, Mother? Are you suggesting that I do something *physical*?"

"Darling sweet fairy daughter of mine," said Dorabella, "it's not for *you* and it's not for *me*. It's for Ender Wiggin's own good."

Alessandra rolled her eyes. She was such a teenager.

"Eye-rolling is not an answer, darling sweet fairy daughter."

"Mother, people who are doing the most awful things always say it's for the other person's own good."

"But in this case, I'm quite right. You see, Admiral Morgan and I have become very close. Very very close."

"Are you sleeping with him?"

Dorabella's hand flew up, prepared to strike, before she even knew what she was doing. But she caught herself in time. "Oh, look," she said. "My hand thinks it belongs to your grandmother."

Alessandra's voice shook a little. "When you said you were very *very* close I wondered if you were implying—"

"Quincy Morgan and I have an adult relationship," said Dorabella. "We understand each other. I bring a brightness to his life that he has never had before, and he brings a manly stability that your father, bless his heart, never had. There is also physical attraction, but we are mature adults, masters of our libido, and no, I haven't let him lay a hand on me."

"Then what are we talking about here?" asked Alessandra.

"What I did not know, as a girl your age," said Dorabella, "was that between cold chastity and doing that which produces babies, there is a wide range of steps and stages that can signal to a young man that his advances are welcome, to a point."

"I'm quite aware of that, Mother. I saw other girls at school dressing like whores and putting it all on display. I saw the fondling and grabbing and pinching. We're Italians, I was in an Italian school, and all the boys planned to grow up to be Italian men."

"Don't try to distract me by making me angry at your ethnic stereotypes," said Dorabella. "We have only a few weeks left before we arrive—"

"Two months is not 'a few weeks.' "

"Eight is a few. When we reach Shakespeare, one thing is certain. Admiral Morgan is not going to turn the colony over to a fifteen-year-old boy. That would be irresponsible. He likes Ender—everyone does—but in Battle School all they did was play games all day. It takes someone with experience in leadership to govern a colony. This has never been said outright, mind you. But I have gleaned this from things that were hinted at or almost said or . . . overheard."

"You've been eavesdropping."

"I've been present and human ears don't close. My point is that the very best way it could all turn out is if Ender Wiggin is governor, but taking the advice of Admiral Morgan."

"On everything."

"That's better than Ender being put in stasis and sent home."

"No! He wouldn't do that!"

"It has already been threatened, and there have been hints that it might be necessary. Now, look at this picture: Ender and a beautiful colonist girl fall in love. They pledge to marry. Now he's affianced. It happens that his mother-in-law-to-be—"

"Who happens to be a deranged woman who thinks she's a fairy and the mother of a fairy."

"In-law-to-be is married or about to be married to the admiral who is most definitely *going* to be the power behind the throne, so to speak. Unless Ender gives him trouble, in which case he'll take the throne, so to speak, quite openly. But Ender will *not* give him trouble, because he won't need to. His beautiful young wife will look out for his interests by talking things over with her mother, who will then talk things over with her husband, and everything will work smoothly for everyone."

"In other words, I would marry him in order to be a spy."

"There would be a pair of loving and beloved go-betweens who would make sure there was never any conflict between the admirals on this ship."

"By suppressing Ender and making him dance to Quincy's tune."

"Until he becomes old enough and experienced enough himself," said Dorabella.

"Which would happen exactly never, at least not in Quincy's eyes," said Alessandra. "Mother, I'm not stupid and neither is anyone else involved in this. You're betting that Admiral Morgan will seize power, and so by marrying him, you'll be the wife of the governor of the colony. But because you can't be sure that Ender Wiggin won't prevail, you want me to marry *him*. That way, no matter who wins this little power struggle, *we'll* be able to cash in. Am I correct?"

Alessandra had spoken the phrase "cash in" in English. Dorabella seized on that. "Shakespeare Colony has no cash yet, darling," said Dorabella. "It's all barter and allotment so far. You haven't been studying the lessons on our colony-to-be."

"Mother," said Alessandra. "That *is* your plan, isn't it?"

"Hardly," said Dorabella. "I'm a woman in love. So are you. Don't deny it!"

"I think about him all the time," said Alessandra. "I dream of him every night. If that's being in love, they need a pill to cure it."

"You only feel that way because the boy you love is not aware enough of his own feelings to make things clear to you or even to himself. That's what I've been trying to tell you all along."

"No, Mother," said Alessandra. "You've been trying to do everything *but* tell me. What you want me to do, but refuse to say out loud, is seduce him."

"I do *not*."

"Mother!"

"I've already *said* this. There's a lot of road between pining for him and seducing him. There's little touches."

"He doesn't like being touched."

"He *thinks* he doesn't like being touched because he doesn't yet understand that he's in love with you."

"Wow," said Alessandra. "And all of this without a degree in psychology."

"A fairy woman doesn't need to *study* psychology, she's born with it."

"Mother!"

"You keep saying that. As if you weren't sure I know my title. Yes, dear, I am indeed your mother."

"For once in your life, can't you just say what you mean?"

Dorabella closed her eyes. Saying things plainly had never worked out well for her. Yet Alessandra was right. The girl was so naive she really didn't know what Dorabella was talking about. She didn't understand the need, the urgency—and she didn't understand what she had to do about it.

Candor was probably unavoidable. Might as well get it over with.

"Sit down, darling," said Dorabella.

"So it's going to be a more complicated self-deception," said Alessandra. "One that requires rest."

"I'm cutting you out of my will if you keep that up."

"That threat won't work until you have something to leave me that I want to have."

"Sit down, bratty bad girl," said Dorabella, using her playfully stern voice.

Alessandra lay down on her bed. "I'm listening."

"You can never just do what I ask, can you."

"I'm listening, and you didn't ask, you commanded."

Dorabella took a deep breath and laid it on the line. "If you don't have Ender Wiggin locked down and tied up in a relationship with you within these next four weeks, he almost certainly will be left behind on this ship, under guard or in stasis, when Admiral Morgan goes down to see how the colony is getting along. But if Ender Wiggin is Admiral Morgan's son-in-law-to-be, then he will most definitely be presented to the Shakespearians as their new governor. So either you will be affianced to the titular governor and hero of the human race, or you'll be permanently separated from him and will have to pick one of the local clowns when it comes time for you to marry."

Alessandra closed her eyes for long enough that Dorabella was thinking about throwing a cup of water on her to wake her back up.

"Thank you," said Alessandra.

"For what?"

"For telling me what you actually meant," said Alessandra. "What the plan is. I can see that whatever I do will be for Ender's own good. But I'm fifteen, Mother, and the only thing I know is the way the worst girls in school behaved. I don't think that will have any good results with Ender Wiggin. So even though I would like to do what you say, I have no idea how to do it."

Dorabella went to Alessandra's bed and knelt beside it and kissed her daughter's cheek. "My darling girl, all you had to do was ask."

CHAPTER
14

To: smenach%ShakespeareCol@colmin.gov
From: GovDes%ShakespeareCol@colmin.gov/voy
Subj: As we approach

Dear Dr. Menach,

I have admired—and been grateful for—your work as I've studied it during the voyage. Vitaly Kolmogorov spoke of you with feelings beyond admiration—awe and deep friendship are also inadequate words—and while I have not known you as he did, I have seen your accomplishments. The fact that I and the thousands of new colonists with me will arrive to find Shakespeare Colony a going concern, instead of coming here as rescuers of a failing colony, is owed to all the colonists, of course, but without your solutions for the diseases and protein incompatibilities, it is quite likely we would have come to find no one here at all.

Vitaly told me that you were reluctant to consider accepting the governorship, but I see that you have done so, and governed effectively for nearly five years. Thank you for bending your principles and accepting a political job. I can assure you that I was nearly as reluctant to take the job myself; in my case, I had nowhere else to go.

I am young and inexperienced as a governor, though like you I have served my time as a soldier. I hope to find you in place when I arrive, so I can learn from you and work with you in helping assimilate four thousand "new colonists" and one thousand "old colonists" so that, within a reasonable period of time, they will simply be . . . citizens of Shakespeare.

My name is Andrew Wiggin, but I have usually been called by my child-hood nickname, Ender. Since you served as a pilot during the battle within the system where now you are a colonist, it is quite possible that you heard my voice; certainly you heard the voice of at least one of my fellow com-manders. I grieve for those pilots whom we lost during that action; we may not have known that our mistakes would cost real lives, but that does not re-move our responsibility. I realize that for you, more than forty years have passed; for me, that battle was only three years ago, and has never been far from my thoughts. I am about to face the soldiers who actually fought that battle, and who remember those whose lives were lost because of my mistakes.

I look forward to meeting the children and grandchildren who have been born to your compatriots. They, of course, will have no memory of battles that to them are ancient history. They will have no idea who I am, or why they would be insulted by having a fifteen-year-old boy placed over them as governor.

Fortunately, I have with me the very experienced Admiral Quincy Morgan, who has kindly offered to extend his leadership over the colony as well as the ship, for as long as he remains here. Vitaly and I discussed the nature of lead-ership and command, and we came to think of Quincy Morgan as a man of peace and authority; you will know better than I what that can mean for the colony.

I am sorry for the burdens that our coming will impose on you, and grateful in advance.

Sincerely,
Andrew

To: GovDes%ShakespeareCol@colmin.gov/voy
From: smenach%ShakespeareCol@colmin.gov
Subj: Poor scheduling

Dear Ender,

Thank you for your thoughtful letter. I do understand exactly what you meant about Admiral Morgan being a man of peace and authority, and I wish I were equipped to give him the appropriate greeting. But the only soldiers among us are as old as me; our youngsters have had no reason to learn military discipline or skills of any kind. I fear you would find our attempts at maneuvers an embarrassment. Whatever ceremonies are to take place upon your arrival must be planned entirely from your end. Having seen YOUR work, observing it at least as closely as you have observed mine, I have every confidence that you will handle everything with perfect aplomb.

Not since Vitaly died have I had the opportunity to use "aplomb" in a sentence. Perhaps, since you are to be governor (to my great relief), I have simply transferred to you the style of discourse I always used with him.

It is unfortunate that your arrival coincides with an urgent and long-scheduled trip I must take. I am no longer lead xenobiologist, but my duties in that area have not simply disappeared. Now that you are coming, I can at least make that journey into the broad stretch of land to the south of us, which remains almost completely unexplored. We settled in a semitropical climate, so we wouldn't freeze to death if we could not find adequate fuel and shelter when we first arrived. Now you are bringing Earth vegetation which needs cooler climes to thrive, and I must see if there are appropriate environments for them. I also need to see if there are indigenous fruits, vegetables, and grasses that we might be able to make use of, now that you're bringing means of transportation that could make it practical for us to grow crops in one climate and consume them in another.

For reasons that should be obvious to you, I also believe that having an old man underfoot will not be as helpful to you as you imagine. When two men who have been called "governor" are together, people will turn to the one they have more experience with. And the new people, having been in stasis, will probably follow the practice of the old. My absence will be your greatest asset. Ix Tolo, the head xenobiologist, can acquaint you with ongoing projects.

I'm sure you will understand that my taking this journey does not reflect any wish on my part not to meet you or help you. If I thought my presence would be better for the colony than my absence, one of my greatest pleasures would be to shake the hand of the commander who led us to victory. Among the old coots of the colony, you'll find many who are still in awe of you. Please be patient with them if they're a bit tongue-tied.

Sincerely,
Sel

Sel began quietly to prepare for an expedition southward. It would be on foot—there had been no beasts of burden in the original expedition, and he was not going to deprive the colony of any of its vehicles. And even though many of the new edible hybrids had spread widely, he meant to pass out of their optimum climate, which meant he would have to carry his food with him. Fortunately, he didn't eat much, and he would bring along six of the new dogs he had genetically altered to be able to metabolize the local proteins. The dogs would hunt, and then he would harvest two of them—and turn the other four loose, two breeding pairs that could live off the land.

New predators turned loose in the wild—Sel knew exactly how dangerous this could be to the local ecology. But they could not eat *all* the native species and would not interfere with the vegetation. It would be important during later exploration and colonization to find edible and tamable creatures loose in the wild.

We aren't here to preserve the local ecology like a museum. We're here to colonize, to suit the world for ourselves.

Which is precisely what the formics had started to do to Earth. Only their approach was much more drastic—burn all, and then plant vegetation from the formics' native planet.

Yet for some reason they had not done so here. He had found none of the species the formics had planted on Earth during the Scouring of China nearly a century ago. This was one of the formics' oldest colonies, and its flora and fauna seemed to be too distant, genetically, to have shared common ancestors with the formic varieties. It must have been settled before they developed the formification strategy they had begun to use on Earth.

In all the years till now, Sel had had to devote himself entirely to the genetic research required to keep the colony viable, and then, for the past five years, to governing the colony. Now he could go into unexplored lands and learn what he could.

He could not go any great distance—he supposed a few hundred kilometers would be his limit—for it would do no good to range so far that he could not return and report his findings.

Ix Tolo helped him pack, griping about this and that—his normal behavior. Not taking enough equipment, taking too much, not enough food, too much water, why this, why not that . . . it was his constant attention to detail that made him effective in his job and Sel bore it with good humor.

And, of course, Ix had a mind of his own.

"You can unpack that other bag," Sel told him, "because you're not going with me."

"Other bag?"

"I'm not an idiot. Half the equipment I decided not to take, you've put into another pack, along with more food and an extra bedroll."

"I never thought you were an idiot. But I'm not so stupid I'd endanger the colony by sending both our lead xenobiologists on the same journey."

"So who's the pack for?"

"My son Po."

"I've always been bothered that you named him for an insanely romantic Chinese poet. Why nobody from Mayan history?"

"All the characters in the Popol Vuh have numbers instead of names. He's a sensible kid. Strong. If he had to, he could carry you back home."

"I'm not *that* old and wizened."

"He could do it," said Ix. "But only if you're alive. Otherwise, he'll watch and record the process of decomposition, and then sample the microbes and worms that manage to feed on your old Earthborn corpse."

"Glad to see you still think like a scientist and not a sentimental fool."

"Po is good company."

"And he'll allow me to carry enough equipment for the trip to be useful. While you stay here and play with the new stuff from the colony ship."

"And train the xenobiologists they've sent along," said Ix. "No doubt you've told Wiggin that I'll help him. That will not happen. I'll have plenty of work to do in my own field without babysitting the new governor."

Sel ignored his kvetching. He knew Ix would help in whatever way Wiggin needed him to. "And Po's mother is happy about his going with me?"

"No," said Ix. "But she knows he'd never speak to her again if she barred him from it. So we have her blessing. More or less."

"Then first thing in the morning, we're off."

"Unless the new governor forbids you."

"His authority doesn't begin until he sets foot on this planet. He isn't even in orbit yet."

"Haven't you looked at their manifest? They have four skimmers."

"If we need one, we'll radio back for it. Otherwise, don't tell them where we went."

"Good thing the formics got rid of all the major predators on this planet."

"There's no self-respecting predator would eat an old wad of gristle like me."

"I was thinking of my son."

"He won't want to eat me either, even if we run out of food."

That night, Sel went to bed early and then, as usual, got up to pee after only a few hours of sleep. He noticed that the ansible was blinking. Message.

Not my problem.

Well, that wasn't true, was it? If Wiggin's authority didn't begin until he set foot on the planet, then Sel was still acting governor. So any messages from Earth, he had to receive.

He sat down and signaled that he was ready to receive.

There were two messages recorded. He played the first one. It consisted of the face of the Minister of Colonization, Graff, and his message was brief.

"I know you're planning to skip town before Wiggin gets there. Talk to Wiggin before you go. He won't try to stop you, so relax."

That was it.

The other message was from Wiggin. He looked his age, but his adult height was coming on him. In the colony, teenagers his size were expected to do a man's work, and got a man's vote in the meetings. So maybe his position wouldn't be as awkward as Sel expected.

"Please contact me by ansible as soon as you get this," said Ender. "We're in radio distance, but I don't want anyone else to be able to intercept the signal."

Sel toyed with the idea of turning the message over to Ix to answer, but decided against it. The point wasn't to hide from Wiggin, was it? Only to leave the field clear for him.

So he signaled his intention to make a connection. It took only a few minutes for Wiggin to appear. Now that the colony ship wasn't traveling at a relativistic speed, there was no time differential, and therefore the ansible transmitted instantly. Not even the time lag of radio.

"Governor Menach," said Ender Wiggin. He smiled.

"Sir," Sel replied. He tried to smile back, but . . . this was Ender Wiggin he was talking to.

"When we got word that you were leaving, my first thought was to beg you to stay."

Sel ignored him. "I was glad to see on the manifest a full range of beasts of burden as well as milk, wool, egg, and meat beasts. Are they Earth-natural, or have they been genetically altered to digest the local vegetation?"

"Your methods were very promising at the time we left, but did not prove out until we were well under way. So all the animals and plants we brought with us are Earth-natural. They're all in stasis, and can be maintained in that condition on the surface for some time, even after the ship leaves. So there'll be time to make the alterations on the next generation."

"Ix Tolo has ongoing projects of his own, but I believe he'll be able to train your new xenos in the techniques."

"Ix Tolo will remain the head xenobiologist, in your absence," said Wiggin. "I've seen his work in recent weeks—years, to you. You've trained him to an exacting standard, and the xenos on this ship intend to learn from him. Though they're hoping you'll return soon. They want to meet you. You're something of a hero to them. This is the only world that has non-formiform flora and fauna. The other colonies have been work-ing with the same genetic groups—this is the only world that posed unique challenges, so you had to do, alone, what all the other colonies were able to do cooperatively."

"Me and Darwin."

"Darwin had more help than you," said Wiggin. "I hope you'll keep your radio dormant instead of off. Because I want to be able to ask for your counsel, if I need it."

"You won't. I'm going back to bed now. I have a lot of walking to do tomorrow."

"I can send a skimmer after you. So you don't have to carry your sup-plies. It would increase your range."

"But then the old settlers will expect me to come back soon. They'll be waiting for me instead of relying on you."

"I can't pretend that we're not able to track you and find you."

"But you can tell them that you're showing me the respect of not try-ing. At my request."

"Yes," said Ender. "I'll do that."

There was little more to say. They signed off and Sel went back to bed. He slept easily. And, as usual, woke just when he wanted to—an hour be-fore dawn.

Po was waiting for him.

"I already said good-bye to Mom and Dad," he said.

"Good," said Sel.

"Thanks for letting me come."

"Could I have stopped you?"

"Yes," said Po. "I won't disobey you, Uncle Sel." All the grandchil-dren generation called him that.

Sel nodded. "Good. Have you eaten?"

"Yes."

"Then let's go. I won't need to eat till noon."

———

You take a step, then another. That's the journey. But to take a step with your eyes open is not a journey at all, it's a remaking of your own mind. You see things that you never saw before. Things never seen by the eyes of human beings. And you see with your particular eyes, which were trained to see not just a plant, but *this* plant, filling *this* ecological niche, but with this and that difference.

And when your eyes have been trained for forty years to be familiar with the patterns of a new world, then you are Antonie van Leeuwenhoek, who first saw the world of animalcules through a microscope; you are Carl Linnaeus, first sorting creatures into families, genera, species; you are Darwin, sorting lines of evolutionary passage from one species to another.

So it was not a rapid journey. Sel had to force himself to move with any kind of haste.

"Don't let me linger so long over every new thing I see," he told Po. "It would be too humiliating for my great expedition to take me only ten kilometers south of the colony. I must cross the first range of mountains, at least."

"And how will I keep you from lingering, when you have me photographing and sampling and storing and recording notes?"

"Refuse to do it. Tell me to get my bony knees up off the ground and start walking."

"All my life I'm taught to obey my elders and watch and learn. I'm your assistant. Your apprentice."

"You're just hoping we don't travel very far so when I die you don't have so long to carry the corpse."

"I thought my father told you—if you actually die, I'm supposed to call for help and observe your decomposition process."

"That's right. You only carry me if I'm breathing."

"Or do you want me to start now? Hoist you onto my shoulders so you can't discover another whole family of plants every fifty meters?"

"For a respectful, obedient young man, you can be very sarcastic."

"I was only slightly sarcastic. I can do better if you want."

"This is good. I've been so busy arguing with you, we've gone this far without my noticing anything."

"Except the dogs have found something."

It turned out to be a small family of the horned reptile that seemed to fill the bunny rabbit niche—a big-toothed leaf-eater that hopped, and would only fight if cornered. The horns did not seem to Sel to be weapons—too blunt—and when he imagined a mating ritual in which these creatures leapt into the air to butt their heads together, he could not see how it could help but scramble their brains, since their skulls were so light.

"Probably for a display of health," said Sel.

"The antlers?"

"Horns," said Sel.

"I think they're shed and then regrown," said Po. "Don't these animals look like skin-shedders?"

"No."

"I'll look for a shed skin somewhere."

"You'll have a long look," said Sel.

"Why, because they eat the skins?"

"Because they don't shed."

"How can you be sure?"

"I'm not sure," said Sel. "But this is not a formic import, it's a native species, and we haven't seen any skin shedding from natives."

So went the conversation as they traveled—but they did cover the ground. They took pictures, yes. And now and then, when it was something really new, they stopped and took samples. But always they walked. Sel might be old and need to lean on his walking stick now and then, but he could still keep up a steady pace. Po was likely to move ahead of him more often than not, but it was Po who groaned when Sel said it was time to move on after a brief rest.

"I don't know why you have that stick," said Po.

"To lean on when I rest."

"But you have to carry it the whole time you're walking."

"It's not that heavy."

"It *looks* heavy."

"It's from the balsa tree—well, the one I *call* 'balsa,' since the wood is so light."

Po tried it. Only about a pound, though it was thick and gnarled and widened out at the top like a pitcher. "I'd *still* get tired of carrying it."

"Only because you put more weight in your backpack than I did."

Po didn't bother arguing the point.

"The first human voyagers to Earth's moon and the other planets had an easy time of it," said Po, as they crested a high ridge. "Nothing but empty space between them and their destination. No temptation to stop and explore."

"Like the first sea voyagers. Going from land to land, ignoring the sea because they had no tools that would let them explore to any depth."

"We're the conquistadores," said Po. "Only we killed them all before we ever set foot on land."

"Is that a difference or a similarity?" asked Sel. "Smallpox and other diseases raced ahead of the conquistadores."

"If only we could have talked to them," said Po. "I read about the conquistadores—we Mayans have good reason to try to understand them. Columbus wrote that the natives he found 'had no language,' merely because they didn't understand any of the languages his interpreters knew."

"But the formics had no language at all."

"Or so we think."

"No communication devices in their ships. Nothing to transmit voice or images. Because there was no need of them. Exchange of memory. Direct transfer of the senses. Whatever their mechanism was, it was better than language, but worse, because they had no way to talk to us."

"So who were the mutes?" asked Po. "Us, or them?"

"Both of us mutes," said Sel, "and all of us deaf."

"What I wouldn't give to have just one of them alive."

"But there couldn't be just one," said Sel. "They hived. They needed hundreds, perhaps thousands to reach the critical mass to achieve intelligence."

"Or not," said Po. "It could also be that only the queen was sentient. Why else would they all have died when the queens died?"

"Unless the queen was the nexus, the center of a neural network, so they all collapsed when she did. But until then, all of them individuals."

"As I said, I wish we had one alive," said Po, "so we could know something instead of guessing from a few desiccated corpses."

Sel silently rejoiced that yet another generation of this colony had produced at least one who thought like a scientist. "We have more of them preserved than any of the other colonies. Here, there are so few scavengers that can eat them, the corpses lasted long enough for us to get to the planet's surface and freeze some of them. We actually got to study structure."

"But no queens."

"The sorrow of my life," said Sel.

"Really? That's your greatest regret?"

Sel fell silent.

"Sorry," said Po.

"It's all right. I was just considering your question. My greatest regret. What a question. How can I regret leaving everything behind on Earth, when I left it in order to help save it? And coming here allowed me to do things that other scientists could only dream of. I have been able to name more than five thousand species already and come up with a rudimentary classification system for an entire native biota. More than on any of the other formic worlds."

"Why?"

"Because the formics stripped those worlds and then established only a limited subset of their own flora and fauna. This is the only world where most of the species evolved here. The only place that's messy. The formics brought fewer than a thousand species to their colonies. And their home world, which might have had vastly more diversity, is gone."

"So you don't regret coming here?"

"Of course I do," said Sel. "And I'm also glad to be here. I regret being an old wreck of a man. I'm glad I'm not dead. It seems to me that all my regrets are balanced by something I'm glad of. On average, then, I have no regrets at all. But I'm also not a bit happy. Perfect balance. On average, I don't feel anything at all. I think I don't exist."

"Father says that if you get absurd results, you're not a scientist, you're a philosopher."

"But my results are not absurd."

"You *do* exist. I can see you and hear you."

"Genetically speaking, Po, I do not exist. I am off the web of life."

"So you choose to measure by the only standard that allows your life to be meaningless?"

Sel laughed. "You are your mother's son."

"Not father's?"

"Both, of course. But it's your mother who won't put up with any bull-shit."

"Speaking of which, I can hardly wait to see a bull."

Now that the ship was rapidly decelerating as they approached Shakespeare, the crew were far busier than usual. The first order of business would be docking with the transport ship that had brought the war fleet here to this world forty years before. Without supplies for a return journey, the ship was left as a huge satellite in geosynchronous orbit directly over the colony site. Solar power was enough to keep its computers and communications running for these past decades.

The original crew, colonists now, had used their fighters as landing vehicles; their supplies and equipment for the first years of the colony had been designed to fit in or on the fighters. And all of them were equipped with ansibles. But the fighters were land-once vehicles, and had no ability to leave the surface of the planet.

Admiral Morgan's crew would service and refit the transport. They had brought new communications and weather satellites with them, which they would place in geosync at intervals all the way around the planet. Then the old transport would be given a captain and crew, and would voyage, not back to Eros, but on to another colony.

Despite all this business, Ender had no illusion that Admiral Morgan himself was at all distracted from watching over Ender's activities. The man was a planner, a plotter, and while a "man of peace" like him might seem to plod along, never doing much, he was always poised to strike.

So as they approached the key moment—the arrival on Shakespeare— Ender had to give Morgan no reason at all for suspecting that Ender was plotting anything. Morgan expected Ender to be a bright, eager boy of fifteen, and those expectations had to be fulfilled; yet Morgan was also wary of Ender's unassailable claim to the governorship. He had to be confident that Ender was content to let him be the power behind the throne.

That's why Ender went to Morgan for permission to use the ansible to communicate with the Shakespeare xenobiologists. "You know I've been studying the formics' biological systems, and now I can communicate with them in real time. I have a lot of questions."

"I don't want you bothering them," said Morgan. "There's too much to do already, working out the landing."

Ender knew that there was nothing whatsoever for the landside colony to do except stand out of the way. Morgan would land and then decide what supplies to requisition for the return trip. Whether Morgan was on it or not, the ship would return to Earth.

"Sir, the XBs need to know what grazing species we have so they can prepare to adapt them to use the alien proteins. It's a massive project, and until we have a new generation of adapted animals, there'll be no meat. You have no idea how eager they are. And I'm fully up to speed, since I worked on the manifest when we left Eros."

"I've already sent them the manifest."

Actually, Ender had sent the manifest before the ship departed. But why quibble? "The list says things like 'cows' and 'pigs.' They need way more information than that. I have it; I can send it; and nobody's using the ansible, sir. This is really important." Ender almost said "really really really" but decided that would be too over-the-top boyish and Morgan might suspect something.

Morgan sighed. "This is why children should not be given adult assignments. You don't respect priorities the way adults do. But . . . as long as you drop whatever you're doing whenever the crew needs to use the ansible, go ahead. Now, if you don't mind, I have *real* work to do."

Ender knew that Morgan's "real" work had more to do with preparing to have a shipboard wedding than anything to do with the landing. Dorabella Toscano had him so frantic with lust—no, it was affection, the deep bonds of permanent companionship—that he had agreed that she would arrive on Shakespeare as the admiral's wife, not just as an ordinary colonist.

And that was fine with Ender. He would not interfere with that in any way.

Ender went to the ansible room to send his messages directly. If he had linked from his desk, the message would certainly have been intercepted and stored, to be puzzled over at leisure. Ender toyed with the idea of switching off the observation system so that nothing he said to Sel Menach could be overheard, but decided against it. Though the security was I.F. standard, which meant that a significant number of kids in

Battle School had been able to tweak it or hack it or, like Ender, get inside it and spoof it completely, he still couldn't risk having Morgan ask to see the vid of Ender in the ansible room and have the report come back that there was no vid for that timeframe.

Apart from that, he had only one short message to send to Graff, asking for a bit of help with his present situation, and then he could have a few moments of blissful privacy before doing the work he had told Morgan he was coming here to do.

He did what he always did when he had a chance to be completely alone. He rested his head on his arms and closed his eyes, hoping for a few moments of sleep to refresh his mind.

He awoke because somebody was gently rubbing his shoulders. "You poor thing," said Alessandra. "Fell asleep in the middle of your work."

Ender sat up, as she kept kneading the muscles of his shoulders and back and neck. They really *were* tight, and what she was doing felt good. If she had asked him, he would have refused—he didn't want physical contact between them—and if she had come upon him when he was awake and simply started doing it, he would have recoiled because he hated it when anyone thought they had the right to touch him without his consent.

But waking up to it, it felt too good to stop. "I'm not doing much," he said. "Busywork, mostly. Let the adults do the hard stuff. I've put in my time." By now, he lied to Alessandra by reflex.

"You don't fool me," she said. "I'm not as dumb as you think."

"I don't think you're dumb," said Ender. And he didn't. She wasn't Battle School material, but she wasn't stupid, either.

"I know you don't like it that Mother and Admiral Morgan are getting married."

Why would I care about that? "No, it's fine," said Ender. "I suppose you take love where you find it, and your mother's still young. And beautiful."

"She is, isn't she," said Alessandra. "I hope my body turns out like hers. The women in my father's family were all scrawny. No curves."

Ender knew at once what she was there for. Talking about "curves" while she massaged him was too obvious to miss. But he wanted to see where this was heading, and why. More specifically, why *now*.

"Scrawny or curvy, everybody's attractive under the right circumstances."

"What are those circumstances for you, Ender? When will anyone be attractive to you?"

He knew what was expected. "You're attractive, Alessandra. But you're too young."

"I'm the same age as you."

"I'm too young, too," said Ender. They had had this discussion before—but in the abstract. As they congratulated each other on being such good friends without any kind of sexual interest in each other. Clearly, there had been a change of program.

"I don't know," said Alessandra. "Back on Earth, people married later and later. And had sex earlier and earlier. It was wrong to divide them, I know, but who can say which direction was wrong? Maybe the biology of our bodies is wiser than all the reasons for waiting to marry. Maybe our bodies want to raise children when we're still young enough to keep up with them."

Ender wondered how much of this had been scripted by her mother. Probably not much. Alessandra really did think about things like this—they'd had enough conversations on socio-political topics that this didn't seem out of line for her.

The problem was that even though Ender understood perfectly well what was going on, he was enjoying it. He didn't want it to stop.

But it had to stop. Stop or change. The back-rubbing thing couldn't go on forever.

And he couldn't stop it abruptly. He had a role to play. Morgan had to believe that Ender was devoted to Alessandra, so that by marrying Dorabella, he would become Ender's future father-in-law. One more set of levers to control him by. Ender had planned to do it platonically. The time he spent with Alessandra, the attention he devoted to her, that would do the job.

Until now. Now they were pushing him. Through Alessandra—for Ender did not believe she had thought of this little encounter herself. "Thinking about your mother and Admiral Morgan?" said Ender. "Getting jealous?"

That got her to pull her hands away. "No," she said. "Not at all. What does rubbing your shoulders have to do with them getting married?"

Now, with her no longer touching him, Ender could swivel the chair around to face her. She was dressed . . . differently. Nothing obvious, not like the vids he'd seen of supposedly sexy fashions on Earth. She was wearing clothing he'd seen before. But a button less was fastened. Was that the only difference? Perhaps, because she had been touching him until a moment before, he was seeing her through new eyes.

"Alessandra," he said, "let's not pretend we don't know what's happening here."

"What do you think is happening?" she said.

"I was asleep, and you did what you've never done before."

"I never felt like that before," she said. "I saw how heavy a weight you carry. Not just the governorship and all that, I mean . . . all that came before. The weight of being Ender Wiggin. I know you don't like to be touched, but that doesn't mean other people can't want to touch you."

Ender reached out and touched her hand, hooked it lightly in his fingers. He knew even as he did it that he shouldn't. Yet the desire to do it was almost overwhelming, and a part of him said, There's no danger in this. Touching hands? People do it all the time.

Yes, and they do other things all the time, another part of his mind said.

Shut up, said the part that liked touching Alessandra.

What if this did go according to Alessandra's script—or her mother's. Were there worse fates? He was coming to a colony world. Colonies were all about reproduction. He liked this girl. There wasn't going to be a huge pool of girls to choose from in the colony; there were few his age among the passengers in stasis, so it would be mostly the girls born on Shakespeare that he would have to choose from, and they would be—not from Earth.

While he argued with himself, she held his hand more tightly and moved closer to him. Beside him. Now he could feel her warmth—or imagined he could. Now her body touched his upper arm; now her other hand, the one he was not holding, stroked his hair. Now she brought his hand up to her chest. Pressed the back of his hand, not to her breast—that would be too obvious—but to her chest, where her heart was beating. Or was that his own pulse he felt pounding in his hand?

"On this voyage I've come to know you," she whispered. "Not the famous boy who saved the world, but this teenager, this young man of about my own age, so careful, so thoughtful of other people, so patient with them. With me, with my mother. You think I haven't seen that? Never wanting to hurt anyone, never wanting to offend, but never letting anyone come close, either, except your sister. Is that your future, Ender? You and your sister, in a circle that lets no one else inside?"

Yes, thought Ender. That's what I decided. When Valentine showed up, I thought: Yes, I can let her in. I can trust this one person.

I can't trust you, Alessandra, thought Ender. You're here in service of someone else's plans. Maybe you mean what you're saying, maybe you're sincere. But you're also being used. You are a weapon aimed at my heart. Someone dressed you today. Someone told you what to do, and how to do it. Or if you really know all this yourself, then you're too much for me. I'm too caught up in this. I want too much for it to go forward as you seem to be offering.

I will not let this go on, thought Ender.

But even with that decision, he couldn't just leap to his feet and say, Get thee hence, temptress, like Joseph did with Potiphar's wife. He would have to make her *want* to stop, so that it would never seem to Admiral Morgan that he refused her. Morgan would certainly watch the playback of this. On the eve of his own marriage, Morgan could not see Ender absolutely refuse Alessandra.

"Alessandra," said Ender, speaking just as softly as she was. "Do you really want to live your mother's life?"

For the first time, Alessandra hesitated, uncertain.

Ender took his hand back, leaned on the chair's armrests, rose to his feet. He reached for her, gathered her into an embrace, and decided that for this to work, he would need to kiss her.

So he did. He was not good at it. To his relief, neither was she. It was awkward, they missed each other a little and had to re-center, and neither of them knew what they were actually supposed to do. Oddly enough, this kiss broke the mood and when they were done with it, they both laughed. "There," said Ender. "We've done it. Our first kiss. *My* first kiss, of anyone, ever."

"Mine too," she said. "The first one I've even wanted."

"We *could* go farther," said Ender. "We're both equipped for it—we make a complete matching set, I'm sure."

She laughed again. That's right, thought Ender. Laughing is the right mood, not the other.

"I meant what I said, about your mother," said Ender. "She did this, right at your age. Conceived you when she was fourteen, you were born when she was fifteen. The age you are now. And she married the boy, yes?"

"And it was wonderful," said Alessandra. "Mother told me, so many times, how happy she was with him. How good it was. How much they both loved me."

Of course your mother said that, thought Ender. She's a good person, she wouldn't want to tell you what a nightmare it was, being fifteen and having so much responsibility.

But maybe it *was* good, said another part of his mind. The part that was keenly aware that their bodies were still pressed together, that his fingers were pressing gently against the back of her shirt, moving slightly, caressing the skin and body under the cloth.

"Your mother was under the domination of someone stronger than her," said Ender. "Your grandmother. She wanted to get free."

That did it. Alessandra pulled away from him. "What are you saying? What do you know about my grandmother?"

"Only what your mother told me herself," said Ender. "In front of you."

He could see on her face that she remembered, and the flash of anger subsided. But she did not come back into his embrace. Nor did he invite her to. He thought more clearly when she was standing a half-meter away. A meter would be even better.

"My mother isn't anything like my grandmother," said Alessandra.

"Of course not," said Ender. "But the two of you have lived together your whole life. Very close all the time."

"I'm not trying to get away from her," said Alessandra. "I wouldn't use you like that." But her face showed something else. A recognition, perhaps, that she *had* been using him—that her whole visit to him was prompted by her mother.

"I was just thinking," said Ender, "that even the cheerful fairyland she likes to pretend she lives in—"

"When did you—" she began, and then stopped herself, because of course Dorabella had done her queen-of-the-fairies bit several times, to the delight of the other colonists.

"I was thinking," said Ender, "that after such a long while, you might not want to spend the rest of your life in her fairyland. Maybe your world is better for you than her imaginary places. That's all I was thinking. She's made a lovely cocoon for you, but maybe you still want to break out of it and fly."

Alessandra stood there, her hand to her mouth. Then tears came to her eyes. "Per tutte sante," she said. "I was . . . doing what she wanted. I thought it was my own idea, but it was hers, it was . . . I wanted you to like me, I really did, that wasn't made up, but the idea of coming here . . . I wasn't getting away from her, I was *obeying* her."

"You were?" Ender said, trying to act as if he hadn't already guessed.

"She told me just what to do, how far to . . ." Alessandra started unbuttoning her blouse, tears flowing. She was wearing nothing under it. "What you were going to see, what you could touch, but no more . . ."

Ender stepped to her, embraced her again, to stop her from unbuttoning any more. Because even in this emotional moment, there was a part of him that only cared about the blouse and what would be revealed, not about the girl who was doing it.

"You do care about me," she said.

"Of course I do," said Ender.

"More than she does," she said. Her tears were dampening his shirt.

"Probably not," said Ender.

"I wonder if she cares for me at all," said Alessandra into his chest. "I wonder if I've ever been anything more than her puppet, just the way she was Grandmother's. Maybe if Mother had stayed home and hadn't married and hadn't had *me*, Grandmother would have been full of fairyland and beauty—because she was getting her way."

Perfect, thought Ender. Despite my own impulses, my biological distractibility, this has gone exactly right. Admiral Morgan would see that even though the sex angle didn't play according to script, Ender and Alessandra were still close, still bonding—whatever he wanted to read into it. The game was still on. Even if the romance was definitely on hold.

"The door to this room can't lock," said Ender.

"I know," she said.

"Someone might come in at any time." He thought it was best not to point out that surveillance cameras were in every room, including most particularly this one, and someone could be watching them right now.

She took the hint, pulled away from him, rebuttoned her blouse. This time all the way up to where she usually buttoned it. "You saw through me," she said.

"No," said Ender. "I saw *you*. Maybe your mother doesn't."

"I know she doesn't," said Alessandra. "I know it. I'm just—it's just—Admiral Morgan, that's what it is, she said she was bringing me here to find a young man with prospects, but she found an old man with even *better* prospects, that's what it is, and I just fit into her plans, that's all, I—"

"Don't do this," said Ender. "Your mother loves you, this wasn't cynical, she thought she was helping you get what you wanted."

"Maybe," said Alessandra. Then she laughed bitterly. "Or is this just *your* version of fairyland? Everybody wants me to be happy, so they construct a fake reality around me. Yes, I want to be happy, but not with a lie!"

"I'm not lying to you," said Ender.

She looked at him fiercely. "Did you desire me? At all?"

Ender closed his eyes and nodded.

"Look at me and say it."

"I wanted you," said Ender.

"And now?"

"There are lots of things I want that aren't right for me to have."

"You sound as if your mother taught you to say that."

"If I'd been raised by my mother, maybe she would have," said Ender. "But as it is, I learned that when I decided to go to Battle School, when I decided to live by the rules of that place. There are rules to everything, even if nobody made them up, even if nobody calls it a game. And if you want things to work out well, it's best to know the rules and only break them if you're playing a different game and following *those* rules."

"Do you think that made sense of some kind?"

"To me it did," said Ender. "I want you. You wanted me. That's a nice thing to know. I had my first kiss."

"It wasn't bad, was it? I wasn't awful?"

"Let's put it this way," said Ender. "I haven't ruled out doing it again. Sometime in the future."

She giggled. The crying had stopped.

"I really do have work to do," said Ender. "And believe me, you woke me right up. Not sleepy at all. Very helpful."

She laughed. "I get it. Time for me to go."

"I think so," he said. "But I'll see you later. As we always do."

"Yes," said Alessandra. "I'll try not to act too giggly and strange."

"Act like yourself," said Ender. "You can't be happy if you're pretending all the time."

"Mother is."

"Which? Pretending? Or happy?"

"Pretending to be happy."

"So maybe you can grow up to be happy without having to pretend."

"Maybe," she said. And then she was gone.

Ender closed the door and sat down. He wanted to scream in frustration at thwarted desire, in rage at a mother who would send her daughter on such an errand, at Admiral Morgan for making all this necessary, at himself for being such a liar. "You can't be happy if you're pretending all the time." Well, his life certainly didn't contradict that statement. He was pretending all the time, and he certainly was not happy.

CHAPTER
15

To: GovDes%ShakespeareCol@colmin.gov/voy
From: vwiggin%ShakespeareCol@colmin.gov/voy
Subj: relax about it, kid

E:

Nothing about your behavior with A should either surprise or embarrass you. If desire did not dim the brain, nobody would ever get married, drunk, or fat.

-V

By the time Sel and Po had been a fortnight gone, with almost two hundred kilometers behind them, they had talked about every conceivable subject at least twice, and finally walked along in companionable silence most of the time, except when the exigencies of their journey forced them to speak.

One-sentence warnings: "Don't grab that vine, it's not secure."

Scientific speculations: "I wonder if that bright-colored froglike thing is venomous?"

"I doubt it, considering that it's a rock."

"Oh. It was so vivid I thought—"

"A good guess. And you're not a geologist, so how could you be expected to recognize a rock?"

Mostly there was nothing but their breathing, their footfalls, and the sounds and smells and sights of a new world revealing itself to the first of the human species to pass through this portion of it.

At two hundred clicks, though, it was time to stop. They had rationed carefully, but their food was half gone. They pitched a more permanent camp by a clear water source, chose a safe spot and dug a latrine, and pitched the tent with the stakes deeper and the ground more padded under the floor of it. They would be here for a week.

A week, because that's about how long they expected to be able to live on the meat of the two dogs they slaughtered that afternoon.

Sel was sorry that only two of the dogs were smart enough to extrapolate from the skins and carcasses that their human masters were no longer reliable companions. Those two left—they had to drive the other pair away with stones.

By now, like everyone else in the colony, both Sel and Po knew how to preserve meat by smoking it; they cooked only a little of the meat fresh, but kept the fire going to smoke the rest as it hung from the bending limbs of a fernlike tree . . . or treelike fern.

They marked out a rough circle on the satellite map they carried with them and each morning they set out in a different direction to see what they might find. Now they collected samples in earnest, and took photographs that they bounced to the orbiting transport ship for storage on the big computer there. The pictures they sent up, the test results, those were secure—they would not be lost, no matter what happened to Sel and Po.

The physical samples, though, were by far the most valuable items. Once they brought them back, they could be studied at great length using far more sophisticated equipment—the new equipment the xenos on the new colony ship would bring.

At night, Sel lay awake for long hours, thinking of what he and Po had seen, classifying it in his mind, trying to make sense of the biology of this world.

But when he woke up, he could not remember having had any great insights the night before, and certainly had none by morning light. No great breakthroughs; just a continuation of the work he had already done.

I should have gone north, into the jungles.

But jungles are far more dangerous to explore. I'm an old man. Jungles could kill me. This temperate plateau, colder than the colony because it's a little closer to the poles and higher in elevation, is also safer—at least in summer—for an old man who needs open country to hike through and nothing unusually dangerous to snag or snap at him.

On the fifth day, they crossed a path.

There was no mistaking it. It was not a road, certainly not, but that was no surprise, the formics had built few roads. What they made were paths, and those inadvertent, the natural result of thousands of feet treading the same route.

Those feet had trodden here, though it was forty years before. Trodden so long and often that after all these years, and overgrown as it was, the naked eye could trace the path of it through the pebbly soil of a narrow alluvial valley.

There was no question now of pursuing any more flora and fauna. The formics had found something of value here, and archaeology took precedence, at least for a few hours, over xenobiology.

The path wound upward into the hills, but not terribly far before it led to a number of cave entrances.

"These aren't caves," said Po.

"Oh?"

"They're tunnels. These are too new, and the land hasn't shaped itself around them the way that it does with real caves. These were dug as doorways. All the same height, do you see?"

"That damnably inconvenient height that makes it such a pain for humans to go inside."

"It's not our purpose here, sir," said Po. "We've found the spot. Let's call for others to explore the tunnels. We're here for the living, not the dead."

"I have to know what they were doing here. Certainly not farming—there's no trace of their crops gone wild here. No orchards. No middens, either—this wasn't a great settlement. And yet there was so much traffic, along that single path."

"Mining?" asked Po.

"Can you think of any other purpose? There's something in those tunnels that the formics thought was worth the trouble of digging out. In large quantities. For a long time."

"Not such large quantities," said Po.

"No?" said Sel.

"It's like steel-making back on Earth. Even though the purpose was smelting iron to make steel, and they mined coal only to fire their smelters and foundries, they didn't carry the coal to the iron, they carried the iron to the coal—because it took far more coal than iron to make steel."

"You must have gotten very good marks in geography."

"My parents and I were born here, but I'm human. Earth is still my home."

"So you're saying that whatever they took out of these tunnels, it wasn't in such large quantities that it was worth building a city here."

"They put their cities where the food was, or the fuel. Whatever they got here, they took little enough of it that it was more economical to carry it to their cities, instead of building a city here to process it."

"You may grow up to amount to something, Po."

"I'm already grown up, sir," said Po. "And I already amount to something. Just not enough to get any girl to marry me."

"And knowing the principles of Earth's economic history will attract a mate?"

"As surely as that bunny-toad's antlers, sir."

"Horns," said Sel.

"So we're going in?"

Sel mounted one of the little oil lamps into the flared top of his walking stick.

"And here I thought that opening at the top of your stick was decoration," said Po.

"It *was* decorative," said Sel. "It was also the way the tree grew out of the ground."

Sel rolled up his blankets and put half the remaining food into his pack, along with their testing equipment.

"Are you planning to spend the night down there?"

"What if we find something wonderful, and then have to climb back out of the tunnels before we get a chance to explore?"

Dutifully, Po packed up. "I don't think we'll need the tent in there."

"I doubt there'll be much rain," Sel agreed.

"Then again, caves can be drippy."

"We'll pick a dry spot."

"What can live in there? It's not a natural cave. I don't think we'll find fish."

"There are birds and other creatures that like the dark. Or that find it safer and warmer indoors. And maybe a species of some chordate or insect or worm or fungus we haven't seen yet."

At the entrance, Po sighed. "If only the tunnels were higher."

"It's not *my* fault you grew so tall." Sel lit the lamp, fueled by the oils of a fruit Sel had found in the wild. He called it "olive" after the oily fruit on Earth, though in no other attribute were they alike. Certainly not flavor or nutrition.

The colonists grew it in orchards now, and pressed and filtered it in three harvests a year. Except for the oil the fruit was good for nothing except fertilizer. It was good to have clean-burning fuel for light, instead of wiring every building with electricity, especially in the outlying settlements. It was one of Sel's favorite discoveries—particularly since there was no sign the formics had ever discovered its usefulness. Of course, the formics were at home in the dark. Sel could imagine them scuttling along in these tunnels, content with smell and hearing to guide them.

Humans had evolved from creatures that took refuge in trees, not caves, thought Sel, and though humans had used caves many times in the past, they were always suspicious of them. Deep dark places were at once attractive and terrifying. There was no chance the formics would have allowed any large predators to remain at large on this planet, particularly in caves, since the formics themselves were tunnel makers and cave dwellers.

If only the formic home world had not been obliterated in the war. What we could have learned, tracing an alien evolution that led to intelligence!

Then again, if Ender Wiggin had not blown the whole thing up, we would have lost the war. Then we wouldn't have even *this* world to study. Evolution here did not lead to intelligence—or if it did, the formics already wiped it out, along with any traces the original sentient natives might have left behind.

Sel bent over and squat-walked into the tunnel. But it was hard to keep going that way—his back was too old. He couldn't even lean on his stick, because it was too tall for the space, and he had to drag it along, keeping it as close to vertical as possible so the oil didn't spill out of the canister at the top.

After a while he simply could not continue in that position. Sel sat down and so did Po.

"This is not working," said Sel.

"My back hurts," said Po.

"A little dynamite would be useful."

"As if you'd ever use it," said Po.

"I didn't say it would be morally defensible," said Sel. "Just convenient." Sel handed his stick, with the lamp atop it, to Po. "You're young. You'll recover from this. I've got to try a new position."

Sel tried to crawl but instantly gave up on that—it hurt his knees too much to rest them directly on the rocky floor. He finally settled for sitting, leaning his arms forward, putting weight on them, and then scrabbling his legs and hips after him. It was slow going.

Po also tried crawling and soon gave up on it. But because he was holding the stick with the light, he was forced to return to walking bent over, knees in a squat.

"I'm going to end up a cripple," said Po.

"At least I won't have to hear your mother and father complain about what I did to you, since I don't expect to get out of here alive."

And then, suddenly, the light went dim. For a moment Sel thought it had gone out, but no—Po had stood up and lifted the stick to a vertical position, so that the tunnel where Sel was creeping along was now in shadow.

It didn't matter. Sel could see the chamber ahead. It was a natural cavern, with stalactites and stalagmites forming columns that supported the ceiling.

But they weren't the straight-up-and-down columns that normally formed when lime-laden water dripped straight down, leaving sediment behind. These columns twisted crazily. Writhed, really.

"Not natural deposits," said Po.

"No. These were made. But the twisting doesn't seem designed, either."

"Fractal randomness?" asked Po.

"I don't think so," said Sel. "Random, yes, but genuinely so, not fractal. Not mathematical."

"Like dog turds," said Po.

Sel stood looking at the columns. They did indeed have the kind of curling pattern that a long dog turd got as it was laid down from above. Solid yet flexible. Extrusions from above, only still connected to the ceiling.

Sel looked up, then took the stick from Po and raised it.

The chamber seemed to go on forever, supported by the writhing stone pillars. Arches like an ancient temple, but half melted.

"It's composite rock," said Po.

Sel looked down at the boy and saw him with a self-lighting microscope, examining the rock of a column.

"Seems like the same mineral composition as the floor," said Po. "But grainy. As if it had been ground up and then glued back together."

"But not glued," said Sel. "Bonded? Cement?"

"I think it's been glued," said Po. "I think it's organic."

Po took the stick back and held the flame of the lamp under an elbow of one of the twistiest columns. The substance did not catch fire, but it did begin to sweat and drip.

"Stop," said Sel. "Let's not bring the thing down on us!"

Now that they could walk upright, they moved forward into the cavern. It was Po who thought of marking their path by cutting off bits of his blanket and dropping them. He looked back from time to time to make sure they were following a straight line. Sel looked back, too, and saw how impossible it would be to find the entrance they had come through, if the path were not marked.

"So tell me how this was made," said Sel. "No toolmarks on the ceiling or floor. These columns, made from ground-up stone with added glue. A kind of paste, yet strong enough to support the roof of a chamber this size. Yet no grinding equipment left behind, no buckets to carry the glue."

"Giant rock-eating worms," said Po.

"That's what I was thinking, too," said Sel.

Po laughed. "I was joking."

"I wasn't," said Sel.

"How could worms eat rock?"

"Very sharp teeth that regrow quickly. Grinding their way through. The fine gravel bonds with some kind of gluey mucus and they extrude these columns, then bind them to the ceiling."

"But how could such a creature evolve?" said Po. "There's no nutrition in the rock. And it would take enormous energy to do all this. Not to mention whatever their teeth were made of."

"Maybe they didn't evolve," said Sel. "Look—what's that?"

There was something shiny ahead. Reflecting the lamplight.

As they got closer, they saw reflections from spots on the columns, too. Even the ceiling.

But nothing else was as bright as the thing lying on the floor.

"A glue bucket?" asked Po.

"No," said Sel. "It's a giant bug. Beetle. Ant. Something like—look at this, Po."

They were close enough now to see that it was six-legged, though the middle pair of limbs seemed more designed for clinging than walking or grasping. The front ones were for grasping and tearing. The hind ones, for digging and running.

"What do you think? Bipedal?" asked Sel.

"Six or four, and bipedal at need." Po nudged it with his foot. No response. The thing was definitely dead. He bent over and flexed and rotated the hind limbs. Then the front ones. "Climb, crawl, walk, run, all equally well, I think."

"Not a likely evolutionary path," said Sel. "Anatomy tends to commit one way or the other."

"Like you said. Not evolved, bred."

"For what?"

"For mining," said Po. He rolled the thing over onto its belly. It was very heavy; it took several tries. But now they could see much better what it was that caught the light. The thing's back was a solid sheet of gold. As smooth as a beetle's carapace, but so thick with gold that the thing must weigh ten kilos at least.

Twenty-five, maybe thirty centimeters long, thick and stubby. And its entire exoskeleton thinly gilt, with the back heavily armored in gold.

"Do you think these things were mining for gold?" asked Po.

"Not with that mouth," said Sel. "Not with those hands."

"But the gold got inside it somehow. To be deposited in the shell."

"I think you're right," said Sel. "But this is the adult. The harvest. I think the formics carried these things out of the mine and took them off to be purified. Burn off the organics and leave the pure metal behind."

"So they ingested the gold as larvae . . ."

"Went into a cocoon . . ."

"And when they emerged, their bodies were encased in gold."

"And there they are," said Sel, holding up the light again. Only now he went closer to the columns, where they could now see that the glints of reflection were from the bodies of half-formed creatures, their backs embedded in the pillars, their foreheads and bellies shiny with a layer of thin gold.

"The columns are the cocoons," said Po.

"Organic mining," said Sel. "The formics bred these things specifically to extract gold."

"But what for? It's not like the formics used money. Gold is just a soft metal to them."

"A useful one. What's to say they didn't have bugs just like these, only bred to extract iron, platinum, aluminum, copper, whatever they wanted?"

"So they didn't need tools to mine."

"No, Po—these *are* the tools. And the refineries." Sel knelt down. "Let's see if we can get any kind of DNA sample from these."

"Dead all this time?"

"There's no way these are native to this planet. The formics brought them here. So they're native to the formic home world. Or bred from something native there."

"Not necessarily," said Po, "or other colonies would have found them long before now."

"It took *us* forty years, didn't it?"

"What if this is a hybrid?" asked Po. "So it exists only on this world?"

By now, Sel was sampling DNA and finding it far easier than he thought. "Po, there's no way this has been dead for forty years."

Then it twitched reflexively under his hand.

"Or twenty minutes," said Sel. "It still has reflexes. It isn't dead."

"Then it's dying," said Po. "It has no strength."

"Starving to death, I bet," said Sel. "Maybe it just finished its metamorphosis and was trying to get to the tunnel entrance and stopped here to die."

Po took the samples from him and stowed them in Sel's pack.

"So these gold bugs are still alive, forty years after the formics stopped bringing them food? How long *is* the metamorphosis?"

"Not forty years," said Sel. He stood up, then bent over again to look at the gold bug. "I think these cocooned-up bugs embedded in the columns are young. Fresh." He stood up and started striding deeper into the cavern.

There were more gold bugs now, many of them lying on the ground—but unlike the first one they found, many of these were destroyed, hollowed out. Nothing but the thick golden shells of their backs, with legs discarded as if they had been . . .

"Spat out," said Sel. "These were eaten."

"By what?"

"Larvae," said Sel. "Cannibalizing the adults because otherwise there's nothing to eat here. Each generation getting smaller—look how large this one is? Each one smaller because they only eat the bodies of the adults."

"And they're working their way back toward the door," said Po. "To get outside where the nutrients are."

"When the formics stopped coming . . ."

"Their shells are too heavy to make much progress," said Po. "So they get as far as they can, then the larvae feed on the corpse of the adult, then they crawl toward the light of the entrance as far as they can, cocoon up, and the next generation emerges, smaller than the last one."

Now they were among much larger shells. "These things are supposed to be more than a meter in length," said Sel. "The closer to the entrance, the smaller."

Po stopped, pointed at the lamp. "They're heading toward the light?"

"Maybe we'll be able to see one."

"Rock-devouring larvae that grind up solid rock and poop out bonded stone columns."

"I didn't say I wanted to see it up close."

"But you do."

"Well. Yes."

Now they were both looking around them, squinting to try to see movement somewhere in the cavern.

"What if there's something it likes much better than light?" asked Po.

"Soft-bodied food?" asked Sel. "Don't think I haven't thought of it. The formics brought them food. Now maybe we have, too."

At that moment, Po suddenly rose straight up into the air.

Sel held up the stick. Directly above him, a huge sluglike larva clung to the ceiling. Its mouth end was tightly fastened on Po's back.

"Unstrap and drop down here!" called Sel.

"All our samples!"

"We can always get more samples! I don't want to have to extract bits of *you* from one of these pillars!"

Po got the straps open and dropped to the floor.

The pack disappeared into the larva's maw. They could hear hard metal squeaking and scraping as the larva's teeth tried to grind up the metal instruments. They didn't wait to watch. They started toward the entrance. Once they passed the first gold bug's body, they looked for the bits of blanket to mark the path.

"Take my pack," said Sel, shrugging it off as he walked. "It's got the radio and the DNA samples in it—get out the entrance and radio for help."

"I'm not leaving you," said Po. But he was obeying.

"You're the only one who can get out the entrance faster than that thing can crawl."

"We haven't seen how fast it can go."

"Yes we have," said Sel. He walked backward for a moment, holding up the lamp.

The larva was about thirty meters behind them and coming on faster than they had been walking.

"Is it following the light or our body heat?" asked Po as they turned again and began to jog.

"Or the carbon dioxide of our breath? Or the vibrations of our footfalls? Or our heartbeats?" Sel held out the stick toward him. "Take it and run."

"What are you going to do?" said Po, not taking the stick.

"If it's following the light, you can stay ahead of it by running."

"And if it's not?"

"Then you can get out and call for help."

"While it has you for lunch."

"I'm tough and gristly."

"The thing eats stone."

"Take the light," said Sel, "and get out of here."

Po hesitated a moment longer, then took it. Sel was relieved that the boy would keep his promise of obedience.

Either that, or Po was convinced the larva would follow the light.

It was the right guess—as Sel slowed down and watched the larva approach, he could see that it was not heading directly toward him, but rather listed off to the side, heading for Po. And as Po ran, the larva began speeding up.

It went right past Sel. It was more than a half-meter thick. It moved like a snake, with a back-and-forth movement, writhing along the floor, shaping itself exactly like the columns, only horizontally and, of course, *moving*.

It was going to reach Po while he was scrambling through the tunnel.

"Leave the light!" shouted Sel. "Leave it!"

In a few moments, Sel could see the light leaning against the wall of the cavern, beside where the low tunnel began, leading toward the outside world. Po must already be inside the tunnel.

The larva was ignoring the light and heading into the tunnel behind Po. The larva didn't have to crawl or walk bent over—it would catch Po easily.

"No. No, stop!" But then he thought: What if Po hears me? "Keep going, Po! Run!"

And then, wordlessly, Sel shouted inside his mind: Stop and come back here! Come back to the cavern! Come back to your children!

Sel knew it was insane, but it was all he could think of to do. The formics communicated mind to mind. This was also a large insectoid life form from the formics' home world. Maybe he could speak to it the way the hive queens spoke to the individual worker and soldier formics.

Speak? That was asinine. They had no language. They wouldn't *speak*.

Sel stopped and formed in his mind a clear picture of the gold bug lying on the cavern floor. Only the legs were writhing. And as he pictured it, Sel tried to feel hungry, or at least remember how it felt to be hungry. Or to find hunger within himself—after all, he hadn't eaten for a few hours.

Then he pictured the larva coming to the gold bug. Circling it.

The larva reemerged from the tunnel. There had been no screaming from Po—it hadn't caught him. Maybe it got too near the sunlight and it blinded the larva and it couldn't go on. Or maybe it had responded to the images and feelings in Sel's mind. Either way, Po was safely outside.

Of course, maybe the larva had simply decided not to bother with the prey that was running, and had come back for the prey that was standing very still, pressing himself against a column.

To: GovDes%ShakespeareCol@ColMin.gov/voy
From: MinCol@ColMin.gob
Subj: As requested
Handshake key: 3390ac8d9afff9121001

Dear Ender,

As you have requested, I have sent a holographic message from me and Pole-march Bakossi Wuri to the ship's system, using the hook you inserted into the ship's ansible software. If your program runs as advertised, it will take over all the ship's communications. In addition, I have attached the official notification to Admiral Morgan for you to print out and hand to him.

I hope you have won his trust well enough that he will let you have the access you need to use any of this.

This message will leave no trace of its existence, once you delete it.

Good luck,
Hyrum

Admiral Morgan had been in communication with the *acting* acting governor, Ix Tolo—ridiculous name—because the official acting governor had had the bad manners to take off on a completely meaningless trip right when he was needed for the official public transfer of power. The man probably couldn't stand being displaced from his office. The vanity of some people.

Morgan's executive officer, Commodore das Lagrimas, confirmed that, as far as could be ascertained from orbit, the runway the colonists had constructed for the shuttle met the specifications. Thank heaven they didn't have to pave these things anymore—it must have been tedious in the days when flying vehicles had to land on wheels.

The only thing that worried him was bringing the Wiggin boy down with him for the first landing. It would be easy enough to tell the old settlers that Morgan had come ahead of Wiggin to prepare the way. That would give him plenty of chance to make sure they were aware that Wiggin was a teenage boy and hardly likely to be the real governor.

Dorabella agreed with him. But then she pointed out, "Of course, all the older people in this colony are the pilots and soldiers who fought under Ender's command. They might be disappointed not to see him. But no, it will make it all the more special when he comes down later."

Morgan thought about it and decided that having Wiggin with him might be more of an asset than not. Let them *see* the legendary boy. Which was why he called the Wiggin boy to his quarters.

"I don't know that you need to say anything to the colonists on this first occasion," said Admiral Morgan. This was the test—would Wiggin be miffed at being held in silence?

"Fine with me," said Wiggin instantly. "Because I'm not good at speeches."

"Excellent," said Morgan. "We'll have marines there in case these people are planning some sort of resistance—you never know, all their cooperation might be a ruse. Four decades on their own here—they might resent the imposition of authority from forty lightyears away."

Wiggin looked serious. "I never thought of that. Do you really think they might rebel?"

"No, I don't," said Morgan. "But a good commander prepares for everything. You'll acquire habits like that in time, I'm sure."

Wiggin sighed. "There's so much stuff to learn."

"When we get there, we'll put the ramp down at once and the marines will secure the immediate perimeter. When the people have assembled around the base of the ramp, then we'll come out. I'll introduce you, I'll say a few words, then you'll go back inside the shuttle until I can secure appropriate quarters for you in the settlement."

"Toguro," said Wiggin.

"What?"

"Sorry. Battle School slang."

"Oh, yes. Never went to Battle School myself." Of course the little brat had to give his little reminder that he had gone to Battle School and Morgan had not. But his use of slang was encouraging. The more childish Wiggin appeared, the easier it would be to marginalize him.

"When can Valentine come down?"

"We won't start bringing down the new colonists for several days. We have to make sure we do this in an orderly way—we don't want to swamp the old settlers with too many new ones before there's housing and food for them all. The same thing with supplies."

"We're going down empty-handed?" asked Wiggin, sounding surprised.

"Well, no, of course not," said Morgan. He hadn't thought of it that way. It *would* be a nice gesture to have some key supplies with them. "What do you think, some food? Chocolates?"

"They have better food than we do," said Ender. "Fresh fruits and vegetables—that's going to be their gift to *us*. I bet they'd go boky over the skimmers, though."

"Skimmers! That's serious technology."

"Well, it's not like they're any use up here in the ship," said Ender, laughing. "But some of the xeno equipment, then. Something to show them how much it's going to help them, now that we're here. I mean, if you're worried they'll resent us, giving them some really useful tech will make us heroes."

"Of course—that's what I was planning. I just didn't think of the skimmers on our *first* landing."

"Well, it'd sure help with carrying cargo to wherever it's going to be warehoused. I know they'd appreciate not having to lug stuff by hand or in carts or whatever they use for transportation."

"Excellent," said Morgan. "You're catching on to this leadership thing already." The kid really *was* clever. And Morgan would be the one to reap the good will that bringing the skimmers and other high-tech equipment would create. He would have thought of all this himself if he ever had a chance to stop and think about things. The boy could sit around and think about things, but Morgan couldn't afford the time. He was constantly on call, and though das Lagrimas handled most things well, Morgan also had to deal with Dorabella.

Not that she was demanding. In fact, she was amazingly supportive. Never interfered with anything, didn't try to butt in when it was none of her business. She never complained about anything, always fit in with his plans, always smiled and encouraged and sympathized but never tried to advise or suggest.

But she distracted him. In a good way. Whenever he wasn't actually busy with a meeting, he would find himself thinking about her. The woman was simply amazing. So willing. So eager to please. It was as if Morgan only had to think of something and she was doing it. Morgan found himself looking for excuses to go back to his quarters, and she was always there, always happy to see him, always eager to listen, and her hands, touching him, making it impossible for him to ignore her or leave as quickly as he should.

He'd heard from other people that marriage was hellish. The honeymoon lasts a day, they said, and then she starts demanding, insisting, complaining. All lies.

Maybe it was only like this with Dorabella. But if so, he was glad he had waited, so he could marry the one in a million who could make a man truly happy.

For he was besotted. He knew the men joked about it behind his back—he caught their smirks whenever he came back from a rendezvous with Dorabella for an hour or two in the middle of the working day. Let them have their laughs! It was all about envy.

"Sir?" asked Wiggin.

"Oh, yes," said Morgan. It had happened again—in the middle of a conversation, he had drifted off into thinking about Dorabella. "I have a lot on my mind, and I think we're through here. Just be in the shuttle at 0800—that's when we're closing the doors, everything loaded by the dawn watch. The descent will take several hours, the shuttle pilot tells me, but nobody will be able to sleep—you'll want to get to bed early tonight so you're well rested. And it's better to enter the atmosphere on an empty stomach, if you know what I mean."

"Yes sir," said Wiggin.

"Dismissed, then," said Morgan.

Wiggin saluted and left. Morgan almost laughed out loud. The kid didn't realize that even on Morgan's ship, Wiggin's seniority as a rear admiral entitled him to courtesies, including the right to leave when he felt like it instead of being dismissed like a subordinate. But it was good to keep the boy in his place. Just because he had the office of admiral bestowed on him before Morgan actually *earned* his didn't mean Morgan had to pretend to show respect to an ignorant teenager.

Wiggin was in his place before Morgan got there, dressed in civilian clothes instead of military uniform—which was all to the good, since it would not be helpful for people to see that they had identical dress uniforms and rank insignias, while Ender had markedly more battle decorations. Morgan merely nodded to Wiggin and went to his own seat, in the front of the shuttle with a communications array at his disposal.

At first the shuttle flight was normal space travel—smooth, perfectly controlled. But as they orbited the planet and then dipped down into their point of entry, the shuttle reoriented itself to have the shield meet and dissipate the heat, which is when the bouncing and yawing and rolling began. As the pilot told him beforehand, "Roll and yaw mean nothing. If we start to pitch, *then* we've got problems."

Morgan found himself quite nauseated by the time they steadied out into smooth flight at ten thousand meters. But poor Wiggin—the boy practically *flew* back to the head, where he was no doubt retching his poor head off. Unless the kid had forgotten not to eat and really had something to puke up.

The landing went smoothly, but Wiggin hadn't returned to his seat— he took the landing in the head. And when the marines reported that the people were gathering, Wiggin was still inside.

Morgan went to the door of the head himself and rapped on it. "Wiggin," he said, "it's time."

"Just a few more minutes, sir," said Wiggin. His voice sounded weak and shaky. "Really. Looking at the skimmers will keep them busy for a few minutes, and then they'll meet us with a cheer."

It hadn't crossed Morgan's mind to send the skimmers out ahead of his own entrance, but Wiggin was right. If the people had already seen something wonderful from Earth technology, it would make them all the more enthusiastic when he came out himself. "They can't watch the skimmers forever, Wiggin," said Morgan. "When it's time to go out, I hope you're ready to join me."

"I will," said Wiggin. But then another retching sound gave the lie to that statement.

Of course, retching sounds could be made with or without nausea. Morgan had a momentary suspicion and so he acted on it, opening the door without any warning.

There was Wiggin, kneeling in front of the john, his belly convulsing as his body arched with another retch. He had his jacket and shirt off, tossed on the floor near the door—at least the kid had thought ahead and arranged not to get vomit on his suit. "Anything I can do to help?" asked Morgan.

Wiggin looked at him, his face a mask of barely controlled nausea. "I can't keep this up forever," he said weakly, managing a faint smile. "I'll be fine in a minute."

And then he turned his face toward the bowl again. Morgan closed the door and suppressed a smile. So much for any worries that the kid might not cooperate. Wiggin was going to miss his own grand entrance, and it wasn't even going to be Morgan's fault.

Sure enough, the midshipman he sent for Wiggin returned with a message, not the boy. "He says he'll come out as soon as he can."

Morgan toyed with sending back word that he was *not* going to have Wiggin's late arrival distract from his own speech. But no, he could afford to be magnanimous. Besides, it didn't look as if Wiggin would be ready any time soon.

The air of Shakespeare was pleasant but strange; there was a light breeze, and it carried some kind of pollen on it. Morgan was quite aware that just by breathing, he might be poisoning himself with the blood-sucking worm that almost killed this colony at the start, but they had treatments for it, and they'd get their first dose in plenty of time. So he savored the smell of planetside air for the first time in ages—he had last been on Earth six years before this voyage began.

In the middle distance, the scenery was savannah-like—trees dotting the landscape here and there, lots of bushes. But on either side of the runway, there were crops growing, and he realized that the only way they could accommodate the runway was in the midst of their fields. They had to resent that—it was a good thing he had thought of sending out the skimmers first, to take their minds off the damage their landing had done to the crops.

The people were surprisingly numerous. He vaguely remembered that the hundreds in the original invasion force would now be more than two thousand, since they'd been reproducing like rabbits, even with the relatively few women in the original force.

What mattered most was that they were applauding when he came out. Their applause might be more for the skimmers than for him, but he was content with that, as long as there was no resistance.

His aides had set up a public address system, but Morgan didn't think they'd need it. The crowd was numerous, but many of them were children, and were so crowded together that from the top of the ramp they were all within easy hailing distance. Still, now that the lectern had been set up, it would look foolish of Morgan not to use it. So he strode to it and gripped it with both hands.

"Men and women of Shakespeare Colony, I bring the greetings of the International Fleet and the Ministry of Colonization."

He had expected applause for that, but . . . nothing.

"I am Rear Admiral Quincy Morgan, the captain of the ship that brought the new colonists, and new equipment and supplies, to your settlement."

Again, nothing. Oh, they were attentive, and not at all hostile, but they only nodded, and only a few of them. As if they were waiting. Waiting for what?

Waiting for Wiggin. The thought came to him like bile into his throat. They know that Wiggin is supposed to be their governor, and they're waiting for him.

Well, they'll find out soon enough just what Wiggin is—and isn't.

Then Morgan heard the sound of running footfalls from inside the shuttle and coming out onto the ramp. Wiggin couldn't have timed it better. This really *would* go more smoothly with him for the crowd to look at.

The crowd's attention shifted toward Wiggin, and Morgan smiled. "I give you . . ."

But they didn't hear his answer. They knew who it was. The applause and shouting overpowered Morgan's voice, even with the amplification, and he did not need to say Wiggin's name, because the crowd was shouting it.

Morgan turned to give a welcoming gesture to the boy, and was shocked to see that Wiggin was in full dress uniform. His decorations were almost obscenely vast—dwarfing anything on Morgan's chest. It was so ridiculous—Wiggin had been playing videogames, for all he knew, and here he was wearing decorations for every battle in the war, along with all the other medals he was given after his victory.

And the little bastard had deliberately deceived him. Wearing civilian clothes, and then changing in the bathroom, just so he could upstage him. Was the nausea all faked, too, so that he could make this grand entrance? Well, Morgan would wear a phony smile and then he'd make the kid pay for this later. Maybe he wouldn't keep Wiggin as a figurehead after all.

But Wiggin didn't go to the place that Morgan was gesturing him to take at his side, behind the lectern. Instead, Wiggin handed a folded piece of paper to Morgan and then jogged on down the ramp to the ground— where he was immediately surrounded by the crowd, their shouts of "Ender Wiggin!" now giving way to chatter and laughter.

Morgan looked at the paper. On the outside, in pencil, Wiggin had written: "Your supremacy ended when this shuttle touched ground. Your authority ends at the bottom of this ramp." And he signed it, "Admiral Wiggin"—reminding him that in port, Wiggin was senior to him.

The gall of the boy. Did he think such claims would hold up here, forty years away from any higher authority? And when it was Morgan who commanded a contingent of highly trained marines?

Morgan unfolded the paper. It was a letter. From Polemarch Bakossi Wuri and Minister of Colonization Hyrum Graff.

Ender recognized Ix Tolo immediately, from Vitaly's description of him, and ran right up to him. "Ix Tolo," he shouted as he came. "I'm glad to meet you!"

But even before he reached Tolo and shook his hand, Ender was looking for old men and women. Most of them were surrounded by younger people, but Ender sought them out and tried to recognize the younger faces he had studied and memorized before this voyage even launched.

Fortunately, he guessed right about the first one, and the second one, calling them by rank and name. He made it solemn, that first meeting with the pilots who had actually fought in the war. "I'm proud to meet you at last," he said. "It's been a long wait."

At once the crowd caught on to what he was doing, and backed away, thrusting the old people forward so Ender could find them all. Many of them wept as they shook Ender's hands; some of the old women insisted on hugging him. They tried to speak to him, to tell him things, but he smiled and held up a hand, signaling, Wait a minute, there are more to greet.

He shook every soldier's hand, and when he occasionally guessed at the wrong name, they laughingly corrected him.

Behind him, there was still silence from the loudspeakers. Ender had no idea what Morgan would do about the letter, but he had to keep things moving forward here on the ground, so there was never a gap in which Morgan could insert himself.

The moment he had shaken the last old man's hand, Ender raised that hand up and then turned around, signaling for the people to gather around him. They did—in fact, they already had, so he was now completely surrounded by the crowd. "There are names I didn't get to call," he said. "Men and women I didn't get to meet." Then, from memory, he spoke the names of all those who had died in the battle. "Too many lost. If only I had known what price was being paid for my mistakes, maybe I could have made fewer of them."

Oh, they wept at that, even as some of them called out, "What mistakes!"

And then Ender reeled off another list of names—the colonists who had died in those first weeks of the settlement. "By their deaths, by your heroic efforts, this colony was established. Governor Kolmogorov told me about how you lived, what you accomplished. I was still a twelve-year-old boy on Eros when you were fighting the war against the diseases of this land, and you triumphed without any help from me."

Ender raised his hands to face level and clapped them, loudly and solemnly. "I honor those who died in space, and those who died here."

They cheered.

"I honor Vitaly Kolmogorov, who led you for thirty-six years of war and peace!" Another cheer. "And Sel Menach, a man so modest he could not bear to face the attention he knew would be paid to him today!" Cheers and laughter. "Sel Menach, who will teach me everything I need to know in order to serve you. Because I'm here, he will now have time to get back to his *real* work." A roar of laughter, and a cheer.

And now, from the back of the crowd, from the loudspeakers, came the sound of Morgan's voice. "Men and women of Shakespeare Colony, please forgive the interruption. This was not how the program for today was supposed to go."

The people around Ender glanced in puzzlement toward the top of the ramp. Morgan was speaking in a pleasant, perhaps jocular tone. But he was irrelevant to what had just been happening. He was an intruder in this ceremony. Didn't he see that Ender Wiggin was a victorious commander meeting with his veterans? What did Quincy Morgan have to do with that?

Hadn't he read the letter?

Morgan could only spare half his attention for the letter, he was so furious at Wiggin for heading straight into the crowd. What was he doing? Did he actually know these people's *names*?

But then the letter began to register with him and he read it with his full attention.

Dear Rear Admiral Morgan,

Former Polemarch Chamrajnagar, before his retirement, warned us that there was some risk that you would misunderstand the limited nature of your responsibilities upon reaching Shakespeare Colony. He takes full responsibility for any such misunderstanding, and if he was mistaken, we apologize for the actions we have taken. But you must understand that we were compelled to take preventive measures in case you had been misled into thinking that you were to exercise even momentary authority on the surface of the planet. We have been careful to make sure that if you behave with exact correctness, no one but you and Vice-Admiral Andrew Wiggin will ever know how we were prepared to deal with the situation if you acted inappropriately.

Correct action is this: You will recognize that upon setting foot on Shakespeare, Vice-Admiral Wiggin becomes Governor Wiggin, with absolute authority over all matters concerning the colony and all transfers of persons and material to and from the colony. He retains his rank of Vice-Admiral, so that outside your actual ship, he is your superior officer and you are subject to his authority.

You will return to your ship without setting foot on the planet. You will not meet with any persons from the colony. You will provide a full and orderly transfer of all cargos and persons from your ship to the colony, exactly as Governor Wiggin specifies. You will make all your actions transparent to IFCom and ColMin by reporting hourly by ansible on all actions taken in compliance with Governor Wiggin's orders.

We assume that this is what you intended to do all along. However, because of Polemarch Chamrajnagar's warning, we anticipate the possibility that you had different plans, and that you might consider acting on them. The forty-year voyage between us and you made it necessary for us to take actions which we can and will reverse upon your successful completion of this mission and your return to lightspeed.

Every twelve hours, Governor Wiggin will report to us by holographic ansible, assuring us of your compliance. If he fails to report, or seems to us to be under duress of any kind, we will activate a program now embedded in your ship's computer. The program will also be activated by any attempt to rewrite the program itself or restore an earlier state of the software.

This program will consist of the vocal and holographic transmission to the ansibles aboard your ship and shuttles, through every speaker and computer display on your ship and shuttles, and to every ansible in Shakespeare Colony, stating that you are charged with mutiny, ordering that no one obey you, and that you be arrested and placed in stasis for the return voyage to Eros, where you will be tried for mutiny.

We regret that the existence of this message will certainly cause offense to you if you did not plan to behave any way other than correctly. But in that case, your correct actions will ensure that no one sees this message, and when you have returned to lightspeed flight after successfully carrying out your mission, the message will be eliminated from your ship's computer and there will be no record whatsoever of this action. You will return with full honors and your career will continue without blemish.

A copy of this letter has been sent to your executive officer, Commodore Vlad das Lagrimas, but he cannot open it as long as Governor Wiggin continues to certify to us that you are taking correct actions.

Since yours is the first colony ship to arrive at its destination, your actions will establish the precedent for the entire I.F. We look forward to reporting on your excellent actions to the entire fleet.

> Sincerely,
> Polemarch Bakossi Wuri
> Minister of Colonization Hyrum Graff

Morgan read the letter, filled with rage and dread at first, but gradually taking a very different attitude. How could they imagine that he planned anything other than to oversee Wiggin's orderly assumption of power? How dare Chamrajnagar tell them anything that would lead them to think he intended anything else?

He would have to send them a very stiff letter informing them of his disappointment that they would treat him in this high-handed and completely unnecessary way.

No, if he sent a letter it would go into the record. He had to keep his record clean. And they were going to make a lot of hoopla about his being the first captain of a colony ship to complete his mission—that would be a huge plus for his career.

He had to act as if this letter didn't exist.

The crowd was cheering. They had been cheering and clapping over and over again while Morgan read the letter. He looked out to see that they were now completely surrounding Wiggin, none of them even glancing at the shuttle, at the ramp, at Admiral Morgan. Now that he was looking at them, he could see that everyone was gazing intently at Ender Wiggin, devotedly, eagerly. Every word he said, they cheered at, or laughed, or wept.

Incredibly, they loved him.

Even without this letter, even without any intervention from IFCom or ColMin, Morgan lost this power struggle from the moment Ender Wiggin appeared in full uniform and called the veterans by name and invoked their memories of the dead. Wiggin knew how to win their hearts, and he did it without deception or coercion. All he did was care enough to learn their names and faces and remember them. All he did was lead them in victory forty-one years ago. When Morgan was in charge of a supply operation in the asteroid belt.

For all I know, this letter is a complete bluff. Wiggin wrote it himself. Just to keep me distracted while he carried out his public relations coup. If I decided to be obstructive, if I decided to work behind his back to undermine their confidence in him, to destroy him as governor so that I would *have* to step in and . . .

The people cheered again, as Wiggin invoked the name of the acting governor.

No, Morgan would never be able to undermine their confidence in Wiggin. They wanted him to be their governor. While to them, Morgan was nothing. A stranger. An interloper. They weren't in the I.F. anymore. They didn't care about authority or rank. They were citizens of this colony now, but they had the legend of how they were founded. The great Ender Wiggin, by his victory, slew all the formics on the surface of this world, opening the land to these humans so they could come and dwell here. And now Wiggin had come among them in person. It was like the second coming of Christ. Morgan had zero chance now.

His aides were watching him intently. They had no idea what was in the letter, but he was afraid that his face might not have been as impassive as he'd meant, while he was reading it; in fact, his impassivity would be a strong message in itself. So now Morgan smiled at them. "Well, so much for our script. It seems Governor Wiggin had his own plans for how this day would go. It would have been nice of him to inform us, but . . . there's no accounting for the pranks that boys will play."

His aides chuckled, because they knew he expected them to. Morgan knew perfectly well that they understood exactly what had happened here. Not the threats in the letter, but Wiggin's complete triumph. Nevertheless, Morgan would act as if this was exactly how things were always meant to turn out, and they would join him in acting that way, and ship's discipline would be maintained.

Morgan turned to the microphone. In a lull in the cheering and shouting of the crowd, he spoke, taking a friendly, joking tone. "Men and women of Shakespeare Colony, please forgive the interruption. This was not how the program for today was supposed to go."

The crowd turned toward him, distractedly, even annoyed. They immediately turned back to Wiggin, who faced Morgan, not with the jaunty smile of victory, but with the same solemn face that he always presented on the ship. The little bastard. He'd been plotting this the whole time, and never showed a sign of it. Even when Morgan looked over the vids of him in his quarters, even when he watched Wiggin with Dorabella's daughter, the boy never let his pretense lapse, not for a second.

Thank the stars he'll be staying on this world, and not returning to be my rival for preeminence in the I.F.

"I won't take but a moment more of your time," said Morgan. "My men will immediately unload all the equipment we brought with us, and the marines will stay behind to assist Governor Wiggin however he might desire. I will return to the ship and will follow Governor Wiggin's instructions as to the order and timing of the transfer of materials and persons from the ship to the ground. My work here is done. I commend you for your achievements here, and thank you for your attention."

There was scattered applause, but he knew that most of them had tuned him out and were merely waiting for him to be done in order to get back to lionizing Andrew Wiggin.

Ah well. When he got back to the ship, Dorabella would be there. It was the best thing he had ever done, marrying that woman.

Of course, he had no idea how she would take the news that she and her daughter would not be colonists after all—that they would be staying with him on his voyage back to Earth. But how could they complain? Life in this colony would be primitive and hard. Life as the wife of an admiral—the very admiral who was first to bring new settlers and supplies to a colony world—would be a pleasant one, and Dorabella would thrive in such social settings; the woman really was brilliant at it. And the daughter—well, she could go to university and have a normal life. No, not normal, exceptional—because Morgan's position would be such that he could guarantee her the finest opportunities.

Morgan had already turned to go back inside the shuttle when he heard Wiggin's voice calling to him. "Admiral Morgan! I don't think the people here have understood what you have done for us all, and they need to hear it."

Since Morgan had the words of Graff's and Wuri's letter fresh in his mind, he could not help but hear irony and bad intent in Wiggin's words. He almost decided to keep moving back into the shuttle, as if he hadn't heard the boy.

But the boy was the governor, and Morgan had his own command to think about. If he ignored the boy now, it would look to his own men like an acknowledgment of defeat—and a rather cowardly one at that. So, to preserve his own position of respect, he turned to hear what the boy had to say.

"Thank you, sir, for bringing us all safely here. Not just me, but the colonists who will join with the original settlers and native-born of this world. You have retied the links between the home of the human race and these far-flung children of the species."

Then Wiggin turned back to the colonists. "Admiral Morgan and his crew and these marines you see here did not come to fight a war and save the human race, and none of them will die at the hands of our enemies. But they made one great sacrifice that is identical to one made by the original settlers here. They cut themselves loose from all that they knew and all that they loved and cast themselves out into space and time to find a new life among the stars. And every new colonist on that ship has given up everything they had, betting on their new life here among you."

The colonists spontaneously began applauding, a few at first, but soon all of them, and then cheering—for Admiral Morgan, for the marines, for the unmet colonists still on the ship.

And the Wiggin boy, damn him, was saluting. Morgan had no choice but to return the salute and accept the gratitude and respect of the colonists as a gift from him.

Then Wiggin strode toward the shuttle—but not to say anything more to Morgan. Instead, he walked toward the commander of the marine squad and called out to him by name. Had the boy learned the names of all of Morgan's crew and marines as well?

"I want you to meet your counterpart," Wiggin said loudly. "The man who commanded the marines with the original expedition." He led him to an old man, and they saluted each other, and in a few moments the whole place was chaotic with marines being swarmed by old men and women and young ones as well.

Morgan knew now that little of what Wiggin had done was really about him. Yes, he had to make sure Morgan knew his place. He accomplished that in the first minute, when he distracted Morgan with the letter while he showed that he knew all the original settlers by name, and acted—with justification—as the commander of veterans meeting with them forty-one years after their great victory.

But Wiggin's main purpose was to shape the attitude that this community would have toward Morgan, toward the marines, toward the starship's crew, and, most important, toward the new colonists. He brought them together with a knowledge of their common sacrifice.

And the kid claimed that he didn't like making speeches. What a liar. He said exactly what needed saying. Next to him, Morgan was a novice. No, a fumbling incompetent.

Morgan made his way back inside the shuttle, pausing only to tell the waiting officers that Governor Wiggin would be giving them their orders about unloading the cargo.

Then he went to the bathroom, tore the letter into tiny pieces, chewed them into pulp, and spat the wad into the toilet. The taste of paper and ink nauseated him, and he retched a couple of times before he got control of himself.

Then he went into his communications center and had lunch. He was still eating it when a lieutenant commander supervised a couple of the natives in bringing in a fine mess of fresh fruits and vegetables, just as Wiggin had predicted. It was delicious, and afterward, Morgan napped until one of his aides woke him to tell him the unloading was finished, they had taken aboard a vast supply of excellent foodstuffs and fresh water, and they were about to take off to return to the ship.

"The Wiggin boy will make a fine governor, don't you think?" Morgan said.

"Yes, sir, I believe so, sir," said the aide.

"And to think I imagined that he might need help from me to get started." Morgan laughed. "Well, I have a ship to run. Let's get back to it!"

Sel watched warily as the larva made its way back into the cavern. Was it heading for him, or just returning the way he came? He might test it by moving, but then his very motion might draw its attention to him.

"Nice larva," whispered Sel. "How about some nice dried dog?"

When he reached for his pack, to extract the food, it wasn't there. Po had his pack.

But Sel had the little bag at his waist where he carried his own food for each day's hike. He opened it, took out the dried dog meat and the vegetables that he carried there, and tossed them toward the larva.

It stopped. It nudged the food lying on the ground. Just in case sending mental images had actually worked, Sel created a mental image of the food as being part of the belly of a dying gold bug. This is magical thinking, he told himself, to believe that what I form in my mind will affect the behavior of this beast. But at least it occupied his mind while he waited to see whether the larva liked its food in small batches, or large and on the hoof.

The larva rose up and plunged its gaping mouth down on the food like a remora attaching itself to a shark.

Sel could imagine a smaller version of the larva being exactly that—a remora, attaching itself to larger creatures to suck the blood out of them. Or to burrow into them?

He remembered the tiny parasites that had killed people when the colony was first formed. The ones Sel had invented blood additives to repel.

This creature *is* a hybrid. Half native to this world. Half derived from organisms of the formic world.

No, not "organisms." Derived from the formics themselves. The body structure was basically formicoid. It would take very creative and knowledgeable gene-splicing to construct a viable creature that combined attributes of two species growing out of such disparate genetic heritages. The result would be a species that was half formic, so that perhaps the hive queens could communicate with them mentally, control them like any other formics. Only they were still different enough that they didn't completely bond with the queen—so when this world's hive queen died, the gold bugs didn't.

Or maybe they already had a species they used for menial tasks, one that had a weak mental bond with the hive queens, and *that's* what they interbred with the parasitic worms. Those incredible teeth that could burrow right through leather, cloth, skin, and bone. But sentient, or nearly so. It could still be ruled by the hive queen's mind.

Or my mind. Did it come back at my summoning? Or was it simply taking the easy food first?

By now the larva had plunged down onto each of the bits of food and devoured them—along with a thin layer of the stone floor at each spot. The thing *was* hungry.

Sel formed a picture in his mind—a complicated one now. A picture of Sel and Po bringing food into the tunnel. Feeding the larva. He pictured himself and Po going in and out of the cave, bringing food. Lots of food. Leaves. Grain. Fruit. Small animals.

The larva came toward him, but then circled around him. Writhed around his legs. Like a constrictor? Did it have that snakelike pattern, too?

No. It didn't get tighter. It was more like a cat.

Then it pushed from behind. Nudging him toward the tunnel.

Sel obeyed. The thing understood. There was rudimentary communication going on.

Sel hurried to the tunnel, then knelt and sat and started to try to slide along as he had coming in.

The larve slid past him in the tunnel and then stopped. Waiting.

The image came into his mind, just a flash of it: Sel holding on to the larva.

Sel took hold of the creature's dry, articulated surface, and it began moving forward again. It was carefully not thrashing him against the wall, though he scraped now and then. It hurt and probably drew blood, but none of his bones broke and none of the lacerations were deep. Perhaps it was bred to give rides like this to formics when they were still alive. It wouldn't have bothered a formic to bash against the walls a little.

The larva stopped. But now Sel could see the light of day. So could the larva. It didn't go out there; it shied from the light and backed down the tunnel past Sel.

When Sel emerged into the daylight and stood up, Po ran to him and hugged him. "It didn't eat you!"

"No, it gave me a ride," he said.

Po wasn't sure how to make sense of this.

"All our food," said Sel. "I promised we'd feed it."

Po didn't argue. He ran to the pack and started handing food to Sel, who gathered it into a basket made by holding his shirt out in front of him. "Enough for the moment," said Sel.

In a few moments, he had his shirt off and stuffed with food. Then he started laboriously down the tunnel again. In moments the larva was there again, coiling around him. Sel opened the shirt and dropped the food. The larva began eating ravenously. Sel was still close enough to the entrance that he could squat-walk out again.

"We'll need more food," said Sel.

"What's food to the larva?" asked Po. "Grass? Bushes?"

"It ate the vegetables from my lunch pack."

"There's not going to be anything edible growing around here."

"Not edible to *us*," said Sel. "But if I'm right, this thing is half native to this world, and it can probably metabolize the local vegetation."

If there was one thing they knew how to do, it was identify the local flora. Soon they were shuttling shirtfuls of tuberous vegetables down the tunnel. They took turns carrying food to the larva.

———

Morgan had gone inside the shuttle; Ender had given his orders and the ship's crew was unloading the shuttle while the locals loaded up the skimmers and transported the cargo to the right places. Other people knew better than Ender how to direct and carry out these tasks, so he left them to it while Ix took him to the xeno station where Sel's ansible was waiting, amid the other communications equipment. "I just need to transmit a quick message back to Eros," Ender said.

While he was still composing it, the voice of young Po Tolo came in on the radio.

"No, I'm not your father," said Ender. "I'll call him."

He didn't have to—Ix had heard his voice, probably heard Po's voice on the radio, and he was there in a moment. Ender quickly finished his message while catching the gist of Ix's conversation with his son. Ender transmitted to Graff and Wuri just as Ix said, "We'll be there quicker than you can guess."

Ix turned to Ender. "We need to take a skimmer to Sel and Po. They're out of supplies."

Ender couldn't believe Sel would plan so badly that he could do anything as foolish as that. But before he could say anything, Ix went on.

"They've found a creature," said Ix. "At least a hybrid. Cave dweller. Six legs in the adult form. Huge wormlike larva. It can chew rock, but it doesn't metabolize it. It was starving, so they gave it all their food."

"He's such a generous man," said Ender.

"The skimmer can travel that far? Two hundred clicks, over uneven terrain?"

"Easily," said Ender. "It charges by solar, but the normal range is five hundred kilometers without a pause for recharge."

"I'm very glad you got here when you did."

"Not a coincidence," said Ender. "Sel left *because* I was coming, re-member?"

"But he didn't need to," said Ix.

"I know. But as I said, he's a generous man."

They had two of the skimmers loaded with food in about twenty min-utes, and along with experienced marines to pilot the things, Ender brought along Ix himself. They rode together on the more lightly loaded of the two.

Too bad none of the new xenos had been wakened yet—they would have killed for a chance to be along for the ride. But all in good time.

On the way, Ix explained to Ender as much as he had gleaned from talking to his son. "Po didn't want to leap to conclusions—he's a cau-tious boy—but from what he says, Sel thinks it's some kind of genetic merge between a formicoid species and a local worm—conceivably even the bloodworm that tried to wipe out our first generation."

"The one you take injections to control?"

"We have better methods now," said Ix. "Preventive rather than maintenance. They can't take hold. The original problem was that we were already deeply infected before we knew the problem existed—they had to be rooted out. But my generation never got the infection. You won't either. You'll see."

"Define 'formicoid,' " said Ender.

"Look, I'm not sure myself, Po and I didn't talk long. But . . . my guess is that he meant 'formicoid' the way we'd say 'mammalian' or even 'chordate,' rather than 'humanoid.' "

Ender looked a little disappointed. "You've got to understand, I'm a little obsessed with the formics. My old enemy, you know? Anything that might bring me closer to understanding them . . ."

Ix said nothing. Either he understood or he didn't. Either way, what *he* cared about was that both his son and his mentor were out there, without food and with a vastly important scientific discovery that would make waves on Earth and in all the colonies.

With only one satellite in the sky so far—the original transport ship— there was no way to triangulate a global positioning system. That would come later, when Morgan's people placed their network of geosyncs into orbit. For now, they depended entirely on the maps that had been generated before they landed, and Po's description of the route they would need to follow. Ender was impressed that the kid's instructions were perfect. Not a missed landmark, not a wrong turn. No delays at all.

Even proceeding cautiously, they made good time. They were there five hours after the call from Po, and it was still daylight, though it wouldn't be for much longer. As they skimmed into the valley with all its cave entrances, Ender saw with some amusement that the young man waving to them was no more than a year or two older than he was. Why had he been surprised that Po could do a good, reliable job? Hadn't Ender himself been doing a man's job for years?

Ix was off the skimmer almost before it stopped, and ran to his son and embraced him. Ender might be governor, but Ix was in charge here, giving instructions to the marines about where to park and unload. Ender authorized the instructions with a wink, and then set to work helping the men with their work. He was tall enough now that he could do a decent share of it, though not as much as two adult men with marine training. They found things to chat about while they worked, and Ender broached a subject that he'd been thinking about through most of the voyage.

"A world like this," said Ender, "almost makes you sorry to leave again, doesn't it?"

"Not me," said one of them. "Everything's so dirty. Give me shipboard life and crappy food!"

But the other one said nothing, just glanced at Ender and then looked away. So he was considering it. Staying. That was something Ender would have to negotiate with Morgan. He would be sorry if the way he thwarted Morgan's plans made it impossible to work out a way for some of the crew to stay. Still, there'd be time to figure it out. Work out a trade— because there had to be at least a few of the younger generation born here on Shakespeare who were longing to get out of this place, this tiny village, and see a wider world. It was the old tradition of the sea. And of the circus. Lose a few crew members in every port or town, but pick up a few others who have an itchy foot or a dreamy eye.

Out of the cavern emerged an old man, who took more than a few moments to straighten up from being inside the cave. He spoke for a few moments to Po and Ix, and then, as they headed inside the cavern, dragging a sledge filled with roots and fruits—a sledge that Ix had made sure they loaded onto a skimmer—Sel Menach turned to look at Ender for the first time.

"Ender Wiggin," he said.

"Sel Menach," said Ender. "Po said you had a giant worm situation going on here."

Sel looked at the marines, who had their hands on their sidearms. "No weapons needed. We're not exactly talking with the things, but they understand rudimentary images."

"Things?" asked Ender.

"While we were feeding the one, two others came up. I don't know if it's enough to sustain a breeding population, but it's better than coming upon a species when only one specimen is left alive. Or none."

" 'Formicoid' is a word that's been bandied about," said Ender.

"Can't be sure till we get the genetic material scoped and scanned," said Sel. "If they were really formics, they'd be dead. The adult bodies have carapaces; they're not furred, with an endoskeleton. Might not even be as close to formics as lemurs are to us—or they might be as close as chimps. But Ender," said Sel, his eyes glistening. "I talked to it. No, I thought to it. I gave it an image and it responded. And it gave me one back. Showed me how to hitch a ride on it through the tunnel."

Ender looked at Sel's scraped and torn clothing. "Rough ride."

"Rough *road*," said Sel. "The ride was fine."

"You know I came here for the formics," said Ender.

"Me too," said Sel, grinning. "To kill them."

"But now to understand them," said Ender.

"I think we've found a key here. Maybe not to every last door, but it'll open something." Then he put an arm across Ender's shoulder and led him away from the others. Ender usually disliked the arm-across-the-shoulder move—it was how one man asserted superiority over another. But there was no hint of that in Sel. It was more like an assertion of camaraderie. Even conspiracy. "I know we can't talk openly," said Sel, "but give it to me straight. Are you governor or not?"

"In fact as well as name," said Ender. "The threat was averted and he's back on the ship, cooperating as if that's all he ever intended."

"Maybe it was," said Sel.

Ender laughed. "And maybe this larva you've found will teach us calculus before the day is out."

"I'll be happy if it knows how to count to five."

Later, after night fell and the men sat around a fire eating the fresh, easily spoiled food Po's mother had sent for tonight's supper, Sel was expansive, full of speculation, full of hope. "These creatures metabolize gold and extrude it in their carapaces. Maybe they do it with whatever metal is in the ore, or maybe they bred separate subspecies for each metal they needed. Maybe this isn't the only population with survivors. Maybe we can locate iron miners, copper miners, tin, silver, aluminum, anything we need. But if this group is average, then we'll find some groups that are all dead, and some that have larger populations. It would be too freakish for this to be the last surviving group in the world."

"We'll get on it right away," said Ender. "While we still have marines from the ship to help in the search. And they can take . . . locals with them to learn how to fly the skimmers like experts before the ship goes away."

Ix laughed. "You almost said 'natives' instead of 'locals.' "

"Yes," Ender admitted freely. "I did."

"It's all right," said Ix. "The formics didn't evolve here either. So 'native' just means 'born here,' and that describes me and Po—everybody except the ancient ones of Sel's generation. Natives and newcomers, but in the next generation, we'll all be natives."

"Then you think that's the term we should use?"

"Native Shakespearians," said Ix. "That's what we are."

"I hope we don't have to do some kind of blood ceremony or initiation to be accepted into the tribe."

"No," said Ix. "White man bringing skimmer is always welcome."

"Just because I'm white doesn't mean—" Then Ender saw the laughter in Ix's eyes and smiled. "I'm too eager not to give offense," said Ender. "So eager I was too quick to *take* offense."

"You'll get used to our Mayan sense of humor eventually," said Ix.

"No he won't," said Sel. "Nobody else has gotten used to it, anyway."

"Everybody but you, old man," said Ix.

Sel laughed along with the others, and then the conversation took another turn, with the marines describing their training, and talking about what life was like on Earth and in the high-tech society that moved throughout the solar system.

Ender noticed Sel getting a faraway look in his eyes, and misunderstood what it meant. As they prepared for sleep, Ender took a moment to ask Sel, "Do you ever give any thought to going back? Home? To Earth?"

Sel visibly shuddered. "No! What would I do there? Here's where everyone and everything I love and care about are." Then he got that wistful look again. "No, I just can't help but think that it's just a damn *shame* that I didn't find this place thirty or twenty or even ten years ago. So busy, so much work right around the settlement, always meant to make this trip, and if I'd only done it back then, there'd have been more of them alive, and I'd have had more years to take part in the work. Missed opportunity, my young friend! There is no life without regret."

"But you're glad that you found them now."

"Yes I am," said Sel. "Everybody misses some things, finds others. This is something I helped to find. With not a minute to spare." Then he smiled. "One thing I noticed. I don't know if it matters, but . . . the larva hadn't eaten the gold bug we found, the one that was still alive. And those larvae, they're voracious."

"They only eat carrion?" asked Ender.

"No, no, they went down on the turtles just fine. Not Earth turtles, but we call them that. They like living meat. But eating the gold bugs, that was cannibalism, you understand? That was their parents' generation. Eating them because there was nothing else. But they waited until they were dead. You see?"

Ender nodded. He saw perfectly. A rudimentary sense of respect for the living. For the rights of others. Whatever these gold bugs were, they were not mere animals. They weren't formics, but maybe they would give Ender his chance to get inside the formic mind, at least at one remove.

CHAPTER
17

To: MinCol@ColMin.gov
From: Gov%ShakespeareCol@ColMin.gov
Subj: Let's have a very quiet revolution

Dear Hyrum,

I have been warmly received as governor here, in no small part due to your long-distance intervention, as well as the enthusiasm of the natives.

We are still bringing colonists down from the ship as quickly as housing can be constructed for them. We are branching out into four settlements—the original, Miranda; and Falstaff, Polonius, and Mercutio. There was some enthusiasm for a Caliban village, but it quickly dissipated when people contemplated a future village school and what the mascot might look like.

You do understand, don't you, that local self-government is inevitable in the colonies, and the sooner the better. Well-intentioned as you are, and vital as it is that Earth continue to pay the astronomical (pun intended) expenses of starflight in the faint hope that it will eventually pay for itself, there is no way that the I.F. can force an unwanted governor on an unwilling populace—not for long.

Far better that I.F. ships come with ambassadorial status, to promote trade and good relations and deliver colonists and supplies to compensate for the burden they place on the local economy.

In token of which good counsel, I intend to serve for two years as governor, during which time I will sponsor the writing of a constitution. We will submit it to ColMin, not for approval—if we like it, it's our constitution—but for your judgment as to whether ColMin can recommend Shakespeare as a destination for colonists. That's where your power comes from—your ability to decide whether colonists can join an existing colony or not.

And perhaps some regulatory commission can meet by ansible, with a representative and single vote from every colony, to certify each other as worthy trading partners. In this way, a colony that sets up an intolerable government can be ostracized and cut off from trade and new colonists—but no one will commit the absurdity of trying to wage war (another word for enforcing policy) against a settlement that it takes half a lifetime to reach.

Does this letter constitute a declaration of independence? Not a very principled one. It's more a simple recognition that we're independent whether we make it official or not. These people survived for forty-one years completely on their own. They're glad to have received the supplies and the new breeding stock (plant, animal, human), but they did not have to have them.

In a way, each of these colonies is a hybrid—human by gene and cultural forebear, but formic by infrastructure. The formics built well; we don't have to clear land or search for water or process it, and their sewage systems seem to have been built for the ages. A fine monument! They still serve us by carrying away our poo. Because of what the formics prepared and what good scientists like Sel Menach accomplished in the colonies, the I.F. and ColMin don't have the clout that they might have had.

I say all this along with the sincere hope that we can eventually reach a point where every colony is visited every single year. Not in your lifetime or mine, probably, but that should be the goal.

Though if history is any guide, that ambition will seem absurdly modest within fifty years, as ships may very well come and go every six months, or every month, or every week of the year. May we both live to see it.

—Andrew

There is no accounting for the whims of children. When Alessandra was a toddler, Dorabella merely chuckled at the strange things she tried to do. When Alessandra was old enough to speak, her questions seemed to come from thought processes so random that it made Dorabella half believe that her child really *was* sent to her by fairies.

But by school age, children tended to become more reasonable. It was not teachers or parents who did it to them, but the other children, who either ridiculed or shunned a child whose actions and utterances did not conform with their standard of ordinariness.

Still, Alessandra never ceased to be able to come up with complete surprises, and of all times, with poor Quincy so frustrated at the way Ender had bested him in bureaucratic maneuvering, she picked this one to be completely unreasonable.

"Mother," said Alessandra, "most of the sleepers have woken now and gone down to Shakespeare, and I've been packed for days. When are we going?"

"Packed?" said Dorabella. "I thought you had been seized by a fit of tidiness. I was going to ask the doctors to test you for some odd disease."

"I'm not joking, Mother. We signed on to go to the colony. We're at the colony. Just one shuttle trip away. We have a contract."

Dorabella laughed. But the girl really wasn't going to be teased out of this. "Darling daughter of mine," said Dorabella. "I'm married now. To the admiral who captains this ship. Where the ship goes, he goes. Where he goes, I go. Where I go, you go."

Alessandra stood there in utter silence. She seemed poised to argue.

And then she didn't argue at all. "All right, Mother. So it's clean indoor living for another few years."

"My dear Quincy tells me that our next destination is another colony, nowhere near so far from us as Earth. Only a few months of flying time."

"But very tedious for me," said Alessandra. "With all the interesting people gone."

"Meaning Ender Wiggin, of course," said Dorabella. "I did so hope that you might manage to attract that fine young man with prospects. But he seems to have chosen to cast us aside."

Alessandra looked puzzled. "Us?" she said.

"He's a very smart boy. He knew that by forcing my dear Quincy to leave Shakespeare, he was sending you and me away, too."

"I never thought of that," said Alessandra. "Why, I'm very cross with him, then."

Dorabella felt a sudden tingling of awareness. Alessandra was taking things too well. This was not like her. And this hint of childish petulance directed against Ender Wiggin seemed to be almost a parody of Dorabella's deliberately childish fairy talk.

"What are you planning?" asked Dorabella.

"Planning? How can I plan anything when the crew are all so busy and the marines are down on the planet?"

"You're planning to sneak onto the shuttle without permission and go down to the planet's surface without my knowing it."

Alessandra looked at Dorabella as if she were crazy. But since that was her normal expression, Dorabella fully expected to be lied to, and her daughter did not disappoint. "Of course I wasn't," said Alessandra. "I fully expect to *have* your permission."

"Well, you don't."

"We came all this way, Mother." Now she sounded like her petulant self, so that her arguments might be sincere. "I at least want to *visit*. I want to say good-bye to all our friends from the voyage. I want to see the sky. I haven't seen sky for two years!"

"You've been *in* the sky," said Dorabella.

"Oh, that was a smart answer," said Alessandra. "That makes my longing to be outdoors go away . . . just. Like. That."

Now that Alessandra mentioned it, Dorabella realized that she, too, longed for a bit of a walk outdoors. The gym on the ship was always full of marines and crew members, and even though they were required to walk for a certain number of minutes a day on the treadmill, it was not as if that ever felt like you had truly *gone* somewhere.

"That's not unreasonable," said Dorabella.

"You're joking," said Alessandra.

"What, do you think it *is* unreasonable?"

"I didn't think *you* would ever think it was reasonable."

"I'm hurt," said Dorabella. "I'm a human being, too. I long for the sight of clouds in the sky. They do have clouds here, don't they?"

"How would *I* know, Mother?"

"We'll go together," said Dorabella. "Mother and daughter, saying good-bye to our friends. We never got to do that when we left Monopoli."

"We didn't have any friends," said Alessandra.

"We certainly did too, and they must have thought we were so rude to leave without them."

"I bet they brood about it every day. 'What ever happened to that rude girl Alessandra, who left us without saying good-bye—*forty years ago.*'"

Dorabella laughed. Alessandra did have such biting wit. "That's my smart little fairy daughter. Titania had nothing on you when it came to bitchiness."

"I wish you had stopped reading Shakespeare with *Taming of the Shrew.*"

"I've been living inside *A Midsummer Night's Dream* my whole life and I never knew it," said Dorabella. "*That* was what felt like coming home to me, not reaching some strange planet."

"Well, *I* live inside *The Tempest,*" said Alessandra. "Trapped on an island and desperate to get *off.*"

Dorabella laughed again. "I'll ask your father to let us ride down with one of the shuttles and come back up with another. How's that?"

"Excellent. Thank you, Mother."

"Wait a minute," said Dorabella.

"What do you mean?"

"You agreed too quickly. What are you planning? Do you think you can sneak away into the woods and hide till I go off and leave without you? That will never happen, my dear. I will not go without you, and Quincy will not go without me. If you try to run away, marines will track you down and find you and *drag* you back to me. Do you understand?"

"Mother," said Alessandra, "the last time I ran away was when I was six."

"My dear, you ran away only a few weeks before we left Monopoli. When you skipped school and went to visit your grandmother."

"That wasn't running away," said Alessandra. "I came back."

"Only after you found out that your grandmother was Satan's widow."

"I didn't know the devil was dead."

"Married to *her,* can you imagine he *wouldn't* kill himself?"

Alessandra laughed. That's how it was done—you lay down the law, but then you make them laugh and be happy about obeying you.

"We'll visit Shakespeare, and then we'll come back home to the ship. The ship *is* home now. Don't forget that."

"Of course not," said Alessandra. "But Mama."

"Yes, darling fairy girl?"

"He's not my father."

Dorabella took a moment to figure out what she was talking about. "Who's not your what?"

"Admiral Morgan," said Alessandra. "Not my father."

"I'm your mother. He's my husband. What do you think that makes him, your nephew?"

"Not. My. Father."

"Oh, I'm so sad," said Dorabella. "Here I thought you were happy for me."

"I'm very happy for you," said Alessandra. "But my father was a real man, not the king of the fairies, and he didn't prance off into the woods, he died. Anyone you marry now will be your husband, but not my father."

"I didn't marry *anyone,* I married a wonderful man with whom I am bound to have more children, so that if you reject him as your father, he will have no shortage of other heirs on whom to bestow his estate."

"I don't want his estate."

"Then you'd better marry well," said Dorabella, "because you don't want to raise your own children in poverty the way I did."

"Just don't call him my father," said Alessandra.

"You have to call him something, and so do I. Be reasonable, darling."

"Then I'll call him Prospero," said Alessandra, "because that's what he is."

"What? Why?"

"A powerful stranger who has us completely under his control. You're Ariel, the sweet one who loves your master. I'm Caliban. I just want to be set free."

"You're a teenager. You'll grow out of it."

"Never."

"There is no such thing as freedom," said Dorabella, getting impatient. "Sometimes, though, there's a chance to choose your master."

"Very well, Mother. You chose your master. But I haven't chosen mine."

"You still think the Wiggin boy even notices you."

"I know that he does, but I'm not pinning my hopes on him."

"You offered yourself to him, my dear, and he turned you down flat. It was quite humiliating, even if you didn't realize it."

Alessandra's face turned a bit red and she stalked to the door of their quarters. Then she whirled around, real pain and fury on her face. "You watched," she said. "Quincy *recorded* it and you watched!"

"Of course I did," said Dorabella. "If I hadn't, *he* or some *crewman* would have watched. Do you think I wanted *them* ogling your body?"

"You sent me to Ender expecting me to get naked with him, and you knew they were recording it, and you *watched* it. You *watched* me."

"You didn't get naked, did you? And so what if you had? I saw your naked body from angles you've never even thought of during the butt-wiping years."

"I hate you, Mother."

"You love me, because I always watch out for you."

"And Ender didn't humiliate me. Or reject me. He rejected *you*. He rejected the way *you* made me act!"

"What happened to, 'Oh thank you, Mother! Now I shall have the man I love'?"

"I never said that."

"You thanked me and giggled and thanked me again. You stood there and let me make you up like a whore to entice him. At what point did I force you to do something against your will?"

"You told me what I had to do if I wanted Ender to love me. Only a man like Ender doesn't fall for tricks like yours!"

"A *man*? A *boy* is what you mean. The only reason he didn't fall for that 'trick' was because he probably hasn't reached sexual maturity. *If* he's even a heterosexual."

"Listen to yourself, Mother," said Alessandra. "One minute Ender is the beginning and end of the world, the best chance for a great man that I'll ever have a chance to find. The next minute, he's a gay little boy who shamed me. You judge him according to whether he's useful to you."

"No, my pet. Whether he's useful to my little girl."

"Well, he isn't," said Alessandra.

"That was my point," said Dorabella. "And yet you gave me a tongue-lashing for saying so. Do make up your mind, my little Caliban." Then Dorabella burst into laughter, and, completely against her will, so did Alessandra. The girl was so angry at herself for laughing, or at Dorabella for making her laugh, that she fled from the room, slamming the door behind her. Or trying to—the pneumatics caught it and it closed quite gently.

Poor Alessandra. Nothing went the way she wanted.

Welcome to the real world, my child. Someday you'll see that my getting dear Quincy to fall in love with me was the best thing I ever did for you. Because I do everything for you. And all I ask in return is that you hold up your end and *take* the opportunities I get for you.

—

Valentine tried to walk normally into the room, to remain perfectly calm. But she was so disgusted with Ender that she could hardly contain herself. The boy was so busy making himself "available" to all the new colonists and old settlers, answering questions, chatting about things that he could not possibly remember from half-hour interviews two years ago, when he was so tired he could hardly speak. Yet when someone with whom he had a genuine personal relationship was looking for him, he was nowhere to be found.

It was just like the way he had refused to write to their parents. Well, he hadn't refused. He had always promised to do it. Then he simply never did.

For the past two years, he had promised—by implication, if not by word—that if the poor Toscano girl fell in love with him, it would not be unwelcome. Now she and her mother had come down to the planet's surface, to do some "sightseeing." The girl was obviously looking for only one sight: Ender Wiggin. And he was nowhere.

Valentine was fed up. The boy could be bold and brave indeed, except when there was something emotionally demanding that he didn't actually *have* to do. He *could* evade this girl, and maybe he thought that was some kind of clear message, but he owed her words. He owed her at least a good-bye. It didn't have to be a fond one, it just had to *happen.*

She finally found him in the XB's ansible room, writing something—probably a letter to Graff or someone equally irrelevant to their life on this new world.

"The fact that you're here," said Valentine, "leaves you without any excuse at all."

Ender looked up at her, seeming to be genuinely puzzled. Well, he probably wasn't faking it—he probably blocked the girl out of his mind so thoroughly that he had no clue what Valentine was talking about.

"You're looking through your mail. That means you got the passenger log for this shuttle trip."

"I already met the new colonists."

"Except one."

Ender raised an eyebrow. "Alessandra isn't a colonist anymore."

"She's looking for you."

"She could ask anybody where I am and they'll tell her. It's no secret."

"She can't *ask.*"

"Well, then, how does she expect to find me?"

"Don't put on this stupid act. I'm not so stupid as to believe you're stupid, even if you're *acting* as stupid as can be."

"OK, I've got the stupid part. Can you be more specific?"

"*Extremely* stupid."

"Not the degree, dear sister."

"Emotionally insensitive."

"Valentine," said Ender, "doesn't it occur to you that I actually know what I'm doing? Can't you have a little faith in me?"

"I think you're evading an emotionally difficult confrontation."

"Then why don't I hide from *you?*"

She wasn't sure whether to be even more annoyed at him for turning the tables on her, or to be a bit relieved that he considered a confrontation with her to be emotional. She wasn't actually sure she had enough of a hold on him for their confrontations to *be* emotional—on his side, anyway.

Ender glanced at the time in the computer display and sighed. "Well, your timing, as usual, is impeccable, even if you don't have a clue."

"I'd have a clue if you gave me one," said Valentine.

Ender was standing now, and to her surprise, he really was taller than her. She had noticed he was getting tall, but hadn't realized that he had passed her. And it wasn't thick shoes—he wasn't wearing any.

"Val," he said softly. "If you looked at what I say and do, it would be obvious to you what's going on. But you don't analyze. You see something that doesn't look right, and you leap past all the thinking part and go straight to 'Ender is doing something wrong and I must put a stop to it.'"

"I think! I analyze!"

"You analyze everything and everybody. That's what makes your history of Battle School so wonderful and truthful."

"You've read it?"

"You gave it to me three days ago. Of course I've read it."

"You didn't say anything."

"This is the first time I've seen you since I finished it. Val, think, please."

"Don't patronize me!"

"*Feeling* patronized isn't *thinking*," he said, sounding irritated at last. That made her feel a little better. "Don't judge me until you understand me. You can't understand me if you've already judged me. You think I've treated Alessandra badly, but I haven't. I've treated her extremely well. I'm about to save her life. But you can't trust me to do the right thing. You don't even bother to think what the right thing *is* before you decide that I'm not doing it."

"What is it that I think you're not doing that you *are* doing? That girl is pining for you—"

"Her *feelings*. Not her *needs*. Not what's actually good for her. You think the worst danger she faces is having her feelings hurt."

Valentine felt the righteous anger bleed out of her. What danger was he talking about? What *need* did Alessandra have, beyond her need for Ender? What was Valentine missing?

Ender put his arms around her, hugged her, and then moved past her, out of the room, then out of the building. Valentine had no choice but to follow.

He moved briskly across the grassy square in the middle of the science complex—really, just four one-story structures where the handful of scientists worked on the biology and technology that kept the colonists and the colony running. Now, though, with the newcomers from the ship, the houses were teeming with people, and Ender had already asked the foremen of the crews to shift their priorities and get additional science buildings. The noise of building wasn't deafening, because there were few power tools. But the calling out of instructions, the shouted warnings, the pounding of axes and hammers, it was a vigorous sound, taken all together. The sound of deliberate, welcome change.

Did Ender really know exactly where the Toscanos would be? He certainly walked straight toward the place. And now that Valentine thought about it—*analyzed,* yes, Ender—she realized that Ender must have been waiting till the end of their visit, until the shuttle was loading up for the return trip. Not quite the last one, but the last that wouldn't be full of marines and crew. The last shuttle with room for nonessential passengers.

He cut it rather close, even so. Alessandra was standing forlorn at the bottom of the ramp, with her mother tugging at her sleeve, urging her to move on into the shuttle. Then she saw Ender coming toward her and broke away from her mother, running to Ender. Could the poor girl be any more obvious?

She flung her arms around Ender, and to his credit, he embraced her willingly. In fact, Valentine was surprised at the way he held her, nuzzling her shoulder with real affection. What did he mean by that? What was the girl going to think he meant? Ender, are you really that insensitive?

—

When she practically jumped into his arms, Ender took a step back to bear the sudden momentum; but he made sure to get his face down close to her ear.

"Sixteen is old enough to join a colony without parental permission," he said softly.

Alessandra pulled away from him, looked searchingly in his eyes.

"No," said Ender. "Nothing will happen between us. I'm not asking you to stay for me."

"Then why would you ask me to stay at all?"

"I'm not," said Ender. "I'm telling you *how*. Right now, right here, I can set you free from your mother. Not to take her place, not to take control of your life, but to let *you* take control of it. The question is, do you want it?"

Alessandra's eyes filled with sudden tears. "You don't love me?"

"I care about you," said Ender. "You're a good person who has never had a moment's freedom. Your mother controls your coming and going. She spins stories around you and eventually you always believe them and do what she wants. You barely *know* what you want. Here in Shakespeare, you'll find out. Up there, with your mother and Admiral Morgan, I wonder if you'll ever know."

She nodded, understanding. "I know what I want. I want to stay."

"Then stay," said Ender.

"Tell her," said Alessandra. "Please."

"No."

"If I talk to her, she'll find some reason why I'm being stupid."

"Don't believe her."

"She'll make me feel guilty. Like I'm doing something really awful to her."

"You're not. In a way, you're setting *her* free, too. She can have Morgan's children and not worry about you."

"You know about that? You know she's going to have children with him?"

Ender sighed. "We don't have time for this conversation now. Your mother's coming because the shuttle has to leave and she expects you to be on it. If you decide to stay, I'll back you up. If you go with her willingly, I won't lift a hand to stop you."

Then Ender stepped away from her, just as Dorabella arrived.

■

"I can see what he's doing," said Mother. "Promising you anything you want, just to get you to stay and become his *plaything*."

"Mother," said Alessandra, "you don't know what you're talking about."

"I know that whatever he promised you is a lie. He doesn't love you."

"I know he doesn't," said Alessandra. "He told me he doesn't."

It was rather satisfying to see how surprised Mother looked. "Then what was all that hugging about? The way he nuzzled you?"

"He was whispering in my ear."

"What did he say?"

"He only reminded me of something I already knew," said Alessandra.

"Tell me on the shuttle, my dear little fairy princess, because they're getting quite impatient. They don't want to make your father angry by arriving late."

It hadn't been a whole day since Alessandra told her mother *never* to call Quincy her "father," and she was already doing it again. That's how it always was—Mother decided how things should be, and nothing Alessandra did could change her. Instead Alessandra always had to change. Whatever Mother wanted, eventually Alessandra would go along with because it was easier. Mother made sure that doing things her way was always easier.

The only time I ever defied her was behind her back. When she wasn't looking, when I could pretend she wouldn't know. I walk in fear of her, even though she's not a monster like my grandmother. Or . . . or maybe she is, but I never defied her enough to find out.

I don't have to go with her. I can stay here.

But Ender doesn't love me. Who do I have here? No friends, really. People I know from the voyage, but they all related to Mother, not to me. They talked *about* me, right in front of me, because Mother did. When they did speak to me, it was to say the things that Mother had virtually commanded them to say. I have no friends.

Ender and Valentine were the only ones who treated me like a person in my own right. And Ender doesn't love me.

Why doesn't he love me? What's wrong with me? I'm pretty, I'm smart. Not as smart as he is, or Valentine is, but *nobody's* that smart, not even on Earth. He said he desired me, that time back on the ship. He wants me, but he doesn't love me. I'm just a body to him, just a big nothing, and if I stay here, I'll be reminded of that all the time.

"My fairy darling," said Mother, tugging at her sleeve again. "Come with me. We're going to be so happy together, voyaging among the stars! You'll get a superb education with the midshipmen—your father already promised me that—and by the time you're the right age, we'll certainly be back near Earth, so you can go to a real university and you can find a *man* instead of this obnoxious, self-centered *boy*."

By now Mother was almost dragging her toward the shuttle. It was how things always went. Mother made it seem so inevitable to go along with her plans. And the alternatives were always so awful. Other people never understood Alessandra the way Mother did.

But Mother doesn't, thought Alessandra. She doesn't understand *me*. She just understands the insane picture she has of me. Her fairy changeling daughter.

Alessandra looked back over her shoulder, looking for Ender. There he was, showing nothing on his face at all. How can he do that? Has he no feelings? Won't he miss me? Won't he call me back? Won't he plead for me?

No. He said he wouldn't. He told me . . . my own choice . . . willingly . . .

Am I going with her willingly?

She's dragging at me, but not with very much force at all. She's talking me into it with every step, and I'm going. Like the rats following the pied piper of Hamelin. The music of her voice entrances me, and I follow, and then I find myself . . . here, on the ramp, heading to the shuttle.

Going back to where I'll be under her thumb all the time. A rival to the children she and Quincy have together. A nuisance, ultimately. What will happen then, when she turns on me? And even if she doesn't, it will only be because I'm complying completely with what she wants for me.

Alessandra stopped.

Mother's hand slipped away from her arm—she really *hadn't* been gripping her, or just barely.

"Alessandra," said Mother. "I saw you look back at him, but you see? He doesn't want you. He isn't calling for you. There's nothing for you here. But up there, in the stars, there's my love for you. There's the magic of our wonderful world together."

But their wonderful world together wasn't magic, it was a nightmare that Mother only *called* magic. And now there was someone else in that "wonderful world," someone that Mother was sleeping with and going to have babies with.

Mother isn't just lying to me, she's lying to herself. She doesn't really want me there. She has found her own new life, and she's only pretending that nothing will be changed by it. The fact is that Mother desperately needs to be rid of me, so she can get on with her happiness. For sixteen years I've been the weight dragging her down, holding her to the ground, keeping her from doing any of the things she dreamed of. Now she has the man of her dreams—well, a man who can give her the *life* of her dreams. And I am in the way.

"Mother," said Alessandra. "I'm not going with you."

"Yes you are."

"I'm sixteen," said Alessandra. "The law says I can decide for myself whether to join a colony."

"Nonsense."

"It's true. Valentine Wiggin joined this colony when *she* was only fifteen. Her parents didn't want her to, but she did it."

"Is that the lie she told you? It may seem romantic and brave, but you'll just be *lonely* all the time."

"Mother," said Alessandra. "I'm lonely all the time anyway."

Mother recoiled from her words. "How can you say that, you ungrateful little brat," she said. "I'm with you. You're *never* lonely."

"I'm always lonely," said Alessandra. "And you're *never* with me. You're with your darling angel fairy changeling child. And that's *not me.*"

Alessandra turned away and headed back down the ramp.

She heard Mother's footsteps. No, she *felt* them, as the ramp bounced slightly under the impact of her feet.

Then she felt Mother shove her from behind, a brutal shove that threw her completely off balance. "Go, then, you little bitch!" Mother screamed.

Alessandra struggled to get her feet under her, but her upper body was moving far faster than her feet could match, and she felt herself falling forward, the ramp looking so steep, she was going to hit so *hard* and her hands wouldn't be able to hold her up—

All of those thoughts in a split second, and then she felt her arm grabbed from behind and instead of hitting the ramp she swung down and then up again and it wasn't Mother who caught her, Mother was still a few steps away, where she had been when she shoved her. This was Ensign Akbar, and his face looked so concerned, so kind.

"Are you all right?" he said, once he had her standing up.

"That's right!" Mother shouted. "Bring that ungrateful little brat right inside here."

"Do you want to go back to the ship with us?" asked Ensign Akbar.

"Of course she does," said Mother, who was now at Akbar's elbow. Alessandra could see the transformation in Mother's face as she switched from the screamer who called Alessandra a bitch and a brat to the sweet fairy queen. "My darling fairy child is only happy when she's with her mother."

"I think I want to stay here," said Alessandra softly. "Will you let me go?"

Ensign Akbar leaned over to her and whispered in her ear, exactly as Ender had done. "I wish I could stay here with you," he said. Then he stood up to military attention. "Good-bye, Alessandra Toscano. Have a happy life here in this good world."

"What are you saying! My husband will court-martial you for this!" The Mother moved past him, heading for Alessandra, a hand reaching out for her like the bony hand of death.

Ensign Akbar caught her by the wrist.

"How dare you," she hissed directly into his face. "You've signed your death warrant for mutiny."

"Admiral Morgan will approve of my preventing his wife from breaking the law," said Ensign Akbar. "He will approve of my allowing this free colonist to exercise her right to fulfil her contract and stay in this colony."

Mother put her face right up into his, and Alessandra could see how flecks of her spittle sprayed right into his mouth, his nose, and onto his chin and cheeks. Yet he didn't budge. "It won't be about this, you fool," she said. "It will be about the time you tried to rape me in a darkened room on the ship."

For a moment, Alessandra found herself wondering when such a thing might have happened, and why Mother didn't mention it at the time.

Then she realized: It hadn't happened. Mother only intended to say it had. She was threatening Ensign Akbar with a lie. And there was one thing for sure—Mother was a good liar. Because she believed her own lies.

But Akbar only smiled. "The lady Dorabella Morgan has forgotten something."

"What is that?"

"Everything is recorded." Then Akbar let go of Mother's wrist, turned her around, and gave her a gentle nudge up the ramp.

Alessandra couldn't help herself. She gave one short, sharp laugh.

Mother whirled around, her face full of rage. Looking so much like Grandmother. "Grandmother," Alessandra said aloud. "I thought we left her behind, but look, we brought her with us."

It was the cruelest thing Alessandra could have said, that was plain. Mother was dumbstruck with the pain of it. Yet it was also the simple truth, and Alessandra hadn't said it to hurt her mother, it had simply spilled out of her mouth the moment she realized it was so.

"Good-bye, Mother," said Alessandra. "Have lots of babies with Admiral Morgan. Be happy all the time. I wish you would. I hope you will." Then she let Ensign Akbar take her down the ramp.

Ender was there—he had come closer while Mother was distracting her, and Alessandra hadn't realized it. He had come for her after all.

She and Akbar reached the base of the ramp; she noticed that Ender did not set foot on it.

"Ensign Akbar," said Ender, "you're mistaken about Admiral Morgan. He *will* believe her, if only to have peace with her."

"I'm afraid you're right," he said. "But what can I do?"

"You can resign your commission. Both by real time and relativistic time, your term of enlistment has expired."

"I can't resign in mid-voyage," said Akbar.

"But you're not in mid-voyage," said Ender. "You're in a port that is under the authority of the Hegemony, in the person of myself, the governor."

"He won't let it happen," said Akbar.

"Yes he will," said Ender. "He will obey the law, because it's the same law that gives him his absolute authority during a voyage. If he breaks it against you, then it can be broken against him. He knows that."

"And if he didn't," said Akbar, "you're telling him right now."

Only then did Alessandra realize that their words were still being recorded.

"I am," said Ender. "So you don't have to face the consequences of defying Mrs. Morgan. You acted with complete propriety. Here in the town of Miranda, you'll be treated with the respect that a man of your integrity deserves." Ender turned and with a sweep of his hand indicated the whole settlement. "The town is very small. But look—it's so much larger than the ship."

It was true. Alessandra could see that now for the first time. That this place was huge. There was room to get away from people if you didn't like them. Room to carve out a space for yourself, to say things that nobody else could hear, to think your own thoughts.

I've made the right choice.

Ensign Akbar stepped off the end of the ramp. So did Alessandra. Back on the ramp, Mother howled something. But Alessandra did not make any sense of the sound. She could hear no words in it, though surely words were being said.

She didn't *have* to hear it. She didn't have to understand it. She no longer lived in Mother's world.

CHAPTER
18

From: MinCol@ColMin.gov
To: Gov%ShakespeareCol@ColMin.gov
Subj: Unexpected colonists

Dear Ender,

I'm glad to hear that things are going so well in Shakespeare Colony. The successful assimilation of the new colonists is not being matched everywhere, and we have granted the petition of the governor of Colony IX that we not send them colonists—or a new governor—after all. In short, they have declared themselves even more independent than you have. (Your declaration that Shakespeare would accept no more offworld governors was cited as having prompted them to decide whether they wanted new colonists, so in a way this is all your fault, don't you think?)

Unfortunately, their declaration came when I already had a ship with several thousand colonists, a new governor, and a huge amount of supplies most of the way toward their planet. They left not very long after your ship. Now they're thirty-nine lightyears from home, and the party they were invited to has been canceled.

However, Shakespeare is close to the route they were taking, and at this moment, they are in such a position that we can bring them out of lightspeed, start turning them as soon as that becomes feasible, and get them to your planet in about a year.

These colonists will all be strangers to you. They have their own governor—again, someone you do not know or even know of. It would almost certainly work best if they establish their own settlement, accepting guidance and medical help and supplies from you, but governing themselves.

Since you have already divided your colony into four villages, the settlement they form will be larger than any of yours. It will be a far more difficult assimilation than when your ship arrived, and I suggest a federation of two colonies rather than incorporating them in your colony. Or, if you prefer, a federation of five cities, though having the new colonists outnumbered four-to-one in such a federation will cause its own tensions.

If you tell me not to send them, I will follow your wishes; I can keep them on a holding pattern, even putting most of the crew in stasis, until one of the planets we're terraforming is ready for them.

But if anyone can adapt to this situation, and induce his colony to accept the newcomers, it is you.

I am attaching full information, including bios and manifest.

—Hyrum

From: Gov%ShakespeareCol@ColMin.gov
To: MinCol@ColMin.gov
Subj: Re: Unexpected colonists

Dear Hyrum,

We'll find a site for them and have habitations prepared when they arrive. We will put them near a formic city, so they can mine their technology and farm their fields, as we did; and because you've given us a year's notice, we'll have time to plant fields and orchards for them with human-adapted local crops and genetically altered Earth crops. The people of Shakespeare voted on this and are embracing the project with enthusiasm. I will leave shortly to choose an appropriate site.

—Andrew

In all eleven years of Abra's life, only one thing had ever happened that mattered: the arrival of Ender Wiggin.

Until then, it was all work. Children were expected to do whatever was within their ability, and Abra had the misfortune to be clever with his hands. He could untie knots and tie them before he could make sentences. He could see how machinery worked and when he became strong enough to use adult tools, he could fix it or adapt it. He understood the flow of power through the metal parts. And so there were jobs for him to do even when other children were playing.

His father, Ix, was proud of his son, and so Abra was proud of himself. He was glad to be a child who was needed for grownup tasks. He was much smaller than his older brother Po, who had gone along with Uncle Sel to find the gold bugs; but he was sent to help rig the low trolley that people rode into and out of the cave, and on which food was taken to the colony of bugs, and gold carcasses removed.

Yet Abra also looked wistfully as the children his age (he couldn't call them friends, because he spent so little time with them) headed for the swimming hole, or climbed trees in the orchard, or shot at each other with wooden weapons.

Only his mother, Hannah, saw him. She urged him sometimes to go with the others, to leave whatever job he was doing. But it was too late. Like a baby bird that a child has handled, so it has the scent of man on it, Abra was marked by his work with adults. There was no resentment on their part. They just didn't think of him as one of them. If he had tried to come along, it would have seemed to all of them as inappropriate as if some adult had insisted on playing their games with them. It would ruin things. Especially because Abra was secretly convinced that he would be very bad at children's games. When he was little, and tried to build with blocks, he would weep when other children knocked down his structures. But the other children couldn't seem to understand why he would build, if *not* to see things get knocked down.

Here is what Ender's coming meant to Abra: Ender Wiggin was the governor, and yet he was young, the same age as Po. Adults talked to Ender as if he were one of them. No, as if he were their superior. They brought problems to him for solutions. They laid their disputes before him and abided by his decisions, listening to his explanations, asking him questions, coming to accept *his* understanding.

I am like him, thought Abra. Adults consult me about their machines the way they consult Ender about their other problems. They stand and listen to my explanations. They do what I tell them they should do to fix the problem. He and I live the same life—we are not really children. We have no friends.

Well, Ender had his sister, of course, but she was a strange recluse, who would stay indoors all day, except for her morning walk in summer, her afternoon walk in winter. They said she was writing books. All the adult scientists wrote things and sent them off to the other worlds, and then read the papers and books that were sent back. But what she was writing wasn't science at all. It was history. The past. Why would that matter, when there was so much to do and discover in the present? Ender could not possibly be interested in such things. Abra could not even imagine what they would talk about. "Today I gave Lo and Amato permission to divorce." "Did it happen a hundred years ago?" "No." "Then I don't care."

Abra also had siblings. Po treated him well. They all did. But they did not play with him. They played with each other.

Which was fine. Abra didn't *want* to "play." He wanted to do things that were real, things that mattered. He took as much pleasure from fixing machines and building things as they ever did from their games and mock fights and knocking-down. And now that Mother said he didn't have to go to school anymore, so there wouldn't be the constant humiliation of being unable to read and write, Abra spent his free time following Ender Wiggin everywhere.

Governor Wiggin noticed him, because he spoke to Abra from time to time—explaining things sometimes; just as often asking him questions. But mostly he let Abra tag along, and if other adults who were talking about serious matters sometimes glanced at Abra as if to ask Ender why he had this *child* with him, Ender simply ignored their silent question and soon they all carried on as if Abra were not there.

So when Ender left on his expedition to search for an appropriate site for the new starship to land and found another colony, no one even questioned the fact that Abra would be going with him. Father did take Abra aside and talk to him, though. "This is a heavy responsibility," he said. "You are not to do anything dangerous. If something happens to the governor, your first responsibility is to report it to me by satfone. Your location will already be tracked and we'll send help at once. Don't try to deal with it yourself until we have been notified. Do you understand?"

Of course Abra understood. To Father, Abra was merely going along as backup. Mother's advice was a bit less pessimistic about Abra's value. "Don't argue with him," she said. "Listen first, argue after."

"Of course, Mom."

"You say 'of course,' but you aren't good at listening, Abra, you always think you know what people are going to say, and you have to let them say it because sometimes you're wrong."

Abra nodded. "I'll listen to *Ender,* Mother."

She rolled her eyes—even though she yelled at the other children when they did that to her. "Yes, I suppose you will. Only Ender is wise enough to know more than my Abra!"

"I don't think I know everything, Mom." How could he get her to see that he only got impatient with adults when they thought they understood machinery and didn't? The rest of the time, he didn't speak at all. But since most of the time adults thought they knew what had gone wrong with a broken machine, and most of the time they were mistaken, most of his conversation with adults consisted of correcting them—or ignoring them. What else would they talk about except machinery, and Abra knew it better than they did. With Ender, though, it was almost never about machines. It was about *everything,* and Abra drank it all in.

"I'll try to keep Po from marrying Alessandra before you get home," said Mom.

"I don't care," said Abra. "They don't have to wait for me. It's not like they'll need me for the wedding night."

"Sometimes your face just needs slapping, Abra," said Mom. "But Ender puts up with you. The boy's a saint. Santo André."

"San Énder," said Abra.

"His Christian name is Andrew," said Mom.

"But the name that makes him holy is Ender," said Abra.

"My son the theologian. And you say you don't think you know everything!" Mother shook her heads, apparently disgusted with him.

Abra never understood how such arguments began, or why they usually ended with adults shaking their heads and turning away from him. He took *their* ideas seriously (except for their ideas about machinery); why couldn't they do the same for him?

Ender did. And he was going to spend days—weeks, maybe—with Ender Wiggin. Just the two of them.

They loaded the skimmer with supplies for three weeks, though Ender said he didn't think they'd be gone that long. Po came along to see them off, Alessandra clinging to him like a fungus, and he said, "Try not to be a nuisance, Abra."

"You're jealous that he's taking me and not you," said Abra.

Alessandra spoke up. A talking fungus, apparently. "Po doesn't want to go anywhere." Meaning, of course, that he couldn't bear to be away from her for a single second.

Po's face stayed blank, however, so that Abra knew perfectly well that while he might be completely imasen over the girl, he would still rather go on the trip with Ender than stay behind with her. Contrary to Mother's opinion of him, however, Abra said nothing at all. He didn't even *wink* at Po. He just kept his face exactly as blank as Po's. It was the Mayan way of laughing at somebody right in front of them, without being rude or starting a fight.

The journey was a strange experience for Abra. At first, of course, they simply skimmed along above the fields of home. Familiar ground. Then they followed the road to Falstaff, which was due west of Miranda; this was also familiar, since Abra's married sister Alma lived there with her husband, that big stupid eemo Simon, who always tickled younger children until they wet themselves and then made fun of them for peeing themselves like babies. Abra was relieved that Ender only paused to greet the mayor of the village and then moved on without any further delay.

They camped the first night in a grassy glen, sheltered from the wind that was coming up. It brought a storm in the night, but they were snug inside a tent, and without Abra even asking, Ender told him stories about Battle School and what the game was like, in the battleroom, and how it wasn't really a game at all, it was training and testing them for command. "Some people are born to lead," said Ender. "They just think that way, whether they want to lead or not. While others are born craving authority, but they have no ability to lead. It's very sad."

"Why would people want to do something they're not good at?" Abra tried to imagine himself wanting to be a scholar, in spite of his reading problem. It was just absurd.

"Leading is a strange thing," said Ender. "People see it happening, but they don't have a clue how it works."

"I know," said Abra. "Most people are like that with machines. But they try to fix them anyway and make everything worse."

"So you understand exactly," said Ender. "They don't see what a leader *does,* they just see how everybody respects a good leader, and they want to have the attention and respect without understanding what you actually have to do to earn it."

"Everybody respects *you,*" said Abra.

"And yet I do almost nothing," said Ender. "I have to learn other people's jobs well enough to help them at their work, because I just don't have enough work of my own to do. Leading this colony is too easy to be a fulltime job."

"Easy for you," said Abra.

"I suppose," said Ender. "But then, even when I'm doing other jobs, I'm still doing my job as governor. Because I'm always getting to know people. You can't lead people you don't know or at least understand. In war, for instance, if you don't know what your soldiers can do, how can you lead them into battle and hope to succeed? The enemy, too. You have to know the enemy."

Abra thought about that as they lay there in the darkness inside the tent. He thought about it so long that maybe he even dreamed for a while, about Ender sitting down and talking to the buggers—only the newcomers called them formics—and then exchanging Christmas gifts with them.

But maybe he only imagined it while awake, because he *was* awake when he whispered, "Is that why you spend so much time with the gold bugs?"

It was as if Ender had been thinking about the same thing, because he didn't give one of those impatient adult answers, like, What are you talking about? He knew that Abra was still holding to the thread of their prior conversation. In fact, Ender sounded sleepy, and Abra wondered if he had been dozing and Abra's voice had woken him and *still* Ender knew what he was talking about.

"Yes," said Ender. "I understood the hive queens well enough to defeat them. But not well enough to understand why they let me."

"They *let* you?"

"No, they fought hard against me, to prevent my victory. But they also brought themselves together where I *could* kill them all in a single battle. And they knew I had the weapon that could do it. A weapon they understood better than we did, because we got it from them. We *still* don't fully understand the science of it. But they must have. And yet they gathered together and waited for me. I don't understand it. So . . . I try communicating with the gold bug larvae. To get some idea of how the hive queens thought."

"Po says nobody's better at it than you."

"Does he?"

"He says everybody else has to work and work to get a glimmer of an image into or out of the gold bugs' heads, but you could do it the very first time."

"I didn't realize I was all that unusual," said Ender.

"They talk about it when you're not there. Po talks about it with Papa."

"Interesting," said Ender. He didn't sound like he felt flattered, or like he was acting modest—Ender truly sounded like he thought of his unusual talent for talking with the gold bugs as a simple fact.

When he thought about it, this made sense to Abra. You shouldn't be *proud* of being good at something, if you were born with it. That would be as dumb as being proud of having two legs, or speaking a language, or pooping.

Because he was with Ender, Abra felt free to say what he had just thought of, and Ender laughed. "That's right, Abra. Something you work to achieve, that's one thing. Why not be proud of it? Why not feel good about it? But something you were born with, that's just the way you are. Do you mind if I quote you?"

Abra wasn't sure what he meant by quoting. Was he going to write a scholarly paper? A letter to somebody? "Go ahead," said Abra.

"So . . . I'm unusually good at talking to the gold bugs," said Ender. "I had no idea. It's not talking, though. It's more like they show you what they remember, and put a feeling with it. Like, here's my memory of food, and they put hunger with it. Or the same image of food, plus a feeling of revulsion or fear, meaning, this is poisonous or I don't like the taste or . . . you get the idea."

"No words," said Abra.

"Exactly."

"The way I see machinery," said Abra. "I have to find words to explain it to people, but when I see it, I just know. I don't think the machinery is talking to me, though. No feelings."

"It may not be talking," said Ender, "but that doesn't mean you can't hear."

"Exactly! Yes! That's right!" Abra almost shouted the words, and his eyes filled with tears, and he didn't even know why. Or . . . yes he did. No adult had ever known what it felt like before.

"I had a friend once, and I think he saw battles that way. I had to think things through, the way the forces were arranged, but Bean just *saw*. He didn't even realize that other people took longer to understand—or never did at all. To him it was simply obvious."

"Bean? Is that a name?"

"He was an orphan. It was a street name. He didn't find out his real name until later, when people who cared about him did enough research to find out that he had been kidnapped as an embryo and genetically altered to make him such a genius."

"Oh," said Abra. "So that's not what he really was."

"No, Abra," said Ender. "We really *are* what our genes make us. We really have whatever abilities they give. It's what we start with. Just because his genes were shaped deliberately, by a criminal scientist, doesn't mean they're any less his than *our* genes, which are shaped by random selection between the genes of our father and the genes of our mother. *I* was shaped deliberately, too. Not by illegal science, but my parents chose each other partly because they were each so brilliant, and then the International Fleet asked them to have a third child because my older brother and sister were so brilliant but still were not quite what the I.F. wanted. Does that mean that I'm not *really* me? Who would I be, if my parents hadn't given birth to me?"

Abra was having a hard time following the conversation. It made him sleepy. He yawned.

Then Ender came up with a comparison Abra understood. "It's like saying, What would this pump be, if it weren't a pump?"

"That's just dumb. It *is* a pump. If it weren't a pump, it wouldn't *be* anything at all."

"So now you understand."

Abra whispered the next question. "So you're like my father, and you don't believe people have souls?"

"No," said Ender. "I don't know about souls. I just know that while we're alive, in these bodies, we can only do what our body can do. My parents believe in souls. I've known people who were absolutely sure. Smart people. Good people. So just because I don't understand it doesn't mean I'm sure it can't be true."

"That's like what Papa says."

"See? He doesn't *disbelieve* in souls."

"But Mom talks like . . . she says that she can look in my eyes and see into my soul."

"Maybe she can."

"Like you can look into a gold bug larva and see what it's thinking?"

"Maybe," said Ender. "I can't see what it's thinking, though. I can only see what it pushes into my mind. I try to push thoughts into *its* mind, but I don't think I'm actually pushing. I think the ability to communicate by thoughts belongs completely to the larva. It pushes things into my mind, and then takes from my mind whatever I show it. But I'm not doing anything."

"Then how can you be better at it than other people, if you're not doing anything?"

"*If* I'm really better—and remember, your father and Po can't really know whether I am or not—then maybe it's because I have a mind that it's easier for a gold bug to get inside of."

"Why?" asked Abra. "Why would a human being born on Earth have a brain that was easier for a gold bug to get inside of?"

"I don't know," said Ender. "That's one of the things I came to this world to find out."

"That's not even true," said Abra. "You couldn't have come here to find out why your brain was easier for the buggers to understand because you didn't know your brain could do that until you got here!"

Ender laughed. "You just don't have any tolerance for kuso, do you?"

"What's kuso?"

"Mierda," said Ender. "Bullshit."

"Were you lying to me?"

"No," said Ender. "Here's the thing. I had dreams when I was fighting the war on Eros. I didn't know I was fighting the war, but I was. I had one dream where a bunch of formics were vivisecting me. Only instead of cutting open my body, they were cutting up my memories and displaying them like holographs and trying to make sense of them. Why did I have that dream, Abra? After I won the war and found out that I had really been fighting the hive queens and not just a computer simulation, or my teacher, I thought back to some of my dreams and I wondered. Were they trying just as hard to understand me as I was trying to understand them? Was that dream because on some level I was aware that they were getting inside my head, and it frightened me?"

"Wow," said Abra. "But if they could read your mind, why couldn't they beat you?"

"Because my victories weren't *in* my mind," said Ender. "That's the weird thing. I thought through the battles, yes, but I didn't *see* them like Bean did. Instead, I saw the *people*. The soldiers under me. I knew what those kids were capable of. So I put them in a situation where their decisions would be crucial, told them what I wanted them to do, and then I trusted them to make the decisions that would achieve my objective. I didn't actually know what they'd do. So being inside my head would never show the hive queens what I was planning, because I had no plan, not of a kind they could use against me."

"Is that why you thought that way? So they couldn't read your plans?"

"I didn't know the game was real. I've only thought of these things afterward. Trying to understand."

"But if that's true, then you were communicating with the buggers—formics—hive queens all along."

"I don't know. Maybe they were *trying,* but they couldn't make sense of it. I'm sure they didn't push anything into my head, or at least not clearly enough for me to understand it. And what could they take *from* my thoughts? I don't know. Maybe it didn't happen at all. Maybe I only dreamed about them because I kept thinking about them. What will I do when I face *real* hive queens? If this simulation were a real battle, how would a hive queen think? That sort of thing."

"What does Papa think?" asked Abra. "He's really smart and he knows more than anybody about the gold bugs now."

"I haven't discussed this with your father."

"Oh." Abra digested that thought in silence.

"Abra," said Ender. "I haven't talked about this with *anybody.*"

"Oh." Abra felt overwhelmed by Ender's trust. He could not speak.

"Let's go to sleep," said Ender. "I want us to be wide awake and on our way at first light. This new colony needs to be several days' journey away, even by skimmer. And once we find the general area, I have to mark out specific places for buildings and fields and a landing strip for the shuttle and all that."

"Maybe we'll find another gold bug cave."

"Maybe," said Ender. "Or some other metal. Like the bauxite cave you found."

"Just because the aluminum bugs were all dead doesn't mean we won't find another cave that has living bugs, right?" said Abra.

"We might have found the only survivors," said Ender.

"But Papa says the odds are against that. He says it would be too co-incidental if the longest-surviving gold bugs just *happened* to be the ones that Uncle Sel and Po *happened* to discover."

"Your father's not a mathematician," said Ender. "He doesn't under-stand probability."

"What do you mean?"

"Sel and Po *did* find the cave with living gold bug larvae in it. There-fore the chance of their finding it, in this causal universe, is one hundred percent. Because it happened."

"Oh."

"But since we don't know how many other bug caves there are, or where they're situated, any guess at how likely we are to find one isn't about probability—it's just a guess. There's not enough data for mathematical probabilities."

"We know there was a second one," said Abra. "So it's not like we know *nothing*."

"But from the data we actually have, one cave with living gold bugs and one with dead aluminum ones, what would you conclude?"

"That we have as much chance of finding live ones as dead. That's what Father says."

"But that isn't really true," said Ender. "Because in the cave Sel and Po found, the bugs weren't thriving. They had *almost* died out. And in the other cave, they *had* died out. So now what are the odds?"

Abra thought hard about it. "I don't know," he said. "It depends on how big each colony was, and whether they would think of eating their own parents' bodies like these bugs did, and maybe other stuff I don't even know about."

"Now you're thinking like a scientist," said Ender. "Now, please think like a sleeping person. We have a long day tomorrow."

They traveled all day the next day, and it all began to look the same to Abra. "What's wrong with any of these places?" said Abra. "The . . . formics farmed there, and they did fine. And a landing strip could go *there*."

"Too close," said Ender. "Not enough room for the newcomers to develop their own culture. So close that if they became envious of Falstaff village, they might try to take it over."

"Why would they do that?"

"Because they're human," said Ender. "And, specifically, because then they'd have people who knew everything that we know and can do everything we do."

"But they'd still be *our* people," said Abra.

"Not for long," said Ender. "Now that the villages are separate, the Falstaffians will start thinking about what's good for Falstaff. They might resent Miranda for thinking we should be their boss, and maybe they'd want to join these new people voluntarily."

Abra thought about that for about ten clicks. "What would be wrong with that?" he said.

This time it took Ender a moment of thought before he was able to answer. "Ah, Falstaff joining the new people voluntarily. Well, I don't know if anything would be wrong with it. I just know that what I *want* to happen is for all the villages—including the new one—to be separate enough to develop their own traditions and cultures, and far enough apart that they won't fight over the same resources, yet close enough to intermarry and trade. I'm hoping that there's some perfect distance apart that will make it so they don't start fighting each other, or at least not for a long time."

"As long as we have you as governor, we'll just win anyway," said Abra.

"I don't care who wins," said Ender. "It's having a war at all that would be terrible."

"That's not how you felt when you beat the formics!"

"No," said Ender. "When the survival of the human race is at stake, you can't help but care who wins. But in a war between colonists on this planet, why would I care which side won? Either way, there'd be killing and loss and grief and hate and bitter memories and the seeds of wars to come. And both sides would be human, so no matter what, humans would lose. And lose and keep on losing. Abra, I sometimes say prayers, did you know that? Because my parents prayed. I sometimes talk to God even though I don't know anything about him. I ask him: Let the wars end."

"They *have* ended," said Abra. "On earth. The Hegemon united the whole world and nobody's at war anywhere."

"Yes," said Ender. "Wouldn't it be ridiculous if they finally got peace on Earth and we just started up the whole warfare thing again here on Shakespeare?"

"The Hegemon is your brother, right?" asked Abra.

"He's Valentine's brother," said Ender.

"But she's your sister," said Abra.

"He's Valentine's brother," said Ender, and his face looked sort of dark and Abra didn't ask him what in the world he was talking about.

███

On the third day of their trip, as the sun got to about two hands above the western horizon—time on clocks and watches meant nothing here, since they had all been made on Earth for Earth days, and nobody liked any of the schemes for dividing up the Shakespearian day into hours and minutes— Ender finally stopped the skimmer on the crest of a hill overlooking a broad valley with overgrown orchards and fields with forty years' growth of trees in them. There were tunnel entrances in some of the surrounding hills, and chimneys that showed there had been manufacturing here.

"This place looks as likely as any," said Ender. So, just like that, the site of the new colony was chosen.

They pitched the tent and Ender fixed dinner and he and Abra walked down into the valley together and looked inside a couple of the caves. No bugs, of course, since this wasn't that kind of settlement, but there was machinery of a kind that they hadn't seen before and Abra wanted to plunge right in and figure it all out but Ender said, "I promise you'll be the first one to get a look at these machines, but not now. Not tonight. That's not our mission. We have to lay out a colony. I have to determine where the fields will be, the water source—we have to find the formic sewer system, we have to see if we can wake up their generating equipment. All the things that Sel Menach's generation did, long before you were born. But before too long, we'll have time for the formic machines. And then, believe me, they'll let you spend days and weeks on them."

Abra wanted to wheedle like a little kid, but he knew Ender was right. And so he accepted Ender's promise and stayed with him for the rest of that night's walk.

The sun had set before they got back to camp—they had only a faint light in the sky when they turned in to sleep. This time their conversation consisted of Ender asking Abra to tell stories that his parents had told him, his father's Mayan stories and his mother's Chinese stories and the Catholic stories they both had in common, and that took until Abra could hardly keep his eyes open, and then they slept.

The next day, Ender and Abra marked out fields and laid out streets, recording everything on the holomaps in Ender's field desk, which were automatically transmitted to the orbiting computer. No need even to call Papa on the satfone, because he would get all this information automatically and he could see the work they were doing.

Late in the afternoon, Ender sighed and said, "You know, this is actually kind of boring."

"Really?" said Abra sarcastically.

"Even slaves get time off now and then."

"Who?" Abra was afraid this was some school-learning thing that he didn't know because he couldn't read and stopped going to school.

"You have no idea how happy it makes me that you don't know what I'm talking about."

Well, if Ender was happy, Abra was happy.

"For the next hour, I say we do whatever we want," said Ender.

"Like what?" asked Abra.

"What, you mean I have to decide for you what *you* think would be fun?"

"What are *you* going to do?"

"I'm going to see if the river's good for swimming."

"That's dangerous and you shouldn't do it alone."

"If I drown, call your father to come get you."

"I could drive the skimmer home, you know."

"But you couldn't get my corpse up onto it," said Ender.

"Don't talk about dying!" Abra said. He meant to sound angry. Instead his voice shook and he sounded scared.

"I'm a good swimmer," said Ender. "I'm going to test the water to make sure it won't make me sick, and I'll only swim where there's no current, all right? And you're free to swim with me, if you want."

"I don't like to swim." He'd never really learned, not well.

"So—don't go climbing into any caves or fiddling with machinery, all right?" said Ender. "Because machinery really *is* scary."

"Only because you don't understand it."

"Right," said Ender. "But what if something went wrong? What if I had to take *your* mangled or incinerated body back to your parents?"

Abra laughed. "So I can let the governor die, but you can't let one dumb kid get killed."

"Exactly right," said Ender. "Because I'm responsible for you, but you're only responsible for reporting my death if it happens."

So Ender went back to the skimmer and got the water testing equipment. And since Abra knew perfectly well Ender was going to have to test the river anyway, he realized that Ender wasn't really taking a break, he was giving *Abra* a break. Well, two could play this game. Abra would use the time to scout out the crest of the far ridge and see what lay on the other side. That was useful. That was a real job that would have to be done. So while Ender swam around in the river, Abra would be adding to the map.

It was a longer walk than Abra thought it would be. The far hills looked deceptively close. The higher he got, though, the easier it was to spot the place where Ender was, in fact, swimming. He wondered if Ender could also see him. He turned and waved a couple of times, but Ender didn't wave back, probably because he would look like a speck to Ender, just as Ender looked like a speck to him. Or else Ender wasn't looking, and that was fine, too. It meant Ender trusted him not to screw up and get hurt or lost.

At the top of the hill, Abra could see why the river in the valley behind him widened—there was an irrigation dam between the hills so the widening of the river was really a pond behind the dam. The drop wasn't very severe, though, and certain sluices were permanently open so that the river flowed permanently into three channels. One was the original riverbed, and the other two carried water through slightly higher canals skirting the north side of the valley. Here on the south side of the river, the canals were permanently empty, and so Abra could easily see the difference that the irrigation made. Both sides of the lower valley were lush with life, but on the wet side, trees were growing, and on the drier side, it was grass and low shrubs.

But as he gazed at the south side—the grassy side—he realized that there was something wrong with the landscape. Instead of being a smooth flood plain, like the upper valley behind him where Ender was, there were several mounds in the plain below him. And there was nothing natural about the way they were laid out.

The formics had to have built them. But what were they for?

And now that he looked closely, he could see that there were even-more-artificial-looking structures here and there. They didn't look like normal formic buildings, either. This was something new and strange, and even though they were overgrown with grass and vines, they were still plainly visible.

Abra scrambled down the slope—not running, because it was unfamiliar ground, and the last thing he wanted was to sprain an ankle and become a burden on Ender. He came to the largest of the artificial mounds. It was steep-sided but covered with grass, so climbing it wasn't very hard. He reached the top and realized that it was hollow inside, and there was water gathered in it.

Abra walked the ridge line and found that at one end, two ridges extended out like legs, making a widening vale between them. And when he turned around, he realized that there were also low ridges that could be arms, and where a head would be, a large white rock glistened in the sunlight, looking for all the world like a skull.

It was shaped like a man. Not like a formic—a man.

He felt a thrill go through him—of fear, of dread, of excitement. Such a place as this could not exist. And yet it did.

He heard a voice calling his name. He looked up and saw that Ender had driven the skimmer over the ridge from the other valley and was looking for him. Abra waved and called out, "Ho, Ender!"

Ender saw him and skimmed over to the base of the steep hill where Abra had climbed. "Come up," said Abra.

When Ender had scrambled up the slope—displacing a few turves in the process, since he was bigger than Abra and weighed more—Abra gestured to the body-like structure of the artificial hills. "Can you believe this?"

Apparently Ender didn't see it the way Abra did. He simply looked, and said nothing.

"It's like a giant died here," said Abra, "and the earth grew up to cover his carcass."

Abra heard a sharp intake of breath from Ender, so he knew now that he had seen.

Ender looked around and pointed wordlessly at some of the smaller, vine-covered structures. He pulled out his binoculars and looked for a long time. "Impossible," he muttered.

"What? What are they?"

Ender didn't answer. Instead he walked the length of the hill, toward the "head." Abra scrambled down onto the neck and up the chin. "Somebody had to build this," Abra said. He scratched at the white surface. "Look, this skull place, it's not rock, look at it. This is concrete."

"I know," said Ender. "They built it for me."

"What?"

"I know this place, Abra. The buggers built it for me."

"They were all dead before Grandpa and Grandma even got here," said Abra.

"You're right, it's impossible, but I know what I know." Ender put a hand on Abra's shoulder. "Abra, I shouldn't take you with me."

"Where?"

"Over there." Ender pointed. "It might be dangerous. If they knew me well enough to build this place, they might be planning to—"

"To get even with you," said Abra.

"For killing them," said Ender.

"So don't go, Ender. Don't do what they want you to do."

"If they want to get revenge, Abra, I don't mind. But perhaps they don't. Perhaps this is the closest they could come to talking. To writing me a note."

"They didn't know how to read and write." They didn't even know the *idea* of reading and writing—that's what Father said. So how would they know about leaving notes?

"Maybe they were learning when they died," said Ender.

"Well I'm sure as hell not sticking around here if you're taking off somewhere. I'm going with you."

Ender looked amused when Abra said "hell." He shook his head, smiling. "No. You're too young to take the risk of—"

"Come on!" said Abra with disgust. "You're Ender *Wiggin*. Don't tell me what eleven-year-old kids can do!"

So they rode in the skimmer together until they got to the first set of structures. Ender stopped and they got off. The shape of the structures came from metal frameworks underlying and supporting the vines. Now Abra realized they were swings and slides, just like those in the town park in Miranda. The ones in Miranda were smaller, because they were just for the little kids. But there was no mistaking what they were.

But formics didn't have babies, they had larvae. Worms would hardly needs swings and slides.

"They made human stuff," said Abra.

Ender only nodded.

"They really were taking stuff out of your head," said Abra.

"That's one explanation," said Ender. Then they got on the skimmer and went on. Ender seemed to know the way.

They neared the farthest structure. It was a thick tower and some lower walls, all covered with ivy. There was a window near the top of the tower.

"You knew this would be here," said Abra.

"It was my nightmare," said Ender. "My memory of the fantasy game."

Abra had no idea what "the fantasy game" was, but he understood that this place represented one of those dreams that the formics were taking out of Ender when they vivisected him in that nightmare he had talked about.

Ender got out of the skimmer. "Don't come after me," he said. "If I'm not back in an hour, it means it's dangerous here, and you *must* go home at once and tell them everything."

"Eat it, Ender, I'm coming with you," said Abra.

Ender looked at him coldly. "Eat it yourself, Abra, or I'll stuff you with mud."

His words were jocular, and so was his tone. But his eyes were not joking, and Abra knew that he meant it.

So Abra stayed with the skimmer and watched Ender jog over to the castle—for that's what it was. And then Ender climbed up the outside of the tower and went in through the window.

Abra stayed, watching the tower, for a long time. He checked the skimmer's clock now and then. And finally his gaze began to wander. He watched birds and insects, small animals in the grass, clouds moving across the sky.

That's why he didn't see Ender come out of the tower. He only saw him walking toward the skimmer, carrying his jacket in a wad under his arm.

Only it wasn't a wad. There was something inside the jacket. But Abra didn't ask what Ender had found. He figured that if Ender wanted him to know, he'd tell him.

"We aren't building the new colony here," said Ender.

"OK," said Abra.

"Let's go back and strike camp," said Ender.

They searched for five more days, well to the east and south of the place they had first found, until they had another colony site. It was a bigger formic settlement, with a much larger area of fields and all the signs of a much larger annual rainfall. "This is the right place," said Ender. "Better climate, warmer. Good, rich soil."

They spent a week laying out the new site.

Then it was time to go home. The night before they left, lying out on the open ground—it was too hot at night inside the tent—Abra finally asked. Not what it was that Ender brought back from the tower—he would never ask that—but the deeper question.

"Ender, what did they mean? Building this for you?"

Ender was silent for a long time. "I'm not going to tell you the whole truth, Abra. Because I don't want anyone to know. I don't even want them to know what we found there. I hope it's all decayed and crumbled away before people go back there. But even if it's not, nobody else will understand it. And in the far future, nobody will believe that the formics made that place. They'll think it's something that human colonists did."

"You don't have to tell me everything," said Abra. "And I won't tell anybody else what we found."

"I know you won't," said Ender. He hesitated again. "I don't want to lie to you. So I'll only tell you true things. I found the answer, Abra."

"To what?"

"My question."

"Can't you tell me any of it?"

"You've never asked the question. I hope to God you never know what it is."

"But the message really was for you."

"Yes, Abra. They left a message that told me why they died."

"Why?"

"No, Abra. It's my burden, truly. Mine alone." Ender reached out a hand, gripped Abra by the arm. "Let there be no rumors of what Ender Wiggin found when he came to this place."

"There never will be," said Abra.

"You mean that at the age of eleven, you're prepared to take a secret to your grave?"

"Yes," said Abra without hesitation. "But I hope I don't have to do that very soon."

Ender laughed. "I hope the same. I hope you live a long, long time."

"I'll keep the secret all my life. Even though I don't actually know what it is."

—

Ender came into the house where Valentine was working on the next-to-last volume of her history of the Formic Wars. He set his own desk on the table across from her. She looked up at him. He smiled—a jokey, mechanical smile—and started typing.

She wasn't fooled. The smile was fake, but the happiness behind it was real.

Ender was actually *happy*.

What happened on that trip to lay out the new colony?

He didn't say. She didn't ask. It was enough for her that he was happy.

CHAPTER

19

To: jpwiggin%ret@gso.nc.pub, twiggin%em@uncg.edu
From: Gov%ShakespeareCol@MinCol.gov
Subj: Third

Dear Mother and Father,

Some things cannot be helped. For you, it has been 47 years of silence from your third and youngest child. For me, it has been my six years in Battle School, where I lived for one reason only, to destroy the formics; the year after our victory, in which I learned that I had twice killed other children, that I destroyed an entire sentient species that I don't believe I ever understood, and that every mistake I made caused the deaths of men and women in places lightyears away; and then two years of a voyage in which I could never for a moment speak or show my true feelings about anything.

Through all of this, I have been trying to sort out what it meant that you gave life to me. To have a child, knowing that you have signed a contract to give him up to the government upon demand—isn't there a bit of the story of Rumpelstiltskin in this? In the fairy tale, someone happens to overhear the secret name that will free them from their pledge to give their child to the dwarf.

In our case, the universe did not conspire in our favor, and when Rumpelstiltskin showed up, you handed over the boy. Me.

I made a choice myself—though what I really understood at six years of age is hard to fathom. I thought I was already myself; I was aware of no deficiencies of judgment. But now, looking back, I wonder why I chose. It was partly a desire to flee from Peter's threats and oppression, since Valentine really couldn't stop him and the two of you had no idea what was going on among us children. It was partly a desire to save the people I knew, most particularly my own protector, Valentine, from the predations of the formics.

It was partly a hope that I might turn out to be a very important boy. It was partly the challenge of it, the hope of victory over the other children competing to be great commanders. It was partly a wish to leave a world where every day I was reminded that Thirds are illegal, unwanted, despised, taking more than their family's share of the world's resources.

It was partly my sense that while you cried (Mother) and you blustered (Father) it would make a positive difference in our family's life for me to go. No longer would you be the ones who had an extra child and yet were not suffering the penalties of law. With that monitor gone, there'd be no more visible excuse. I could hear you telling people, "The government authorized his birth so he could enter military training, only when the time came, he refused to go."

I existed for one reason only. When the time came, I believed I had no decent choice but to fulfil the purpose of my creation.

I did it, didn't I? I dominated the other children in Battle School, though I was not the best strategist (that was Bean). I led my jeesh and, unwittingly, many pilots to complete victory in the war—though again at a crucial moment it was Bean who helped me see my way through. I am not ashamed of having needed help. The task was too great for me, too great for Bean, and too great for any of the other children, but my role was to lead by getting the best from everyone.

But when the victory was won, I could not go home. There was Graff's court martial. There was the international situation, with nations fearing what might happen if America had the great war hero to command their Earthbound troops.

But I confess that there was something else. I became aware that both my brother and my sister were writing essays whose deliberate effect was to keep me from coming home to Earth again. Peter's reasons I could guess at; they were an outgrowth of our relationship as young children. Peter cannot live in the same world with me. Or at least he could not then.

Here was the mystery to me. I was a twelve-year-old boy during most of my year on Eros. I was barred from returning to Earth. My siblings were siding with those who wanted me kept away. And not once on any of the newsvids did I see a quotation or a statement from my parents, pleading with the powers-that-be to let their boy come home. Nor did I hear of any effort on your part to come and see me, since I could not go to you.

Instead, once Valentine showed up, I got hints, ranging from the blunt to the oblique, that for some reason it was my obligation to write to YOU. Through the two years of our voyage—forty years to you—Valentine reported to me on her correspondence with you, and told me that I should write, I must write. And through all of this, knowing that you could easily obtain my address and that your letters would get through to me as easily as they got through to Valentine, I never heard from you.

I have waited.

Now you are getting rather old. Peter is nearly sixty years of age and he rules the world—all his dreams have come true, though there seem to have been many nightmares along the way. From news reports I gather that you have been at his side almost continuously, working for him and his cause. You have made statements to the press in support of him, and at times of crisis you stood by him quite bravely. You have been admirable parents. You know how the job is done.

And still I waited.

Recently, having learned the answers to a set of questions unrelated to you, I determined that because half of this silence between us has been mine, I would wait no longer to write to you. Still, I do not understand how it became my obligation to open this door. How did I skip directly from the irresponsibility of a six-year-old to the complete responsibility that seemed to devolve on me to reestablish our relationship after it became possible again?

I thought: You were ashamed of me. My "victory" came along with the scandal of my killings; you wanted to put me from your mind. Who am I, then, to insist that you recognize me? Yet I killed Stilson when I was still a child living in your house. You cannot blame the Battle School for that. Why didn't you stand up and take responsibility for creating me, and for raising me those first six years?

I thought: You were so in awe of my great achievement that you felt unworthy to insist on a relationship, and as with royalty, you waited for me to invite you. Here, though, the fact that you are not too much in awe of Peter to be with him, though his achievements are arguably greater—peace on Earth, after all!— tells me that awe is not a powerful motive in your lives.

Then I thought: They have divided the family. Valentine is their co-parent, and she has been assigned to me, while they assigned themselves to Peter. Other people had taken care of training me to save the world; but who would train Peter, who would watch out for him, who would pull him up short if he over-reached or became a tyrant? That was where you were needed; that was your life's work. Valentine would give her life to me, and you would give yours to Peter.

But if that was your thinking, then I think you made a poor choice. Valentine is as good as I remembered her to be, and as smart. But she cannot understand me or what I need, she does not know me well enough to trust me, and it drives her crazy. She is not my mother or father, she is only my sister, and yet she has been assigned—or assigned herself—to take on a motherly role. She does her best. I hope she is not too unhappy with the bargain she made, to come along on this voyage. The sacrifice she made in order to come with me was far too great. I fear she thinks the results in me have amounted to little of worth.

I do not know you, a man and a woman in their eighties. I knew a young man and woman in their early thirties, busy with their own extraordinary careers, raising extraordinary children who, for a time, each wore the monitor of the I.F. at the base of their skulls. There was always someone else watching over me. I always belonged to someone else. You never felt that I was fully your son.

Yet I am your son. There is in me, in the abilities I have, in the choices that I make without realizing that I've chosen, in my deep feelings about the religions that you believed in secretly, which I have studied when I could, there is in all these things a trace of you. You are the explanation of much that is unexplainable.

And my ability to shut certain things completely from my mind—to set them aside so I can work on other projects—that also comes from you, for I think that is what you have done with me. You have set me aside, and only by directly asking for it can I win your attention once again.

I have watched painful relationships between parents and children. I have seen parents who control and parents who neglect, parents who make terrible mistakes that hurt their children deeply, and parents who forgive children who have done awful things. I have seen nobility and courage; I have seen dreadful selfishness and utter blindness; and I have seen all these things in the SAME parents, raising the same children.

What I understand now is this: There is no harder job than parenting. There is no human relationship with such potential for great achievement and awful destructiveness, and despite all the experts who write about it, no one has the slightest idea whether any decision will be right or best or even not-horrible for any particular child. It is a job that simply cannot be done right.

For reasons truly out of your control, I became a stranger to you; for reasons I do not understand, you made no effort to come to my defense and bring me home, or to explain to me why you did not or could not or should not. But you let my sister come to me, giving her up from your own lives. That was a great gift, jointly offered by her and you. Even if she now regrets it, that does not reduce the nobility of the sacrifice.

Here is why I am writing. No matter how hard I try to be self-sufficient, I am not. I have read enough psychology and sociology, and I have observed enough families over the past two years, to realize that there is no replacement for parents in a person's life, and no going on without them. I have achieved, at the age of fifteen, more than any but a handful of the greatest men in history. I can look at the records of what I did and see, clearly, that it is so.

But I do not believe it. I look into myself and all I see is the destroyer of lives. Even as I prevented a tyrant from usurping the control of this colony, even as I helped a young girl liberate herself from a domineering mother, I heard a voice in the back of my mind, saying, "What is this, compared to the pilots who died because of your clumsiness in command? What is this, compared to the death at your hands of two admittedly unpleasant but nevertheless young children? What is this, compared to the slaughter of a species that you killed without first understanding whether they needed killing?"

There is something that only parents can provide, and I need it, and I am not ashamed to ask it from you.

From my mother, I need to know that I still belong, that I am part of you, that I do not stand alone.

From my father, I need to know that I, as a separate being, have earned my place in this world.

Let me resort to the scriptures that I know have meant much to you in your lives. From my mother, I need to know that she has watched my life and "kept all these sayings in her heart." From my father, I need to hear these words: "Well done, thou good and faithful servant. . . . Enter into the joy of the Lord."

No, I don't think I'm Jesus and I don't think you're God. I just happen to believe that every child needs to have what Mary gave; and the God of the New Testament shows us what a father must be in his children's lives.

Here is the irony: Because I had to ask for these things, I will be suspicious of your replies. So I ask you not only to give me these gifts, but also to help me believe that you mean them.

In return, I give you this: I understand the impossibility of having me for a child. I believe that in every case, you chose to do what you believed would be best for me. Even if I disagree with your choices—and the more I think, the less I disagree—I believe that no one who knew no more than you did could have chosen better.

Look at your children: Peter rules the world, and seems to be doing it with a minimal amount of blood and horror. I destroyed the enemy that terrified us most of all, and now I'm a not-bad governor of a little colony. Valentine is a paragon of selflessness and love—and has written and is writing brilliant histories that will shape the way the human race thinks about its own past.

We're an extraordinary crop of children. Having given us our genes, you then had the terrible problem of trying to raise us. From what I see of Valentine and what she tells me of Peter, you did very well, without your hand ever being heavy in their lives.

And as for me, the absent one, the prodigal who never did come home, I still feel your fingerprints in my life and soul, and where I find those traces of your parenthood I am glad of them. Glad to have been your son.

For me, there have been only three years in which I COULD have written you; I'm sorry that it took me all this time to sort out my heart and mind well enough to have anything coherent to say. For you, there have been forty-one years in which I believe you took my silence as a request for silence.

I am far away from you now, but at least we move through time at the same pace once more, day for day, year for year. As governor of the colony I have constant access to the ansible; as parents of the Hegemon, I believe you have a similar opportunity. When I was on the voyage, you might have taken weeks to compose your reply, and to me it would have seemed that only a day had passed. But now, however long it takes you, that is how long I will wait.

> With love and regret and hope,
> your son Andrew

Valentine came to Ender, carrying the printed-out pages of his little book. "What are you calling this?" she asked, and there was a quaver in her voice.

"I don't know," said Ender.

"To imagine the life of the hive queens, to see our war from their perspective, to dare to invent an entire history for them, and tell it as if a hive queen herself were speaking—"

"I didn't invent it," said Ender.

Valentine sat down on the edge of the table. "Out there with Abra, searching for the new colony site. What did you find?"

"You're holding it in your hand," said Ender. "I found what I've been searching for ever since the hive queens let me kill them."

"You're telling me that you found living formics on this planet?"

"No," said Ender, and technically it was true—he had found only one formic. And was a dormant pupa truly describable as "living"? If you found only one chrysalis, would you say that you had found "living butterflies"?

Probably. But I have no choice except to lie to everyone. Because if it was known that a single hive queen still lived in this world, a cocoon from which she would emerge with several million fertilized eggs inside her, and the knowledge of all the hive queens before her in her phenomenally capacious mind, the seeds of the technology that nearly destroyed us and the knowledge to create even more terrible weapons if she wanted to—if that became known, how long would that cocoon survive? How long would be the life of anyone who tried to protect it?

"But you found something," said Valentine, "that makes you certain that this story you wrote is not just beautiful, but true."

"If I could tell you more than that, I would."

"Ender, have we ever told each other everything?"

"Does anyone?"

Valentine reached out and took his hand. "I want everyone on Earth to read this."

"Will they care?" Ender hoped and despaired. He wanted his book to change everything. He knew it would change nothing.

"Some will," said Valentine. "Enough."

Ender chuckled. "So I send it to a publisher and they publish it and then what? I get royalty checks here, which I can redeem for—what exactly can we buy here?"

"Everything we need," said Valentine, and they both laughed. Then, more seriously, Valentine said, "Don't sign it."

"I was wondering if I should."

"If it's known that this comes from you, from Ender Wiggin, then the reviewers will spend all their time psychoanalyzing you and say almost nothing about the book itself. The received wisdom will be that it's nothing more than your conscience trying to deal with your various sins."

"I expect no better."

"But if it's published with real anonymity, then it'll get read on its own merits."

"People will think it's fiction. That I made it up."

"They will anyway," said Valentine. "But it doesn't sound like fiction. It sounds like truth. And some will take it that way."

"So I don't sign it."

"Oh, you do," said Valentine, "because you want to give them some name to refer to you by. The way I'm still using Demosthenes."

"But nobody thinks it's the *same* Demosthenes who was such a rabble-rouser back before Peter took over the world."

"Come up with a name."

"How about 'Locke'?"

Valentine laughed. "There are still people who call him that."

"What if I call it 'Obituary' and sign it . . . what, Mortician?"

"How about 'Eulogy' and you sign it 'Speaker at the Funeral'?"

In the end, he called it simply The Hive Queen and he signed it "Speaker for the Dead." And in his anonymous, untraceable correspondence with his publisher, he insisted that it be printed without any kind of copyright notice. The publisher almost didn't go through with it, but Ender became even more insistent. "Put a notice on the cover that people are free to make as many copies of this book as they want, but that your edition is especially nice, so that people can carry it with them and write in it and underline it."

Valentine was amused. "You realize what you're doing?" she said.

"What?"

"You're having them treat it like scripture. You really think that people will read it like that?"

"I don't know what people will do," said Ender, "but yes, I think of it as something holy. I don't want to make money from it. What would I use money for? I want everyone to read it. I want everyone to know who the hive queens were. What we lost when we took them out of existence."

"We saved our lives, Ender."

"No," said Ender. "That's what we thought we were doing, and that's what we should be judged for—but what we really did was slaughter a species that wanted desperately to make peace with us, to try to understand us—but they never understood what speech and language were. This is the first time they've had a chance to find a voice."

"Too late," said Valentine.

"Tragedies are like that," said Ender.

"And their tragic flaw was . . . muteness?"

"Their tragic flaw was arrogance—they thought they could terraform any world that didn't have intelligence of the kind they knew how to recognize—beings that spoke to each other mind to mind."

"The way the gold bugs speak to us."

"The gold bugs are grunting—mentally," said Ender.

"You found one," said Valentine. "I asked you if you found 'formics' and you said no, but you found *one*."

Ender said nothing.

"I will never ask again," said Valentine.

"Good," said Ender.

"And that one—it's alone."

Ender shrugged.

"You didn't kill it. It didn't kill you. It told you—no, showed you—all the memories that you put into your book."

"For someone who was never going to ask again, you sure have a lot of questions, missy," said Ender.

"Don't you dare talk down to me."

"I'm a fifty-four-year-old man," said Ender.

"You may have been born fifty-four years ago," said Valentine, "but you're only sixteen, and no matter how old you are, I'm two years older."

"When the colony ship arrives, I'm getting on it," said Ender.

"I think I knew that," said Valentine.

"I can't stay here. I have to take a long journey. To get away from every living human."

"The ships only go from world to world, with people on all of them."

"But they take time doing it," said Ender. "If I take voyage after voyage, eventually I'll leave behind the human race as it now is."

"That's a long, lonely journey."

"Only if I go alone."

"Is that an invitation?"

"To come with me as long as you find it interesting," said Ender.

"Fair enough," said Valentine. "My guess is that you'll be better company now that you aren't in a perpetual funk."

"I don't think so," said Ender. "I intend to remain in stasis through every voyage."

"And miss the play readings on the way?"

"Can you finish your book before it's time to leave?" asked Ender.

"Probably," she said. "Certainly this volume."

"I thought this was the last one."

"Last but one," said Valentine.

"You've covered every aspect of the Formic Wars and you're writing the last battle now."

"There are two great knots to unravel."

Ender closed his eyes. "I think my book unravels one of them," he said.

"Yes," said Valentine. "I'd like to include it at the end of my last volume."

"It's not copyrighted," said Ender. "You can do what you want."

"Do you want to know what the other knot is?" asked Valentine.

"I assume it's Peter bringing the whole world together after the war was over," said Ender.

"What does that have to do with a history of the Formic Wars?" she said. "The last knot is you."

"I'm a Gordian knot. Don't unravel, just slice."

"I'm going to write about you."

"I won't read it."

"Fine," said Valentine. "I won't show it to you."

"Can't you please wait?" He wanted to say: Until I'm dead. But he didn't get that specific.

"Maybe a while," said Valentine. "We'll see."

Ender filled his days now with the business of the new colony, laying the groundwork for their arrival, making sure there were plenty of surplus crops being grown at all four of the villages as well as the new colony site, so that the newcomers could have failed harvests for two, even three years, and there'd still be no hunger. "And we'll need money," said Ender. "Here where we all know each other, this sort of ad hoc communism we've been using has worked out. But for trade to work well, we need a medium of exchange."

"Po and I found you the gold bugs," said Sel Menach. "So you've got the gold. Make coins."

Abra figured out how to adapt an oil press to make a coin stamper, and one of the chemists came up with an alloy that wouldn't constantly be shedding gold as the coins passed from hand to hand. One of the talented youngsters drew a picture of Sel Menach and one of the old women drew, from memory, the face of Vitaly Kolmogorov. Sel insisted that Kolmogorov get the cheaper coin, "Because that's the face they'll see the most. You always give the greatest man the smallest denomination."

They practiced using the money, so the prices would be set before the new colonists arrived. It was a joke at first. "Five chickens don't make a cow." And instead of calling the coins "fives" and "ones," they became "sels" and "vits." "Render unto Sel that which is Sel's, but hang on to Vit." "Sel wise, Vit foolish."

Ender wrestled with trying to set a value for the coins relative to the international dollar of the Hegemony, but Valentine stopped him. "Let it find its own value, tied to whatever people eventually pay for whatever it is we eventually export to other worlds." So the currency floated within their own private universe.

The first edition of The Hive Queen sold slowly at first, but then faster and faster. It was translated into many languages, even though almost everyone on Earth had a working knowledge of Common, since that was the official language of Peter's "Free People of Earth"—the propagandistic name he had chosen for his new international government.

Meanwhile, free copies circulated on the nets, and one day it was included in a message one of the xenobotanists received. She started telling everyone in Miranda about it, and copies were printed out and handed around. Ender and Valentine made no comment; when Alessandra pressed a copy on Ender, he accepted it, waited a while, and returned it. "Isn't it wonderful?" Alessandra asked.

"I think it is, yes," said Ender.

"Oh, yes, that analytical voice, that dispassionate attitude."

"What can I say?" said Ender. "I am who I am."

"I think this book has changed my life," said Alessandra.

"For the better, I hope," said Ender. And then, glancing at her swollen belly, he asked, "Changed your life more than that?"

Alessandra smiled. "I don't know yet. I'll tell you in a year."

Ender did not say: In a year I'll be on a starship and far away.

Valentine finished her penultimate volume and when it was published, she included the full text of The Hive Queen at the end, with an introductory note:

"We know so little of the formics that it is impossible for me, as a historian, to tell of this war from their point of view. So I will include an artistic imagining of the history, because even if it can't be proved, I believe this is the true story."

Not long after, Valentine came to Ender. "Peter read my book," she said.

"I'm glad someone did," said Ender.

"He sent me a message about the last chapter. He said, 'I know who wrote it.'"

"And was he right?"

"He was."

"Isn't he the clever one."

"He was moved, Ender."

"People seem to be liking it."

"More than liking, and you know it. Let me read what Peter said: 'If he can speak for the buggers, surely he can speak for me.'"

"What's that supposed to mean?"

"He wants you to write about him. About his life."

"When I last saw Peter I was six and he had threatened to kill me just a few hours before."

"So you're saying no."

"I'm saying that I'll talk to him and we'll see what happens."

On the ansible, they talked for an hour at a time, Peter in his late fifties, with a weak heart that had the doctors worried, Ender still a boy of sixteen. But Peter was still himself, and so was Ender, only now there was no anger between them. Maybe because Peter had achieved everything he dreamed of, and Ender hadn't stood in his way or even, at least in Peter's mind, surpassed him.

In Ender's mind, too. "What you did," said Ender, "you knew you were doing."

"Is that good or bad?"

"Nobody had to trick Alexander into conquering Persia," said Ender. "If they had, would we call him 'the Great'?"

When Peter had told of his whole life, everything he did that mattered enough to come up in these conversations, Ender spent only five days writing a slim volume called "The Hegemon."

He sent a copy to Peter with a note: "Since the author will be 'Speaker for the Dead,' this can't be published until after you die."

Peter wrote back: "It can't happen a moment too soon for me." But in a letter to Valentine, he poured out his heart about what it meant to him to feel so completely understood. "He didn't conceal any of the bad things I did. But he kept them in balance. In perspective."

Valentine showed the letter to Ender and he laughed. "Balance! How can anybody know the relative weight of sins and great achievements? Five chickens do *not* make a cow."

CHAPTER 20

To: MinCol@ColMin.gov
From: Gov%ShakespeareCol@MinCol.gov
Subj: Is that job still open?

Dear Hyrum,

I have reasons of my own that I won't go into, but I also believe that Shakespeare will be well served if, when this colony ship leaves, I am on it. I will be here throughout the arrival and establishment of the new colonists. The present settlers have already passed through a profound change: The colonists who arrived with me are now included in the term "old settlers" in anticipation of the arrival of the ship. The old folks who fought the formics are now called "originals" but there is no common term to distinguish between their descendants and the people who arrived with me.

If I remained, then both the governor of the new settlement and I would be appointees from ColMin. If I leave, replaced by an elected council of the four settlements, with an elected president and elected mayors, it will create almost irresistible pressure on the new governor to limit himself to a single two-year term, as I did, and allow himself to be replaced by an elected mayor.

Meanwhile, the "old settlers" have planted their crops for them, but have built only half enough houses. That is at my suggestion, so that the new colonists can join with them in building the rest. They need to experience how much work it takes, so they'll appreciate better just how much work was done *for* them by the old settlers. And working side by side will help keep the two groups from being strangers—even though I have located them far enough away that your goal of separate development will also have a chance of being met. They can't be completely separated, however, or exogamy would be impractical and genes are more important than culture at this moment for the future health of this world's human stock.

Human stock . . . but we ARE having to concern ourselves with the physical bodies in just the way herders always have. Uncle Sel would be the first to laugh and say that this is exactly right. We're mammals before we're humans, and if we ever forget the mammal, then all that makes us human will be overwhelmed by the hungry beast.

I've been studying everything I can about Virlomi and the wars she fought. What an astonishing woman! Her Battle School records show only an ordinary student (in an admittedly extraordinary group). But Battle School is about war, not revolution or national survival; nor did your tests measure anyone's propensity for becoming a demigod. If you had such a test, I wonder what you would have found out about Peter, back when he was a child and not ruler of the world.

Speaking of Peter, he and I are in conversation; perhaps you knew. We're not messaging, we're using ansible bandwidth for conversation. It's bittersweet to see him at nearly sixty years of age. Hair turning steely grey, face lined, carrying a little weight (but still fit), and the lines of responsibility etched on his face. He's not the boy I knew and hated. But the existence of this man does not erase that boy from my memory. They are simply two separate people in my mind, who happen to have the same name.

I find myself admiring the man; even loving him. He has faced choices every bit as terrible as mine ever were—and he dealt with them with his eyes open. He knew before he made his decisions that people would die from them. And yet he has more compassion than he—or I, or Valentine for that matter—ever expected of him.

He tells me that in his childhood, after I was in Battle School, he decided that the only way to succeed in his work was to deceive people into thinking he was as lovable as me. (I thought he was joking, but he was not; I don't believe my reputation in Battle School was "lovable" but Peter was dealing with the way I was remembered at home.) So from then on, he looked at all his choices and said, What would a good person do, and then did it. But he has now learned something very important about human nature. If you spend your whole life pretending to be good, then you are indistinguishable from a good person. Relentless hypocrisy eventually becomes the truth. Peter has made himself into a good man, even if he set out on that road for reasons that were far from pure.

This gives me great hope for myself. All I have to do now is find some work to do that will lay to rest the burden that I carry. Governing a colony has been interesting and valuable work, but it does not do for me what I hoped it would. I still wake up with dead formics and dead soldiers and dead children in my head. I still wake up with memories that tell me that I am what Peter used to be. When those go away, I can be myself again.

I know that it troubles you that I have this mindset. Well, that's your burden, isn't it? Let me assure you, however, that my burden is half of my own making. You and Mazer and the rest of the officers training and using me and the other children did what you did in a righteous cause—and it worked. Toward me you have the same responsibility that commanders always have for those soldiers who survive, but maimed. The soldiers are still responsible for the lives they make for themselves after the fact; it's bitterly ironic that your true answer to them is: It's not my fault that you lived. If you had been killed you would not have to deal with all these wounds. This is the portion of life that was given back to you; it was the enemy who took from you the wholeness that you do not have. My job was to make it so that your death or injuries meant something, and I have done that.

That is what I have learned from the soldiers here. They still remember their comrades who fell; they still miss the life they left behind on Earth, the families they never saw again, the places they can revisit only in their dreams and memories. Yet they do not blame me. They're proud of what we did together. Almost every one of them has said to me, at one time or another, "It was worth it." Because we won.

So I say that to you. Whatever burden I'm carrying, it was worth it because we won.

So I appreciate your warning about this little book that's going around, The Hive Queen. Unlike you, I don't believe it's nonsense; I think this "Speaker for the Dead" has said something truthful, whether it's factual or not. Suppose the hive queens were every bit as beautiful and well-meaning as they are in this Speaker for the Dead's imagination. That does not change the fact that during the war they could not tell us that their intentions had changed and they regretted what they had done. It does not change our blamelessness (though blamelessness does not relieve us of responsibility).

I have a suspicion that I cannot verify: I think that even though the individual formics were so dependent on the hive queens that when the queens died, so did the soldiers and workers, that does not mean that they were a single organism, or that the hive queens did not have to take the deep needs, the *will* of the individuals, into account. And because the formics were individually so very stupid, the hive queens could not explain subtleties to them. Isn't it possible that if the hive queens had refused to fight those initial battles, letting us slaughter them like true pacifists, the survival instinct of the individual formics would have asserted itself with so much strength as to overwhelm the power of their mistresses? We would have had the battles anyway—only the formics would have fought without coherence or real intelligence. This in turn might have caused formics everywhere to rebel against their queens. Even a dictator has to respect the will of the pawns, for without their obedience, he has no power. Those are my thoughts about The Hive Queen, since you asked. And about everything else, because you need to hear my thoughts as much as I need to say them. You were my hive queen, and I was your formic, during this war. Twice I wanted to reject your overlordship; twice, Bean stepped in and put me back under the yoke. But all that I did, I did of my own free will, like any good soldier or servant or slave. The task of the tyrant is not to compel, but to

persuade even the unwilling that compliance better serves their interest than resistance.

So if you wish to send this arriving ship to Ganges Colony, I will go and see
what I can do to help Virlomi deal with Bean's kidnapped son and his very
strange mother (though it is *not* her spitting on you that proves her to be
strange; there are—or were—hundreds who would have stood in line for the
privilege). I have a feeling that Virlomi will indeed find herself over her head,
because her colony is so overwhelmingly Indian. It will make all her decisions
seem unjust to the non-Indians, and if this Randall Firth is anything like as smart
as his father, and if his mother has raised him to hate any who ever stood in
Achilles Flandres's way, which certainly includes Virlomi, then this is the
wedge that Randall will exploit to try to destroy her and gain power.

And while there are those in the I.F. and even in ColMin who believe that
nothing that happens in the colonies can threaten Earth, I'm glad you recognize that this is not so. A warrior-rebel in a colony world can capture the imagination of millions on Earth. Billions, perhaps. And The Hive Queen may turn
out to be part of this. A clever demagogue from the colonies can wrap himself
in the mantle of the vanished hive queens, playing upon the powerful senti-
ment that the colony worlds were somehow "wronged" by Earth and are
owed something. It is irrational, but there are precedents for even more illogi-
cal leaps of judgment.

Even if you cannot or no longer wish to send me to Ganges, however, I will
be aboard that ship, so I hope our flight plan will send me somewhere interesting. Valentine has not yet decided whether to come with me, but since,
because of working on her histories, she has remained completely detached
from this colony, emotionally and socially, I think she'll come with me, having
no incentive to remain here without me.

Your lifelong worker bee,
Ender

Achilles came to the hut where Governor Virlomi lived in her lofty
poverty. She made such a show of having the simplest of habitations—

but it was completely unnecessary to build adobe walls and a thatched roof, with so much fine lumber nearby. Virlomi's every action was calculated to enhance her prestige among the Indian colonists. But the whole display filled Achilles with contempt.

"Randall Firth," he said to the "friend" standing outside. Virlomi had said, "My friends stand watch to protect my time," she said, "so I can meditate sometimes." But her "friends" ate at the common table and drew their full share at harvest, so that their service to her was, in effect, paid. They were cops or guards, and everyone knew it. But no, the Indians all said, they really are volunteers, they really do a full day's labor besides.

A full day's labor . . . for an Indian. It gets a little hot and they go lie down when regular fullsize people have to take up the slack for them.

No wonder my father, Achilles the Great, led the Chinese to conquer the Indians. Someone had to teach them how to work. Nothing, though, could teach them how to think.

Inside the hut, Virlomi was spinning yarn by hand. Why? Because Gandhi did it. They had four spinning jennies and two power looms, and spare parts to keep them running for a hundred years, by which time they should have the ability to manufacture new ones. There was no need for homespun. Even Gandhi only did it because he was protesting against the way English power looms were putting Indians out of work. What was Virlomi trying to accomplish?

"Randall," she said.

"Virlomi," he answered.

"Thank you for coming."

"No one can resist a command from our beloved governor."

Virlomi lifted weary eyes to him. "And yet you always find a way."

"Only because your power here is illegitimate," said Achilles. "Even before we founded our colony, Shakespeare declared its independence and started electing governors to two-year terms."

"And we did the same," said Virlomi.

"They always elect *you*," said Achilles. "The person appointed by ColMin."

"That's democracy."

"Democracy only because the deck was stacked. Literally. With

Indians. And you play this holy-woman game to keep them in your thrall."

"You have far too much time to read," said Virlomi, "if you know words like 'thrall.' "

Such an easy opening. "Why do you feel the need to discourage citizens from educating themselves?" asked Achilles.

Virlomi's pleasant expression didn't crack. "Why must everything be political with you?"

"Wouldn't it be nice if other people ignored politics, so you could have it all to yourself?"

"Randall," said Virlomi, "I didn't bring you here because of your agitation among the non-Indian colonists."

"And yet that's why I came."

"I have an opportunity for you."

Achilles had to give her credit: Virlomi kept on plugging away. Maybe that's one of the attributes of Indian goddesshood. "Are you going to offer me another placeholder job to assuage my ego?"

"You keep saying that you're trapped on this world, that you've never been anywhere else, so your entire life will be lived under the dominion of Indians, surrounded by Indian culture."

"Your spies have reported accurately."

He expected her to get sidetracked on whether her informants were spies or not, since they were ordinary citizens who freely attended public events and then talked about them afterward. But apparently she was as weary of that topic as he was. And besides, she clearly had an urgent agenda.

"A starship is arriving here in about a month," said Virlomi. "It comes from Shakespeare Colony, and it's bringing us several of their highly successful hybrids and genetic alterations to augment our agricultural resources. A very important visit."

"I'm not a farmer," said Achilles.

"When starships come here," said Virlomi, "it's never permanent. They come, and then they go."

Now Achilles understood exactly what she was offering him. If it *was* an offer, and not an involuntary exile. "Go where?" he asked.

"In this case, I am assured that the pilot is taking his starship back to Earth—well, *near* to Earth—so that the samples from Shakespeare, along with our own poor offerings, can be examined, propagated, studied, and shared with all the colonies. Some may even be cultivated on Earth itself, because the high yields and climatic adaptations are so favorable."

"Are they naming one of the species after you?" asked Achilles.

"I'm offering you a chance to go to that big wide world and see it for yourself. Indians are only about a quarter of Earth's population at the moment, and there are many places you can go where you'll almost never see an Indian."

"It's not Indians that I don't like," said Achilles blandly.

"Oh?"

"It's smug authoritarian government pretending to be democratic."

"Indians are in the majority here. By definition democratic, even if smug," said Virlomi.

"Earth is ruled by an evil dictatorship."

"Earth is ruled by an elected Congress, and presided over by an elected hegemon."

"A hegemony established through the murder of—"

"Of the man you mistakenly believe to be your father," said Virlomi.

That sentence struck Achilles like a blow with a sledgehammer. In all his life, he and his mother had kept his parentage a secret, just as no one had ever heard him called by his secret—but true—name, Achilles. It was always Randall this and Randall that; only in moments of tender privacy did Mother ever speak to him as Achilles. Only in his own mind did he call himself that name.

But Virlomi knew. How?

"I watched your supposed father murder children in cold blood," said Virlomi. "He murdered a good friend of mine. There was no provocation."

"That's a lie," said Achilles.

"Ah. You have a witness who will contradict me?"

"There was provocation. He was trying to unite the world and establish peace."

"He was a psychotic who murdered everyone who ever helped him—or saw him helpless."

"Not everyone," said Achilles. "He let *you* live."

"I didn't help him. I didn't thwart him. I stayed invisible, until at last I was able to escape from him. Then I set out to liberate my country from the cruel oppression he had unleashed upon us."

"Achilles Flandres was establishing world peace, and you brought war back to a country that *he* had pacified."

"But you have no problem with admitting that you believe the fantasy that he is your father."

"I think my mother knows more than anyone else about that."

"Your mother knows only what she was told. Because she's a surrogate—not your genetic mother. Your embryo was implanted in her. She was lied to. She has passed that lie down to you. You are nothing but another of Achilles' kidnap victims. And your imprisonment by him continues to this day. You are his last and most pathetic victim."

Achilles' hand lashed out before he could stop himself. The blow he struck was not hard—not as hard as his height and strength could have made it.

"I have been assaulted," said Virlomi quietly.

Two of her "friends" came into the hut. They took Achilles by the arms.

"I charge Randall Firth with assault on the governor. Under penalty of perjury, Randall, do you admit that you struck me?"

"What an absurd lie," said Achilles.

"I thought you'd say that," said Virlomi. "Three vids from different angles should substantiate the charge *and* the perjury. When you're convicted, Randall, I will recommend that your sentence be exile. To Earth—the place you seem to think would be infinitely preferable to Ganges. Your mother can go with you or not, as she chooses."

She played me like a fish, thought Achilles. My father would never have stood for this. Humiliation—the unbearable offense. That's how my father lived, and that's how I will live.

"The whole recording," said Achilles. "That's what they'll see—how you goaded me."

Virlomi rose smoothly to her feet and came close to him, putting her mouth close to his ear. "The whole recording," said Virlomi, "will show who you think your father is, and your approval of his actions, which still are seen as the epitome of evil by the entire human race."

She stepped back from him. "You can decide for yourself whether the whole record or an edited portion will be shown."

Achilles knew that this was the point where he was expected to make threats, to bluster pathetically. But the recording was still running.

"I see that you know how to manipulate a child," said Achilles. "I'm only sixteen, and you provoked me to anger."

"Ah, yes, sixteen. Big for your age, aren't you?"

"In heart and mind, as well as skin and bone," said Achilles—his standard answer. "Remember, Your Excellency the Governor, that setting me up is one thing, and knocking me out is another."

He turned—and then waited as the men clinging to his arms scrambled to move around again to be beside him. They left the hut together. Then Achilles stopped abruptly. "You do know that I can shake you off like houseflies if I feel like it."

"Oh, yes, Mr. Firth. Our presence was as witnesses. Otherwise our taking hold of you was merely symbolic."

"And you hoped I'd knock one of you down on camera."

"We hope that all men and women can live together without violence."

"But you don't mind being the victim of violence, if you can use it to discredit or destroy your enemy."

"Are you our enemy, Mr. Firth?"

"I hope not," said Achilles. "But your goddess wants me to be."

"Oh, she is not a goddess, Mr. Firth." They laughed as if the idea were absurd.

As Achilles walked away, he was already formulating his next move. She was going to use his father's reputation against him—and he did not believe she would keep it a secret, since she was right and any link between him and Achilles the Great would permanently besmirch him.

If my father is widely believed to be the worst man in human history, then I must find a worse one to link *her* with.

As for the claim that Mother was only a surrogate, Randall would not let Virlomi's lie come between him and his mother. It would break her heart for him even to question her motherhood of him. No, Virlomi, I will not let you turn me into a weapon to hurt my mother.

CHAPTER
21

To: AWiggin%Ganges@ColLeague.adm
From: hgraff%retlist@IFCom.adm
Subj: Welcome back to the human universe

Of course my condolences on the passing of your parents. But I understand from them that you and they corresponded to great mutual satisfaction before they died. The passing of your brother must have come as more of a surprise. He was young, but his heart gave out. Pay no attention to the foolish rumors that always attend the death of the great. I saw the autopsy, and Peter had a weak heart, despite his healthy lifestyle. It was quick, a clot that stopped his life while he slept. He died at the peak of his power and his powers. Not a bad way to go. I hope you'll read the excellent essay on his life written by supposedly the same author as The Hive Queen. It's called The Hegemon, and I've attached it here.

An interesting thing happened to me while you were in stasis, sailing from Shakespeare to Ganges. I was fired.

Here is something I hadn't foreseen (believe it; I have foreseen very little in my long life; I survived and accomplished things because I adapted quickly), though I should have: When you spend ten months of every year in stasis, there is a side effect: Your underlings and superiors begin to regard your awakenings as intrusions. The ones who were fiercely loyal to you retire, pursue their careers into other avenues, or are maneuvered out of office. Soon, everyone around you is loyal to themselves, their careers, or someone who wants your job.

Everyone put on such a show of deference to me whenever I awoke. They reported on how all my decisions from my last awakening had been carried out—or had explanations as to why they had not.

For three awakenings, I should have noticed how unconvincing those explanations had become, and how ineffectively my orders had been carried out. I should have seen that the bureaucratic soup through which I had navigated for so many years had begun to congeal around me; I should have seen that my long absences were making me powerless.

Just because I wasn't having any fun, I didn't realize that my months in stasis were, in effect, vacations. It was an attempt to prolong my tenure in office by not attending to business. When has this ever been a good idea?

It was pure vanity, Ender. It could not work; it could not last. I awoke to find that my name was no longer on my office door. I was on the retired list of IFCom— and at a colonel's pay, to add insult to injury. As for any kind of pension from ColMin, that was out of the question, since I had not been retired, I had been dismissed for nonperformance of my duties. They cited years of missed meetings when I was in stasis; they cited my failure to seek any kind of leave; they even harked back to that ancient court martial to show a "pattern of negligent behavior." So . . . dismissed with cause, to live on a colonel's half pay.

I think they actually assumed that I had managed to enrich myself during my tenure in office. But I was never that kind of politician.

However, I also care little for material things. I am returning to Earth, where I still own a little property—I did make sure the taxes were kept up. I will be able to live in peaceful retirement on a lovely piece of land in Ireland that I fell in love with and bought during the years when I traveled the world in search of children to exploit and quite possibly destroy in Battle School. No one there will have any idea of who I am—or, rather, who I was. I have outlived my infamy.

One thing about retirement, however: I will have no more ansible privileges. Even this letter is going to you with such a low priority that it will be years before it's transmitted. But the computers do not forget and cannot be misused by anyone vindictive enough to want to prevent my saying good-bye to old friends. I saw to the security of the system, and the leaders of the I.F. and the FPE understand the importance of maintaining the independence of the nets. You will see this message when you come out of stasis yourself upon arriving at Ganges four years from now.

I write with two purposes. First, I want you to know that I understand and remember the great debt that I and all the world owe to you. Fifty-seven years ago, before you went to Shakespeare, I assembled your pay during the war (which was all retroactively at admiral rank), the cash bonuses voted for you and your jeesh during the first flush of gratitude, and your salary as governor of Shakespeare, and piggybacked them onto six different mutual funds of impeccable reputation.

They will be audited continuously by the best software I could find, which, it may amuse you to know, is based on the kernel of the Fantasy Game (or "mind game," as it was also called in Battle School). The program's ability to constantly monitor itself and all data sources and inputs, and to reprogram itself in response to new information, made it seem the best choice to make sure your best interests, financially, were well watched out for. Human financial managers can be incompetent, or tempted to embezzle, or die, only to be replaced by a worse one.

You may draw freely from the accruing interest, without paying taxes of any kind until you come of age—which, since so many children are voyaging, is now legally accounted using the sum of ship's time during voyages added to the days spent in real time between voyages, with stasis time counting zero. I have done my best to shore up your future against the vicissitudes of time.

Which brings me to my second purpose. I am an old man who thought he could manipulate time and live to see all his plans come to fruition. In a way,

I suppose I have. I have pulled many strings, and most of my puppets have finished their dance. I have outlived most of the people I knew, and all of my friends.

Unless you are my friend. I have come to think of you that way; I hope that I do not overstep my bounds, because what I offer you now is a friend's advice.

In rereading the message in which you asked me to send you to Ganges, I have seen in the phrase "reasons of my own" the possibility that you are using starflight the way I was using stasis—as a way to live longer. In your case, though, you are not seeking to see all your plans to fruition—I'm not sure you even have plans. I think instead that you are seeking to put decades, perhaps centuries, between you and your past.

I think the plan is rather clever, if you mean to outlast your fame and live in quiet anonymity somewhere, to marry and have children and rejoin the human race, but among people who cannot even conceive of the idea that their neighbor, Andrew Wiggin, could possibly have anything to do with the great Ender Wiggin who saved the world.

But I fear that you are trying to distance yourself from something else. I fear that you think you can hide from what you (all unwittingly) did, the matters that were exploited in my unfortunate court martial. I fear that you are trying to outrun the deaths of Stilson, of Bonzo Madrid, of thousands of humans and billions of formics in the war you so brilliantly and impossibly won for us all.

You cannot do it, Ender. You carry them with you. They will be freshly in your mind long after all the rest of the world has forgotten. You defended yourself against children who meant to destroy you, and you did it effectively; if you had not done so, would you have been capable of your great victories? You defended the human race against a nonverbal enemy who destroyed human lives carelessly in the process of taking what it wanted—our world, our home, our achievements, the future of planet Earth. What you blame yourself for, I honor you for. Please hear my voice in your head, as well as your own self-condemnation. Try to balance them.

You are the man you have always been: one who takes responsibility, one who foresees consequences and acts to protect others and, yes, yourself. That man will not easily surrender a burden.

But do not use starflight like a drug, using it to seek oblivion. I can tell you from experience that a life lived in short visits to the human race is not a life. We are only human when we are part of a community. When you first came to Battle School, I tried to isolate you, but it could not be done. I surrounded you with hostility; you took most of your enemies and rivals and made friends of them. You freely taught everything you knew, and nurtured students that we teachers had, frankly, given up on; some of them ended up finding greatness in themselves, and achieved much. You were a part of them; they carried you inside them all their lives. You were better at our job than we were.

Your jeesh loved you, Ender, with a devotion I could only envy—I have had many friends, but never the kind of passion that those children had for you. They would have died for you, every one of them. Because they knew you would have died for them. And the reports I had from Shakespeare Colony—from Sel Menach, from Ix Tolo and his sons Po and Abra, and from the colonists who never even knew you, but found the place you had prepared for them—I can tell you that you were universally loved and respected, and all of them regarded you as the best member of their communities, their benefactor and friend.

I tell you this because I fear that the lesson I taught you first was the one you learned the best: that you are always alone, that no one will ever help you, that whatever must be done, only you can do. I cannot speak to the deep recesses of your mind, but only to the uppermost part, the conscious mind that has spoken and written to me so eloquently all these years. So I hope you can hear my message and pass it along to the part of you that will not at first believe it:

You are the least-alone person I have ever known. Your heart has always included within it everyone who let you love them, and many who did not. The meetingplace of all these communities you formed was your own heart; they knew you held them there, and it made them one with each other. Yet the gift you gave them, none was able to give you, and I fear this is because I did my evil work too well, and built a wall in your mind that cannot let you receive the knowledge of what and who you are.

It galls me to see how this "Speaker for the Dead" with his silly little books has achieved the influence that YOU deserved. People are actually turning it into a religion—there are self-styled "speakers for the dead" who presume to talk at funerals and tell "the truth" about the dead person, an appalling desecration—who can know the truth about anyone? I have left instructions in my will that none of these poseurs is to be allowed anywhere near my funeral, if anyone even bothers to have one. You saved the world and were never allowed to come home. This mountebank makes up a fake history of the formics and then writes an apologia for your brother Peter and people make a religion out of it. There's no accounting for the human race.

You have Valentine with you. Show her this letter, and see if she does not affirm that every word I've said about you is true. I may not be alive when you read this, but many who knew you as students in Battle School are still alive, including most of your jeesh. They are old, but not one of them has forgotten you. (I still write to Petra now and then; she has been widowed twice, and yet remains an astonishingly happy and optimistic soul. She keeps in touch with all the others.) They and I and Valentine can all attest to the fact that you have belonged to the human race more deeply and fully than most people could even imagine.

Find a way to believe that, and don't hide from life in the unfathomable, lightless depths of relativistic space.

I have achieved much in my life, but the greatest of my achievements was finding you, recognizing what you were, and somehow managing not to ruin you before you could save the world. I only wish I could then have healed you. But that will have to be your own achievement—or perhaps Valentine's. Or perhaps it will come from the children that you must, you *must* have someday.

For that is my greatest personal regret. I never married and had children of my own. Instead I stole other people's children and trained them—not raised them. It is easy to say that you can adopt the whole human race as your children, but it is not the same as living in a home with a child and shaping all you do to help him learn to be happy and whole and good. Don't live your life without ever holding a child in your arms, on your lap, in your home, and feeling a child's arms around you and hearing his voice in your ear and seeing his smile, given to you because you put it into his heart.

I had no such moments, because I did not treat my kidnapped Battle School children that way. I was no one's father, by birth or adoption. Marry, Ender. Have children, or adopt them, or borrow them—whatever it takes. But do not live a life like mine.

I have done great things, but now, in the end, I am not happy. I wish I had let the future take care of itself, and instead of skipping forward through time, had stopped, made a family, and died in my proper time, surrounded by children.

See how I pour out my heart to you? Somehow, you took me into your jeesh as well.

Forgive the maudlinness of old men; when you are my age, you will understand.

I never treated you like a son when I had you in my power, but I have loved you like a son; and in this letter I have spoken to you as I'd like to think I might have spoken to the sons I never had. I say to you: Well done, Ender. Now be happy.

Hyrum Graff
I.F. Col. Ret.

Ender was shocked at the difference in Valentine when he emerged from stasis at the end of the voyage. "I told you I wasn't going into stasis until my book was finished," she said when she saw his expression.

"You didn't stay awake for the whole voyage."

"I did," she said. "This wasn't a forty-year voyage in two years like our first one, it was only an eighteen-year voyage in a bit over fourteen months." Ender did the arithmetic quickly and saw that she was right. Acceleration and deceleration always took about the same amount of time, while the length of the voyage in between determined the difference in subjective time.

"Still," he said. "You're a woman."

"How flattering that you noticed. I was disappointed that I didn't have any ship's captains falling in love with me."

"Perhaps the fact that Captain Hong brought his wife and family with him had an effect on that."

"Bit by bit, they're learning that you don't have to sacrifice everything to be a star voyager," said Valentine.

"Arithmetic—I'm still seventeen, and you're nearly twenty-one."

"I *am* twenty-one," she said. "Think of me as your Auntie Val."

"I will not," he said. "You finished your book?"

"I wrote a history of Shakespeare Colony, up to the time of your arrival. I couldn't have done it if you had been awake."

"Because I would have insisted on accuracy?"

"Because you wouldn't have let me have complete access to your correspondence with Kolmogorov."

"My correspondence is double-password encrypted."

"Oh, Ender, you're talking to *me,*" said Valentine. "Do you think I wouldn't be able to guess 'Stilson' and 'Bonzo'?"

"I didn't use their names just like that, naked."

"To me they were naked, Ender. You think nobody really understands you, but I can guess your passwords. That makes me your password buddy."

"That makes you a snoop," said Ender. "I can't wait to read the book."

"Don't worry. I didn't mention your name. His emails are cited as 'letter to a friend' with the date."

"Aren't you considerate."

"Don't be testy. I haven't seen you in fourteen months and I missed you. Don't make me change my mind."

"I saw you yesterday, and you've snooped my files since then. Don't expect me to ignore that. What else did you snoop?"

"Nothing," said Valentine. "You have your luggage locked. I'm not a *yegg.*"

"When can I read the book?"

"When you buy it and download it. You can afford to pay."

"I don't have any money."

"You haven't read Hyrum Graff's letter yet," said Valentine. "He got you a nice pension and you can draw on it without paying any taxes until you come of age."

"So you didn't confine yourself to your research topic."

"I can never know whether a letter contains useful data until I read it, can I?"

"So you read all the letters ever written in the history of the human race, in order to write this book?"

"Only the ones written since the founding of Colony One after the Third Formic War." She kissed his cheek. "Good morning, Ender. Welcome back to the world."

Ender shook his head. "Not Ender," he said. "Not here. I'm Andrew."

"Ah," she said. "Why not 'Andy,' then? Or 'Drew'?"

"Andrew," Ender repeated.

"Well, you should have told the governor that, because her letter of invitation is addressed to 'Ender Wiggin.' "

Ender frowned. "We never knew each other in Battle School."

"I imagine she *thinks* she knows you, having been so intimately involved with half your jeesh."

"Having had her army beaten into the ground by them," said Ender.

"That's a kind of intimacy, isn't it? A sort of Grant-and-Lee thing?"

"I suppose Graff had to warn her that I was coming."

"Your name was also on the manifest, and it included the fact that you were governor of Shakespeare until your two-year term ended. That narrows you down among all the possible Andrew Wiggins in the human race."

"Have you been down to the surface?"

"No one has. I asked the captain to let me wake you so you could be on the first shuttle. Of course he was pleased to do anything for the great Ender Wiggin. He's of that generation—he was on Eros when you won that final victory. He says he saw you in the corridors there, more than once."

Ender thought back to his brief meeting with the captain before going into stasis. "I didn't recognize him."

"He didn't expect you to. He really is a nice man. Much better at his job than old what's-his-name."

"Quincy Morgan."

"I remembered his name, Ender, I just didn't want to say it or hear it."

Ender cleaned himself up. Stasis left him with a sort of scum all over his body; his skin seemed to crackle just a little when he moved. This can't be good for you, he thought as he scrubbed it off and the skin protested by giving him little stabbing pains. But Graff does stasis ten months of the year and he's still going strong.

And he got me a pension. Isn't that nice. I can't imagine Ganges is using Hegemony money any more than Shakespeare was, but once interstellar trade starts up, maybe there'll start being some buying power in the FPE dollar.

Dried and dressed, Ender got his luggage out of storage and, in the privacy of Valentine's locked stateroom, from which she had discreetly absented herself, Ender opened the case containing the cocoon of the last hive queen in the universe.

He was afraid, for a moment, that she had died during the voyage. But no. After he had held the cocoon in his bare hands for a few minutes, an image flickered into his mind. Or rather a rapid series of images—the faces of hundreds of hive queens, a thousand of them, in such rapid succession that he couldn't register any of them. It was as if, upon waking—upon rebooting—all the ancestors in this hive queen's memory had to make an appearance in her mind before settling back and letting her have control of her own brain.

What ensued was not a conversation—it could not be. But when Ender thought back on it, it seemed to him like a conversation, complete with dialogue. It was as if his brain was not designed to remember what had passed between them—the direct transfer of shaped memory. Instead, it translated the exchange into the normal human mode of interresponsive language.

"Is this my new home? Will you let me come out?" she asked him—or rather, she showed herself emerging from the cocoon into the cool air of a cave, and the feeling of a question—or a demand?—came along with the image.

"Too soon," he said—and in his mind there really were words, or at least ideas shapable into language. "Nobody's forgotten anything yet. They would be terrified. They'd kill you as soon as they discovered you or any of your children."

"More waiting," she said. "Wait forever."

"Yes," he said. "I will voyage as often as I can, as far as I can. Five hundred years. A thousand years. I don't know how long it will be before I can safely bring you out, or where we'll be."

She reminded him that she was not affected by the relativistic effects of time travel. "Our minds work on the principle of your ansible. We are always connected to the real time of the universe." For this she used images of clocks that she drew from his own memory. Her own metaphor for time was the sweep of sun across sky for days, and its drift northward and south again to show years. Hive queens never needed to subdivide time into hours and minutes and seconds, because with her own children— the formics—everything was infinitely *now*.

"I'm sorry that you have to experience all the time of the voyage," said Ender. "But you want me in stasis during the voyage, so I'll stay young long enough to find you a home."

Stasis—she compared his hibernation with her own pupation. "But you come out the same. No change."

"We humans don't change in cocoons. We stay awake through our maturation process."

"So for you, this sleep isn't birth."

"No," said Ender. "It's temporary death. Extinguishment, but with a spark left glowing in the ash. I didn't even dream."

"All I do is dream," she said. "I dream the whole history of my people. They are my mothers, but now they are also my sisters, because I remember doing all the things they do."

For this, she had drawn on the images of Valentine and Peter to say "sisters." And when Peter's face appeared, there was fear and pain in the memory.

"I don't fear him anymore," said Ender. "Or hate him. He turned out to be a great man."

But the hive queen didn't believe him. She drew from his mind the image of the old man from their ansible conversations, and compared it with the child Peter in Ender's deepest memory. They were too different to be the same.

And Ender could not argue the point. Peter the Hegemon was not Peter the monster. Maybe he never was. Maybe both were an illusion. But

Peter the monster was the one buried deep in Ender's memory, and he was unlikely to expunge him from it.

He put the cocoon back in its hiding place, locked it, and then left it on the cart of luggage being taken down to the surface.

Virlomi actually came to meet the shuttle; and in moments she made it clear she was extending this courtesy only for Ender's sake. She came aboard the shuttle to talk to him.

Ender did not take this as a good sign. While they waited for her to come aboard, Ender said to Valentine, "She doesn't want me here. She wants me to go back onto the ship."

"Wait and see what she wants," said Valentine. "Maybe she just wants to know what you intend."

When she came in, Virlomi looked so much older than the girl whose face Ender had seen on the vids of the Sino-Indian War. A year or two of brooding over defeat, and then sixteen years of governing a colony—they were bound to take their toll.

"Thank you for letting me visit you so early," she said.

"You have flattered us beyond measure," said Ender. "To come out and receive us yourself."

"I had to see you," she said, "before you emerged into the colony. I swear to you that I told no one of your coming."

"I believe you," said Ender. "But your remark seems to imply that people know I'm here."

"No," she said. "No, there's no rumor of that, thank God."

Which God, Ender wondered. Or, being reputed a goddess, did she thank herself?

"When Colonel Graff—oh, whatever his title was then—he'll always be Colonel Graff to me—when he told me he had asked you to come, it was because he anticipated problems with a particular mother and son."

"Nichelle and Randall Firth," said Ender.

"Yes," she said. "It happens that I had also noticed them as a potential problem during setup back in Battle School—Ellis Island—whatever the name of the place was by then. So I understood his concern. What I didn't know was why he thought you could handle them better than I could."

"I'm not sure he thought I could. Perhaps he only wanted you to have a resource to draw on, in case I had some ideas. Have they been a problem?"

"The mother was your ordinary reclusive paranoid," said Virlomi. "But she worked hard, and if she seemed obsessively protective of her son, there was nothing perverse about their relationship—she never tried to keep him in her bed, for instance, and she never bathed him after infancy—none of the danger signs. He was such a tiny baby. Almost like a toy. But he walked and talked incredibly young. Shockingly young."

"And he stayed small," said Ender, "until he was in his teens. Just kept growing at an ordinary pace and then didn't stop. I imagine he's something of a giant now."

"Two full meters in height with no sign of stopping," said Virlomi. "How did you know this?"

"Because of who his parents are."

Virlomi gasped. "Graff knows who the real father is. And he didn't tell me. How was I supposed to deal with this situation if he didn't give me all the information?"

"Forgive me for reminding you," said Ender, "but you were not widely trusted at the time."

"No," she said. "But I thought if he made me governor, he'd give me . . . but that's past and gone."

Ender wondered if, indeed, Graff was gone. He wasn't on any of the registries he could access—but he didn't have ansible privileges like those he'd had before, as a new governor coming to his colony. There were deep searches he simply wasn't given time to pursue.

"Graff didn't want to leave you without knowledge. But he gave it to me, and left it to me to judge how much to tell you."

"So you don't trust me either?" Her voice sounded jocular, but there was pain under it.

"I don't know you," said Ender. "You made war against my friends. You liberated your country from the invaders. But then you became a vengeful invader yourself. I don't know what to do with this information. Let me make up my mind as I come to know you."

Valentine spoke up for the first time since their initial greetings. "What is it that has happened that made you assure us that you told no one Ender was coming?"

Virlomi turned to her respectfully. "It's part of the longstanding struggle between me and Randall Firth."

"Isn't he still a child?"

Virlomi laughed bitterly. "Do Battle School graduates really say such things to each other?"

Ender chuckled. "Apparently so. How long has this struggle gone on?"

"By the time he was twelve, he was such a precocious . . . orator . . . that he had the old settlers and the non-Indian colonists who came with me eating out of his hand. At first he was their clever mascot. Now he is something closer to a spiritual leader, a . . ."

"A Virlomi," said Ender.

"He has made himself into their equivalent of the way the Indian colonists regard me, yes," she said. "I never claimed to be a goddess."

"Let's not argue such old issues."

"I just want you to know the truth."

"No, Virlomi," said Valentine, intruding again, or so Virlomi's expression seemed to say. "You deliberately constructed the goddess image, and when people asked you, you gave nondenial denials: 'Since when do goddesses walk the earth?' 'Would a goddess fail so often?' And the most loathsomely deceptive of them all: "What do you think?' "

Virlomi sighed. "You have no mercy," she said.

"No," said Valentine. "I have a lot of mercy. I just don't have any manners."

"Yes," said Virlomi. "He has learned from watching me, how I handle the Indians, how they worship me. His group has no shared religion, no traditions in common. But he constructed one, especially because everyone knew that evil book The Hive Queen."

"How is it evil?" asked Ender.

"Because it's a pack of lies. Who could know what the hive queens thought or felt or remembered or tried to do? But it has turned the formics into tragic figures in the minds of the impressionable fools who memorize that damnable book."

Ender chuckled. "Smart boy."

"What?" Virlomi asked him, looking suspicious.

"I assume you're telling me this because he somehow claims that he is the heir of the hive queens."

"Which is absolutely absurd because ours is the first colony that was *not* founded on the ruins of formic civilization."

"So how does he manage it?" asked Ender.

"He claims that the Indian population—eighty percent of the total—are merely trying to reestablish here the exact culture they had on Earth. While he and the others are the ones who are trying to create something new. He really does have the gall to call his little movement the 'Natives of Ganges.' And he says we Indians are like the jackals who have settled other worlds—destroying the natives and then stealing all that they accomplished."

"And people buy this?"

"Oddly enough," she said, "not that many do. Most of the non-Indian colonists are trying to get along."

"But some believe him," said Ender.

"Millions."

"There aren't that many colonists," said Valentine.

"He isn't just playing to the local crowd," said Virlomi. "He sends his writings out by ansible. There are chapters of the Natives of Ganges in most of the major cities of Earth. Even in India. Millions, as I told you."

Valentine sighed. "I saw them referred to only as 'the Natives' on the nets and I wasn't interested. That originated here?"

"They regard The Hive Queen as their scripture, and the formics as their spiritual forebears," said Virlomi. "On Earth, their doctrine is almost the opposite of what Randall preaches here. They claim that the FPE should be abolished because it erases all the 'genuine,' 'native' cultures of Earth. They refuse to speak Common. They make a big show of following native religions."

"While here, Randall condemns your people for doing exactly that," said Ender. "Preserving your culture from Earth."

"Yes," said Virlomi. "But he claims it isn't inconsistent—this is not where Indian culture originated. It's a new place, and so he and his 'Natives of Ganges' are creating the real native culture of this world, instead of a warmed-over copy of an old one from Earth."

Ender chuckled.

"It's funny to you," Virlomi said.

"Not at all," said Ender. "I'm just thinking that Graff really was such a genius. Not as smart as the kids he trained in Battle School, but . . . with Randall just an infant in his mother's arms, he knew that they would cause trouble."

"And sent you to save me," she said.

"I doubt you need saving," said Ender.

"No, I don't," she said. "I've already dealt with it. I provoked him into assaulting me in my house. It's on vid and we've already held the trial and sentenced him to be exiled. He's going back to Earth—along with any of his malcontents who want to go with him."

Ender shook his head. "And it doesn't occur to you that that's exactly what he wants you to do?"

"Of course it did. But I also don't care, as long as I don't have to deal with him."

Ender sighed. "Of course you care, Virlomi. If he already has a following there, and then he returns to Earth as an exile from what he calls his 'native world,' then you have just sown the seed that can bring down the FPE and restore the Earth to the miserable chaos of war and hatred that Peter Wiggin ended such a short time ago."

"That's not my problem," said Virlomi.

"Our generation is gone from power, Virlomi," said Ender, "except in a few remote colonies. Peter is dead. His successors are lackluster placeholders. Do you think they'll be competent to deal with this Randall Firth?"

Virlomi hesitated. "No."

"So if you knowingly infect someone with a virus that you know their body can't fight off, have you not murdered them?"

Virlomi buried her face in her hands. "I know," she said. "I tried not to know, but I know."

"What I can't yet determine," said Valentine, "is why your first words to us were a protest that you hadn't told anyone that Ender was coming. Why would that matter?"

Virlomi raised her face. "Because at the trial and ever since then, he has been using you. And linking himself to his monster of a father. Who he *thinks* his father is."

"Specifically," prompted Valentine.

"He calls you 'Ender the Xenocide,' " said Virlomi. "He says you're the worst war criminal in all of history, because you were the one who slaughtered the native people of all these worlds so that the robbers could come in and steal their houses and lands."

"Predictable," said Ender.

"And Peter is called the 'Brother of the Xenocide,' who tried to extinguish all the native cultures of Earth."

"Oh my," said Ender.

"While Achilles Flandres was not a monster—that's just propaganda from the pro-xenocide party. He was the only one who stood against Peter's and Ender's evil plans. He tried to stop you in Battle School, so your friends got him sent back to be imprisoned in an insane asylum on Earth. Then, when he escaped and began his work of opposing the threat of the Hegemon becoming dictator of the world, Peter's propaganda mill went to work, slandering him." Virlomi sighed. "Here's the irony. Through all of this, he pretends to honor me greatly. As a hero who stood against the jeesh of the xenocides—Han Tzu, Alai, Petra, all who served with you."

"And yet he struck you."

"He states that he was provoked. That it was all a setup. That a man of his size—if he had meant to hurt me, I'd be dead. He was merely trying to wake me up to the enormity of the lies I was telling and believing. His followers accept this explanation completely. Or don't care whether it's true or not."

"Well, it's nice that even while I'm in stasis, somebody found me useful," said Ender.

"It's not a joke," said Virlomi. "All over the nets, his revisionist view is gaining more and more acceptance. All the nonsense from Graff's court martial came into even more prominence. Pictures of the dead bodies of . . . those bullies . . ."

"Oh, I can guess," said Ender.

"You had to know before you got off the shuttle," said Virlomi. "He can't have known you were coming. He just chose this time to invoke your name. I think it's because I was using Achilles' name as the symbol of a monster. So he decided to use your name to outmonster Achilles. If it weren't for that horrible pack of lies called The Hive

Queen, he wouldn't have found so much fertile ground for his non-sense."

"I did everything he accuses me of," said Ender. "Those boys died. So did all the formics."

"But you're not a murderer. I read those trial transcripts too, you know. I understood—I was in Battle School, I talked to people who knew you, we all knew how the adults shaped our lives and controlled us. And we all recognized that your devastating self-defense was perfect military doctrine."

Ender did what he always did when somebody tried to exonerate him—he shunted her words aside without comment. "Well, Virlomi, I'm not sure what you think I should do about this."

"You could get back on the ship and go."

"Is that what you're asking me to do?" asked Ender.

"He's not here to take over your job," said Valentine. "He's not a threat to you."

Virlomi laughed. "I'm not trying to get rid of your brother, Valentine. He's welcome to stay. If he does, then I will definitely need and take his help and advice. For my own sake, I'm happy he's here. Randall will have no choice but to turn all his hatred onto you. Please, stay."

"I'm glad you asked," said Ender. "I accept."

"No," said Valentine. "This is the kind of situation that leads to violence."

"I promise not to kill anybody, Valentine," said Ender.

"I'm talking about violence *against* you," she said.

"So am I," said Ender.

"If he chooses to whip a mob into a frenzy—"

"No," said Virlomi. "You have nothing to fear on that score. We will protect you fully."

"Nobody can protect anybody fully," said Valentine.

"Oh, I'm sure Virlomi's people will do a splendid job," said Ender. "As I said, I accept your kind invitation. Now, let's leave this boat and go ashore, neh?"

"As you wish," said Virlomi. "I'll be glad to have you. But I also warned you, and as long as this ship is still here, you're free to move on. You won't like it when Randall turns his wrath on you. He has a way with words."

"Just words?" said Ender. "So he's nonviolent?"

"So far," said Virlomi.

"Then I'm safe," said Ender. "Thank you for the great honor you paid me. Please let it be known that I'm here. And that I really am *that* Andrew Wiggin."

"Are you sure?" asked Virlomi.

"Insane people are always sure," said Valentine.

Ender laughed, and so Virlomi did, too—a nervous chuckle.

"I'd invite you to join me for supper tonight," said Virlomi, "only one of my affectations is to eat little, and of course, as a Hindu, I eat an entirely vegetarian cuisine."

"Sounds excellent," said Valentine.

"Tell us when and where, and we'll be there," said Ender.

With a few more parting words, Virlomi left.

Valentine turned on Ender, angry and sad, both at once. "Did you bring me here to watch you die?"

"I didn't bring you anywhere," said Ender. "You just came."

"That doesn't answer my question."

"Everyone dies, Valentine. Mother and Father are dead. Peter is dead. Graff is probably dead by now."

"You forget that I know you, Ender," said Valentine. "You have decided to die. You've decided to provoke this boy into killing you."

"Why would you think that?"

"Look at the names you chose for passwords, Ender! You can't live with the guilt."

"Not guilt, Val," said Ender. "Responsibility."

"Don't make this boy kill you," said Valentine.

"I won't make anybody do anything. How about that?"

"I should have stayed home and watched Peter conquer the world."

"Oh, no, Valentine. We're on a much more interesting trajectory through space-time."

"I'm not going to sleep through my life like you are, Ender. I have work to do. I'm going to write my histories. I'm not burdened with a death wish."

"If I wished to be dead," said Ender, "I would have let Bonzo Madrid and his friends beat my brains out in a bathroom in Battle School."

"I know you," said Valentine.

"I know you think you do," said Ender. "And if I die, you'll think I chose to. The truth is much more complicated. I don't intend to die. But I'm not afraid of the risk of death. Sometimes a soldier has to put himself in harm's way in order to achieve victory."

"It's not your war," said Valentine.

Ender laughed. "It's always my war."

CHAPTER
22

To: VWiggin%Ganges@ColLeague.Adm/voy
From: AWiggin%Ganges@ColLeague.Adm/voy
Subj: If I am dead

Dear Val,

I don't expect to be dead. I expect to be alive, in which case, you won't receive this, because I will keep sending the do-not-deliver code until after the coming confrontation.

This is about the case. The code to unlock it is the name of your favorite stuffed animal when you were six. When you open it, hold what you find in your hands for a good long time. If you come up with some good ideas, then act on them; otherwise, please repack the item exactly as you found it, and arrange to ship it to Abra Tolo on Shakespeare with a message: "This is what I found that day. Please don't let it be destroyed."

But you won't need this, because, as is my fashion, I expect to win.

> Love,
> your demanding and mysterious little brother,
> Ender
> or, I suppose I should now say: Ended

Since the starship had not arrived full of new colonists, it was almost inconsequential to most of the people of the city of Andhra. Of course everyone turned out to watch the shuttle land. And there was some commotion as a few trade goods were loaded off and many supplies were loaded on. But the tasks being carried out were repetitive and people quickly lost interest and went back to their work. Governor Virlomi's visit to the shuttle was taken as good manners by those who heard about it—few knew or cared what the ordinary protocol would be, and so didn't realize that it had been altered. And those who did know simply took it as part of Virlomi's character—or her pose—that she did not make the visitors come to her.

Only when that evening's supper saw strangers come to Virlomi's house—which Achilles and his fellow "Natives of Ganges" liked to refer to as "the governor's mansion"—did anyone's curiosity get aroused. A teenage boy; a young woman of about twenty. Why were they the only passengers on the starship? Why was Virlomi giving them special honors? Were they new colonists or government officials or . . . what?

Since this was the ship that was supposed to take Achilles into exile for his "crime" of striking the governor, he was, quite naturally, anxious to find out anything he could to derail the plan. These guests were unusual, unexpected, unannounced, unexplained. That had to mean they presented an opportunity to embarrass Virlomi, at the very least—to stymie her or destroy her, if things went well.

It took two days of having his supporters consort with the crew before someone finally got their hands on the manifest and discovered the names of the passengers. Valentine Wiggin, student. Andrew Wiggin, student.

Student?

Achilles didn't even have to look anything up. The ship's last call had been to Shakespeare Colony. Up to the time of that ship's arrival, the governor of Shakespeare had been Andrew Wiggin, retired admiral of the I.F. and much-cited commander of the I.F. forces in the Third Formic War. Two starflights at relativistic speed explained the boy's age. Boy? One year older than Achilles.

Wiggin was tall, but Achilles was taller; strong, but Achilles was stronger. Wiggin was chosen for Battle School because he was smart, but

Achilles had never encountered anyone in his life who was as intelligent as he. Virlomi was Battle School bright—but she forgot things that he remembered, overlooked things that he noticed, thought two moves ahead instead of ten. And she was the closest to being in his league.

Achilles had learned to conceal just how intelligent he was, and to treat others as if he thought them his equal. But he knew the truth and counted on it: He was quicker, smarter, deeper, subtler than anyone else. Hadn't he, as a mere boy on a faraway colony world, using only the lowest-priority ansible messaging, created a significant political movement on Earth?

Even intelligent people are sometimes just plain lucky. Wiggin's arrival just at this time clearly fell into that category. Wiggin couldn't have known that he was coming to the colony where dwelt the son of Achilles the Great, whom Ender's brother had arranged to murder. And when Achilles-who-was-called-Randall launched his attack on the reputation of Ender Wiggin, labeling him as Ender the Xenocide, he had no idea that within the month that very Andrew Wiggin would be having supper at Virlomi's house.

It was an easy thing to get pictures of Virlomi and Wiggin together. It was just as easy to get, from the nets, pictures of Peter the Hegemon at roughly the same age as Ender was now. Juxtaposing their pictures made it easy to see they were brothers, the resemblance was so strong. Achilles then put pictures of Ender and Virlomi, so that anyone could see that Peter's brother was consorting with the anti-native governor of Ganges.

Never mind that it was Peter who had sent Virlomi into exile. Achilles dismissed that as an obvious fraud—Virlomi had been part of Peter's conspiracy all along. Her consorting with Ender Wiggin proved it, if anyone had doubts.

Now Achilles could paint his exile as the result of an obvious conspiracy between Virlomi and her Wiggin masters—Ender's sister was along for the ride. They were exiling him so that Wiggin's xenocidal, anti-native plots could proceed on Ganges without opposition.

It would take a week for any of this story to reach Earth, but the computers worked impartially, and Virlomi couldn't stop him from sending them. And locally, the story and pictures went up immediately.

Achilles watched with delight as people began watching the Wiggins' every move. Everything he did or said was seen through the lens of Achilles' accusations. Even the Indians, who regarded Achilles with suspicion or hostility, were convinced by the pictures that Achilles was not lying. What was going on?

It's costing you, Virlomi. You attacked my father, and through him, me. You tried to exile me—hoping my troublesome mother would disappear along with me. Well, I have attacked Ender Wiggin, and through him, you—and you very kindly have taken him in as your honored guest at precisely the moment when it was most useful to me.

Three days after his public tagging of Ender Wiggin, Achilles made his next move. This time, he used a surrogate writer—one of his brighter supporters, who could actually put sentences together coherently—to put out the allegation, disguised as a denial, that Virlomi's plan was to have Ender Wiggin himself murder Randall Firth on the trip to Earth. He would be sent into exile, supposedly, but he would never be seen again.

Randall Firth has offended, not just the Wiggin stooge Virlomi, but the whole hegemonistic conspiracy. He has to be eliminated, or so the story goes. But we have found no evidence to corroborate this account, and therefore we must dismiss it as nothing but a rumor, a mere suspicion. How else can we explain Wiggin's multiple secret meetings with Virlomi?

Randall Firth himself, when questioned, asserted that Virlomi is too intelligent to consort openly with Wiggin if she were planning any violent action against Firth. Therefore he fears nothing.

But we wonder: Does Virlomi count on Firth making that assumption, so that his guard will be down? Will she insist that he goes into stasis, from which Wiggin, aboard the ship, will make sure he never wakes up? It would be so easy to call it an accident.

Firth is too brave for his own good. His friends are more worried about him than he is about himself.

This time Achilles' foray brought a response from Virlomi—which was, after all, what he wanted. "Andrew Wiggin's visit here is an obvious coincidence—he set out on his voyage when Randall Firth was still an infant on a starship and Ganges Colony had not even been founded."

"This is an obvious nondenial denial," wrote Achilles' surrogate. "Virlomi says that it is a coincidence that Wiggin is here. She does not say that Randall Firth will not be at Wiggin's mercy on his voyage of 'exile'— or, as some assert, 'death.'"

The colony was now riven with heated arguments, and Achilles noted with delight that there were even Indians now on the side that said, "You can't send Randall out on the same ship with Wiggin." "Isn't Wiggin the one who already murdered two children?" "Randall Firth's crime is not worthy of the death penalty."

There was a groundswell building to commute Randall Firth's sentence and keep him on Ganges. Meanwhile, there was even talk of arresting Ender Wiggin for his crimes against humanity. Achilles publicized these proposals by making statements opposing them. "The statute of limitations has surely passed, even for the monstrous crime of xenocide," he wrote. "It has been sixty-one years since Ender Wiggin wiped out the hive queens. What court has jurisdiction now?"

By now the demand from Earth was so great that any writings of Achilles or his surrogates were being moved up to a higher priority in the queue. On Earth, there were open demands that the I.F. arrest Andrew Wiggin and bring *him* back to Earth for trial, and polls showing that a small but growing minority was demanding justice for the murder of the hive queens.

It was time for Randall Firth to meet Ender Wiggin face to face.

It was easy enough to arrange. Achilles' supporters kept watch on Wiggin, and when he, his sister, and the governor passed along the banks of the great river one morning, Achilles was there—alone.

Virlomi stiffened when she saw him, and tried to draw Ender away, but Wiggin strode forward to meet Achilles and held out his hand. "I've wanted to meet you, Mr. Firth," he said. "I'm Andrew Wiggin."

"I know who you are," said Achilles, letting scorn and amusement into his voice.

"Oh, I doubt that," said Ender, his apparent amusement even greater. "But I've been wanting to see you, and I think the governor has been trying to keep us apart. I know *you* have been aching for this moment."

Achilles wanted to say, What do *you* know about *me*? But he knew that's what Wiggin wanted him to say—that Wiggin wanted to determine the course of the conversation. So instead he asked, "Why would you want to see me? You're the celebrity, I think."

"Oh, we're both quite famous enough," said Ender, now chuckling outright. "Me for what I've *done*. You for what you've *said*."

And with that, Ender smiled. Mockingly?

"Are you trying to goad me into some ill-considered action, Mr. Wiggin?"

"Please," said Ender. "Call me Andrew."

"The name of a Christian saint," said Achilles. "I prefer to call you by the name of a monstrous war criminal . . . Ender."

"If there were some way to bring back the hive queens," said Ender, "and restore them to their former glory and power, would you do it, Mr. Firth?"

Achilles recognized the trap at once. It was one thing to read The Hive Queen and shed a tear for a vanished race. It was quite another to wish for them to return—it was an invitation for headlines saying, "Leader of Natives Movement would bring back formics," along with grisly pictures from the Scouring of China.

"I don't indulge in hypotheticals," said Achilles.

"Except the hypothetical charge that I plan to kill you in your sleep during the voyage back to Earth."

"Not *my* accusation," said Achilles. "I was quoted in your defense."

"Your 'defense' is the only reason anyone heard of the accusation," said Ender. "Please don't think that I'm fooled."

"Who would hope to fool a genius like you?"

"Well, we've sparred long enough. I just wanted to look at you."

Achilles made a flamboyant turn, so Ender could inspect him from all sides. "Is that enough?"

Suddenly tears came into Ender's eyes.

What game was he playing now?

"Thank you," Ender said. Then he turned away to rejoin his sister and the governor.

"Wait," said Achilles. He didn't understand what that teary-eyed thing meant, and it disconcerted him.

But Wiggin didn't wait, or turn back. He simply walked to the others and they turned away from the river, walking back into the city.

Achilles had meant this confrontation—which was being recorded by zoom lens and microphone—for a propaganda vid. He had expected to be able to goad Ender into some rash statement or absurd denial. Even a clip of Ender angry would have done the job. But he was unflappable, he had fallen into no traps, and with that last bit of maudlin emotion he may well have set or sprung one, though Achilles could not think of what the trap might be.

An unsatisfactory encounter in every way. And yet he could not explain to his followers why he didn't want to use the vid they had so painstakingly created. So he allowed them to post it, then waited for the other shoe to drop.

No one on Earth knew what to make of it, either. Commentators noticed the tears in Ender's eyes, of course, and speculated about it. Some Nativists proclaimed it to be crocodile tears—the weeping of the predator at the coming fate of his victim. But some saw something else. "Ender Wiggin did not look the part he's been cast in—the killer, the monster. Instead, he seemed to be a gentle young man, bemused at the obviously planned confrontation. At the end, those infamous tears seemed to me to be a kind of compassion. Perhaps even love for his challenger. Who is trying to pick the fight here?"

That was terrible—but it was only one voice among many. And Achilles' supporters on Earth quickly replied: Who would dare to pick a fight with Ender the Xenocide? It always turns out so badly for those who do.

All his life, Achilles had been able to control things. Even when unexpected things happened, he had adapted, analyzed, and learned. This time he had no idea what to learn.

"I don't know what he's doing, Mother," said Achilles.

She stroked his head. "Oh, my poor darling," she said. "Of course you don't, you're such an innocent. Just like your father. He never saw their plots. He *trusted* that Suriyawong monster."

Achilles didn't actually like it when she talked that way. "It's not our place to *pity* him, Mother."

"But I do. He had such great gifts, but in the end, his trusting nature betrayed him. It was his tragic flaw, that he was too kind and good."

Achilles had studied his father's life and had seen strength and hardness, the willingness to do whatever was necessary. Compassion and a trusting nature were not obvious attributes of Achilles the Great, however.

Let Mother sentimentalize him as she wished. After all, didn't she now "remember" that Achilles the Great had actually visited her and slept with her in order to conceive a son? Yet when he was little she had made no such claim, and had talked of the messenger who arranged to have her ova fertilized with Achilles' precious sperm. From that—and many other examples of shifting memory—he knew that she was no longer a reliable witness.

Yet she was the only one who knew his true name. And she loved him with perfect devotion. He could talk to her without fear of censure.

"This Ender Wiggin," he said. "I can't read him."

"I'm glad you can't understand the mind of a devil."

But she had not called him a devil until Achilles' own propaganda campaign against him. She had ignored Ender Wiggin, because he had never actually fought against her precious Achilles Flandres, even if his brother had.

"I don't know what to do with him now, Mother."

"Well, you'll avenge your father, of course."

"Ender didn't kill him."

"He's a killer. He deserves to die."

"Not at my hands, Mother."

"The son of Achilles the Great slays the monster," said Mother. "No better hands than yours."

"They would call me a murderer."

"They called your father by that name as well," she said. "Are you better than him?"

"No, Mother."

She seemed to think that closed the discussion. He was disconcerted. Was she saying she wanted him to murder a man?

"Let the Hegemon's nearest blood pay for the murder of my Achilles," she said. "Let all the Wiggins be extinguished. All that vicious tribe."

Oh, no, she was in her bloody vengeance mood. Well, he had brought it on, hadn't he? He knew better. Now he'd have to hear her out.

On and on she went, about how great crimes could only be expunged by the shedding of blood. "Peter Wiggin outsmarted us by dying of his heart attack while we were on the voyage," she said. "But now his brother and sister have come to us. How can you pass up what fate has brought into your hands?"

"I'm not a murderer, Mother."

"Vengeance for your father's death is not murder. Who do you think you are, Hamlet?"

And on and on she went.

Usually when she went off like this, Achilles only half-listened. But now the words dug at him. It really *did* feel like some kind of portentous fate that brought Wiggin to him at this very time. It was irrational—but only mathematics was rational, and not always at that. In the real world, irrational things happened, impossible coincidences happened, because probability required that coincidences rarely, but *not* never, occur.

So instead of ignoring her, he found himself wondering: How could I arrange for Ender Wiggin to die without having to kill him myself?

And from there, he went on to a more subtle plan: I have already half destroyed Ender Wiggin—how could I complete the process?

To murder him would make a martyr of him. But if Wiggin could be provoked into killing again—killing another child—he would be destroyed forever. It was his pattern. He sensed a rival; he goaded him into making an attack; then he killed him in self-defense. Twice he had done it and been exonerated. But his protectors weren't here—they were almost certainly all dead. Only the facts remained.

Could I get him to follow the pattern again?

He told his idea to his mother.

"What are you talking about?" she said.

"If he murders again—this time a sixteen-year-old, but still a child, no matter how tall—then his reputation will be destroyed forever. They'll put him on trial, they'll convict him this time—they can't believe he just happened to kill in 'self-defense' three times!—and that will be a far more thorough destruction than a merely ending the life of his body. I'll destroy his *name* forever."

"You're talking about letting him kill *you*?"

"Mother, people don't have to *let* Ender Wiggin kill them. They just have to provide him with the pretext, and he does the rest quite nicely by himself."

"But—you? Die?"

"As you said, Mother. To destroy Father's enemies is worth any sacrifice."

She leapt to her feet. "I didn't give birth to you just so you could throw your life away! You're half a head taller than him—he's a dwarf compared to you. How could he possibly kill you?"

"He was trained as a soldier. And not that long ago, Mother. What have I been trained as? A farmer. A mechanic. Whatever odd jobs have been required of a teenager who happens to be preternaturally large and clever and strong. Not war. Not fighting. I haven't fought anyone since I was so tiny and had to battle constantly to keep them from picking on me."

"Your father and I did not conceive you so that you could die at the hands of a Wiggin, like your father did!"

"Technically, Father died at the hands of a Delphiki. Julian to be precise."

"Delphiki, Wiggin—sides of the same coin. I forbid you to let him kill you."

"I told you, Mother. He'll find a way. It's what he does. He's a warrior."

"No!"

It took two hours to calm her down, and before that he had to put up with crying and screaming—he knew the neighbors had to be listening and trying to make sense of it. But finally she was asleep.

He went to the stock control office and used the computer there to send Wiggin a message:

I believe that I've misjudged you. How can we end this?

He did not expect an answer until the next day. But it came before he could log off.

When and where would you like to meet?

Was it really going to be this easy?

The time and place didn't matter much. It had to be a time and place where they couldn't be stopped by Virlomi and her minions; but there had to be enough light to make a vid. What good would it be to die for his father's sake, only to have the deed unrecorded, so that Wiggin could spin it however he wanted, and thus get away with yet another murder?

They made the appointment. Achilles logged off.

And then he sat there, trembling. What have I done? This really is Ender Wiggin. I really have set up my own death. I'm bigger and stronger than he is—but so were the two boys he already killed. The hive queens were stronger, too, and look what that got them. Ender Wiggin did not *lose*.

This is what I was born for. This is what Mother has instilled in me from infancy. I exist to vindicate my father. To destroy the Hegemony, to bring down all the works of Peter Wiggin. Well, maybe that's not possible. But bringing down Ender Wiggin—I can do that merely by getting him to kill me and letting the world see how it happened. Mother will grieve—but grief is her lifeblood anyway.

If he's so smart, he must know what I'm planning. He can't believe that I'd suddenly change my mind. How could I fool Ender Wiggin with such an obvious plan? He must guess that I'll be having everything recorded.

But maybe he doesn't think he'll *have* to kill me. Maybe he thinks I'm such an easy opponent that he can defeat me without killing me. Maybe he thinks I'm such a giant oaf that I'll never even land a blow.

Or maybe I'm overestimating his cleverness. After all, he went through a whole war against an alien enemy and never once suspected that it wasn't a computer or his teachers playing a simulation with him. How dumb is that?

I'll go. I'll see what happens. I'm ready to die, but only if it will bring him down.

▬

They met two days later, at first light, behind the composting bins. No one would come here—the smell made people avoid it when they didn't have to go there, and vegetative waste was dumped only at the end of a day's work.

His friends had rigged the cameras to cover the whole area. Every word would be recorded. Ender probably guessed that this would be the case— hadn't Achilles done all his work with propaganda on the nets?—but

even if Ender walked away, the confrontation would probably be ran-
corous and work against him. And if he didn't, Achilles simply wouldn't
use it.

Several times during the previous day, Achilles had thought of the possibility of dying and each time it was like a different person was hearing
the news. Sometimes it seemed almost funny—Achilles was so strong,
so much taller, with so much greater a mass and reach. Other times it
seemed inevitable but pointless, and he thought: How stupid am I, to throw
my life away on an empty gesture toward the dead.

But by the end of the day, he realized: I'm not doing this for my father.
I'm not doing it because my mother raised me for vengeance. I'm doing
it for the sake of the human race as a whole. The great monsters of history were almost never held accountable. They died of old age, or lived
out their lives in pampered exile, or—faced with defeat—they killed
themselves.

Being Ender Wiggin's last victim is worth it, not for some private family quarrel, but because the world must see that great criminals like Ender Wiggin did not go unpunished. Eventually they committed one crime
too many and they were brought to account.

And I will be the last victim, the one whose death brought down Ender
the Xenocide.

Another part of him said, Don't believe your own propaganda.

Another part of him said, Live!

But he answered them: If there's one true thing about Ender Wiggin,
it's that he cannot bear to lose. That's how I will tempt him—I will make
him stare defeat in the face, and he will lash out to avoid it—and when he
kills me, *then* he really *will* be defeated. It is his fatal flaw—that he can
be manipulated by facing him with defeat.

Deep inside him, a question tried to surface where he would have to
deal with it: Doesn't this mean that it's not his fault, because he really
had no choice but to destroy his enemies?

But Achilles immediately tamped down that quibble. We're all just the
product of our genes and upbringing, combined with the random events
of our lifetime. "Fault" and "blame" are childish concepts. What matters
is that Ender's actions have been monstrous, and will continue to be
monstrous unless he is stopped. As it is, he might live forever, surfacing

here and there to stir up trouble. But I will put an end to it. Not vengeance, but prevention. And because he will be an example, perhaps other monsters will be stopped before they have killed so often, and so many.

Ender stepped out of the shadows. "Ho, Achilles."

It took half a second—half a step—for Achilles to realize what name Ender had addressed him by.

"The name you call yourself in private," said Ender. "In your dreams."

How could he know? What *was* he?

"You have no access to my dreams," said Achilles.

"I want you to know," said Ender, "that I've been pleading with Virlomi to commute your sentence. Because I have to leave on this ship, when it goes, and I don't want to go back to Earth."

"I would think not," said Achilles. "They're howling for your blood there."

"For the moment," said Ender. "These things come and go."

No apparent recognition that Achilles was the one who had made all this happen.

"I have an errand to run, and taking you back to Earth as an exile will waste my time. I think I've almost got her persuaded that the Free People of Earth never gave governors the right to throw back colonists they don't want."

"I'm not afraid to return to Earth."

"That's what I was afraid of—that you did all this in hopes of being sent there. 'Please don't throw me in the briar patch!' "

"They read you Uncle Remus stories at bedtime in Battle School?" asked Achilles.

"Before I went there. Did your mother read those tales to you?"

Achilles realized that he was being led off on a tangent. He resolutely returned to the subject.

"I said I'm not afraid to return to Earth," said Achilles. "Nor do I think you've been pleading for me with Virlomi."

"Believe what you want," said Ender. "You've been surrounded by lies all your life—who could expect you to notice when a true thing finally came along?"

Here it came—the beginning of the taunts that would goad Achilles into action. What Ender could not understand was that Achilles came here precisely so that he could be goaded, so that Ender could then kill him in "self-defense."

"Are you calling my mother a liar?"

"Haven't you wondered why you're so tall? Your mother isn't tall. Achilles Flandres wasn't tall."

"We'll never know how tall he might have grown," said Achilles.

"I know why you're as big as you are," said Ender. "It's a genetic condition. You grow at a single, steady rate all your life. Small as a child, then about normal size when suddenly all the other kids shoot up with the puberty growth spurt and you fall behind again. But they stop growing; you don't. On and on. Eventually you'll die of it. You're sixteen now; probably by twenty-one or twenty-two your heart will give out from trying to supply blood to a body that's far too large."

Achilles didn't know how to process this. What was he talking about? Telling him that he was going to die in his twenties? Was this some kind of voodoo to unnerve his opponent?

But Ender wasn't through. "Some of your brothers and sisters had the condition; some didn't. We didn't know about you, not with certainty. Not until I saw you and realized that you were becoming a giant, like your father."

"Don't talk about my father," said Achilles. Meanwhile, he thought: Why am I afraid of what you're saying? Why am I so angry?

"But I was so glad to see you, anyway. Even though your life will be tragically short, I looked at you—when you turned around like that, mocking me—I saw your father, I saw your mother in you."

"My mother? I don't look anything like my mother."

"I don't mean the surrogate mother who raised you."

"So you're trying to get me to attack you by goading me exactly the way Virlomi did," said Achilles. "Well it won't work." Yet as he said it, it was working; and he was willing to have the wrath rise within him. Because he had to make it believable, that Ender goaded him into attacking, so that when Ender killed him everyone who saw the vids would know that it wasn't really self-defense at all. They'd realize it had never been self-defense.

"I knew your father best of all the kids in Battle School. He was better than I was—did you know that? All of the jeesh knew it—he was quicker and smarter. But he always was loyal to me. At the last moment, when it all looked so hopeless, he knew what to do. He virtually *told* me what to do. And yet he left it to me. He was generous. He was truly great. It broke my heart to learn how his body betrayed him. The way it's betraying you."

"Suriyawong betrayed him," said Achilles. "Julian Delphiki killed him."

"And your mother," said Ender. "She was my protector. When I got put into an army whose commander hated me, she was the one who took me under her wing. I relied on her, I trusted her, and within the limitations of a human body, she never let me down. When I heard that she and your father had married, it made me so happy. But then your father died, and eventually she married my brother."

Comprehension almost blinded him with fury. "Petra Arkanian? You're saying Petra Arkanian is my mother? Are you insane? She was the one that first set the traps for my father, luring him—"

"Come now, Achilles," said Ender. "Surely by the age of sixteen you've recognized that your surrogate mother is insane."

"She's my mother!" cried Achilles. And then, only as an afterthought, and weakly, he said, "And she's not insane."

This is not going right. What is he saying? What kind of game is this?

"You look exactly like them. More like your father than like your mother. When I see you, I see my dear friend Bean."

"Julian Delphiki is not my father!" Achilles could hardly see for rage. His heart was pounding. This was exactly how it was supposed to go.

Except for one thing. His feet were rooted to the ground. He wasn't attacking Ender Wiggin. He was just standing there and taking it.

It was in that moment that Valentine Wiggin jogged into the clearing behind the compost bins. "What are you doing? Are you insane?"

"There's a lot of that going around," said Ender.

"Get away from here," she said. "He's not worth it."

"Valentine," he said, "you don't know what you're doing. If you interfere in any way, you'll destroy me. Do you understand me? Have I ever lied to you?"

"Constantly."

"Neglecting to tell you things is not lying," said Ender.

"I'm not going to let this happen. I know what you're planning."

"With all due respect, Val, you don't know anything."

"I know you, Ender, better than you know yourself."

"But you don't know this boy who calls himself by the name of a monster because he thinks the madman was his father."

For a few moments Achilles' anger had dissipated, but now it was coming back. "My father was a genius."

"Not incompatible concepts," said Valentine dismissively. To Ender, she said, "It won't bring them back."

"Right now," said Ender, "if you love me, you'll stop talking."

His voice was like a lash—not loud, but sharp and with true aim. She recoiled as if he had struck her. Yet she opened her mouth to answer.

"If you love me," he said.

"I think what your brother is trying to tell you," said Achilles, "is that he has a plan."

"My plan," said Ender, "is to tell you who you are. Julian Delphiki and Petra Arkanian lived in hiding because Achilles Flandres had agents seeking them, wanting to kill them—especially because he had once desired Petra, after his sick fashion."

The rage was rising in Achilles again. And he welcomed it. Valentine's coming had almost ruined everything.

"They had nine fertilized eggs that they entrusted to a doctor who promised he could purge them of the genetic condition that you have— the giantism. But he was a fraud—as your present condition indicates. He was really working for Achilles, and he stole the embryos. Your mother gave birth to one; we found seven others that were implanted in surrogate mothers. But Hyrum Graff always suspected that they found those seven because Achilles meant them to be found, so that the searchers would think their methods were working. Knowing Achilles, Graff was sure the ninth baby would not be found by the same methods. Then your mother spat on Hyrum Graff and he began to look into her past and found out that her name wasn't Nichelle Firth, it was Randi. And when he looked at the DNA records, he found that you had no genes in common with your supposed mother. You were not in any way her genetic child."

"That's a lie," said Achilles. "You're saying it only to provoke me."

"I'm saying it because it's true, in the hope that it will liberate you.

The other children were found and returned to their parents. Five of them didn't have your genetic disorder, your giantism, and all five of them are still alive on Earth. Bella, Andrew—named for me, I must point out—Julian the Third, Petra, and Ramon. Three of your siblings were giants, and of course they're gone now—Ender, Cincinnatus, Carlotta. You're the extra one, the missing one that they gave up looking for. The one they never got to name. But your last name is Delphiki. I knew your parents and I loved them dearly. You are not the child of a monster, you're the child of two of the best people who ever lived."

"Julian Delphiki is the monster!" cried Achilles, and he lunged at Ender.

To his surprise, Ender made no evasive maneuver. Achilles' blow landed squarely and sent Ender sprawling onto the ground.

"No!" cried Valentine.

Ender picked himself up calmly and rose to face him again. "You know that I'm telling you the truth," said Ender. "That's why you're so angry."

"I'm angry because you say I'm the son of the killer of my father!"

"Achilles Flandres murdered everyone who showed him kindness. A nun who arranged for his crippled leg to be restored. The surgeon who fixed the leg. A girl who took him in when he was the least successful street bully in Rotterdam—he pretended to love her, but then he strangled her and threw her body in the Rhine. He blew up the house where your father was living, in the effort to kill him and his whole family. He kidnapped Petra and tried to seduce her but she despised him. It was Julian Delphiki that she loved. You are their child, born of their love and hope."

Achilles rushed at him again—but deliberately made it a clumsy move, so that Ender would have plenty of time to block him, to strike at him.

But again Ender made no move to step away. He took the blow, this time a deep punch in the stomach, and fell to the ground, gasping, retching.

And then rose up again. "I know you better than you know yourself," said Ender.

"You're the father of lies," said Achilles.

"Never call yourself by that vile name again. You're not Achilles. Your father is the hero who rid the world of that monster."

Again Achilles struck at him—this time walking up slowly and bringing his fist hugely into Ender's nose, breaking it. Blood spurted from his nostrils and covered the front of his shirt almost instantly.

Valentine cried out as Ender staggered and then fell to his knees.

"Fight me," hissed Achilles.

"Don't you get it?" said Ender. "I will never raise my hand against the son of my friends."

Achilles kicked him in the jaw so hard it flung him over backward. This was no staged fight like in the silly vids, where the hero and the villain delivered killing blows, yet their opponent got up to fight again. The damage to Ender's body was deep and real. It made him clumsy and unbalanced. An easy target.

He's not going to kill me, thought Achilles.

It came to him as such a relief that he laughed aloud.

And then he thought: It's Mother's plan after all. Why did I ever imagine I should let him *kill* me? I'm the son of Achilles Flandres. His true son. I can kill the ones who need killing. I can end this pernicious life, once and for all, avenging my father and the hive queens and those two boys that Ender killed.

Achilles kicked Ender in the ribs as he lay on his back in the grass. The ribs broke so loudly that even Valentine could hear them; she screamed.

"Hush," said Ender. "This is how it goes."

Then Ender rolled over—wincing, then crying out softly with the pain. Yet he managed, somehow, to rise to his feet.

Whereupon he put his hands in his pockets.

"You can destroy the vids you're recording," said Ender. "No one will know that you murdered me. They won't believe Valentine. So you can claim self-defense. Everyone will believe it—you've made them hate me and fear me. Of course you had to kill me to save your own life."

Ender wanted to die? Now? At Achilles' hand? "What's your game?" Achilles asked.

"Your supposed mother raised you to take vengeance for her fantasy lover, your fraudulent father. Do it—do what she raised you to do, be who she planned you to be. But I will not raise my hand against the son of my friends, no matter how deluded you are."

"Then you're the fool," said Achilles. "Because I *will* do it. For my father's sake, and my mother's, for that poor boy Stilson, and Bonzo Madrid, and the formics, and the whole human race."

Achilles began the beating in earnest then. Another blow to the belly. Another blow to the face. Two more kicks to the body as he lay unmoving on the ground. "Is this what you did to the Stilson boy?" he asked. "Kicking him again and again—that's what the report said."

"Son," said Ender. "Of my friends."

"Please," begged Valentine. Yet she made no move to stop him. Nor did she summon help.

"Now it's time for you to die," said Achilles.

A kick to the head would do it. And if it didn't, two kicks. The human brain could not stand being rattled around inside the skull like that. Either dead or so brain-damaged he might as well be. That was how the life of Ender the Xenocide would end.

He approached Wiggin's supine body. The eyes were looking up at him through the blood still pouring from his broken nose.

But for some reason, despite the hot rage pounding in his own head, Achilles did not kick him.

Stood there unmoving.

"The son of Achilles would do it," whispered Ender.

Why am I not killing him? Am I a coward after all? Am I so unworthy of my father? Ender is right—my father would have killed him because it was *necessary,* without any qualms, without this hesitation.

In that moment, he saw what all of Ender's words really meant. Mother had been deceived. She had been told the child was Achilles Flandres's. She had lied to him as he grew up, telling him that he was her son, but she was only a surrogate. He knew her well enough by now to recognize that her stories were shaped more by what she needed the truth to be than by what it actually was. Why hadn't he reached the obvious conclusion—that everything she said was a lie? Because she never let up, not for an instant. She shaped his world and did not allow any contrary evidence to come to light.

The way the teachers manipulated the children who fought the war for them.

Achilles knew it, had always known it. Ender Wiggin won a war that he didn't know he was fighting; he slaughtered a species that he thought was just a computer simulation. The way that I believed that Achilles Flandres was my father, that I bore his name and had a duty to fulfil his destiny or avenge his murder.

Surround a child with lies, and he clings to them like a teddy bear, like his mother's hand. And the worse, the darker the lie, the more deeply he has to draw it inside himself in order to bear the lie at all.

Ender said he would rather die than raise his hand against the son of his friends. And he was *not* a lunatic like Achilles' mother was.

Achilles. He was not Achilles. That was his mother's fantasy. It was all his mother's fantasy. He knew she was crazy, and yet he lived inside her nightmare and shaped his life to make it come true.

"What is my name?" he whispered.

On the ground at his feet, Ender whispered back: "Don't know. Delphiki. Arkanian. Their faces. In yours."

Valentine was beside them now. "Please," she said. "Can this be over now?"

"I knew," whispered Ender. "Bean's son. Petra's. Could never."

"Could never what? He's broken your nose. He could have killed you."

"I was going to," said Achilles. And then the enormity of it washed over him. "I was going to kill him with a kick to the head."

"And the stupid fool would have let you," said Valentine.

"One chance," said Ender. "In five. Kill me. Good odds."

"Please," said Valentine. "I can't carry him. Bring him to the doctor. Please. You're strong enough."

Only when he bent down and lifted Ender up did he realize how badly he had damaged his own hands, so hard had been his blows.

What if he dies? What if he still dies, even though I don't want him dead now after all?

He bore Ender with studied haste along the ragged ground and Valentine had to jog to keep up. They reached the doctor's house long before he was due to leave for the clinic. He took one look at Ender and had him brought in at once for an emergency examination. "I can see who lost," said the doctor. "But who won?"

"Nobody," said . . . Achilles.

"There's not a mark on *you,*" said the doctor.

He held out his hands. "Here are the marks," he said. "I did this."

"He never landed a blow on you."

"He never tried."

"And you kept on beating him? Like this? What kind of . . ." But then the doctor turned back to his work, stripping the clothes off Ender's body, cursing softly at the huge bruises on his ribs and belly, feeling for the breaks. "Four ribs. And multiple breaks." He looked up at Achilles again, this time with loathing on his face. "Get out of my house," he said.

Achilles started to go.

"No," said Valentine. "This was all according to his plan."

The doctor snorted. "Oh, yes, he plotted his own beating."

"Or his own death," said Valentine. "Whatever happened, he was content."

"*I* planned this," said Achilles.

"You only thought you did," said Valentine. "He manipulated you from the start. It's the family talent."

"My mother manipulated," said Achilles. "But I didn't have to believe her. I did this."

"No, Achilles," said Valentine. "Your mother's training did this. The lies Achilles told *her* did this. What *you* did was . . . stop."

Achilles felt his body convulse with a sob and he sank to his knees. "I don't know what to call myself now," he said. "I hate the name she taught me."

"Randall?" asked the doctor.

"Not . . . no."

"He calls himself Achilles. *She* calls him that."

"How can I . . . undo this?" he asked her.

"Poor boy," said Valentine. "That's what Ender's spent the past few years trying to figure out for himself. I think he just used you to get a partial answer. I think he just got you to give him the beating that Stilson and Bonzo Madrid both intended. The only difference is, you're the son of Julian Delphiki and Petra Arkanian, and so there's something deep inside you that cannot do murder—cold or hot. Or maybe it has nothing to do with your parents. It has to do with being raised by a mother who you know was mentally ill, and feeling compassion for her—such deep compassion that you could never challenge her fantasy world. Maybe that's it. Or maybe it's your soul. The thing that God wrapped in a body and turned into a man. Whatever it was, *you* stopped."

"Arkanian Delphiki," he said.

"That would be a good name," said Valentine. "Doctor, will my brother live?"

"He took blows to the head," said the doctor. "Look at his eyes. There's serious concussion. Maybe worse. We have to get him to the clinic."

"I'll carry him," said . . . not Achilles . . . Arkanian.

The doctor grimaced. "Letting the beater carry the beaten? But I don't want to wait for anyone else. What a hideous time of day for you to have this . . . duel?"

As they walked along the road to the clinic, a few early risers looked at them quizzically, and one even approached, but the doctor waved her off.

"I meant for him to kill *me*," said Arkanian.

"I know," said Valentine.

"What he did to those other boys. I thought he'd do again."

"He meant for you to think he'd fight back."

"And then the things he said. The opposite of everything."

"But you believed him. Right away, you knew it was true," she said.

"Yes."

"Made you furious."

Arkanian made a sound, somewhere between a whimper and a howl. He didn't plan it; he didn't understand it. Like a wolf baying at the moon, he only knew that the sound was in him and had to come out.

"But you couldn't kill him," she said. "Because you're not such a fool as to think you can hide from the truth by killing the messenger."

"We're here," said the doctor. "And I can't believe you're reassuring the one who beat your brother like this."

"Oh, didn't you know?" said Valentine. "This is Ender the Xenocide. He deserves whatever anyone does to him."

"Nobody deserves this," the doctor said.

"How can I undo this," said Arkanian. And this time he did not mean Ender's injuries.

"You can't," said Valentine. "And it was already there, it was inherent in that book, The Hive Queen. If you hadn't said it, somebody else would have. As soon as the human race understood that it was a tragedy to destroy the hive queens, we had to find someone to blame for it, so that the rest of us could be absolved. It would have happened without you."

"But it didn't happen without me. I have to tell the truth—I have to admit what I was . . ."

"No you don't," she said. "You have to live your life. *Yours*. And Ender will live his."

"And what about you?" asked the doctor, sounding even more cynical than before.

"Oh, I'll live Ender's life, too. It's so much more interesting than my own."

CHAPTER
23

To: ADelphiki%Ganges@ColLeague.Adm, PWiggin%ret@FPE.adm
From: EWiggin%Ganges@ColLeague.Adm/voy
Subj: Arkanian Delphiki, behold your mother. Petra, behold your son.

Dear Petra, Dear Arkanian,

In so many ways too late, but in the ways that count, just in time. The last of your children, Petra; your real mother, Arkanian. I will let him tell you his story, and you can tell him yours. Graff did the genetic testing long ago, and there is no doubt. He never told you, because he could never bring you together and I think he believed it would only make you sad. He might be right, but I think you deserve to have the sadness, if that's what it is, because it belongs to you by right. This is what life has done to the two of you. Now let's see what YOU do for each other's lives.

Let me tell you this much, though, Petra. He's a good boy. Despite the madness of his upbringing, in the crisis, he was Bean's son, and yours. He will never know his father, except through you. But Petra, I have seen, in him, what Bean became. The giant in body. The gentle heart.

Meanwhile, I voyage on, my friends. It's what I already planned to do, Arkanian. I'm on another errand. You did not deflect me from my course. Except that they won't let me go into stasis on this ship until my wounds are healed—there's no healing in stasis.

With love,
Andrew Wiggin

In his little house overlooking the wild coast of Ireland, not far from Doonalt, a feeble old man knelt in his garden, pulling up weeds. O'Connor rode up on his skimmer to deliver groceries and mail, and the old man rose slowly to his feet to receive him. "Come in," he said. "There's tea."

"Can't stay," said O'Connor.

"You can never stay," said the old man.

"Ah, Mr. Graff," said O'Connor, "that's the truth. I can never stay. But it's not for lack of will. I have a lot of houses waiting for me to bring them what I brought you."

"And we have nothing to say to each other," said Graff, smiling. No, laughing silently, his frail chest heaving.

"Sometimes you don't need to say a thing," said O'Connor. "And sometimes a man has no time for tea."

"I used to be a fat man," said Graff. "Can you believe it?"

"And I used to be a young man," said O'Connor. "Nobody believes *that*."

"There," said Graff. "We had a conversation after all."

O'Connor laughed—but he did not stay, once he had helped put the groceries away.

And so Graff was alone when he opened the letter from Valentine Wiggin.

He read the account as if he was hearing it in her own voice—that was her gift as a writer, now that she had left off being the Demosthenes that Peter made her create, and had become herself, even if she did still use that name for her histories.

This was a history that she would never publish. Graff knew he was the only audience. And since his body was continuing to lose weight, slowly but surely, and he grew more feeble all the time, he thought it was rather a shame she had spent so much time to put memories into a brain that would hold them for so little time before letting all the memories go at once into the ground.

Yet she had done this for him, and he was grateful to receive it. He read of Ender's contest with Quincy Morgan on the ship, and the story of the poor girl who thought she loved him. And the story of the gold bugs, some of which Ender had told him—but Valentine's version relied also on interviews with others, so that it would include things that Ender either did not know or deliberately left out.

And then, on Ganges. Virlomi seemed to have turned out well. That was a relief. She was one of the great ones; it had turned to ashes because of her pride, yes, but not until after she had singlehandedly taught her people how to free themselves of a conqueror.

Finally, the account of Ender and the boy Randall Firth, who once called himself Achilles, and now was named Arkanian Delphiki.

At the end of it, Graff nodded and then burned the letter. She had asked him to, because Ender didn't want a copy of it floating around somewhere on Earth. "My goal is to be forgotten," she quoted Ender as saying.

Not likely, though whether he would be remembered for good or ill, Graff could not predict.

"He thinks he finally got the beating Stilson and Bonzo meant to give him," Graff said to the teapot. "The boy's a fool, for all his brains. Stilson and Bonzo would not have stopped. They weren't this boy of Bean's and Petra's. That's what Ender has to understand. There really is evil in the world, and wickedness, and every brand of stupidity. There's meanness and heartlessness and . . . I don't even know which of them is me."

He fondled the teapot. "I don't even have a soul to hear me talk."

He sipped from the cup before the teabag had really done its job. It was weak, but he didn't mind having it weak. He didn't really mind much of anything these days, as long as he kept breathing in and out and there was no pain.

"Going to say it anyway," said Graff. "Poor fool of a boy. Pacifism

only works with an enemy that can't bear to do murder against the innocent. How many times are you lucky enough to get an enemy like *that*?"

———

Petra Arkanian Delphiki Wiggin was visiting with her son Andrew and
his wife Lani and their two youngest children, the last ones still at home,
when the letter came from Ender.

She came into the room where the family was playing a card game,
her face awash with tears, brandishing the letter, unable to speak.

"Who died!" Lani cried out, but Andrew came up to her and folded her
into a giant hug. "This isn't grief, Lani. This is joy."

"How can you tell?"

"Mother tears things when she's grieving, and this letter is only wrin-
kled and wet."

Petra slapped him lightly but still she laughed enough that she could
talk. "Read it aloud, Andrew. Read it out loud. Our last little boy is found.
Ender found him for me. Oh, if only Julian could know it! If only I could
talk to Julian again!" And then she wept some more, until he started to
read. The letter was so short. But Andrew and Lani, because they had
children of their own, understood exactly what it meant to her, and they
joined her in her tears, until the teenagers left the room in disgust, one of
them saying, "Call us when you get some *control*."

"Nobody has control of anything," said Petra. "We're all beggars at
the throne of fate. But sometimes he has mercy!"

———

Because it was not carrying Randall Firth into exile, the starship did not
have to go back to Eros by the most direct route. It added four months to
the subjective voyage—six years to the realtime trip—but it was cleared
at IFCom and the captain didn't mind. He would drop off his passengers
wherever they wanted, for even if no one at IFCom understood just who
Andrew and Valentine Wiggin were, the captain knew. He would justify
the detour to his superiors. His crew had started when he did, and also remembered, and did not mind.

In their stateroom, Valentine nursed Ender back to health between
shifts of writing her history of Ganges Colony.

"I read that stupid letter of yours," she said one day.

"Which? I write so many," he answered.

"The one that I was only supposed to see if you died."

"Not my fault the doctor put me under total anesthetic to reset my nose and pull out the shards of bone that didn't fit back in place."

"I suppose you want me to forget what I read."

"Why not? I have."

"You have not," she said. "You're not just hiding from your infamy, with all this voyaging, are you?"

"I'm also enjoying the company of my sister, the professional nosy person."

"That case—you're looking for a place where you can open it."

"Val," said Ender, "do I ask you about your plans?"

"You don't have to. My plan is to follow you around until I get too bored to stand it anymore."

"Whatever you think you know," said Ender, "you're wrong."

"Well, as long as you explain it so clearly."

Then, a little later: "Val, you know something? I thought for a minute there that he was really going to kill me."

"Oh, you poor thing. It must have been *devastating* to realize you had bet wrong on the outcome."

"I had thought that if it came to that moment, if I really knew that I was going to die, it would come as a relief. None of this would be my problem anymore. Someone else could clean up the mess."

"Yes, me, I'm so grateful that you were going to dump it all on me."

"But when he was coming back to finish me off—I knew he planned a kick or two in the head, and my head was already so foggy from concussion that I knew it would finish me—when he came walking up to me, I wasn't relieved at all. I wanted to get up. Would have if I could."

"And run away, if you had any brains."

"No, Val," said Ender sadly. "I wanted to get up and kill him first. I didn't want to die. It didn't matter what I thought I deserved, or how I thought it would bring me peace, or at least oblivion. None of that was in my head by then. It was just: Live. Live, whatever it takes. Even if you have to kill to do it."

"Wow," said Valentine. "You've just discovered the survival instinct. Everybody else has known about it for years."

"There are people who don't have that instinct, not the same way," said Ender, "and we give them medals for throwing themselves on grenades or running into a burning house to save a baby. Posthumously, mind you. But all sorts of honors."

"They have the instinct," said Valentine. "They just care about something else more."

"I don't," said Ender. "Care about anything more."

"You let him beat you until you *couldn't* fight him," said Valentine. "Only when you knew you couldn't hurt him did you let yourself feel that survival instinct. So don't give me any more of this crap about how you're still the same evil person who killed those other boys. You proved that you could win by deliberately losing. Done. Enough. Please don't pick a fight with anybody again unless you intend to win it. All right? Promise?"

"No promises," said Ender. "But I'll try not to get killed. I still have things to do."

AFTERWORD

I never meant this book to go this way. I was supposed to spend a few chapters getting Ender from Eros to Shakespeare and on to Ganges. But I found that all the real story setting up the confrontation on Ganges took place earlier, and to my own consternation, I ended up with a novel which mostly takes place between chapters 14 and 15 of *Ender's Game*.

But as I wrote it, I knew this was the true story, and one that had been missing. The war ends. You come home. Then you deal with all the things that happened in the war. Only Ender doesn't get to come home. He has to deal with that, too.

Yet none of this material was "missing" from the original novel, any more than anything was missing from the novelette version before the novel was written. If, at the end of chapter 14, we had then had *Ender in Exile,* neither story would have worked. For one thing, *Exile* is partly a sequel to *Shadow of the Giant*—that's where Virlomi's, Randi's, and Achilles/Randall/Arkanian's stories are left hanging, in need of this resolution. For another, *Ender's Game* ends as it should. The story you've just read works better as it is here—in a separate book. The book of the soldier after the war.

Except for one tiny problem. When I wrote the novel *Ender's Game* back in 1984, my focus in the last chapter, chapter 15, was entirely on setting up *Speaker for the Dead.* I had no notion of any sequel between those two books. So I was rather careless and cavalier with my account of Ender's time on the first colony. I was so careless I completely forgot that on all but the last formic planet, there would have been human pilots and crew left alive. Where would they go? Of course they would begin colonizing the formic worlds. And those who sent them would have at least allowed for that possibility, sending people trained to do whatever jobs they anticipated would be necessary.

So while the meat of chapter 15 of *Ender's Game* is exactly right, the details and timeline are not. They aren't what they should have been then, and they certainly aren't what they need to be now. Since writing that chapter, I have written stories like "Investment Counselor" (in *First Meetings*), where Ender meets Jane (a major character in *Speaker*) when he is legally coming of age on a planet called Sorrelledolce; but this contradicted the timeline stated in *Ender's Game.* All in all, I realized, it was chapter 15 that was wrong, not the later stories, which took more details into account and developed the story in a superior way.

Why should I be stuck now with decisions carelessly made twenty-four years ago? What I've written since is right; those contradictory but unimportant details in the original novel are wrong.

Therefore I have rewritten chapter 15 of *Ender's Game,* and at some future date there will be an edition of the novel that includes the revised chapter. Meanwhile, the entire text is online for anyone who has ever bought or ever buys any issue of my magazine *Orson Scott Card's Inter-Galactic Medicine Show* (oscIGMS.com). I have linked it to that magazine because every issue of it contains a story from the *Ender's Game* universe. My hope is that if you buy an issue in order to read that revised chapter, you'll also sample all the stories in that issue and find out what an excellent group of writers we've been publishing there.

But rest assured that nothing significant is changed in that chapter. You have not missed anything if you don't read it.

In fact, the most important purpose for that revised chapter is to keep people from writing to me about contradictions between the original version of chapter 15 and this novel. So if you're content to take my word for it that all the contradictions are now resolved, you won't need to look it up online.

In preparing this novel, I had to venture back into old territory. It's not just that I had to fit in with *Ender's Game* (where that was even possible). This story also had to fit in with every casual decision I made in *Ender's Shadow, Shadow of the Hegemon, Shadow Puppets, Shadow of the Giant, Speaker for the Dead, Xenocide,* and *Children of the Mind,* not to mention all the short stories.

There was no way I had the time or the inclination to reread all those books. It would just depress me to notice all the things in all those books that now, being a better or at least more experienced writer, I would like to change.

Fortunately, I had the aid of people who have read my fiction more carefully and more recently than I have.

First and foremost, **Jake Black** recently wrote *The Ender's Game Companion,* in which he deals with every event, character, location, and situation in all the Ender novels and stories. He was a consultant on this book (as he is on the Marvel Comics adaptation of *Ender's Game*) and vetted everything.

And in preparing *his* book, he also had the help of **Ami Chopine,** a writer in her own right, who also has been the mother superior and/or nanny of PhiloticWeb.Net, and **Andy Wahr** (alias "Hobbes" on my website at Hatrack.com), who also helped me directly by answering many questions I had in preparing to write this book. I hope I never have to write an Ender novel without their help; and in the meantime, I count them all as good friends.

I also have the benefit of a community of kind people and friends at http://www.hatrack.com, whom I exploit mercilessly as a resource. As I set out to write this novel, I had several questions I needed to have answered. If I had never addressed the issue in any of the books, I needed to know that; if I had, I needed to know what I had said so I could try not to contradict it.

Here is the original request I posted at Hatrack.com:

I can't trust my memory about details in *Ender's Game* and the Shadow books, and I'm afraid that in writing *Ender in Exile* I might be contradicting some points in the EG universe. Perhaps someone can help on the following questions:

1. Who decided Ender should not come back to Earth, and why? Peter was involved, but I think he gives different motives from what Valentine and/or the narrator of EG specifies.

2. I think there's already a contradiction between EG and the Shadow books (Giant?) about the circumstances surrounding Ender's governorship and who commanded the colony ship. But was it already fully resolved? That is, Mazer was announced as commander of the ship, but then didn't go? I remember that in conversation with Han Tzu, this was solved (after Hatrack citizens helped by pointing out the contradiction in the first place!).

I'm referring to that last chapter in EG, but what I can't do is ferret out details from the four Shadow books or any stray references elsewhere in EG or the Speaker series. I'll be grateful for any reminders people can give me of details from this time period—from the end of Ender's last battle to the arrival on his new colony world, not just what happens to Ender, but what happens to Peter and Valentine, Mazer and Graff, and the world at large.

I had valuable responses to this cri de coeur, from **C. Porter Bassett, Jaime Benlevy, Chris Wegford, Marc Van Pelt, Rob Taber, Steven R Beers, Shannon Blood, Jason Bradshaw, Lloyd Waldo, Simeon Anfinrud, Jonathan Barbee, Adam Hobart, Beau Pearce,** and **Robert Prince.** Thank you to all of them for plunging back into the books to find the answers to my questions.

In addition, **Clinton Parks** found an issue I hadn't even thought of, and sent my staff this letter:

I know you guys probably got this already, but I wanted to put it out there just in case. Did you remember that there was a discussion in "Shadow of the Giant" where the first colony's name is revealed as "Shakespeare"? It stuck in my mind cause I wondered why Ender would name his colony that. Anyway, I just wanted to be vigilant and send a reminder. Take care!

This was, in fact, a real contradiction—elsewhere, I definitely stated that the first colony was named Rov. That's because in writing those earlier books I did *not* have the resource of a community of generous readers, or didn't think to ask for their help as I should have, and so thought up cool new ideas for things that I had already dealt with in earlier books, but forgot about in the years that followed.

This, too, I have resolved.

I was once a professional proofreader. I know from experience that even the brightest, most careful readers, working in teams so we could catch each other's mistakes, still missed errors. A world as complex, with as many stories set in it, as this one is bound to contain other contradictions as yet undetected. Please post any that you find (except the ones from the former chapter 15 of *Ender's Game*) at Hatrack.com, and maybe I can find a way to fix them later.

Or take it philosophically, and realize that if these were genuine histories or biographies instead of works of fiction, there would be contradictions between them anyway—because even in factual accounts of the real world, errors and contradictions creep in. There are few events in history that were recounted identically by all witnesses. Pretend, then, that any remaining contradictions are the result of errors in historical transmission. Even if it's a "history" of events hundreds of years in the future.

Besides these helpful friends, I showed my chapters as I wrote them to my usual crew of unbelievably patient friends. Getting a novel piecemeal is an old tradition—Charles Dickens's fans always had to read his novels as they came out in installments in the newspaper. But getting a chapter every few days and having to respond quickly because I'm on such a tight writing schedule is making more demands than I should rightly make of friends.

Jake Black was, for the first time, one of those first readers, in order to bring his encyclopedic knowledge of the Ender universe to bear. Kathryn H. Kidd, my longsuffering collaborator on the long-overdue-and-entirely-my-fault sequel to *Lovelock,* called *Rasputin,* has been one of my first readers for years. Erin and Phillip Absher have also been longtime prereaders of mine, and Phillip bears the distinction of making me throw out several chapters in order to follow up on a plot thread that I had thought was a throwaway, and he convinced me was at the heart and soul of the story. He was right, I was wrong, and the book was better for it. This time, fortunately, he didn't make me rewrite whole swaths of my book. But his,

Erin's, Kathy's, and Jake's encouragement helped me feel as though I was telling a story that was worth the time spent on it.

My very first reader, however, remains my wife, Kristine, who also bears the brunt of the burden of the family when I'm in writing mode. Her suggestions might seem small to her, but they're large to me, and if she has any doubts, I rewrite until they go away.

Kristine and our youngest child, Zina, the last at home, have to deal with a father who haunts the house like a distracted, irritable ghost during the writing of a book. But we do have those nights watching *Idol* and *So You Think You Can Dance,* where we actually inhabit the same universe for an hour or two at a time.

I have also had the help of Kathleen Bellamy, the managing editor of *The InterGalactic Medicine Show*—who does *not* read my books until they are in page proofs, whereupon she reads them for the first time—as our very last proofreader before the book goes to press. That makes her our final line of defense. And our webwright and IT manager, Scott Allen, keeps Hatrack and oscIGMS going so that I *have* that community to call upon.

On this book, Beth Meacham, my editor at Tor, played a larger role than I usually ask of my editors. Because this book was so quirky—being a "midquel" that overlapped with my most popular novel—I did not want to proceed without her assurance that the book was actually something Tor wanted to publish! Her suggestions and caveats were wise and helpful at every stage of the development and writing of this book.

And I thank the production team at Tor for the sacrifices they had to make because I was so late with this manuscript. That this book still came out on time is owed to their extra work and sharp concern for quality. Even when rushing, they do their work with pride and so I end up with a book I can be proud of. Where would I be, if other good souls did not make up for my shortcomings?

The character of Ender as depicted in the original novel was in some ways drawn from my son Geoffrey, who was five and then six when I was writing that book. He is now thirty years old and the father of two children (with the good offices of his wife, the former Heather Heavener). To my great relief, Geoffrey was never called upon to serve his country in war.

So in examining what Ender's experience might be like, I have drawn upon much reading, of course, but also from correspondence and conversation with good men and women who have served our country in Afghanistan, Iraq, and other trouble spots where our responsibilities as the only nation with the strength and the will to help beleaguered people against tyranny have been fulfilled. You bear a burden for us all, and I salute you.

I grieve for those who have fallen, or who, surviving with dire injuries or broken hearts, have been deprived of much or most of the future that you once dreamed of. As a citizen of the United States, I bear some of the responsibility for sending you where you have gone, and certainly reap the benefits. Like Ender, I might not have known what was being sacrificed in my name, but I recognize the connection between us.

And for those of you who are visibly whole after your service, but who bear inward changes that no one sees, and carry memories that no one shares, I can only hope that I have done an adequate job of representing, in Ender Wiggin, something of what you feel and think and remember.

Coming in 2009 from Tor Books and Hatrack River Enterprises: *The Ender's Game Companion,* written by Jake Black. This encyclopedic volume is thoroughly researched, and features entries on the characters, planets, technology, and more from the *Ender's Game* Universe—the novels, short stories, comics, and screenplay. The following is a sample entry from the *Companion.*

HUNDRED WORLDS

The Hundred Worlds was the name given to the different planets settled by humans during the 3,000 years following Ender Wiggin's victory over the formics: Albion, Armenia, As Fábricas, Associated Planets, Ata Atua, Baía, The Belt, Calicut, Córdoba, Cyrillia, Descoladore, Divine Wind, Etruid, Gales, Ganges, Hegria, Helvetica, Honshu, Jonlei, Jung Calvin Colonies, Lusitania, Lybian Quarter, Memphis, Milagre, Mindanao, Moctezuma, Moskva, Nagoya, Oporto, Otaheti, Outback, Pacifica/Lumana'i', Path/ Tao, Qu, Reykjavik, Rhemis, Rov, Saturn, Shakespeare Colony (formerly Colony I), Sorelledolce, Stumpy Point, Summer Islands, Trondheim, Ugarit.

Ender's and Valentine's Travels

Shortly after defeating the formics, Ender left Earth to govern one of the colonies in the Hundred Worlds. The first colony he visited, as seen in *Ender in Exile* and "Gold Bug," was Shakespeare Colony, also known as Colony I. The term "Colony I" will be changed to "Shakespeare" in future editions of *Speaker for the Dead* and *Xenocide.* This change is being made, in Orson Scott Card's words, "to accommodate the 'true' story" as written in *Ender in Exile.*

Ender and Valentine didn't stay in any one place too long. Their galactic travelogue is as follows:

1. Earth

---

2. Shakespeare Colony

3. Ganges

4. Various planets, including Helvetica and others not yet identified, where Ender was not a speaker for the dead but a research assistant for Valentine as she wrote her books. (Ender had written The Hive Queen and The Hegemon in Shakespeare Colony, but did not list Speaker for the Dead as his occupation.)

5. Sorelledolce

6. Rov, where citizens of the colony first see Ender with Jane's jewel in his ear. He also lists his occupation as speaker for the dead for the first time here.

7. Various planets, including Moctezuma and others not yet identified, where Ender was a fulltime speaker for the dead.

8. Trondheim

9. Lusitania